★ "Though no punches are pulled about the unimaginable atrocity of the death camps, a LIFE-AFFIRMING history."
—*Kirkus Reviews*, starred review

★ "*The Librarian of Auschwitz* is a heartbreaking and ultimately INSPIRING WORK OF ART."
—*Shelf Awareness*, starred review

★ "Iturbe's REMARKABLE account uses an immediate present tense to immerse readers in Dita's story as she goes about what constitutes daily life in Auschwitz, all the while risking everything to distribute and hide the library's books."
—*The Horn Book*, starred review

GUARD TOWERS

WOMEN'S

PRISONERS

MAIN GUARD HOUSE

ENLARGED FROM THE ORIGINAL NEGATIVE AND
CAPTIONED IN 1978 BY THE CIA

AUSCHWITZ-BIRKENAU EXTERMINATION CAMP
OSWIECIM, POLAND
25 AUGUST 1944

PRISONERS

ONERS

CREMATORIUM II

UNDRESSING ROOM

GAS CHAMBER

CREMATORIUM

ENGINE ROOM

ENGINE ROOM

UNDRESSING ROOM

BOXCARS

PRISONERS ON WAY TO GAS CHAMBERS

CREMATORIUM III

GAS CHAMBER

THE LIBRARIAN OF AUSCHWITZ

ANTONIO ITURBE

TRANSLATED BY LILIT ŽEKULIN THWAITES

SQUARE
FISH

GODWINBOOKS

HENRY HOLT AND COMPANY

NEW YORK

SQUARE
FISH

An imprint of Macmillan Publishing Group, LLC
120 Broadway, New York, NY 10271
fiercereads.com

Our books may be purchased in bulk for promotional, educational, or business use.
Please contact your local bookseller or the Macmillan Corporate and Premium
Sales Department at (800) 221-7945 ext. 5442 or by email at
MacmillanSpecialMarkets@macmillan.com.

Library of Congress Cataloging-in-Publication Data

Names: Iturbe, Antonio, 1967– author. | Thwaites, Lilit Žekulin, translator.
Title: The librarian of Auschwitz / Antonio Iturbe ; translated by Lili Thwaites.
Description: New York : Henry Holt and Company, 2017. | Summary: Follows
  Dita Kraus from age fourteen, when she is put in charge of a few forbidden books
  at Auschwitz concentration camp, through the end of World War II and beyond.
  Based on a true story.
Identifiers: LCCN 2017034236 (print) | LCCN 2017007363 (ebook) | ISBN
  978-1-62779-619-4 (Ebook) | ISBN 978-1-250-25803-8 (adult edition)
Subjects: LCSH: Kraus, Dita, 1929– —Juvenile fiction. | CYAC: Kraus, Dita, 1929– —
  Fiction. | Concentration camps—Fiction. | Books and reading—Fiction. | Jews—
  Germany—History—1933–1945—Fiction. | Holocaust, Jewish (1939–1945)—
  Germany—Fiction. | Germany—History—1933–1945—Fiction. | BISAC:
  JUVENILE FICTION / Historical / Holocaust. | JUVENILE FICTION /
  Books & Libraries.
Classification: LCC PZ7.1.I93 (print) | LCC PZ7.1.I93 Lib 2017 (ebook) |
  DDC [Fic]—dc23
LC record available at https://lccn.loc.gov/2017034236

Originally published in the United States by Laura Godwin Books/
Henry Holt and Company
First published in Spain by Editorial Planeta in 2012
First Square Fish edition, 2019
Square Fish logo designed by Filomena Tuosto

1 3 5 7 9 10 8 6 4 2

Dear reader,

I want to tell you how the book you are holding came into being. Some years ago, the Spanish author Antonio Iturbe was searching for someone who could tell him some details about the books on the children's block in the Auschwitz–Birkenau concentration camp.

He received my internet address, and we started exchanging emails. His were short, apologetic questions and mine long, detailed answers. But then we met in Prague, and for two days I showed him where I grew up and where I played in a sandbox and went to school and the house that we—my parents and I—left forever when we were sent to the Terezín ghetto by the Nazi occupants. The next day we even traveled to Terezín itself. Before we parted, Toni said: "Everyone knows about the largest library in the world. But I am going to write a book about the smallest library in the world and its librarian."

This is the book that you are holding. Of course he wrote it in Spanish and this is a translation. He used much of what I told him, but he also diligently collected facts from other sources. Still, despite the historical correctness of the narrative, it is not a documentary. It is a story born both from my own experiences and the rich imagination of the author.

Thank you for reading
and sharing it!

Yours,
Dita Kraus

Courtesy Dita Kraus

While it lasted, Block 31 (in the Auschwitz extermination camp) was home to five hundred children, together with several prisoners who had been named "counselors." Despite the strict surveillance they were under and against all odds, the Block housed a clandestine children's library. It was tiny, consisting of eight books, including *A Short History of the World* by H. G. Wells, a Russian grammar, and another book on analytical geometry. . . . At the end of each day, the books, along with other treasures such as medicine and some food, were entrusted to one of the oldest girls, whose task it was to hide them in a different place every night.

ALBERTO MANGUEL, *The Library at Night*

Literature has the same impact as a match lit in the middle of a field in the middle of the night. The match illuminates relatively little, but it enables us to see how much darkness surrounds it.

JAVIER MARÍAS, citing William Faulkner

1.

Auschwitz–Birkenau, January 1944

THE NAZI OFFICERS ARE DRESSED IN BLACK. THEY LOOK AT DEATH with the indifference of a gravedigger. In Auschwitz, human life has so little value that no one is shot anymore; a bullet is more valuable than a human being. In Auschwitz, there are communal chambers where they administer Zyklon gas. It's cost-effective, killing hundreds of people with just one tank. Death has become an industry that is profitable only if it's done wholesale.

The officers have no idea that in the family camp in Auschwitz, on top of the dark mud into which everything sinks, Alfred Hirsch has established a school. They don't know it, and it's essential that they should not know it. Some inmates didn't believe it was possible. They thought Hirsch was crazy, or naïve: How could you teach children in this brutal extermination camp where everything is forbidden? But Hirsch would smile. He was always smiling enigmatically, as if he knew something that no one else did. *It doesn't matter how many schools the Nazis close,* he would say to them. *Each time someone stops to tell a story and children listen, a school has been established.*

In this life-destroying factory that is Auschwitz–Birkenau, where the ovens burn corpses day and night, Block 31 is atypical, an anomaly. It's a triumph for Fredy Hirsch. He used to be a youth sports instructor, but is now an athlete himself, competing against the biggest steamroller of humans in history. He managed to convince the German camp authorities that keeping the children entertained in a hut would make it easier for their parents to do their work in camp BIIb, the one known as "the family camp." The camp high command agreed, but on the condition that it would be for games and activities only: School was banned. And so Block 31 was formed.

Inside the wooden hut, the classrooms are nothing more than stools, tightly packed into groups. Walls are nonexistent; blackboards are invisible. The teachers trace isosceles triangles, letters of the alphabet, and even the routes of the rivers of Europe with their hands in the air. There are about twenty clusters of children, each with its own teacher. They are so close together that classes are whispered to prevent the story of the ten plagues of Egypt from getting mixed up with the rhythm of a times table.

The barrack door is flung open, and Jakoubek, the lookout, races toward the cubicle of Blockältester Hirsch, the head of Block 31. His clogs leave a trail of moist camp earth across the floor, and the bubble of calm serenity in Block 31 bursts. From her corner, Dita Adler stares, mesmerized by the tiny spots of mud, as Jakoubek calls out:

"Six! Six! Six!"

It's code for the imminent arrival of SS guards at Block 31.

Hirsch pokes his head out of his door. He doesn't need to say a word to his assistants or his teachers, whose eyes are locked on him. His nod is barely perceptible. His look is a command.

The lessons come to a halt and are replaced by silly little German songs and guessing games, to give the impression that all is in order. Normally, the two-soldier patrol barely enters the barrack, casting a routine glance over the children, occasionally clapping along with a song or stroking the head of one of the little ones before continuing their rounds. But Jakoubek adds another note to the customary alert:

"Inspection! Inspection!"

Inspections are another matter altogether. Lines must be formed, and searches are carried out. Sometimes the youngest children are interrogated, the guards hoping to take advantage of their innocence to pry information out of them. They are unsuccessful. Even the youngest children understand more than their snot-covered little faces might suggest.

Someone whispers, "The Priest!" and a murmur of dismay breaks out. That's their name for one of the SS noncommissioned officers, a sergeant who always walks with his hands tucked into the sleeves of his military greatcoat as if he were a priest, though the only religion he practices is cruelty.

"Come on, come on! Juda! Yes, you! Say 'I spy . . .'"

"And what do I spy, Mr. Stein?"

"Anything! For heaven's sake, child, anything!"

Two teachers look up in anguish. They are holding something that's absolutely forbidden in Auschwitz. These items, so dangerous that their mere possession is a death sentence, cannot be fired, nor do they have a sharp point, a blade, or a heavy end. These items, which the relentless guards of the Reich fear so much, are nothing more than books: old, unbound, with missing pages, and in tatters. The Nazis ban them, hunt them down.

Throughout history, all dictators, tyrants, and oppressors, whatever their ideology—whether Aryan, African, Asian, Arab, Slav, or any other racial background; whether defenders of popular revolutions, or the privileges of the upper classes, or God's mandate, or martial law—have had one thing in common: the vicious persecution of the written word. Books are extremely dangerous; they make people think.

The groups are in their places, singing softly as they wait for the guards to arrive, but one girl disrupts the harmony. She launches herself into a noisy run between the clusters of stools.

"Get down!"

"What are you doing? Are you crazy?" teachers shout at her.

One of them tries to stop her by grabbing her arm, but she avoids him and continues with her dash. She climbs up onto the waist-high stove and chimney that splits the hut in two, and jumps down noisily on the other side. She knocks over a stool, and it rolls away with such a thunderous clatter that all activity stops for a moment.

"You wretched girl! You're going to betray us all!" shrieks Mrs. Křižková, purple with rage. Behind her back, the children call her Mrs. Nasty. She doesn't know that this very girl invented the nickname. "Sit down at the back with the assistants, you stupid girl."

But Dita doesn't stop. She continues her frantic run, oblivious to all the disapproving looks. The children watch, fascinated, as she races around on her skinny legs with their woolen socks. She's very thin but not sickly, with shoulder-length brown hair that swings from side to side as she rapidly zigzags her way between the groups. Dita Adler is moving among hundreds of people, but she's running by herself. We always run on our own.

She snakes her way to the center of the hut and clears a path through one group. She brushes aside a stool or two, and a little girl falls over.

"Hey, who do you think you are!" she shouts at Dita from the floor.

The teacher from Brno is amazed to see the young girl come to a halt in front of her, gasping for air. Out of both breath and time, Dita grabs the book from her hands, and the teacher suddenly feels relieved. By the time she responds with her thanks, Dita is already several strides from her. The arrival of the Nazis is only seconds away.

Engineer Maródi, who has seen her maneuvers, is already waiting for her at the edge of his group. He hands her his book as she flies past, as if he were handing off the baton in a relay race. Dita runs desperately toward the back of the hut, where the assistants pretend to sweep the floor.

She's only halfway there when she notices the voices of the groups have momentarily faltered, wavering like candlelight when a window is opened. Dita doesn't need to turn around to confirm that the door of the hut has opened and the SS guards are coming in. She instantly drops to the ground, frightening a group of eleven-year-old girls. She puts the books under her smock and crosses her arms over her chest to prevent them from falling. The amused girls steal a glance at her out of the corners of their eyes while the very nervous teacher prompts them to keep on singing by lifting her chin.

After surveying the scene for a few seconds from the entrance to the hut, the SS guards shout one of their favorite words:

"*Achtung!*"

Silence falls. The little songs and the games of I Spy stop. Everyone freezes. And in the middle of the silence, you can hear someone crisply whistling Beethoven's Fifth Symphony. The Priest is a sergeant to be feared, but even he seems somewhat nervous, because he's accompanied by someone even more sinister.

"May God help us!" Dita hears the teacher nearby whisper.

Dita's mother used to play the piano before the war, and that's why Dita knows for sure that it's Beethoven. She realizes this is not the first time she's heard that particular way of whistling symphonies. It was after they'd been traveling from the Terezín ghetto for three days, crammed into a freight car without food or water. Night had fallen by the time they reached Auschwitz–Birkenau. It was impossible to forget the screeching sound of the metal door as it opened. Impossible to forget that first breath of icy air that smelled of burnt flesh. Impossible to forget the intense glare of the lights in the night: The platform was lit up like an operating room. Then came the orders, the thud of rifle butts against the side of the metal carriage, the shots, the whistles, the screams. And in the middle of all the confusion, that Beethoven symphony being flawlessly whistled by a captain at whom even the SS guards looked with terror.

That day at the station, the officer passed close to Dita, and she saw his impeccable uniform, his spotless white gloves, and the Iron Cross on the front of his military jacket—the medal that can be won only on the battlefield. He stopped in front of a group of mothers and children and patted one of the children in a friendly manner with his gloved hand. He even smiled. He pointed to a pair of fourteen-year-old twins—Zdeněk and Jirka—and a corporal hurried to remove them from the line. Their mother grabbed the guard by the bottom of his jacket and fell on her knees, begging him not to take them away. The captain calmly intervened.

"No one will treat them like Uncle Josef."

And in a sense, that was true. No one in Auschwitz touched a hair of the sets of twins that Dr. Josef Mengele collected for his experiments. No one would treat them as Uncle Josef did in his macabre genetic experiments to find out how to make German women give birth to twins and multiply the number of Aryan births. Dita recalls Mengele walking off holding the children by their hands, still calmly whistling.

That same symphony is now audible in Block 31.

Mengele . . .

Blockältester Hirsch emerges from his tiny cubicle, pretending to be pleasantly surprised by the visit of the SS guards. He clicks his heels together loudly to greet the officer: It's a respectful way of recognizing the soldier's rank, but it's also a way of demonstrating a military attitude, neither submissive nor daunted. Mengele barely gives him a glance; he's still whistling, with his hands behind his back as if none of this had anything to do with him. The sergeant—the one everyone calls the Priest—scrutinizes the hut with his almost transparent eyes, his hands still tucked inside the sleeves of his greatcoat and hovering over his middle, never far from the holster of his gun.

Jakoubek wasn't wrong.

"Inspection," whispers the Priest.

The SS guards repeat his order, amplifying it until it becomes a shout in the prisoners' ears. Dita, sitting in the midst of a ring of girls, shivers and squeezes her arms against her body. She hears the rustle of the books against her ribs. If they find the books on her, it's all over.

"That wouldn't be fair . . ." she murmurs.

She's fourteen years old. Her life is just beginning; everything is ahead of her. She recalls the words her mother has been repeating insistently over the years whenever Dita grumbles about her fate: "It's the war, Edita . . . it's the war."

She is so young that she barely remembers anymore what the

world was like when there was no war. In the same way that she hides the books from the Nazis, she keeps secret the memories in her head. She closes her eyes and tries to recall what the world was like when there was no fear.

She pictures herself in early 1939, aged nine, standing in front of the astronomical clock in Prague's Old Town Hall square. She's sneaking a peek at the old skeleton. It keeps watch over the rooftops of the city with huge empty eye sockets.

They'd told them at school that the clock was a piece of mechanical ingenuity, invented by Maestro Hanuš more than five hundred years ago. But Dita's grandmothers told her a darker story. The king ordered Hanuš to construct a clock with figures, automatons that paraded on the stroke of every hour. When it was completed, the king ordered his bailiffs to blind the clockmaker so that he could never make another wonder like it. But the clock-maker took revenge, putting his hand into the mechanism to disable it. The cogs shredded his hand, the mechanism jammed, and the clock was broken, unfixable for years. Sometimes Dita had nightmares about that amputated hand snaking its way around the serrated wheels of the mechanism.

Dita, hanging on to the books that may take her to the gas chamber, looks back with nostalgia at the happy child she used to be. Whenever she accompanied her mother downtown on shopping expeditions, she loved to stop in front of the astronomical clock, not to watch the mechanical show—the skeleton in fact disturbed her more than she was prepared to admit—but to watch the pass-ersby, many of them foreigners visiting the capital. She had diffi-culty concealing her laughter at the astonished faces and silly giggles of those watching. She made up names for them. One of her favorite pastimes was giving everyone nicknames, especially her neighbors and her parents' friends. She called snooty Mrs. Gottlieb "Mrs. Giraffe" because she used to stretch her neck to give herself airs. And she named the Christian upholsterer in the shop downstairs "Mr. Bowling-Pin-Head" because he was skinny and completely bald. She remembers chasing the tram as, its little bell ringing, it turned the corner at the Old Town Square and snaked its way into the distance through the Josefov neighborhood. Then she would run in the direction of the store, where she knew her mother would be, buying material to make Dita's winter coats and skirts. She hasn't forgotten how much she liked that store, with its neon sign in the door, colored spools of thread lighting up one by one from the bottom to the top and then back down again.

If she hadn't been one of those girls insulated by that happiness typical of children, then perhaps as she passed by the newspaper kiosk she would have noticed that there was a long queue of people waiting to buy the paper. The stack of copies of *Lidové Noviny* that day carried a headline on the front page four columns wide and in an unusually large type. It screamed rather than stated GOVERNMENT AGREES TO GERMAN ARMY'S ENTRY INTO PRAGUE.

Dita briefly opens her eyes and sees the SS guards sniffing around the back of the hut. They leave no stone unturned, even checking behind the drawings that hang on the wall from makeshift barbed wire nails. No one says a word; there is only the sound of the guards rummaging around in the hut. It smells of dampness and mildew. Of fear, too. It's the smell of war.

From the little she remembers of her childhood, Dita recalls that peace smelled of chicken soup left cooking on the stove all night every Friday. It tasted of well-roasted lamb, and pastry made with nuts and eggs. It was long school days, and afternoons spent playing hopscotch and hide-and-seek with Margit and other classmates, now fading in her memory . . .

The changes were gradual, but Dita remembers the day her childhood ended forever. She doesn't recall the date, but it was March 15, 1939. Prague awoke shaking.

The crystal chandelier in the living room was vibrating, but she knew it wasn't an earthquake, because nobody was running around or worried. Her father was drinking his breakfast cup of coffee and reading the paper as if nothing were happening.

When Dita and her mother went out, the city was shuddering. She began to hear the noise as they headed toward Wenceslas Square. The ground was vibrating so strongly that it tickled the soles of her feet. The muffled sounds grew more noticeable as they got closer to the square, and Dita was intrigued. When they reached the square, they couldn't cross the street, which was blocked off by people, or see anything other than a wall of shoulders, coats, necks, and hats.

Her mother came to a dead stop. Her face was strained and suddenly aged. She grabbed her daughter's hand to turn back, but Dita's curiosity was strong. She yanked herself free of the hand that was holding on to her. Because she was small and skinny, she had no trouble wiggling her way through the crowd of people on the sidewalk to the front where the city police were lined up, their arms linked.

The noise was deafening: Gray motorcycles with sidecars led the way one after another. Each carried soldiers in gleaming leather jackets and shining helmets, with goggles dangling from their necks. They were followed by combat trucks, bristling with enormous machine guns, and then tanks thundering slowly down the avenue like a herd of menacing elephants.

She remembers thinking that the people filing past looked like the mechanical figures from the astronomical clock, that after a few seconds, a door would close behind them, and they would disappear, and the trembling would stop. But they weren't automatons; they were men. She would learn that the difference between the two is not always significant.

She was only nine years old, but she felt fear. There were no bands playing, no loud laughter or commotion. . . . The procession was being watched in total silence. Why were those uniformed men here? Why was nobody laughing? Suddenly, it reminded her of a funeral.

With an iron grip, her mother caught her again and dragged her out from the crowd. They headed off in the opposite direction, and Prague became itself again. It was like waking up from a bad dream and discovering that everything was back to normal.

But the ground was still shaking under her feet. The city was still trembling. Her mother was trembling, too. She was desperately pulling Dita along, trying to leave the procession behind, taking hurried little steps in her smart patent-leather shoes.

Dita sighs as she clutches the books. She realizes with sadness that it was on that day, not the day of her first period, that she left her childhood behind. That was the day she stopped being afraid of skeletons and old stories about phantom hands, and started being afraid of men.

2.

THE SS BEGAN THEIR INSPECTION OF THE HUT WITH SCARCELY A glance at the prisoners, focusing their attention on the walls, the floor, and the surroundings. The Germans are systematic like that: first the container, then its contents. Dr. Mengele turns around to speak with Fredy Hirsch, who has remained standing almost at attention all this time. Dita wonders what they're talking about. Few Jews could hold a conversation with Mengele, or Dr. Death as he is called, with such assurance. Some say that Hirsch is a man without fear. Others believe the Germans warm to him because he is German. Some even suggest his impeccable appearance hides something unsavory.

The Priest, who is in charge of the inspection, makes a gesture Dita can't interpret. If the guards order them to stand to attention, how will she hold the books without them falling out?

The first lesson any veteran inmate teaches a recent arrival is that you must always be clear about your goal: survival. To survive a few more hours and, in this way, gain another day that, added to other days, might become one more week. You must continue like this, never making big plans, never having big goals, only surviving each moment. *To live* is a verb that makes sense only in the present tense.

It's her last chance to leave the books; there's an empty stool just a meter away. When they stand up to form lines and the guards

find the books there, they won't be able to accuse her; all of them
and none of them will be guilty. And they won't be able to take all
of them to the gas chambers. Though, without a doubt, they'll shut
down Block 31. Dita wonders if it would really matter. She's heard
how some of the teachers initially questioned the school: Why
make the children study when there's little chance they'll leave
Auschwitz alive? Does it make any sense to talk to them about
polar bears or drill them on multiplication tables, in the shadow of
chimneys belching out the black smoke of burning bodies? But
Hirsch convinced them. He told them that Block 31 would be an
oasis for the children.

Oasis or mirage? Some of them still wonder.

The most logical thing would be to get rid of the books, to fight
for her life. But Dita hesitates.

The sergeant stands to attention in front of his superior. When
he hears the order, he shouts out,

"On your feet! Attention!"

And then the commotion really begins as people start to stand
up. It's the moment of confusion Dita needs. As she relaxes her
arms, the books inside her smock slip down to her lap. But then
she grips them against her body again. With each second she holds
on to them, her life is more at risk.

The SS order silence; no one is to move from their spot. Dis-
order irritates the Germans. When they first set in motion the
Final Solution, the bloody executions gave rise to refusals among
many of the SS officers. They found it difficult to deal with the
mayhem of dead bodies mixed in with those who were still dying;
with the arduous task of having to kill again, one by one, those who
had already been shot; with the quagmire of blood as they stepped
over the fallen bodies; with the hands of the dying coiling around

their boots like creeping vines. But this has ceased to be a problem. In Auschwitz, there is no chaos. The killings are routine.

The people in front of Dita have stood up, and the guards can't see her. She reaches under her smock and grabs hold of the geometry book. As she holds it, she feels the roughness of the pages. She runs a finger over the furrows of the bare spine.

And in that moment, she shuts her eyes and squeezes the books tightly. She acknowledges what she has known right from the start: She's not going to abandon them. She is the librarian of Block 31. She asked Fredy Hirsch to trust her, almost demanded it. And he did. She won't let him down.

Finally, Dita stands up carefully. She holds one arm across her chest, pressing the books to her body. A group of girls obscure her, but she is tall and her posture is suspicious.

Before beginning the inspection, the sergeant had given an order and two SS guards disappeared inside Hirsch's cubicle, where the rest of the books are hidden. Though the hiding place is secure—the books fit in a dugout beneath a wooden floorboard so perfectly as to be undetectable—Dita knows that Hirsch is now in great danger. If they find the books, nothing can save him.

Mengele has moved away, but Hirsch continues to stand stock-still as the Germans root around his cubicle. Two SS guards wait outside, relaxed, their heads tilted back. Hirsch remains upright. The more they relax their posture, the more erect he'll be. He'll take any opportunity, no matter how small, to demonstrate the strength of the Jews. They are a stronger people, and that is why the Nazis fear them, why they must exterminate them. The Nazis are winning only because the Jews don't have an army of their own, but Hirsch is convinced the Jews will never make this mistake again.

The two SS men come out of the cubicle; the Priest holds a few papers in his hand. It seems that this is the only suspicious thing they've found. Mengele gives the papers a cursory look and disdainfully hands them to the sergeant, almost allowing them to fall. They are the reports on the operation of Block 31 that Hirsch writes for the camp high command.

The Priest tucks his hands back into the worn sleeves of his greatcoat. He issues his orders in a low voice, and the guards spring into action. They advance toward the inmates, kicking aside any stools in their path. Fear erupts among the children and the newly arrived teachers, who give way to sobs and cries of anguish. The veterans are less concerned. Hirsch does not move. In a corner, Mengele stands removed, observing.

When the pack reaches the first bunch of prisoners, it slows, and the guards begin their search. They inspect the prisoners, frisking some, moving their own heads up and down in their search for who knows what. The prisoners pretend to look straight ahead, but they cast sidelong glances at the inmates next to them.

The guards order one of the female teachers to step out of the line. She's a tall woman who teaches crafts. In her class, children create small miracles out of old string, wood splinters, broken spoons, and discarded cloth. She doesn't understand what the soldiers are saying; they shout at her and shake her, before returning her to the group. There's probably no reason for it. Shouting and shaking are also part of the routine.

The guards move on. Dita's arm is getting tired, but she pulls the books into her chest even more tightly. They stop at the group beside hers, and the Priest lifts his chin, ordering a man out of the line.

It's the first time Dita has paid any attention to Professor

Morgenstern, an inoffensive-looking man who, based on the folds of skin under his chin, must once have been chubby. He has close-cropped white hair and wears a faded, patched jacket that is too big for him. A pair of round glasses sit in front of his myopic beaver-like eyes. Dita has difficulty hearing what the Priest is saying to him, but she sees Professor Morgenstern hold the spectacles out to him. The Priest takes them and examines them; inmates aren't allowed to keep any personal effects, though glasses for a short-sighted person are no luxury. Even so, the Priest examines them carefully before holding them back out for the old man. When the teacher reaches for them, they fall, smashing against a stool before landing on the floor.

"Clumsy idiot!" the sergeant yells at him.

Professor Morgenstern calmly bends to pick up the broken glasses. He begins to straighten, but a pair of wrinkled origami birds fall from his pocket and he bends again to retrieve them. As he reaches down, his glasses fall to the ground again. The Priest observes this clumsiness with barely contained irritation. Angrily, he turns on his heel and continues the inspection. Mengele misses nothing as he watches from the front of the hut.

Dita senses the SS approach, though she does not look. They stop in front of her group, the Priest directly opposite Dita, not more than four or five paces away. She sees the girls trembling. The sweat on her shoulders is icy cold. There's nothing she can do: Her height makes her stick out, and she's the only one not standing to attention, clearly gripping something with one arm. The Priest's eye is ruthless, inescapable. He's one of those Nazis who, like Hitler, is intoxicated by hatred.

Though she looks straight ahead, Dita feels the Priest's gaze piercing her, and fear forms a lump in her throat. She needs air;

she's suffocating. She hears a male voice, and she's already preparing herself to step out from the middle of the group.

It's all over—

But not yet. It's not the voice of the Priest, but a much more timid one. It's the voice of Professor Morgenstern.

"Excuse me, Sergeant, sir, do you give me permission to go back to my place in the line? If it's all right with you, of course— otherwise I'll stay here until you give me the order. The last thing I'd want to do is to cause you any kind of trouble. . . ."

The Priest looks angrily at the insignificant little man who has dared to address him without permission. The old professor has put his glasses back on, cracked lens and all, and still standing out of line, he looks dopily toward the SS officer.

The Priest strides toward him, and the guards follow behind. For the first time, he raises his voice.

"Stupid old Jewish imbecile! If you're not back in line in three seconds, I'll shoot you!"

"At your service, whatever you order," the professor replies meekly. "I beg you to forgive me, I had no intention of being a nuisance. It's just that I preferred to ask rather than committing an act of insubordination that might be contrary to the rules, because I don't like behaving in an inconvenient manner, and it's my wish to serve you in the most fitting way—"

"Back in line, idiot!"

"Yes, sir. At your orders, sir. Forgive me once again. It wasn't my intention to interrupt, rather—"

"Shut your mouth, before I put a bullet in your head!" yells the Nazi, beside himself.

The professor, bowing his head in an exaggerated manner, steps backward, returning to his group. The enraged Priest does not notice that his guards are now behind him, and as he turns abruptly, he barrels into them. It's a spectacular scene: Nazis bounce off each other like billiard balls. Some of the children laugh quietly, and the teachers, alarmed, elbow them to be quiet.

The sergeant looks to Mengele, who despises nothing more than incompetence, before he angrily thrusts his men aside and resumes the inspection. As he walks in front of Dita's row, she clenches her numb arm. And her teeth. In his agitation, the Priest thinks he's already inspected this group and moves on to the next. There are more shouts, more shoves, the odd search . . . and the soldiers move slowly away from Dita.

The librarian can breathe again, though the danger has not passed: The guards remain in the hut. Her arm aches from holding it in the same position for so long. To distract herself from the pain, she thinks of how fate brought her to Block 31.

It was December when Dita and her family arrived in Auschwitz. On their very first morning in the camp, before the morning roll call, her mother bumped into an acquaintance from Terezín, Mrs. Turnovská, who had owned a fruit shop in Zlín. The encounter was a small joy amidst the misery. Mrs. Turnovská told Dita's mother of the barrack-school for children. There, they held roll call under cover, out of the wet and cold, each morning. There, they didn't have to work all day. Even the food rations were a little better.

When her mother said that Edita was fourteen—just a year too old to join the school—Mrs. Turnovská told her that the director of the school had convinced the Germans he needed a few assistants to help maintain order in the hut. In this way, he'd taken on a few children aged fourteen to sixteen. Mrs. Turnovská, who seemed to know everything, knew the deputy director, Miriam Edelstein, from her hut.

The women found Miriam walking quickly along the *Lagerstrasse*, the camp's main avenue, which stretched from one end to the other. Miriam was in a rush and in a bad mood; things hadn't gone at all well for her since her family's transfer from the Terezín ghetto, where her husband, Yakub, had been chairman of the Jewish Council. When they arrived at the camp, he was put with the political prisoners in Auschwitz I.

Mrs. Turnovská sang Dita's virtues, but before she could finish, Miriam Edelstein cut her off: "The quota for assistants has been filled, and many people before you have asked me for the same favor." With that, Miriam set off in a great hurry.

But just as she was about to disappear down the *Lagerstrasse*, she stopped, then returned to the spot where she had left the women. They had not moved.

"Did you say that this girl speaks perfect Czech and German, and that she reads very well?"

In celebration of Hanukkah, the camp was staging a performance of *Snow White and the Seven Dwarves*, and the prompter who would remind actors of their lines had died that morning. And so that afternoon, Dita entered Block 31 for the first time as the new prompter for *Snow White*.

Thirty-two huts, or barracks, formed camp BIIb. They were in two rows of sixteen, lining either side of the *Lagerstrasse*. Block 31 was the same as those other rectangular barracks, divided by a horizontal brick stove and a chimney, which stood on the foot-flattened dirt floor. But Dita realized that there was one funda-mental difference: Instead of rows of triple bunks where the prisoners slept, there were stools and benches, and instead of rotten wood, the walls were covered with drawings of Eskimos and Snow White's dwarves.

Cheerful chaos reigned as volunteers worked to transform the dismal hut into a theater. Some arranged seating, while others transported colorful costumes and cloth decorations. Another group rehearsed lines with the children, and at the far end of the hut, the assistants positioned mattresses to form a small stage. Dita was struck by the bustling activity: Against all odds, life stubbornly carried on.

They had prepared a small compartment for her at the front of the stage, made out of cardboard and painted black. Rubiček, the director of the play, told Dita to pay particular attention to little Sarah, who forgot to say her lines in German when she became nervous, switching unconsciously to Czech. The Nazis required the performance to be in German.

Dita remembers her nerves before the play began, the weight of responsibility. The audience included some of the top officers of Auschwitz II: Kommandant Schwarzhuber and Dr. Mengele. Whenever she glanced through a hole in her cardboard box, she was astonished to see how much they laughed and clapped. Could these be the same people who sent thousands and thousands of children to their death each day?

Of all the plays performed in Block 31, the December 1943 version of *Snow White* was one of the most memorable. When the performance started, the magic mirror stuttered at the wicked stepmother, "Y-y-y-you are the most beautiful, my q-q-q-queen."

The audience erupted in laughter, thinking it a joke, but Dita was sweating inside her cardboard shell. The stammering wasn't in the script.

When Snow White was abandoned in the forest, the guffaws

stopped. The part was played by a young girl with an air of sadness. She looked fragile as she wandered, lost, pleading for help in her tiny voice, and Dita felt a knot in her chest. She, too, was lost, surrounded by wolves. Little Snow White began to sing, and the audience went completely silent. It was only when the prince—the broad-shouldered Fredy Hirsch—came to her rescue, that the audience came to life again, applauding their approval. The play ended with a huge ovation. Even the impassive Dr. Mengele applauded, though he didn't remove his white gloves, of course.

It is this same Dr. Mengele who now stands at one end of Block 31, taking in the scene. The Priest leads his guards toward the back of the hut, kicking aside stools and hauling inmates out of the line, though they find no excuse to take inmates away. Not this time.

When the Nazis finish inspecting the hut, the sergeant turns to the medical captain, but he has vanished. The guards should be pleased; they have found no escape tunnels or weapons—nothing against the rules. But they are furious; there is nothing to punish. They shout and make threats, violently shaking one boy. And then they leave.

They've gone, but they'll be back.

When the door shuts behind them, there's a murmur of relief. Fredy Hirsch puts the whistle he always wears around his neck to his lips, and blows it loudly, signaling them to fall out. Dita's arm is so numb she can barely move it, and the pain brings tears to her eyes. She is so relieved by the departure of the Nazis that she cries and laughs at the same time.

Nervous chatter breaks out. The teachers want to discuss what has happened, to understand what they have seen. The children run around and let off steam. Dita sees Mrs. Křižková approach her, bearing down on her. As she walks, the flap of skin under her chin wobbles like a turkey's gobbler. She stops just in front of Dita.

"Are you crazy, girl? Don't you know that when the order is given, you have to go to your assigned spot in the assistants' area, not run around like a madwoman? Don't you realize that they can haul you off and kill you? Don't you realize that they can kill all of us?"

"I did what I thought best—"

"What you thought . . ." begins Mrs. Křižková, her face wrinkling. "And who are *you* to change the rules? Do you think you know everything?"

"I'm sorry, Mrs. Křižková . . ."

Dita clenches her fists to stop her tears from falling. She's not going to give her the satisfaction.

"I'm going to report what you've done—"

"That won't be necessary," says a man's voice, speaking Czech with a strong German accent, slow and deliberate, and yet emphatic. It is Hirsch.

"Mrs. Křižková, there's still a little time before classes end. You should take charge of your group."

Mrs. Křižková always brags that she has the most disciplined and hardworking group of girls in all of Block 31. Without a word, she glances furiously at the head of the hut, turns around, and marches stiffly away toward her pupils. Dita sighs with relief.

"Thank you, Mr. Hirsch."

"Fredy. . . ."

"I'm sorry I broke the rules."

Hirsch smiles at her.

"A good soldier doesn't need to wait for orders; he knows what his duty is."

And before he walks off, he turns toward her and looks at the books she's holding against her chest.

"I'm proud of you, Dita. May God bless you."

She watches him leave and remembers the night of the *Snow White* performance. As the assistants were dismantling the stage, Dita emerged from her prompter's den and headed for the exit, thinking she might never again set foot in this wonderful hut that could turn itself into a theater. But a vaguely familiar voice stopped her.

"Young girl . . ." Fredy Hirsch's face was still covered with white chalk makeup. "Your arrival in this camp is timely," he said.

"Timely?"

"Absolutely!" He gestured for her to follow him to the back of the stage, which was now empty of people. Close up, Hirsch's eyes were an odd mix of gentleness and insolence. "I desperately need a librarian for our children's hut."

It astonished Dita that he would remember her. Hirsch had been in charge of the Youth Office in the Terezín ghetto, but she'd caught a glimpse of him only a few times as she helped one of the librarians wheel her trolley of books.

Dita was perplexed, though. She was no librarian. She was just a fourteen-year-old girl.

"Forgive me, but I think there's been a misunderstanding. The librarian was Miss Sittigová; I only helped her."

The director of Block 31 smiled. "I noticed you several times. You were pushing the library cart."

"Yes, because it was very heavy for her, and the little wheels didn't roll easily on the cobblestones."

"You could have spent the afternoon lying on your pallet, going for walks with your girlfriends, or just doing your own thing. But instead, you pushed the cart so that people could have their books."

She was looking at him, perplexed, but Hirsch's words left no room for argument. He was in charge of an army. And like a general, he pronounced, "You are a librarian."

He added, "But it's dangerous. Very dangerous. Handling books here is no game. If the SS catches anyone with a book, they execute them."

As he said it, he raised his thumb and extended his index finger. He aimed that imaginary pistol at Dita's forehead. She tried to appear unbothered, but she was becoming nervous at the thought of this responsibility.

"Count on me."

"It's a huge risk."

"I don't mind at all."

"They might kill you."

"I don't mind."

Dita tried to sound decisive, but she was unsuccessful. She could not control her trembling legs, and Hirsch stared at her shaking limbs.

"Running the library requires a brave person. . . ."

Dita blushed. The more she tried to stay still, the wilder her trembling became. Her hands began to shake, too, and she feared the director might think her too weak for the job.

"S-s-so you're not counting on me, then?"

"You seem like a brave girl to me."

"But I'm trembling!" she replied, devastated.

Then Hirsch smiled in his particular way. "That's why you're brave. Brave people are not the ones who aren't afraid. Those are reckless people who ignore the risk; they put themselves and others in danger. That's not the sort of person I want on my team. I need the ones who know the risk—whose legs shake, but who carry on."

As she listened, Dita's legs began to tremble less.

"Brave people are the ones who can overcome their own fear. You are one of those. What's your name?"

"My name is Edita Adler, Mr. Hirsch."

"Welcome to Block Thirty-One, Edita. May God bless you. Please call me Fredy."

They had waited quietly until everyone had gone. Then Dita entered Fredy Hirsch's cubicle—a narrow rectangle with a pallet and a pair of old chairs. It was almost bare, with only a few food packages, scraps of material left over from the set of *Snow White*, and Fredy's food bowl in sight.

Hirsch told her something that left her dumbstruck: They had a library on legs, a "living library." Teachers who knew particular books well had become book-people. They rotated among the different groups, telling the children stories they knew almost by heart.

"Mrs. Magda is really good with *The Wonderful Adventures of Nils Holgersson,* and the children have fun when she makes them imagine that they're flying over the skies of Sweden holding on to geese. Šašek does a really good job with stories of the American Indians and the adventures of the Wild West. Dezo Kovác is almost like a walking Bible."

But this living library wasn't enough for Fredy Hirsch. He told her about the books that had reached the camp clandestinely. A Polish carpenter called Mietek had brought three, and a Slovak electrician, another two. They were the sorts of prisoners who moved among the camps with greater freedom, as they were employed to do maintenance work. They had managed to sneak some books from the ramp where the luggage from the arriving transports was sorted by privileged prisoners.

As the librarian, Dita would be in charge of keeping track of which books were lent to which teacher, as well as collecting the books when classes were finished and returning them to their secret compartment.

Hirsch made for a corner where scraps of material were piled up, and moved them aside. He removed a wooden board, and books began to emerge. Dita couldn't restrain her joy and clapped.

"This is your library. It's not much." And he looked at her out of the corner of his eye to see what effect it was having on her.

It wasn't an extensive library. In fact, it consisted of eight books, and some of them were in poor condition. But they were books. In this incredibly dark place, they were a reminder of less somber times, when words rang out more loudly than machine guns.

Dita picked up the books one by one, holding them in her hands as carefully as she would a newborn baby. The first one was an unbound atlas, with a few pages missing. It showed a Europe of the past, with empires that had ceased to exist some time ago. The political maps were a mosaic of vermilion, brilliant greens, orange, navy blue, in sharp contrast to the dullness that surrounded Dita: the dark brown of the mud, the faded ocher of the huts, and an ashy clouded sky. She started to leaf through the pages, and it was as if she were flying over the world. She crossed oceans and mountains, navigating with her finger along the rivers Danube and Volga, and then the Nile. To put all those millions of square kilometers of seas, forests, all of Earth's mountain ranges, all the rivers, all the cities and countries into such a tiny space was a miracle that only a book could achieve.

Fredy Hirsch watched her in silence, taking pleasure in her

absorbed expression. If he had any doubts about the responsibility he'd given to the young Czech girl, they dissipated in that moment. He knew that Edita would look after the library carefully.

The *Basic Treatise on Geometry* was somewhat better preserved. It unfurled a different geography in its pages: a countryside of isosceles triangles, octagons, and cylinders, rows of ordered numbers in squads of arithmetical armies, formations that were like clouds, and parallelograms like mysterious cells.

Her eyes opened wide at the third book. It was *A Short History of the World* by H. G. Wells. A book populated by primitive men, Egyptians, Romans, Maya . . . civilizations that formed empires and then collapsed so that new ones could emerge.

The fourth title was *A Russian Grammar*. She didn't understand a thing, but she liked those enigmatic letters. Now that Germany was also at war with Russia, the Russians were her friends. Dita had heard that there were many Russian prisoners of war in Auschwitz and that the Nazis treated them with extreme cruelty.

There was also a French novel in bad condition and a treatise with the title *New Paths to Psychoanalytic Therapy* by a professor named Freud. There was another novel in Russian with no cover. And the eighth book was Czech, only a handful of sheets held together by a few threads along the spine. Before she could take it in her hands, Fredy grabbed it. She looked at him with the expression of a displeased librarian. She wished she had a pair of tortoiseshell glasses so that she could look at him over their rim, as serious librarians do.

"This one's in a very bad state. It's no good."

"I'll fix it."

"And anyway . . . it's not appropriate for children, especially girls."

Dita narrowed her eyes in irritation.

"With all due respect, Fredy, I'm fourteen years old. Do you honestly believe that after observing on a daily basis thousands of people going to the gas chambers at the edge of the *Lager,* what I read in a novel might shock me?"

Hirsch looked at her with surprise. And it wasn't easy to surprise him. He explained to her that the book in question was called *The Adventures of the Good Soldier Švejk* and was written by a blasphemous alcoholic called Jaroslav Hašek, that it contained scandalous opinions about politics and religion, and more than dubious moral situations. In the end, though, he handed her that book.

Dita caressed the books. They were broken and scratched, worn, with reddish-brown patches of mildew; some were mutilated. But without them, the wisdom of centuries of civilization might be lost—geography, literature, mathematics, history, language. They were precious.

She would protect them with her life.

3.

DITA EATS HER TURNIP SOUP VERY SLOWLY—THEY SAY IT FILLS
you more that way—but sipping it barely takes her mind off her
hunger. Between one spoonful and the next, the groups of teachers
discuss the extraordinary behavior of Morgenstern, their scatter-
brained colleague.

"He's a very strange man. Sometimes he talks a lot, but at other
times he hardly says a word to anyone."

"It would be better if he didn't speak at all. He just talks nonsense. He's off his rocker."

"It was painful to watch him bowing down in front of the Priest
in such a servile manner."

"You couldn't exactly call him a Resistance hero."

"I don't know why Hirsch lets a man with a screw loose give
classes to the children."

Dita overhears them and feels sorry for the old man, who reminds her a bit of her grandfather. She sees him sitting on a stool
at the back of the hut, eating by himself, even talking to himself
while, with his little finger raised with a refinement that is so out of
place in this hut, he ceremoniously lifts the spoon to his mouth as
if he were sharing his meal with aristocrats.

They dedicate the afternoon to the usual children's games and
sporting activities, but Dita is desperate for the school day to finish
and the final roll call to be over so she can race off to see her parents.

In the family camp, news travels quickly from hut to hut, but like in a game of telephone, there are distortions in the retellings.

As soon as she can, Dita rushes off to reassure her mother, who will already have found out about the Block 31 inspection. As she runs down the *Lagerstrasse*, she comes across her friend Margit.

"Ditiňka, I hear you had an inspection in Thirty-One!"

"That disgusting Priest!"

"Did they find anything? Did they detain anyone?"

"Absolutely nothing; there's nothing for them to find there." Dita winked. "Mengele was there, too."

"Dr. Mengele? He's a madman. He experimented with injections of blue ink into the pupils of thirty-six children in an attempt to produce blue-eyed people. It was horrible, Ditiňka. Some died of infection, and others were left blind. You were lucky to escape his notice."

The two girls stop talking. Margit is her best friend, and well aware of her work with the secret library, but Margit knows not to say anything to Dita's mother, Liesl. She would try to stop her, say it was too dangerous. She'd threaten to tell Dita's father, or start begging God to save her. It's better not to tell her, or her father, anything. To change the topic, Dita tells Margit about Morgenstern.

"What a fuss he stirred up. You should have seen the Priest's face as the professor kept dumping out the contents of his pocket each time he bent over."

"I know who you mean now. A very old man with a shabby, patched jacket—he always bows when he passes a lady. He's always bobbing his head! I think that man is a bit crazy."

"And who isn't, in this place?"

When Dita reaches her hut, she sees her parents outside, sitting up against one of the long walls, resting. It's cold outside, but very crowded inside the hut. They look tired, especially her father.

It's a long workday: The guards wake them before dawn. They stand outdoors through a lengthy roll call, exposed to the elements, then labor all day. Dita's father works producing shoulder straps for guns, and his hands are often blackened and blistered from the toxic resins and glues they use. Her mother is a cleaner in a workshop where they make hats. They work many hours with very little food, but at least they are sheltered from the elements. There are many who aren't so lucky: Some must collect dead bodies with carts, some clean the latrines or drain the trenches, others spend the day hauling soup barrels.

Her father gives Dita a wink, while her mother quickly gets to her feet.

"Are you all right, Edita?"

"Ye-e-e-ss."

"You're not just pretending?"

"Of course not! I'm here, aren't I?"

Just then, Mr. Tomášek walks past.

"Hans, Liesl! How are you? I see your daughter still has the prettiest smile in Europe."

Dita blushes, and the two girls leave the grown-ups.

"Isn't Mr. Tomášek kind!"

"Do you know him, too, Margit?"

"Yes, he often visits my parents. Here, many people only look after themselves, but Mr. Tomášek looks after others. He asks them how they're doing; he takes an interest in their problems."

"And he listens to them . . ."

"He's a good man."

"Thank goodness there are still people who haven't been corrupted in this hell."

Margit remains silent. Although she is a year older, Dita's direct way of talking makes her feel uncomfortable, but she knows Dita's right. Auschwitz not only kills innocents; it kills innocence as well.

"It's cold, and your parents are outdoors, Dita. Won't they catch pneumonia?"

"My mother prefers not to be inside with her bunkmate, who has lots of horrible boils . . . though she's no worse than my bunkmate!"

"But you're lucky—you both sleep on top bunks. We're spread among the lowest bunks," said Margit.

"You must really feel the damp seeping up from the ground."

"Oh, Ditiňka, Ditiňka. The worst part isn't what comes up from the ground, but what might come down from above. Vomit, diarrhea . . . bucketloads, Ditiňka. I've seen it in other bunks."

Dita pauses for a moment and turns toward her, looking serious.

"Margit . . ."

"What?"

"You could ask for an umbrella for your birthday."

Margit shakes her head. "How did you two manage to get those places on the top bunks?" she shoots back.

"You know what an uproar there was in the camp when our transport train arrived in December."

The two girls stop talking for a moment. The September veterans had not only been fellow Czechs, they'd been friends, acquaintances, even family members who, like them, had been deported from Terezín. But nobody was pleased to see the new arrivals in December. The addition of five thousand new prisoners to the camp meant they'd have to share the water that dribbled from the taps; the roll calls would become interminable; and the huts would be absolutely jam-packed.

"When my mother and I went inside our assigned hut to find a bunk, it was total chaos."

Margit nods. She remembers the arguments, shouts, and fights among women doing battle over a blanket or a filthy pillow.

"In my hut," Margit explains, "there was a very sick woman who couldn't stop coughing. Each time she tried to sit down on a straw mattress, its occupant would shove her onto the floor. 'Idiots!' the German-appointed woman prisoner who was the barrack supervisor, or *Kapo*, would yell at them. 'Do you think you're healthy? Do you really think it makes any difference whether there's a sick woman sharing your bed?' "

"The *Kapo* was right."

"You're kidding! After she said that, the *Kapo* grabbed a stick and started to beat everyone, even the sick woman."

Dita thinks back to the confusion of shouts, scurrying about, and weeping, and then continues.

"My mother wanted us to leave the hut until things calmed down inside. It was cold outside. A woman said that there wouldn't be enough bunks even if we were to share, that some women would have to sleep on the dirt floor."

"So what did you do?" asked Margit.

"Well, we went on freezing to death outside. You know my mother—she doesn't like to call attention to herself. If a streetcar ran over her one day, she wouldn't cry out, because she wouldn't want to be a topic of conversation. But I was about to explode. So I didn't ask her permission. I took off and ran inside before she could say anything. And I realized something. . . ."

"What?"

"The top bunks were almost all occupied. They had to be the best ones. In a place like this, you have to pay attention to what the old hands are doing."

"I've noticed that some will let you share their bunk if you pay them something. I saw one woman agree in exchange for a potato."

"And a potato's worth a fortune," Dita replies. "She must have had no idea about exchange rates. You can buy lots of things and many favors for half a potato."

"Did you have something to exchange?"

"Not a thing. I checked out which veterans still had a bunk to themselves. Where the bunks already had two occupants, those women were sitting on them with their legs dangling over the edge to mark out their territory. Women who had arrived on our train were wandering around begging for a space, top, bottom, or wherever. There were searching for the least-hardened inmates who might allow them to share their mattresses. But such friendly veterans had already agreed to share their beds."

"That happened to us, too," says Margit. "Luckily, we eventually came across a neighbor from Terezín who helped me, my mother, and my sister."

"I didn't know anyone."

"Did you finally find an understanding veteran?"

"It was too late for that. There were only the angry ones and the selfish ones left. So do you know what I did?"

"No."

"I searched for the worst one of the lot."

"Why?"

"Because I was desperate. I saw a middle-aged veteran with short hair that looked as if it had been bitten off, sitting on her bunk. She had a defiant look on her face, which was split in two by a black scar. You could tell she'd been in jail by the blue tattoo on the back of her hand. A woman approached her, begging for space, and the veteran drove her off with yells, even tried to kick the woman with her dirty feet. Huge, twisted feet they were, too!"

"So what did you do?"

"I cheekily stood right in front of her and said, 'Hey, you!'"

"You didn't! I don't believe it! You're kidding! You see an old hand who looks like a criminal and, without knowing anything about her, you go up to her and calmly say, 'Hey, you'?"

"Who said I was calm? I was scared stiff. But with a woman like that, you can't walk up and say, 'Good evening, madam, do you think the apricots will ripen on time this year?' She'd kick you out of there. I had to speak her language if I wanted her to listen to me."

"And did she?"

"First, she threw me a murderous look. I must have been as white as a sheet, but I tried to hide my fear from her. I told her the *Kapo* would end up randomly assigning women who didn't have a bunk. 'There are still twenty or thirty women outside, and you could end up with any one of them,' I said. 'There's a really fat one who would squash you. And another one whose breath smells more than her feet. And there are others who are old and have bad digestion, and they stink.'"

"Dita, you're terrible! And what did she say?"

"She gave me a dirty look—though I don't think she could give you a kind look even if she wanted to. Anyway, she let me continue. 'I weigh less than forty-five kilos. There's no one thinner on the whole train. I don't snore, I wash every day, and I know when to shut up. You won't find a better bunkmate in all of Birkenau, no matter how hard you look.'"

"And what did she do?"

"She stretched out her head toward me and looked at me like you look at a fly when you don't know whether to squash it or leave it alone. If my legs hadn't been shaking so hard, I would have run away."

"Fine, but what did she do?"

"She said, 'Of course you're sharing with me.'"

"You got your way!"

"No, not yet. I said to her, 'As you can see, I will make a great bunkmate, but I'll only share your bunk if you help me to get another top bunk for my mother.' You can't imagine how angry she became! It was obvious that she wasn't the least bit impressed that a puny young girl would tell her what to do. But I could see her checking out the other women wandering around the hut with a look of disgust on her face. Do you know what she asked me—totally serious?"

"What?"

"'Do you wet the bed?' 'Absolutely not. Never,' I replied. 'Lucky for you,' she answered in her booming, vodka-damaged voice. Then she turned to the woman on the bunk next to her, who didn't have a bunkmate.

"'Hey, Boščovič,' she said, 'did you know they've ordered us to share our pallets?' The other woman pretended she didn't: 'We'll see about that. I'm not convinced by your arguments.'"

"And what did your veteran do?"

"She started arguing. She dug around in her straw mattress and pulled out a piece of twisted wire about ten centimeters long, with a really sharp point. She propped herself up with one hand on her neighbor's bunk and held the wire to her neighbor's throat with the other. There was no question which argument was more convincing. The neighbor quickly nodded her head in agreement. The panic made her so bug-eyed it looked as if her eyes would fall out of their sockets!" And Dita laughed.

"There's nothing funny about that. What a horrible woman! God will punish her."

"Well, I once heard the Christian upholsterer who owned the store on the ground floor of our apartment block say that while God's plan is straight, the path to achieving it is twisted. So maybe twisted wires work, too. I thanked her and said, 'My name is Edita Adler. Perhaps we'll become good friends.'"

"And what was her answer?"

"There wasn't one. She must have thought she'd already wasted too much time on me. She turned toward the wall, leaving barely a hand's width of room for me to lie down with my head at her feet."

"And she didn't say another word?"

"She hasn't spoken to me since, Margit. Can you believe it?"

"Oh, Ditiňka. I would believe anything these days. May God watch over us."

It's dinnertime, so the two girls say good-bye to each other and head back to their barracks. Night has fallen, and only the orange lights illuminate the camp. Dita sees two *Kapos* chatting at the entrance to one of the huts. You can recognize them by their better clothes, their brown "special prisoner" armbands, and the triangular badge that identifies them as non-Jews. A red triangle identifies the political prisoners, many of them Communists or social democrats; a brown one is for Gypsies; a green one for criminals and ordinary delinquents. A black triangle is for social misfits, retarded people, and lesbians, while homosexual men wear a pink triangle. *Kapos* with black or pink triangles are rare in Auschwitz, as these are worn by prisoners of the lowest possible category, almost as low as Jews. In camp BIIb, the exception is the rule. The two *Kapos* chatting to each other—a man and a woman—wear a pink and a black triangle respectively; chances are no one else wants to talk to them.

Dita walks toward her hut, thinking about the chunk of bread she's about to receive. She sees it as a feast, the only decent meal of the day, since the soup is a bowl of slops that serves only to soothe her thirst for a moment.

A black shadow, darker than all the rest, is walking along the *Lagerstrasse* in the opposite direction. People give way to it, stepping aside so that it will walk past without stopping. You'd think it was Death itself, and it is. The tune from Wagner's "The Ride of the Valkyries" filters through the darkness.

Dr. Mengele.

As he gets close to her, Dita gets ready to lower her head and move to one side, like everyone else. But the officer stops, and his eyes bore through her.

"You're the one I'm looking for."

"Me?"

Mengele studies her at length.

"I never forget a face."

His words carry a deadly stillness. If Death were to speak, it would do so with precisely this icy cadence. Dita goes back over what happened in Block 31 earlier in the afternoon. The Priest didn't focus on her in the end, thanks to the altercation with the crazy teacher, and she thought she'd escaped. But she hadn't reckoned on Dr. Mengele. He had been farther away, but it was obvious he'd seen her. His forensic eye would definitely have picked up that she wasn't in the correct spot, that she had one arm across her chest, that she was hiding something. She can read all that in the coldness of his eyes, which are, unusually for a Nazi, brown.

"Number?"

"73305."

"I'm going to keep my eye on you. I'll be watching you even when you can't see me. I'll be listening to you, even when you think I can't hear you. I know everything. If you break the camp rules even fractionally, I'll know, and you'll end up stretched out in my autopsy lab. Live autopsies are very enlightening."

And he nods as he says this, as if he were talking only to himself.

"You see the last waves of blood pumped out by the heart reaching the stomach. It's an extraordinary sight."

Mengele becomes lost in thought, thinking about the perfect surgical laboratory he has set up in Crematorium 2, where he has the most up-to-date equipment at his disposal. He is delighted with the red cement floor, the polished marble dissection table with the sinks set in the middle, and its nickel fittings. It's his altar dedicated to science. He feels proud. Suddenly, he remembers there are some Gypsy children waiting for him to complete an experiment on their craniums, and he strides off in a hurry.

Dita, stunned, stands stock-still in the middle of the campground. Her sticklike legs are shaking. A moment ago there were hordes of people on the *Lagerstrasse*, but now she's all on her own. They've all disappeared into the camp's alleyways.

Nobody approaches her to see if she's all right or if she needs anything. Dr. Mengele has marked her. A few of the inmates who stopped a safe distance away to watch what was happening feel sorry for her; she looks so frightened and confused. Some of the women even know her by sight from the Terezín ghetto. But they choose to hurry away. Survival comes above all else. That's one of God's commandments.

Dita reacts and heads off toward her alleyway. She wonders if he really is going to keep tabs on her. That icy look is the answer. As she walks, the questions keep multiplying in her head. What should she do now? It would be wise to quit her job as librarian. How is she going to manage the books with Mengele hot on her heels? Something about him terrifies her, which is unusual for her. She's come across many Nazis in the past few years, but there's something about this one that sets him apart. She senses that he has a special talent for evil.

She whispers a quick good-night to her mother so that Liesl won't notice her anxiety, and carefully lies down alongside her bunkmate's foul-smelling feet. Her quiet good-night disappears among the cracks in the ceiling.

She can't sleep, but she can't move, either. She has to keep her body still while her head spins. Mengele has given her a warning. And maybe she's privileged, because there'll be no more warnings, for sure. Next time he'll simply stick a hypodermic needle into her heart. She can't go on looking after the books in Block 31. But how can she abandon the library?

If she does, they'll think she's scared. She'll present her reasons, all of them understandable. Anyone in her position with any sense at all would do the same. But she's already well aware that news in Auschwitz jumps from one bunk to the next faster than any flea. If someone in the first bunk says that a man has drunk a glass of wine, by the time the news reaches the last bunk, he's drunk an entire barrel. And they don't do it out of spite. All the women are respectable. It even happens with Mrs. Turnovská, who treats her mother so well and is a good woman. Even she can't control her tongue.

Dita can hear her already: *Of course, the little girl got scared.* . . . And they'll say it with that condescending tone that makes her blood boil, pretending to be understanding. And what makes it even worse is that there's always some kind soul who'll say, *Poor little thing! It's easy to understand. She got frightened. She's just a child.*

A child? Dita thinks. Far from it. *You have to have a childhood to be a child!*

4.

CHILDHOOD . . .

It was during one of her many sleepless nights that Dita came up with the idea of turning her memories into photos and her head into the only album that nobody would ever be able to take away from her.

After the Nazis arrived in Prague, the family had to leave their apartment. Dita had really liked that place. It was in the city's most modern building, with a laundry in the basement and an intercom system that was the envy of all her classmates. She remembers coming home from school and seeing her father standing in the living room, dressed as elegantly as he always was, in his gray double-breasted suit, but looking much more serious than he normally did. He told her they were going to swap their marvelous apartment for one across the river in Smíchov. Without looking at her, he told her it was sunnier. He didn't even joke about it, as he usually did when he wanted to make something seem insignificant. Her mother was leafing through a magazine and didn't say a word.

"I have no intention of leaving!" Dita bellowed.

Her father, dismayed, lowered his head. Her mother got up from the armchair and slapped her so hard that her fingers left marks on Dita's cheek.

"But, Mama," Dita said, more puzzled than hurt—her mother wasn't in the habit of even raising her voice, never mind her hand—"you were the one who said that this apartment was a dream come true. . . ."

And Liesl hugged her.

"It's the war, Edita. It's the war."

A year later, her father was again standing in the middle of the living room, in the same double-breasted suit. By that stage he already had less work in the social security office where he was employed as a lawyer. He used to spend many afternoons at home staring at maps and spinning his world globe. He told her they were moving to the Josefov district. The Nazi *Reichsprotektor*, who governed the whole country, had ordered that all Jews must live there. The three of them and her grandparents had to move into a tiny dilapidated apartment on Elišky Krásnohorské Street. She didn't ask questions anymore, nor did she object.

It was the war, Edita. It was the war.

And eventually, the day came when the summons from the Jewish Council of Prague arrived, ordering them to move yet again, this time, out of Prague. They were to move to Terezín, a small town that had once been a military fortification and had been converted into a Jewish ghetto—a ghetto that seemed awful when she first arrived, and for which she now yearns. The ghetto from which they slid into the mud and ashes of Auschwitz.

After that winter of 1939, when everything began, the world around Dita began to collapse, slowly at first, and then faster and faster. Ration cards, bans—no entry into cafés, no shopping at the times when other citizens were doing theirs, no radios, no access to movies or theaters, no buying of new shoes. . . . The expulsion of Jewish children from schools followed. They weren't even permitted to play in the parks. It was as if the Nazis wanted to ban childhood.

Dita smiles briefly as an image pops into her head: two children walking hand in hand in Prague's old Jewish cemetery, wandering among the graves where small stones weighed down slips of paper so they wouldn't blow away in the wind. Prague's Jewish children, banned from the city's parks and schools, had turned the old cemetery into an adventure playground. The Nazis planned to convert the synagogue and cemetery into a museum about the soon-to-be extinguished Jewish race.

In her mind's eye, the children chased each other around the ancient gravestones covered with grass and lost in centuries-old silence.

Under a chestnut tree, and hidden by two thick gravestones leaning so much they had almost fallen over, Dita showed her little classmate Erik the name on an even bigger stone—Judah Loew ben Bezalel. Erik had no idea who he was, so she told him the story her father used to tell her whenever he put his yarmulke on his head and the two of them went for a walk in the cemetery.

Judah was a rabbi in the Josefov district in the sixteenth century, when all the Jews had to live in the ghetto, as they do now. He studied the Kabbalah and found out how to bring a clay figurine to life.

"That's impossible!" Erik burst in, laughing.

She still smiles now as she remembers how she then resorted to her father's trick: She lowered her voice, put her head next to Erik's, and in a deep voice, whispered,

"The Golem."

Erik's face turned a sickly white. Everyone in Prague had heard of the enormous Golem, a monster.

Dita repeated what her father had told her: The rabbi had succeeded in deciphering the sacred word used by Yahweh to instill the gift of life. He made a small clay figurine and placed a piece of paper with the secret word inside its mouth. And the little statue grew and grew until it became a living colossus. But Rabbi Loew didn't know how to control it, and the colossus with no brain began to destroy the neighborhood and cause panic. He was an indestructible titan, and it looked like it would be impossible to defeat him. There was only one way to do it—wait until he was asleep and then screw up the courage to stick a hand in his mouth as he snored and remove the piece of paper with the magic word. Doing this would turn the monster back into an inanimate being. And that's exactly what the rabbi did. He then shredded the piece of paper and buried the Golem.

"Where?" asked Erik anxiously.

"No one knows. In a secret place. And the rabbi left word that when the Jewish people found themselves in a difficult situation again, another rabbi enlightened by God would emerge to decipher the magic word, and the Golem would save us."

Erik gazed at Dita, full of admiration because she knew mysterious stories like the one about the Golem. He gently stroked her face and, sheltered by the strong cemetery walls and their secrets, kissed her innocently on the cheek.

Dita smiles mischievously as she remembers that moment.

The first kiss, no matter how fleeting it might be, is never forgotten. She recalls with pleasure the joy she felt that afternoon, and is surprised at the capacity for happiness to blossom in the emptiness of war. Adults wear themselves out pointlessly searching for a joy they never find. But in children, it bursts out of every pore.

Dita won't let them treat her like a child. She won't quit. She'll carry on; she must. That's what Hirsch said to her: You chew on fear, and you swallow it. And you carry on. No, she won't abandon the library.

Not a single step backward . . .

Dita opens her eyes in the darkness of the hut, and the intensity of her inner flame turns into the flicker of a candle. She hears coughs, snores, the moans of some woman who might be dying. Maybe she doesn't want to admit to herself that it's not so much what Mrs. Turnovská or any of the other inmates might say that worries her. No, what really concerns her is what Fredy Hirsch would think of her.

A few days ago, she heard him talking with a group of older children from the athletics team that runs around the outside of the hut every afternoon even if it's snowing or raining, cold or freezing. Hirsch runs with them, always at the front, leading the way.

"The strongest athlete isn't the one who finishes first. That athlete is the fastest. The strongest athlete is the one who gets up again every time he falls, the one who doesn't stop when he feels a pain in his side, the one who doesn't abandon the race, no matter how far away the finish line is. That runner is a winner whenever he reaches the finish line, even if he comes in last. Sometimes, no matter how much you want it, being the fastest isn't an option, because your legs aren't as long or your lungs as large. But you can always choose to be the strongest. It's up to you—your willpower and your effort. I'm not going to ask you to be the fastest, but I am going to require you to be the strongest."

Dita is certain that if she told him she had to give up the library, he'd offer her kind, extremely polite, even comforting words . . . but she's not sure she could bear his look of disappointment. Dita sees him as an indestructible man, like the unstoppable Golem in the Jewish legend who, one day, would save them all.

Fredy Hirsch. . . . His name gives her courage.

Dita sifts again through the images stored in her head and finds one from a couple of years ago, of the gentle fields of Strašnice, on the outskirts of Prague. Jews could breathe fresh air there, away from all the restrictions of the city. The Hagibor sports grounds were located there.

In her memory, it was summer, and a hot day, so many of the boys were bare-chested. She could see three people surrounded by a bustling huddle of children and teenagers. The first person was a thin twelve- or thirteen-year-old boy with glasses who was wearing nothing more than a pair of white shorts. The one in the middle—a magician who had introduced himself theatrically as Borghini— was bowing. He was elegantly dressed in a shirt, sport coat, and striped tie. There was a young man on the other side of him who was wearing only sandals and a pair of shorts, which emphasized his slim but athletic body. That day, she learned that his name was Fredy Hirsch and that he was in charge of youth activities at the Hagibor sports grounds. The boy with the glasses was holding one end of a piece of string, the magician was holding it in the middle, and Hirsch was holding the other end. Dita remembers the coach's posture: one hand placed somewhat vainly on his waist while the other hand held on to the string. Hirsch was looking at the magician with a slightly mischievous smile.

The show began, and the enterprising Borghini tried to take on the crushing might of the war with his small arsenal of magic tricks: multicolored handkerchiefs up his sleeve versus cannons, the ace of clubs versus fighter-bombers. And, incredible as it might seem, for just a few moments full of smiling, spellbound faces, magic won out.

A very determined young girl holding a bundle of papers approached Dita and held one out to her.

"You can join us. We organize summer camps in Bezpráví, by the Orlice River, where we play sport and strengthen our Jewish spirit. There's more information about our activities on the flyer."

Her father didn't like those sorts of things. She had overheard him telling her uncle that he didn't approve of mixing politics and sport. They said this Hirsch fellow organized guerrilla warfare games with the children, had them digging trenches from which they pretended to shoot weapons, and talked to them about combat techniques as if they were a small army under his command.

If Hirsch is the commander, Dita is now more than ready to get into any trench. Anyway, she's already in it up to her neck. They are Jews, a stubborn people. The Nazis won't be able to crack her, or Hirsch. She won't quit the library . . . but she'll have to be alert, all eyes and ears, keep an eye on the shadows in which Mengele operates so she doesn't get trapped. She's a fourteen-year-old girl, and they are the most powerful military weapon of destruction in history, but she's not going to take part silently in the procession again. Not this time. She's going to stand up to them.

No matter the cost.

Dita isn't the only one suffering insomnia.

Fredy Hirsch, as the head of Block 31, has been granted the privilege of sleeping in his own cubicle, and in a barrack where he is the only resident. After working on one of his reports, he leaves his cubicle and stands by himself in the silence. The whispering has faded, the books have been closed, the songs are over. . . . When the kids race off, the school goes back to being a crude wooden shed.

They're the best thing we've got, he tells himself.

One more day and one more inspection have passed. Each day is a battle won. His chest shrinks and his straight collarbones disappear into his shoulders. He collapses onto a stool and closes his eyes. He's exhausted, but no one must know. He's a leader. He can't let them down.

If they only knew. . . .

He's lying to them all. If they found out who he really is, they would hate him.

He feels drained. So he drops to the floor, beginning a round of push-ups. He's constantly telling the members of his teams that effort overcomes tiredness.

Up, down; up, down.

The whistle he always wears around his neck bangs rhythmically against the foot-flattened earth. His secret feels like an iron ball shackled to his ankle, but he knows he has no choice. He has to keep going. Up and down . . .

"Weakness is a sin," he whispers, almost out of breath.

Growing up in Aachen, all the children walked to school. Fredy was the only one who ran, his schoolbooks tied to his shoulders with a rope. The store owners would jokingly ask him where he was going in such a hurry, and he greeted them politely, but never slowed down. He had no reason to hurry; he just enjoyed running. Whenever an adult asked him why he ran, he would answer that walking made him feel tired, but running never did.

He would race into the little square in front of the main entrance to the school and then, because there were no old people sitting on the bench at that hour, he would leap over it as if he were taking part in a steeplechase. Whenever the opportunity arose, he would tell his classmates that it was his ambition to be a professional athlete.

At the age of ten, his childhood was smashed into a million pieces when his father died. Sitting on the stool in the barrack,

Fredy tries to picture his father, but he can't. His strongest memory of him back then is of the hole left by his absence. That emptiness, which he felt so acutely, has never been filled. He continues to feel that uneasy sense of being alone, even when he's surrounded by people.

After his father's death, Fredy started to lose the strength to run. He stopped enjoying races and lost his bearings. His mother had to spend all day working, and so, to stop him from spending long stretches at home on his own or fighting with his older brother, she signed him up for a German-Jewish version of the Boy Scouts called the Jüdischer Pfadfinderbund Deutschland or JPD. They ran activities for young children and had a separate sports branch called Maccabi Hatzair.

The first time Fredy entered the large and somewhat shabby premises, with its list of rules tacked to the wall, it smelled of bleach. He remembers choking back his tears. Little by little, young Fredy Hirsch found the warmth that was lacking in his empty house. He found companionship, tabletop games on rainy days, excursions that always included a guitar and someone telling an inspiring story about Israel's martyrs. Games of football and basketball, sack races, athletics—they all became a life raft he could cling to. When Saturday rolled around and all the others stayed at home with their families, he would go to the sports grounds by himself to throw balls at the rusty hoops on the basketball court or do endless rounds of sit-ups until his T-shirt was soaked with sweat.

He wiped out all his concerns and banished his insecurities by training to the point of exhaustion. He would set himself small challenges: race to the corner and back five times in under three minutes, do ten push-ups and clap his hands together on the last one, sink four baskets in four attempts from a particular spot on the basketball court. . . . His mind was a blank while he was concentrating on his challenges; he was almost happy.

His mother remarried, and throughout his adolescence, Fredy felt more at home in the JPD headquarters than at home. When school was over, he'd go straight there, staying late into the evening. He always had some reason to give his mother for not coming home: meetings of the youth board—of which he was a member; the need to organize excursions or sports tournaments; maintenance work around the premises. . . . As he got older, he became less and less capable of connecting with kids his own age. Few of them shared either his heightened Zionist mysticism, which encouraged him to see the return to Palestine as a mission, or his passion for endless sports training. His peers invited him to the odd party, where the first couples began to form, but Fredy kept making excuses. Eventually they stopped asking him.

He discovered that what he enjoyed most was coaching teams and organizing tournaments for the youngest children. And he was very good at it, inspiring the kids with his passion. His teams always fought to the bitter end.

"Let's go! Keep going! Try harder, harder!" he'd shout at the children from the sideline. "If you don't fight for victory, then don't cry when you lose!"

Fredy Hirsch never cries.

Up, down. Up, down. Up, down

When he is finished with his push-ups, Fredy stands, satisfied. That is, as satisfied as the secret keeper can be.

5.

RUDI ROSENBERG HAS BEEN INSIDE BIRKENAU FOR ALMOST TWO years, and that's quite an achievement. It's turned him into an old camp hand at the ripe age of nineteen and earned him the position of registrar. The registrar keeps the books on prisoner numbers in a place where the ebb and flow of people is tragically constant. The Nazis, meticulous about everything, including killing, have a high regard for this position. That's why Rudi doesn't wear the regular prisoner's uniform. He proudly sports a pair of riding pants, a luxury item. All the other prisoners wear filthy striped uniforms except for the *Kapos*, the cooks, and those in positions of trust like the barrack secretaries and registrars. And other exceptional cases, like in the family camp.

Rudi passes through the control post of the quarantine camp he's been assigned to, on the other side of the fence from camp BIIb, the family camp. He displays the affable smile of a model prisoner for any guards he comes across. They let him through when he tells them he's headed for camp BIIb to deliver some lists.

He walks along the wide perimeter dirt road connecting the camps of the Birkenau complex and gazes at the distant line of trees that marks the start of the forest. At this hour on a winter afternoon, it forms a dim outline. A gust of wind carries a faint scent of the wet undergrowth, moss and mushrooms. He closes his eyes for a moment to savor it. Freedom is the smell of a damp forest.

He's been summoned to a secret meeting to talk about the mysterious family camp.

When Rudi Rosenberg arrives at the designated meeting point behind one of the barracks in camp BIIb, two men, leaders of the Resistance, are waiting for him. One wears a cook's apron and is sickly pale; he introduces himself as Lem. David Schmulewski, the other man, started out as a roofer and is now assistant to the *Blockältester* of Block 27 in camp BIIb. He is dressed in civilian clothes: worn corduroy pants and a sweater that's as wrinkled as his face.

They've already received basic information about the arrival of the December intake of prisoners to family camp BIIb, but they want Rosenberg to provide them with all the details he has. Rudi confirms the arrival of five thousand Jews from the Terezín ghetto. They arrived at the family camp in two separate trainloads three days apart. As with the September intake, they've been allowed to stay in civilian clothes, their heads haven't been shaved, and children have been allowed entry.

The two Resistance leaders listen silently. It's hard for them to comprehend why a death factory like Auschwitz, where inmates are valuable only for their labor, would convert one of its camps into something as unprofitable as a family compound.

"I still don't get it," mutters Schmulewski. "The Nazis are psychopaths and criminals, but they're not stupid. Why would they want young children in a forced labor camp when they consume food, occupy space, and don't produce anything useful?"

"Could it be some experiment on a grand scale by that lunatic Dr. Mengele?"

No one knows. Rosenberg turns to another mystery. The documentation that arrived with the September shipment of inmates came with a special annotation: "*Sonderbehandlung* (special treatment) after six months." And *SB6* was added to the number tattooed on each prisoner's arm.

"Does anyone know anything more about that 'special treatment'?"

The question hangs in the air, unanswered. The Polish cook continues to scratch away at a bit of dried food stuck to his apron, which hasn't been clean in a long while. Schmulewski whispers what they're all thinking: "In here, treatments are so special that they kill."

"But what's the point?" asks Rudi Rosenberg. "If they plan to get rid of them, why spend money feeding them for six months? It's not logical."

"It has to be. If you learn anything when you're working near the Germans, it's that everything has its rationale, whatever it might be. It might be terrible or cruel . . . but there's always a reason."

"And even if the special treatment consisted in taking them off to the gas chambers, what could we do?"

"Not a lot right now. We're not even sure that's what it is."

Just then, another man arrives. He's young, tall and strong, and he's nervous. He's not wearing the prisoner's uniform, either; instead, he has a turtleneck sweater—a rare privilege for an inmate. Rudi makes as if to leave so they won't think he's meddling, but the Pole gestures for him to stay.

"Thanks for coming, Shlomo. We get very little information about the special operations unit."

"I won't be able to stay long, Schmulewski."

The young man waves his hands around a lot. Rudi deduces from this that he must be a Latin, and he's not wrong. Shlomo comes from a Jewish-Italian community in Thessaloníki.

"We don't know a great deal about what happens in the gas chambers."

"Three hundred more this morning, just in the second crematorium. Most of them were women and children." Shlomo pauses and looks at them. He wonders if you really can explain the inexplicable. He waves his hands in the air and looks up at the sky, but it's overcast. "I had to help a little girl take off her shoes because her mother was holding a baby, and they have to go into the chamber naked. She kept poking her tongue out at me playfully as I was taking off her sandals. She would have been less than four."

"And they don't suspect anything?"

"May God forgive me. . . . They've just arrived after spending three days traveling in a freight car. They're stunned, frightened. An SS guard with a machine gun tells them they're going to have a shower, and they believe him. What else would they think? The guards get them to hang their clothes on hooks and even tell them to take note of the number of the hook so they can retrieve their clothes afterward. That's how they make them believe they'll be coming back. The guards even insist they tie their shoelaces together so they won't lose their shoes. That way, it's easier to gather up all the shoes later on and take them to the hut we call Canada, where they pick out the best articles of clothing to send to Germany. The Germans make use of everything."

"And you can't warn them?" Rudi jumps in.

He immediately feels Schmulewski's hard stare drilling into him. Rudi has no right to a vote or an opinion here. But the Jewish-Italian answers him in that distressed way he has of speaking, as if he were asking for forgiveness with every word that comes out of his mouth.

"May God forgive me. No, I don't warn them. What would a

mother with two children do? Turn on the armed guards? They'd hit her in front of her children; they'd kick her when she fell down. They do that already, in fact. If anyone asks a question, they break his teeth with their rifle butts so he won't talk anymore, and after that no one says another word; everyone looks elsewhere. The SS won't allow anyone to interfere with the process. Once, a well-dressed, erect old woman arrived, holding the hand of her six- or seven-year-old grandson. That woman knew. I don't know how she knew, but she knew they were going to kill them. She threw herself at the feet of an SS guard, she knelt in front of him and begged him to kill her but to let her grandson live. Do you know what that guard did? He dropped his trousers, took out his penis, and started to urinate over her, just like that. The woman, totally humiliated, went back to her place. Today, there was a very elegant woman. I'm sure she came from a good family. She was embarrassed about having to undress. I stood in front of her, with my back to her, to screen her. Then she was so ashamed of being naked in front of us that she put her daughter in front of her to cover herself. But she thanked me with such a sweet smile. . . ."

He stops for a moment, and the others respect his silence. They even look down as if to prevent themselves from looking immodestly at the naked mother hugging her daughter.

"They went into the chamber with the rest of them, may God forgive me. The guards squash them in, you know? They put in more than can really fit. If there are any healthy men in the group, they leave them till last and then they drive them in with blows so that they'll force their way inside and make room for themselves by pushing against those already in there. Then they seal the chamber, which has showerheads so the prisoners won't be suspicious and will keep on thinking they're going to have a shower."

"And then?" asks Schmulewski.

"We remove the lid of the tank and one of the SS guards throws in a canister of Zyklon gas. Then we wait fifteen minutes, maybe a bit less. . . . And then, silence."

"Do they suffer?"

A sigh, followed by another glance heavenward.

"May God forgive me, you have no idea what it's like. When you enter the chamber, you find a mountain of intertwined corpses. I'm sure many of them die of asphyxiation from being crushed. When the poison hits, the body must react horribly: suffocation, convulsions. The corpses are covered in excrement. Their eyes are bulging and their bodies bleeding, as if everything inside had exploded. Their hands are contorted into claws and twisted around other bodies in an act of desperation, and their necks are stretched upward so tautly in the hunt for air that they look as if they're going to snap."

"And what's your job?"

"I have to cut the hair, especially if it's long or in braids. Then it's picked up by a truck. Since my job doesn't require much effort, I take turns with some of the others pulling out any gold teeth. Or dragging the bodies to the freight elevator which takes them up from the basement to the ovens. Dragging them is awful. First you have to untangle them from the other bodies, which are a real confusion of arms covered in blood and who knows what else. You pull them by the hand, and it's wet. It doesn't take long for your hands to become so slimy that you can't grab hold of anything. In the end, we make use of the old people's walking sticks to grab the bodies by their necks. It's the best way to do it. And then they burn them up top."

"How many murders a day are we talking about?"

"Who knows. There's a day shift and a night shift. They never stop. There are at least two to three hundred people per session, and that's just in our crematorium. Sometimes there's one daytime session; other times, there's two. Sometimes the ovens can't cope with the number of bodies, and they tell us to take the corpses to a clearing in the forest. We load them up into a small truck and then we have to unload them again."

"And do you bury them?"

"That would require too many work squads! They don't want that. May God forgive me. The corpses are sprayed with gasoline and burned. Then the ashes are shoveled onto a truck. I think they use them as fertilizer. The hip bones are too large to burn properly, so they have to be crushed."

"My God," whispers Rudi.

"In case anyone hadn't realized it," says Schmulewski sternly, "that's Auschwitz–Birkenau."

While this somber meeting is taking place, two camps away Dita arrives at Barrack 22, next to the second block of latrines. She looks around: No sign of any guards or suspicious persons. Despite that, she can't shake off the unpleasant sensation of being watched. But she goes inside the hut.

That morning, after roll call, her attention had been caught by an older woman wandering close to the barbed wire fence, despite the fact that it was forbidden. Mrs. Turnovská, whom Dita refers to as Radio Birkenau, had told her mother that the guards gave this woman some leeway because she's the seamstress. The woman— everyone knows her as Dudince because that's the name of the city she comes from in southern Slovakia—finds small broken pieces of wire near the fence, which she sharpens with a stone and then forms into sewing needles.

Dita has committed to continuing as librarian, but she has to find a safer way of carrying out her duties. The time between the last roll call and curfew, after which no one is allowed to leave their barracks, is the time for deals and transactions, and that's when Dudince meets with her customers. She says her repairs are the cheapest in Poland: half a bread ration to shorten a jacket; two cigarettes to take in the waistband on a pair of pants; an entire bread ration to patch a big tear.

She sits on her bunk, a cigarette dangling from her lips, as she measures material with a tape measure she's marked off by eye. When she looks up to see what's blocking her light, she finds a skinny adolescent girl with messy hair and a determined look on her face.

"I want you to make me two pockets to wear inside my smock, attached to the side seams under my armpits. They have to be strong."

The woman takes hold of what's left of the cigarette with the tips her fingers and inhales deeply.

"I get it—a couple of holsters under your clothes. And what are you going to use those secret pockets for?"

"I didn't say they were to be secret . . ."

Dita gives an exaggerated smile, trying to look a bit stupid. The woman raises her eyebrows as she looks at her.

Dita begins to regret having made this trip. There are stories all over the camp of informers who sell their fellow prisoners for a bowl of soup or half a pack of cigarettes. And she notices that the seamstress smokes with the air of a ruined vampire—Dita secretly baptizes her with the name Countess Cigarette Butt.

It does also occur to Dita, however, that if the seamstress were receiving an informer's privileges, there'd be no need for her to spend her afternoons sewing by the feeble light of the lamps in the hut. And she feels a certain tenderness toward the seamstress.

No, Countess Patches is a better nickname for her.

"Well, yes, it's a bit secret. I want to carry some mementos of my dead grandmothers."

Dita adopts the air of a naïve young girl again.

"Look, I'm going to give you some advice," says the seamstress. "And I'll even give it to you for free. If you can't do a better job of lying, you'd be better off telling the truth from now on."

The woman takes another deep drag on her cigarette, so deep that the burning embers are right at her yellow-stained fingers. Dita blushes and looks down. Old Dudince is the one who smiles now, like a granny confronted by a naughty granddaughter.

"Child, I don't give a damn about what you're going to put in them. It could be a gun, for all I care; in fact, I hope it is a gun and you shoot some of those bastards," she says, spitting out some dark saliva. "I'm only asking because it sounds like what you want to hide is heavy, and if it weighs a lot, it'll pull your smock out of shape and be very noticeable. So I'd have to add some pleats to the side seams to reinforce them so they can bear the weight."

"It's heavy. But I'm afraid it's not a gun."

"Fine, fine; it's of no interest to me. I don't want to know any more. It will require some work. Have you brought any material? No, of course not. Well, Aunt Dudince has some leftover scraps that'll do. Sewing it will cost you half a ration of bread and a piece of margarine, and the material will be another quarter ration of bread."

"Done," Dita replies.

The seamstress looks at her in amazement—even more than when she thought Dita wanted to hide a gun.

"You're not going to bargain?"

"No. You're doing a job, and it deserves fair recompense."

The woman's laugh turns into a cough, and then she spits off to one side.

"Young people! You know nothing about life. Is that what that handsome director of yours teaches you? Still, a bit of integrity isn't a bad thing, either. Look, forget about the margarine; I'm sick of that yellow fat. Just make it half a ration of bread; the material isn't a big deal, so I'll give it to you for free."

Night has fallen by the time Dita leaves Countess Patches, and she heads quickly for her hut. She doesn't want any more unexpected encounters at this hour of the night. But a hand grabs her arm and a hysterical shriek emerges from her throat.

"It's me—Margit!"

Dita recovers her breath as her friend looks at her with alarm.

"What a yell! You seem upset. Has something happened?"

Margit is the only person she can talk to about Mengele.

"It's that damn doctor's fault. . . ." She can't even think of a nickname for him; her mind goes blank when she thinks about him. "He's threatened me."

"Who are you talking about?"

"Mengele."

Margit's hand covers her mouth in horror, as if Dita has referred to the devil himself. And in fact, she has.

"He told me he'll never take his eye off me, and if he catches me doing anything odd, he'll slit me open like a calf in the slaughterhouse."

"That's terrible. Oh my God! You'll have to be careful!"

"What am I supposed to do?"

"You must be very careful."

"I am already."

"They were telling a terrible story in our row of bunks yesterday!"

"What?"

"I overheard one of my mother's friends telling her that Mengele worships the devil and goes into the forest at night with black candles."

"What nonsense!"

"I swear that's what they were saying. The *Kapo* had told them. She said the Nazi chiefs approve of that sort of thing. They don't have any religion."

"They say lots of things—"

"Pagans do that sort of thing. Worship Satan."

"Well, God protects us—more or less."

"Don't talk like that! It's not right! Of course God protects us."

"Well, I don't feel very protected in here."

"He also teaches us that we have to look after ourselves."

"I'm already doing that."

"That man is the devil. They say he cuts open the stomachs of pregnant women with a scalpel and no anesthetic, and then he cuts open the fetuses as well. He injects healthy people with typhoid bacteria so he can see how the illness develops. He exposed a group of Polish nuns to X-rays until the radiation burned them. They say he makes boys have sex with their twin sisters so he can find out if they'll produce twins. How revolting! He's performed skin grafts, and the patients have died of gangrene. . . ."

They fall silent as they imagine Mengele's laboratory of horrors.

"You've got to be careful, Dita."

"I've already told you that I am!"

"Even more careful."

"We're in Auschwitz. What do you want me to do? Take out life insurance?"

"You've got to treat Mengele's threat more seriously! You've got to pray, Dita."

"Margit . . ."

"What?"

"You sound like my mother."

"And what's wrong with that?"

"I don't know."

The two of them stop talking until Dita decides to speak again.

"My mother mustn't find out, Margit. Please! She'd be worried, she wouldn't sleep, and her concern would end up making me fret."

"And your father?"

"He's not well, though he says he feels fine. I don't want to worry him, either."

"I won't say a word."

"I know."

"But I think you ought to tell your mother—"

"Margit!"

"Okay, okay. It's your decision."

Dita smiles. Margit is the big sister she never had.

She walks back to her hut accompanied by the crunching sound of her shoes on the frozen mud. She's also accompanied by the rare sensation of a pair of eyes staring at her back. When she looks behind her, though, all she can see are the reddish bursts from the ovens, which, seen from afar, have an unreal or nightmarish quality to them. She reaches the hut safe and sound, kisses her mother, and then curls up around the oversized feet of her veteran bunkmate. She thinks that maybe the woman moves her legs away a little to give her a bit more room, but when Dita says good night to her, she doesn't even answer. Dita knows she'll have a hard time going to sleep, but she closes her eyes and squeezes her eyelids tight just to be contrary. She's so stubborn that, in the end, she does fall asleep.

The first thing Dita does after roll call is go to Fredy Hirsch's cubicle. She knocks three times, slowly and distinctly, so that Hirsch will know it's the librarian. He opens the door and then closes it again as soon as she has slipped inside. Then he opens the secret trapdoor just long enough to remove the two books that have been requested for that day's work: the geometry book and *A Short History of the World*.

Hirsch had happily agreed to her suggestion for hiding the books, but four is the limit: It's all that Dita's secret pockets can hold at a time. The thin canvas pockets are tied to each other at the waist so they won't move around.

Dita has to undo the top few buttons of her smock to put the books inside the pockets. Fredy watches, and she hesitates briefly. A respectable young girl shouldn't be by herself in a man's room, and she certainly shouldn't be unbuttoning her dress in front of him. If her mother found out, it would be a disaster. But there's no time to lose. When she unbuttons the smock, one of her small breasts is exposed. Fredy realizes this and immediately looks away in the direction of the door. Dita blushes, but she also feels proud; she's no longer a little girl.

She leaves the *Blockältester*'s cubicle with her hands empty; the two little volumes are perfectly concealed under her clothes.

Anyone who saw her going in and coming out would have no idea she was taking something away. She takes advantage of the flurry of activity after the roll call to make her way to the back of the hut. She hides behind a pile of wood and takes the books out of the hidden pockets. The others have no idea where they've come from. The children look at her with the same smiling admiration they have for a magician and his tricks.

It's Avi Fischer who's asked for the math book for his group of children, the oldest in the school. Dita sees herself as just an ordinary girl whom nobody notices. That's why, when she started as the librarian, she assumed she'd hand the book over to the teacher, and no one would pay any attention to her. She'd melt into the crowd like a shadow. But she was wrong.

When she reaches a group, instinct and curiosity make even the most unruly children suddenly stop what they're doing and watch her. The teacher takes the book by the cover and opens it, reverent.

Many of the children hated books when they were going to regular school. Books were synonymous with boring classes and homework, which prevented them from going outside to play. But here a book is like a magnet; the children are drawn to it.

Dita's attention is caught by Gabriel, a mischievous redhead covered in freckles. He's always making animal noises during class, or pulling a girl's hair, or plotting some prank. But even he looks at the book, totally absorbed.

When Dita hands over her second book, other teachers signal that they, too, would like a book. She crosses paths with Seppl Lichtenstern, a deputy director, and comments on the new interest.

"I don't know what's happened. Suddenly, I'm being flooded with requests for books."

"They've realized the library service works."

Dita smiles, a little overwhelmed by the compliment and the responsibility. Everyone expects so much of her now.

"Seppl, I have a suggestion. Has Fredy told you about my invention for hiding books under my clothing?"

"Yes, he thinks it's very clever."

"Well, it makes things easier if there's a sudden inspection, even if they don't happen too often. What I'm proposing is that you use my secret pockets as a model and have two more made up for another assistant volunteer. That way we could have all the books out here during the day at the disposal of the teachers. Then it really would be like a genuine library."

Lichtenstern stares at her.

"I'm not sure I understand what you're proposing . . ."

"I'd have the books out on top of the chimney during morning classes, and that way, each time there's a class changeover, the teachers could come and ask for a book. Teachers could even request more than one book in the course of a morning, if they wanted to. If there were an inspection, we'd hide the books in the secret pockets under our clothes."

"You want to have the books out on top of the chimney? That's reckless. I don't approve of that."

"Do you think Fredy would agree?"

The naïveté with which Dita asks the question is so exaggerated that the deputy director loses control. Could it be that this child is trying to undermine his authority?

"I'll discuss it with the director, but you might as well forget the idea. I know Fredy."

But Lichtenstern is wrong. Here, no one knows anyone.

6.

LICHTENSTERN OWNS THE ONLY WATCH IN THE CAMP, AND AT THE end of the morning he bangs a gong made from a particularly thin metal bowl, which sounds loudly to signal that classes are over. It's time for soup. First, though, the children must form a straight line and walk to the washroom to rinse their hands.

Dita walks over to Professor Morgenstern's corner and picks up the H. G. Wells book he has been using to explain the fall of the Roman Empire to his students. The professor looks like a shabby Father Christmas with his close-cropped white hair, unshaven white stubble, and eyebrows that look like pieces of white wire. His very worn jacket is coming apart at the shoulder seams and has no buttons. Despite that, he stands very tall in it. He walks with a regal dignity that matches the old-fashioned, if somewhat excessive, politeness of his manners, such as his habit of addressing even the youngest child as "young man" or "young lady."

Dita takes hold of the book with both hands just in case the clumsy old man drops it. She has felt especially curious about him ever since that incident during the inspection, which served her so well in allowing her to elude the Priest. So, some afternoons, she goes to his corner to visit him. Professor Morgenstern always hastens to stand as soon as he sees her coming, and gives her a very deep bow. It amuses her that he starts to talk without preamble.

"Are you aware of the significance of the distance between your eyes and your eyebrows?" he asks, intrigued. "It's hard to find people with the ideal distance—neither too close nor too far away."

His words tumble out as he speaks enthusiastically about the most absurd topics, but he can also suddenly stop talking and gaze up at the ceiling or into space. If anyone tries to interrupt him, he gestures with his hand for them to wait a moment.

"I'm listening to the wheels in my brain turning," he declares very seriously.

He doesn't take part in the conversations the rest of the teachers have at the end of the day. Nor would he be particularly welcome. Most of them think he's crazy. On those afternoons when his students are playing with the other groups at the back of the hut, he's usually sitting by himself. Professor Morgenstern makes origami birds out of the few scraps of paper that have been discarded because there's no more space to write on them.

On this particular afternoon, when Dita approaches him, he leaves a small piece of paper half folded and hastily stands up to greet her with a small dip of his head. He looks at her through his cracked glasses.

"Miss Librarian . . . it's an honor."

His greeting, which flatters her and makes her feel grown up, strikes her as somewhat peculiar. Just for a moment, she wonders if he's making fun of her, but she quickly rejects that possibility. His eyes are kind. The professor talks to her about buildings; he was an architect before the war. When she tells him that he still is one and he'll continue to put up buildings, he smiles.

"I don't have the strength to raise anything anymore, not even my own body from this very low bench."

For several years before he arrived in Auschwitz, he had been unable to pursue his career because he was a Jew, and his memory is starting to fail, he tells her.

Morgenstern confesses to Dita that he sometimes asks her to bring him a book, but then gets distracted and talks about other topics and doesn't even get around to opening it.

"So why do you request it?" Dita asks him reproachfully. "Aren't you aware that we have a limited number of books and you can't ask for them on a whim?"

"You're right, Miss Adler. You're absolutely right. I beg your forgiveness. I'm an egotistical and capricious old man."

And then he stops talking, and Dita doesn't know what to say, because he seems genuinely distressed. And then, for no obvious reason, he suddenly smiles. In a low voice, as if he were telling her a secret, he explains that having a book in his lap while he talks to the children about the history of Europe or the exodus of the Jews makes him feel like a real teacher.

"That way, the children pay attention to me. The words of a crazy old man are of no interest to them, but if the words come from a book . . . that's another matter. Within their pages, books contain the wisdom of the people who wrote them. Books never lose their memory."

And he brings his head up close to Dita as if to entrust something very mysterious to her. She can see his untidy white beard and those tiny eyes.

"Miss Adler . . . books know everything."

Dita leaves Morgenstern absorbed in his origami, attempting to make what looks like a seal. She feels the old professor has a few screws loose, but even so, he makes sense.

Lichtenstern waves Dita over. He looks irritated—the same way he looks when he's out of cigarettes.

"The director says he likes your suggestion."

The deputy director watches her closely for any display of triumph, but her expression is serious and focused. Secretly, she is overjoyed.

"He's given his approval; so be it. But at the first sign of an inspection, the books have to be hidden quickly. That is *your* responsibility."

Dita nods her agreement.

"There is one point on which I have absolutely not compromised," Lichtenstern states more cheerfully, as if this might restore his wounded pride. "Hirsch kept insisting that he would wear the hidden pockets in case there was an inspection. I've made him see the stupidity of this plan. He has to receive the guards—he'll be right next to them, so he can't be found carrying any package. A different assistant will be with you in the library each day."

"Perfect, Seppl! We'll launch the public library right away!"

"I find this business with the books a total madness." And he sighs as he heads off. "But is there anything in this place that isn't mad?"

Dita leaves the hut happy, but also nervous, as she thinks about how she's going to organize things. She's busy thinking when she runs into Margit, who's been waiting for her outside. Just then, they see a man coming out of the makeshift hospital barrack. He pulls a cart; in it, a body covered with a piece of canvas. It's so common to see corpses going past that hardly anyone seems to notice anymore. The two girls walk on in silence until they come across Renée, a young friend of Margit's. Her clothes are covered with mud after a day spent working in the drainage ditches, and the bags under her eyes make her look older.

"You really lucked out with your work assignment, Renée!"

"Bad luck follows me everywhere . . ." she says somewhat enigmatically to make sure she captures the attention of the two girls.

She gestures for them to follow her down an alleyway between two of the huts. They find a spot at the back of one of them, a few meters away from a group of men who, given the way they are whispering and looking around warily, must be talking politics. The three girls huddle together to try and keep warm, and then Renée starts to talk.

"There's a guard who looks at me."

The other two girls exchange puzzled looks. Margit has no idea how to respond, but Dita gets cheeky.

"That's why they pay the guards, Renée. To watch the prisoners."

"But he looks at me in a different way. . . . He stares. He waits until I step out of line once roll call is over, and then he follows me with his eyes; I can feel them. And he does the same thing again with the afternoon head count."

Dita is on the verge of making another joke at Renée's expense, telling her she's very vain, but she notices how worried the girl is and opts to keep quiet.

"At first it didn't seem significant, but this afternoon, while he was patrolling the camp, he detoured from the middle of the *Lagerstrasse* and came over to the drain where we were working. I didn't dare turn around, but I could tell he was very close by. Then he walked away."

"Maybe he was just inspecting the work being done on the ditch."

"But he went right back to the middle of the *Lagerstrasse* and didn't make any other detours till he got to the end. It's as if he was keeping an eye only on me."

"Are you sure it's always the same SS guard?"

"Yes. He's short, so he's easy to spot." And she covers her face with her hands as she says this. "I'm frightened."

"That girl gets too easily flustered," says Dita somewhat contemptuously when Renée leaves them.

"She's scared. I am, too. Aren't you ever afraid, Dita? You're the one who should be most scared, and yet you're the least frightened of all of us."

"Nonsense! Of course I'm afraid. I just don't go around trumpeting it."

"Sometimes you need to talk about things."

They remain silent for a minute and then say good-bye. Dita returns to the *Lagerstrasse*. It has started to snow, and people are gathering in their huts. These are hotbeds of infection, but at least it's not quite so cold inside. Dita can see the door of her hut, Barrack 16, in the distance. There isn't the usual crowd of people milling in the doorway. Married couples often take advantage of the hour before curfew to be together. She soon realizes why no one's there. Notes from Puccini's opera *Tosca* are floating in the air. Dita recognizes it because it's one of her father's favorites. Someone's whistling the notes with precision, and when she looks more carefully, she makes out the figure of a man with the flat cap of an SS officer leaning against the frame of the door.

"My God . . ."

He seems to be waiting for someone. But no one wants him waiting for them. Dita stops; she doesn't know if she's been spotted. A group of four women overtakes her. They chat anxiously about their husbands as they walk briskly. Dita takes two strides, lowers her head, and walks right behind them so they'll provide cover for her. Just as they get to the door of the hut, she scoots around the women and almost races inside.

She runs to her row of bunks and leaps up onto her bed. For the first time ever, she's pleased to see that her bunkmate is already there, and she burrows beside her dirty feet, as if she believes that by doing so, she'll be able to hide from that all-seeing medical captain. There's no sound of hurried footsteps or German commands. Mengele isn't chasing after her, and she feels momentary relief.

She doesn't know that no one has ever seen Mengele running. *Why run?* he thinks. *Prisoners have nowhere to hide. It's like catching fish in a barrel.*

Her mother tells Dita not to worry, there's still time before the curfew. Dita nods and even manages to fake a smile.

Dita says good night first to her mother, and then to her bunkmate's filthy socks, which smell like overripe cheese. She gets no reply; she no longer expects one. She wonders what Mengele was doing there, at the entrance to her hut. If he was waiting for her—if he believes she could be hiding something from the camp commanders—why doesn't he arrest her? She has no idea. Mengele cuts open thousands of stomachs and looks inside them with greedy eyes, but no one has been able to see what's inside his head. The lights are turned off, and she finally feels safe. But then she realizes she's mistaken.

When Mengele threatened her, she was unsure if she should tell the leaders of Block 31. They would relieve her of her responsibility. But everyone would think she'd asked to give up her position out of fear. And so she has made the library more accessible and more visible. She's risked more, so that no one is left in any doubt: Dita Adler is not afraid of any Nazi.

But is this right? she asks herself.

If she puts herself at risk, she's putting everyone else at risk. If they find her with the books, they'll shut down Block 31. The dream of leading anything like a normal life will be over for five hundred children. She has sacrificed sound judgment to her foolish wish to appear brave.

Dita opens her eyes, and the dirty socks still lurk in the dark. She can't hide the truth in the thin canvas compartments under her smock. Truth weighs too much. It ends up tearing the bottom out of any lining, dropping noisily, and shattering everything. She thinks about Hirsch. He is a totally transparent man, and she has no right to hide the facts from him.

Fredy doesn't deserve that.

Dita decides that she'll talk to him the next day. She'll explain that Dr. Mengele is keeping a close eye on her and that the library—and Block 31—is at risk. Hirsch will relieve her of the position, of course. No one will look at her with admiration anymore. That makes her feel a little sad. It's easy to commend the hero whose actions are visible. But how do you measure the bravery of those who step aside?

7.

RUDI ROSENBERG STROLLS UP TO THE FENCE THAT SEPARATES the quarantine camp, BIIa, where he has his office, from the hustle and bustle of the family camp. As registrar, he sent a message to Fredy Hirsch arranging a time to meet and chat across the wire fence. Rosenberg has a great deal of respect for the work the youth instructor is doing in Block 31. There is the odd malicious person who believes that Hirsch collaborates too enthusiastically with the camp commanders, but on the whole, people find him sympathetic and reliable. Schmulewski maintains, in that rasping voice of his, that "he's as trustworthy as any person can be in Auschwitz." Rosenberg has gradually become closer to Hirsch through fleeting conversations and the occasional favor with his lists. And not just because he likes him. Schmulewski has asked him to find out what he can about Hirsch discreetly. Information is far more valuable than gold.

What Rudi isn't expecting this morning is that the head of Block 31 will meet him accompanied by a girl who, in spite of her long, dirty skirt and outsized woolen jacket, has the grace of a gazelle.

Fredy speaks of the problems he's having with supplies for Block 31 and his attempts to get approval for further improvements to rations for the children.

"I've heard tell," says Rosenberg in a neutral tone to suggest that the comment is trivial, "that the play you put on in Block

Thirty-One to celebrate Hanukkah was a real success. They say the SS officers clapped enthusiastically. Apparently, Kommandant Schwarzhuber had a really good time."

Hirsch is well aware that the Resistance still doesn't trust him. He doesn't trust the Resistance, either.

"Yes, they enjoyed it. I took advantage of Dr. Mengele's good mood to ask them to assign us the warehouse next to the hut where they store clothing so we can use it as a day care center for the youngest children."

"Dr. Mengele in a good mood?" Rosenberg's eyes widen at the unlikely possibility that a person who sends hundreds of people to their death on a weekly basis without batting an eyelid could experience such a human emotion.

"The order arrived today with his authorization. It means the little kids can have their space and won't distract the older children."

Rosenberg nods and smiles. He doesn't realize it, but he's staring into the eyes of the girl standing silently a short distance away. Hirsch notices, and introduces her as Alice Munk, one of the young assistants who helps out in Block 31.

Rudi tries to focus on what Hirsch is telling him, but he can't keep his eyes off the young assistant, who smiles back at him cheekily. Hirsch, who is able to stand motionless and fearless in the face of a battalion of SS officers, feels awkward at the sight of the flirting between the two teenagers. Love has been a source of endless problems for him from the time he reached adolescence. Since then, he's tried to fill his time with tournaments and training, and organizing endless events, all to keep his mind occupied. Keeping busy has also allowed him to hide the fact that, despite being incredibly popular, he always ends up on his own.

In the end, Fredy tells the two youngsters he's got something urgent to do. He slips away.

"I'm Rudi."

"I know. And my name is Alice."

As soon as they are on their own, Rudi attempts to demonstrate his finest seduction skills. They are limited; he's never had a girlfriend. He's never had sex. Other than freedom, you can buy and sell everything in Birkenau, including sex. But he's never wanted— or maybe never dared—to try. Rudi rushes to fill the momentary silence. He wants more than anything for her to stay there forever, on the other side of the wire fence, and to smile at him with those pink lips, chapped by the cold, which he'd love to heal with a kiss.

"How's the work in Block Thirty-One?"

"Pretty good. It's our job as assistants to keep everything functioning. Some of us get the fire going when there's coal or wood, which isn't very often. Others help to feed the little ones. And we also sweep the floor. Right now, I'm in the pencils group."

"Pencils?"

"There really aren't a lot of pencils, and they're kept for special occasions. So we make basic ones for everyday use."

"And how do you make them?"

"First, using two stones, we file the edges of some teaspoons until they're really sharp. Then, we use them to sharpen the ends of pieces of wood that can't be used for anything else. I usually do the last bit: scorching the tips in the fire until they're as black as coal. The children can write a few words with each of these, but it means you have to be sharpening the tips and scorching the ends of new bits of wood every day."

"For all the kids you've got! Maybe I could get you some real pencils—"

"Could you?" Alice's eyes sparkled, to Rudi's delight. "But it would be really hard to get them into our camp."

Her words please Rudi even more. This gives him a chance to shine a little.

"All I need is someone I can trust on the other side of the fence. . . . Maybe that could be you."

Alice nods vehemently, happy to be even more useful to Hirsch. She admires Fredy deeply, like all the young assistants.

As soon as he's said it, the registrar feels a stab of doubt. Things have gone well for him so far in Auschwitz, and he's landed a privileged position because he's played his cards well. He's learned how to win over influential inmates, and he's acquired the knack of risking only what is absolutely necessary, dealing in goods and services that are low-risk but highly beneficial to his standing. Acquiring pencils to hand over to a children's hut is neither beneficial nor wise. But he looks at the smile and the sparkle in the girl's black eyes, and forgets everything else.

"Three days from now. At this very spot in the fence, and at the same time."

Alice nods her agreement and runs off nervously, as if she were suddenly in a great hurry. He watches her go, her hair ruffled by the cold afternoon breeze. He'll have to break the rule for survival that has worked so well for him so far: Don't ask for favors for which you don't get any return. He's made a bad deal with that girl and yet, incomprehensibly, he's happy. As he makes his way back to his hut in camp BIIa, he feels weak, as if his legs were giving way. He never figured falling in love would feel so much like the flu.

Dita Adler's legs are shaking, too. The children and their teachers enter the hut, noting that the librarian is on the other side of the chimney with a stack of books in front of her. They haven't seen so many books in one place for months—not since Terezín. The teachers come up and read the spines of the books that are still legible, and then ask with their eyes if they can pick up the books. Dita agrees, but she doesn't take her eyes off them. When one of the women opens the psychology book too forcefully, Dita asks her to be more careful.

"They're very fragile," Dita tells her, forcing a smile.

The books have to come back to her at the end of each class so that they can be rotated, and so Dita knows exactly where they are. She spends the morning observing their movement throughout the hut. She watches a teacher right at the very back gesticulating, the geometry book in her hand. She sees the atlas propped up on a stool nearby; it's a big book but it still fits snugly into her inside pocket. She can easily make out the green cover of the Russian grammar book, which the teachers sometimes use to astonish the children with its mysterious Cyrillic letters. There's less of a call for the novels. Some of the teachers have asked if they can read them, but that can only happen inside Block 31.

She should ask Seppl Lichtenstern if he'll allow her to lend the books to the teachers who are free in the afternoon when the children have games or when Avi Fischer's very popular choir is rehearsing. When the choir sings "Alouette," the whole hut is filled with happy voices.

At the end of the morning, all the books are returned, and Dita gathers them up with relief. She scowls at any teacher who returns a book in worse condition than when it was borrowed. She has come to know every wrinkle, every rip, every scar.

Fredy Hirsch, papers in hand and looking snowed under, walks past Dita's display on top of the chimney. He pauses and looks at the small library. Fredy is one of those people who are always in a hurry but always have time.

"Well, well, young lady. This really is a library now."

"I'm glad you like it."

"This is very good. We Jews have always been a cultured people." And he smiles as he says this. "If there's anything I can do, just let me know."

Hirsch turns around and starts to stride off energetically.

"Fredy!" Dita still feels embarrassed about addressing him so informally, but he insisted that she do so. "There *is* something you could do for me."

He looks at her quizzically.

"Get me some tape, glue, and a pair of scissors. These poor books need attention."

Hirsch nods. As he heads toward the door, he smiles. He never tires of repeating to anyone who'll listen, *The children are the best thing we have.*

In the afternoon, the little kids take advantage of the fact that it's stopped raining to go outside and play tag or hunt for invisible treasures in the wet mud. The older ones place their stools in a large semicircle. Dita has already gathered up her books, so she moves nearer to listen. Hirsch is in the middle of the group, and he's talking to them about one of his favorite topics—the *aliyah*, or march to the lands of Palestine. The children listen, absorbed.

"*Aliyah* is much more than an emigration. No, that's not what it's about. It's not a question of going to Palestine as you might move anywhere else to earn a living and nothing more. No, no, no." There's a long pause, filled by an expectant silence. "It's a journey to connect with the strength of your ancestors. It's picking up a thread that was broken. It's occupying the land and making it yours. It's something much more profound. It's *hagshama atzmit*, or self-fulfillment. You may not have noticed, but you have a light-bulb inside you. Yes, you do—don't give me those looks—it's in there. . . . Even you, Markéta. But it's switched off. You might say, *Who cares? I've lived like this so far, and things have gone all right.* Of course you can live like you have so far, but it will be a mediocre life. The difference between living with the lightbulb switched off or on is like lighting up a dark cave with a match or a spotlight. If you carry out *aliyah* and undertake the march to the land of our ancestors, that light will go on with incredible force and brighten you within as soon as you set foot in Palestine. It's not something I can tell you about. You have to experience it for your-selves. Then you'll understand it all. And that's when you'll know who you are."

The look of concentration on the faces of the teenagers is abso-lute. Their eyes are wide open, and some of them unwittingly stroke their chests as if they were searching for the switch that could turn on those switched-off lights Hirsch says they carry in-side them.

"We look at the Nazis with their modern weaponry and their shiny uniforms, and we think they are powerful, invincible even. Don't be deceived: There is nothing inside those shiny uniforms. They're just an outer shell. They're nothing. We're not interested in shining on the outside. We want to shine on the inside. That's what will give us victory in the end. Our strength isn't in uniforms—it's in faith, pride, and determination."

Fredy pauses and looks at his audience, who are watching him attentively.

"We're stronger than them because our hearts are stronger. We're better than them because our hearts are more powerful.

That's why they won't defeat us. That's why we'll return to the land of Palestine; that's where we'll take a stand. And no one will ever humiliate us again. Because we'll arm ourselves with pride, and with swords . . . very sharp swords. Those who say we are a nation of accountants lie: We are a nation of warriors, and we'll repay all the blows and all the attacks on us a hundred times over."

Dita listens in silence for a while and then slips away.

She waits to see Hirsch when everyone has gone. She doesn't want anyone else to hear about the incident with Mengele. She notices some of the older girls laughing. And some boys, who strike her as silly idiots with pimples, like that Milan who thinks he's so good-looking. Well, he is good-looking, but if an idiot like that tried to flirt with her, she'd tell him to get lost. But Milan would never look at a skinny girl like her anyway.

There are still too many teachers and assistants chatting in little groups, so in the meantime, she hides in the small nook behind a pile of wood that old Professor Morgenstern sometimes sneaks away to. There, Dita sits on a stool and feels a piece of paper brush against her hand: It's a crinkled, spiky little origami bird. She feels like looking through her mental photo album of Prague, perhaps because when you can't dream about the future, you can always dream about the past.

She comes across a very clear image: her mother sewing a horrendous yellow star onto her beautiful deep-blue blouse. It's her mother's face in that snapshot that most upsets her. She's concentrating on her needle, her face as impassive and neutral as if she were sewing the hem on a skirt. Dita remembers that when she angrily asked her mother what she was doing to her favorite blouse, her mother answered what difference did it make? She didn't even look up from what she was doing. Dita recalls clenching her fists, and bursting with outrage. That yellow star made from thick fabric looked awful on top of the satin cloth of her blue blouse. It would look even worse on her green shirt. She couldn't understand how her mother, who was so elegant, who spoke French, and who read those beautiful European fashion magazines she kept on the small coffee table in the living room, could sew such ugly cloth patches on their clothes. *It's the war, Edita . . . it's the war,* her mother whispered, without looking up from her sewing. And Dita didn't say another word, just accepted it as inevitable, as her mother and the other adults had already done. It was the war; there was nothing you could do about it.

She curls up in her hidey-hole and searches for another image, from her twelfth birthday. She can see the apartment, her parents, her grandparents, her aunts and uncles, and some of her cousins. The whole family is around her, and she's in the middle waiting for something. There's a hint of that melancholy smile of hers, the one that appears when she removes her "brave girl" mask and the timid Dita emerges. What's odd is that no one else in the family is smiling.

She remembers that particular party well. It was the last one she ever had, with a delicious cake made by her mother. There haven't been any cakes since then. It's true that that particular strudel, which makes her mouth water now as she remembers it, was much smaller than the ones her mother usually made, but she didn't complain at the time because she had spent the entire week watching her mother going in and out of dozens of stores trying to get hold of more raisins and apples. Impossible! She'd be waiting at the entrance to Dita's school each day with her empty shopping bag and not a hint of annoyance. That was her mother.

On that twelfth birthday, her mother appeared in the living room, smiling nervously and carrying her present. Dita's eyes lit up because it was a shoe box, and she'd been hoping for a new pair of shoes for months. She preferred light-colored ones, with buckles and, if possible, with a small heel.

She hurriedly opened the box, and inside she found a pair of sad-looking, black, everyday shoes with closed toes like school shoes. When she looked at them more closely, she noticed they weren't even new; there were scratches on the toes, which had been covered up with shoe polish. A thick silence suddenly filled the air: Her parents, grandparents, aunts, and uncles were looking at her expectantly, waiting for her reaction. She forced a big smile and said she really loved her present. She went over to kiss her mother, who gave her a big hug, and then her father who, in his typically dashing manner, told her she was a very lucky girl because this autumn, many Parisians would be wearing closed black shoes.

She smiles at the memory. But she had her own wish for her twelfth birthday. That evening, when her mother came to her room to say good night, Dita asked her for one more present. Before her mother could protest, she told her that it wouldn't cost a cent. She had now turned twelve, and she'd like her mother to let her read some grown-up books. Her mother looked at her silently for a moment, finished tucking her in, and left without saying a word.

A little later, just as Dita was starting to fall asleep, she heard her door being opened carefully. Then she saw a hand leaving a copy of A. J. Cronin's *The Citadel* on her bedside table. As soon as her mother had left the room, Dita rushed to block the crack under her door with her dressing gown so her parents wouldn't notice that her light was on. She didn't sleep a wink that night.

Late one October afternoon in the year 1921, a shabby young man gazed with fixed intensity through the window of a

third-class compartment in the almost empty train laboring up the
Penowell valley from Swansea.

Dita settled down in the compartment next to young Dr. Manson and traveled with him to Drineffy, a poor mining town in the mountains of Wales. She had boarded the reading train. That night, Dita felt the thrill of discovery, of knowing that it didn't matter how many hurdles all the Reichs in the world put in her way, she'd be able to jump over all of them by opening a book.

When she now thinks back affectionately, even gratefully, to *The Citadel*, she smiles. Her mother didn't know it, but she used to hide the book in her schoolbag so she could keep reading it during recess. It was the first book that made her angry.

It was also the first book that made her cry.

She smiles again at the thought of all those pages. Since then, she has discovered that her life can be made much more profound, because books multiply your experiences and enable you to meet people like Dr. Manson and, in particular, his wife, Christine. She was a woman who never allowed herself to be dazzled by high society or wealth, who never sacrificed her principles, who was strong and never gave in if she believed something was unjust.

Ever since then, Dita has wanted to be like Mrs. Manson. She wouldn't let herself become discouraged by the war.

In her hiding place behind the woodpile, Dita's head nods as she is overcome by sleep.

When Dita opens her eyes, it's very dark, and there's not a sound in the hut. She panics briefly that she has missed curfew. Not returning to her hut would be a very serious mistake, the sort of mistake Mengele is waiting for so he can turn her into a laboratory specimen. But she calms down when she hears people outside. She can hear voices inside now, too, and realizes that's what has woken her up. They're speaking in German.

She peeps around the woodpile and sees that the door to Hirsch's cubicle is open and his light is on. Hirsch accompanies someone to the hut door, and then cautiously opens it.

"Wait a minute; there are people nearby."

"You seem concerned, Fredy."

"I think Lichtenstern suspects something. We have to do whatever it takes to make sure that neither Lichtenstern nor anyone in Block Thirty-One finds out. If they do, I'm finished."

The other person laughs.

"Come on, stop worrying so much. What can they do to you? After all, they're just Jewish prisoners. . . . They can't shoot you!"

"If they find out how I'm deceiving them, someone would be keen to do that."

The other person finally leaves the hut, and Dita catches a brief glimpse of him. He's a well-built man, and he's wearing a loose-fitting raincoat. She also sees him pulling up the hood even though it's not raining, as if he doesn't want to be recognized. But she can still see his feet, and he's not wearing the clogs the prisoners usually wear, but a gleaming pair of boots.

What's an incognito SS person doing here? Dita asks herself.

The light escaping from Hirsch's cubicle allows her to see him returning to it looking utterly dejected. She's never seen him looking shattered before. The normally proud man hangs his head.

Dita remains behind the woodpile paralyzed. She doesn't understand what she's just seen, but the thought of understanding it terrifies her. Hirsch said he is deceiving them.

But why?

Dita feels as if the ground is shifting under her feet, so she sits down again on the stool. She was feeling ashamed because she hasn't told Hirsch the whole truth . . . but it turns out he's the expert when it comes to hiding the fact that he's secretly meeting with members of the SS, who take advantage of the dark to hide their movements around the camp.

Oh my God . . .

Dita sighs and covers her face with her hands.

How am I going to tell the truth to someone who hides the truth? If Hirsch can't be trusted, who can?

She's so confused that when she stands up, she feels dizzy. As soon as Hirsch shuts himself in his cubicle, Dita quietly leaves the barrack.

At that moment the siren sounds, announcing that curfew is about to start. The last stragglers, who have braved the cold of the night and the fury of the hut *Kapos*, run toward their rickety bunks, but Dita doesn't have the will to run. Her questions are too heavy.

What if the person he was talking with isn't a member of the SS but belongs to the Resistance? But then why would Fredy be worried about the people in Block 31 finding out, if the Resistance is on our side? And how many members of the Resistance speak with that pretentious Berlin accent?

She shakes her head as she walks. It's impossible to deny the obvious. It was an SS man. It's true that Hirsch is obliged to deal with them, but that wasn't an official visit. The Nazi was there incognito and speaking to Fredy in a familiar way, as a friend even. And then there was that image of a Fredy overcome with remorse. . . .

Oh my God . . .

It's rumored all the time in various groups that there are informers and Nazi spies among the prisoners. She can't stop her legs from shaking.

No, no, definitely not.

Hirsch, an informer? If someone had suggested that to her two hours earlier, she would have scratched their eyes out! It wouldn't make any sense for him to be an informer for the SS when he deceives them by running Block 31 as a school. Nothing makes sense. It suddenly occurs to her that maybe he's pretending to be a Nazi informer, but that the information he's passing over to them is irrelevant or inaccurate, and that's how he keeps them mollified.

That would explain everything!

But then she remembers how Hirsch walked back to his cubicle utterly dejected once he was alone. He wasn't a man proud of himself because he was fulfilling a mission. He was weighed down by the burden of guilt. She could see it in his posture.

When she reaches her hut, the *Kapo* is already standing at the door with her stick, ready to hit the women who arrive after the curfew has started, and Dita covers her head with her arms to soften the blow. The *Kapo* hits her hard, but she barely feels the pain. As she clambers into her bunk, she sees a head being raised in the bunk beside her. It's her mother.

"You're very late, Edita. Is everything all right?"

"Yes, Mama."

"Are you sure you're all right? You're not deceiving me?"

"No," Dita answers grudgingly.

It irritates her that her mother treats her like a little girl. She feels like telling her that of course she's fooling her, that in

Auschwitz everybody deceives everyone else. But it wouldn't be fair to take her anger out on her mother.

"So everything's fine?"

"Yes, Mama."

"Shut up, you bitches, or I'll slit your throats!" someone bellows.

"Stop that racket!" orders the *Kapo*.

Silence descends on the hut, but the voice inside Dita's head doesn't stop. *Hirsch isn't who they think he is. Who is he, then?*

She tries to fit together everything she knows about him, and that's when she realizes it's not a lot. After catching a fleeting glimpse of him at the sports ground on the outskirts of Prague, the next time she bumped into him was in Terezín.

The Terezín ghetto . . .

8.

DITA CLEARLY REMEMBERS THE TYPEWRITTEN LETTER WITH THE *Reichsprotektor* stamp lying on top of the table with the dark-red-check oiled tablecloth, in that tiny apartment in Josefov. It was an insignificant piece of paper that changed everything. It changed even the name of the small town of Terezín, sixty kilometers from Prague, its German name written in dark capital letters as if they wanted to proclaim it: THERESIENSTADT. And next to that, the word *relocation*.

Terezín, or Theresienstadt, was a city Hitler generously donated to the Jews—or so Nazi propaganda maintained. They would even film a documentary directed by Kurt Gerron, the Jewish film director, which showed people happily employed in workshops, playing sports, and calmly attending lectures and social events, all presented with a voiceover that explained how content the Jews were in Terezín. The documentary would "prove" that the rumors about the internment and murder of Jews were false. As soon as he finished the documentary, the Nazis would send Kurt Gerron to Auschwitz, where he would die in 1944.

Dita sighs.

The Terezín ghetto . . .

The Jewish Council of Prague had offered *Reichsprotektor* Reinhard Heydrich various options for the location of a such a

Jewish city. But Heydrich had wanted Terezín—nothing else would do—and for a rock-solid reason: Terezín was a walled city.

Dita recalls the sadness of that morning when they had to put their entire lives into two suitcases and drag them to the assembly point near Stromovka park. The Czech police escorted the whole column of deportees to a special train that took them to Terezín.

She sorts through her mental album for a photograph from November 1942. Her father is helping her grandfather, the old senator, get off the train at Bohušovice station. Her grandmother is in the background, carefully watching. The expression on Dita's face now is one of anger and irritation at the biological deterioration that attacks even the most upright and energetic people. Her grandfather had been a stone fortress, and now he was a mere sandcastle. In the background of that frozen image, she can also see her mother with that stubbornly neutral expression of hers, pretending that nothing bad is happening and trying not to attract anyone's attention. She can see herself, too, aged thirteen, more of a girl and outlandishly fat. Her mother had made her wear several sweaters one on top of the other, not because of the cold, but because they were allowed only fifty kilos per person in the suitcases, and layering clothes meant they could bring more. Her father is standing behind her. *It's not the first time I've told you not to eat so much pheasant, Edita*, he said in that serious way he had when he was joking.

The first image her eyes had stored in the Terezín album—after they walked past the guard post at the entrance to the precinct and under the archway bearing the phrase ARBEIT MACHT FREI—work makes you free—was of a dynamic city. It was a place with avenues full of people. It had a hospital, a fire station, kitchens, workshops, a day care center. Terezín even had its own Jewish police, the *Ghettowache*, who wandered about in their jackets and dark caps like any other police in the world. But if you looked more carefully at the hustle and bustle in the streets, you realized that people were carrying baskets with missing handles, threadbare blankets, watches without hands. . . . The inhabitants rushed to and fro as if they were in a hurry, but Dita understood that no matter how fast you walked, you'd always end up bumping into a wall. That was the deception.

Terezín was a city where the streets led nowhere.

That was where she saw Fredy Hirsch again, although her initial memory is of a sound, not an image. It's of the thunderous clatter of a buffalo stampede like the ones in Karl May's adventure novels set in the American prairies. It was during one of her first days in the ghetto, and she was still feeling stunned. She was returning from her assigned work—the vegetable gardens that had been planted at the foot of the walls to provide supplies for the SS garrison.

She was heading back to her small cubicle when she heard a galloping sound coming toward her along a nearby street. She pressed herself against the wall of an apartment block to avoid being mowed down by what she assumed were horses, but what finally came running around the corner was a large group of boys and girls. Their leader was an athletic man with impeccably slicked-back hair and a smooth, elastic stride. He greeted her with a slight nod of his head as he went past. It was Fredy Hirsch, unmistakable, even elegant, in his shorts and T-shirt.

It would be a while before she saw him again. And it would be a stack of books that would lead to their next encounter.

It all started when Dita discovered that, among the sheets,

clothing, underwear, and other belongings her mother had stuffed into the suitcases, her father had hidden a book. Fortunately, her mother didn't know, or she would have hit the ceiling over such a waste of allowable weight. When her mother unpacked the suitcase that first night, she was surprised by the thick volume and glared at Dita's father.

"We could have brought three more pairs of shoes, given what this weighs."

"Why would we want so many shoes, Liesl? We can't go anywhere."

Her mother didn't answer, but Dita thought she lowered her head so they wouldn't see she was smiling. Dita's mother some-times scolded her father for being such a dreamer, but deep down, she adored him because of it.

Papa was right. That book took me much further than any pair of shoes.

Lying on the edge of her bunk in Auschwitz, she smiles as she recalls that moment when she opened the cover of Thomas Mann's *Der Zauberberg* (*The Magic Mountain*).

Starting a book is like boarding a train to go on holiday.

The Magic Mountain tells how Hans Castorp travels from Hamburg to Davos, in the Swiss Alps, to visit his cousin Joachim, who is undergoing treatment for tuberculosis at an elegant health spa. At first Dita didn't know if she identified with the cheerful Hans, who has just arrived at the spa for a few days' holiday, or with the chivalrous and ill Joachim.

> *A year is very important at our age. It brings so many changes with it and so much progress down there in the real world! But I have to stay inside this place like a bat; yes, as if I were*

*inside a putrid hole, and I assure you that the comparison is
not an exaggeration.*

Dita recalls how she unconsciously nodded in agreement as she
read this, and she's still nodding now as she lies awake on her bunk
in Auschwitz. She felt that the characters in that book understood
her better than her own parents, because whenever she complained
about all the misfortunes they were experiencing in Terezín—her
parents having to sleep in separate quarters, her work in the
vegetable gardens, the sense of suffocation from living in a walled
city, the monotonous diet—they'd tell her to be patient; it would all
be over soon. *Maybe by next year the war will be finished*, they'd
say to her as if they were passing on a magnificent piece of news.
For the grown-ups, a year was nothing more than a small segment
of a large apple. Her parents would give her a smile, and she'd bite
her tongue in frustration because they didn't understand anything. When you're young, a year is almost your entire life, the
whole apple.

There were afternoons when her parents would be chatting with
other married couples in the inner courtyard of her building, and
she'd lie on her bed, cover herself with her blanket, and feel a little
like Joachim taking his obligatory rest on the chaise longue in the
spa. Or perhaps more like Hans Castorp, who decides to have a few
more days of holiday, taking advantage of the rest sessions, but in
the more relaxed manner of a tourist rather than a patient.

In Terezín, Dita lay on her bed waiting for night to fall, just
like the two cousins in the book, though her dinner—barely more
than bread and cheese—was much more sparse than the five courses
served in the Berghof International Spa.

Cheese! she thinks now, as she lies on top of her bunk in

Auschwitz. *What did cheese taste like? I don't even remember anymore. Wonderful!*

It is true that in Terezín, despite being wrapped in four layers of sweaters, she felt the same cold as Joachim, the same cold as the patients lying on lounge chairs on the balconies of their rooms at night, wrapped in blankets and breathing in the cold mountain air that was supposed to be so good for restoring their damaged lungs. And lying there in Terezín with her eyes closed, she shared Joachim's view that youth is over in a flash.

It was a long novel, so during the next few months, she shared her own enforced confinement with Joachim and his cheerful cousin Hans. She delved into the secrets, gossip, and obligations of the luxurious Berghof, where illness made time seem to stand still. She shared the conversations between the cousins and the other patients and, in a way, took part in them. The reality in the book became truer and more understandable than the one that surrounded her in that walled city. And it was much more credible than the Auschwitz nightmare of electrified wires and gas chambers that formed the world she currently inhabited.

One afternoon, a half-German girl who used to hang around in the small room they shared in the ghetto, but whom Dita ignored, decided to ask the girl who was always reading if she knew the Russian novel *The Republic of ShKID*, and if she'd heard of the boys in Block L417. Well, of course she'd heard about the boys!

That was when Dita closed her book and pricked up her ears. Curious, she asked Hanka to take her to meet them . . . "Right now!"

Hanka tried to tell her that it was a bit late in the day, so maybe tomorrow, but Dita, smiling now as she remembers that moment, cut her off:

"We don't have a tomorrow. Everything has to be now!"

The two girls set off quickly for Block L417, a boys' block, which they were allowed to visit until seven p.m. At the entrance, Hanka stopped and turned to her roommate with a serious look on her face.

"Watch out for Ludek. . . . He's very handsome! But don't even think about flirting with him, because I saw him first."

Dita raised her right hand with mock solemnity, and the two girls laughed as they headed up the stairs. As soon as they arrived, Hanka started to chat to a tall, slim boy. Not knowing what else to do, Dita approached a boy who was drawing a picture of planet Earth as seen from space.

"What are those really weird mountains in the foreground?" she asked him without any introduction.

"It's the moon."

Petr Ginz was the editor-in-chief of *Vedem*, a clandestine, loose-leaf magazine, which was read out loud every Friday, and which contained information about events in the ghetto. But it also accepted opinion pieces, poems, and fantasies. Petr was a great admirer of Jules Verne, and *From the Earth to the Moon* was one of his favorite books. At night, lying on top of his bunk, he'd think about how incredible it would be to have a cannon like Mr. Barbicane's from which he could launch himself into space inside a giant ball. He stopped drawing for a moment, looked up, and stared at the girl who had questioned him with such self-confidence. He liked the sparkle in her eyes, but he nevertheless addressed her severely.

"You're very curious."

Dita blushed and was overcome with shyness. She regretted being such a chatterbox. And then Petr's attitude changed.

"Curiosity is the primary virtue of a good journalist. I'm Petr Ginz. Welcome to *Vedem*."

Now Dita asks herself what sort of a chronicle Petr Ginz would have written about the activities of Block 31. She wonders what became of that skinny, sensitive boy.

That day, after their first encounter, Dita was walking with Petr in front of the so-called "Dresden barracks." When he had asked her if she'd like to accompany him to do an interview for the magazine, Dita had hesitated for a second—probably not even that—before saying yes. They were going to interview the director of the library.

She was thrilled at the idea of being a journalist, and she felt a shiver of pride when she arrived with the determined Petr Ginz at the entrance to Building L304, where the library was located. They asked the receptionist if the director, Dr. Utitz, could receive two journalists from the magazine, *Vedem*, and the woman smiled amiably and asked them to have a seat.

Emil Utitz appeared a few minutes later. Before the war, he had been a professor of philosophy and psychology at the German University in Prague, and a columnist for various newspapers.

He told them the library had about sixty thousand books. These came from the hundreds of public libraries and private collections belonging to the Jewish community, which the Nazis had closed down and plundered. He also explained that the library still had no reading room, and so for the time being, it was a mobile library, by which he meant that the books were wheeled from building to building and could be borrowed. Petr asked Utitz if it was true that he had been a friend of Franz Kafka. The director nodded.

The editor in chief of *Vedem* then requested permission to

accompany one of the librarians on a book round so that they could explain in the magazine how it all worked. Utitz happily agreed to the request.

On the appointed afternoon, Petr had to attend a poetry recital, so it was Dita who cheerfully accompanied the librarian, Miss Sittigová, as she pushed her trolley of books around the streets of Terezín. After a day's labor in the workshops, factories, and foundries or at agricultural tasks, the opportunity to escape offered by the library-on-wheels was warmly welcomed. But Miss Sittigová told her that books were often stolen, and not always so they could be read. They were also used as toilet paper or as fuel for the stoves.

The librarian didn't even have to announce her arrival in a loud voice: "Library service!" Young and old passed on the news in a chorus of mixed voices, which rang out merrily until people began to emerge from the doors of their buildings and eagerly leaf through the available books. Dita so enjoyed pushing the books that from then on, she began to travel around with them regularly. Once her day's work was over, if she didn't have an art class, she would spend the rest of the afternoon helping the librarian with her work.

And that was when she bumped into Fredy Hirsch again.

He was living in one of the buildings near the main clothing warehouse. But he was rarely to be found there. He was always on the go, organizing sports competitions or taking part in activities with the ghetto youth. Whenever Dita saw him heading toward the trolley, he was always neatly dressed and walking energetically, and he always greeted them with that faint smile of his, which was just enough to make you feel important. He was always on the lookout for songbooks and books of poetry to use during the gatherings he organized with the young people on Friday evenings to celebrate

Shabbat. There'd be singing and storytelling, and Fredy would talk to them about the return to Palestine, where they would go after the war. On one occasion, he even tried to encourage Dita to join the group. She blushed as she told him that it might happen one day, but she felt really embarrassed and didn't think her parents would let her go. Deep down, however, she would have loved to join the older boys and girls who sang, discussed things like adults, and even secretly exchanged kisses.

Dita now realizes how little she knows about Alfred Hirsch. And her life is in his hands. If he tells the German commanders that "inmate Dita Adler hides clandestine books under her clothing," they'll catch her in flagrante at the next inspection. But if he wanted to denounce her . . . why wouldn't he have done it already? And why would Hirsch denounce himself if Block 31 is his initiative? It makes no sense. Dita thinks she'll have to do some digging, but discreetly. Maybe Hirsch is somehow getting preferential treatment for the prisoners and she could ruin it all.

That must be it.

She wants to trust Hirsch. . . . But then why is the block chief afraid that they'll find out about him and hate him?

9.

THE QUARANTINE CAMP IS PACKED WITH NEWLY ARRIVED RUSSIAN prisoners. There's little of their soldier's honor left: Their heads have been shaved, and they're wearing striped prison garb. They are an army of beggars now. They wait their turn, pacing up and down or sitting on the ground. There aren't many groups in huddles, and it is deathly quiet. Some of them look through the wire fence at the Czech women in the family camp who still have their hair, and at the children chasing each other along the *Lagerstrasse*.

Rudi Rosenberg, in his role as the quarantine camp registrar, is working busily, drawing up lists of the new admissions. Rudi speaks Russian, as well as Polish and a little German, which as he well knows, makes life easier for the SS guards who are supervising the registration process. So far, this morning, he's ensured that the three or four pencils at his disposal have made their way into his pockets. He's now talking to a German corporal he's gotten to know who's even younger than he is. He often exchanges a few jokes with the soldier, frequently at the expense of the young women who arrive on the women's transportation trains.

"Corporal Latteck, sir, we really are full to bursting today. You always seem to cop the really hard work!" The Germans always have to be addressed formally, even if they are only eighteen years old.

"True, enough, Rosenberg. You've noticed it, too. I do all the work. You'd think I was the only corporal in this section. That damn sergeant has it in for me. He's a fucking hick from Bavaria, and he can't stand people from Berlin. Let's hope they finally grant me that transfer to the front."

"Corporal, forgive me for troubling you, but I've run out of pencils."

"I'll send a soldier over to the guardroom to find one."

"To make sure it's not a wasted trip, since he's going there, sir, could you perhaps tell him to bring back an entire box?"

The SS guard gives Rudi a long, hard look and then allows a smile to appear on his lips.

"A box, Rosenberg? Why the devil do you want so many pencils?"

Rudi realizes that the corporal isn't as stupid as he seems, so he grins slyly, too, as if they were co-conspirators.

"Well, there's a lot to note down here. And . . . there's no question that if there are any pencils left over, the workers in the clothing area can always use a few to write down their information. Pencils are certainly hard to come by in the *Lager*. And if you provide those people with pencils, they can sometimes return the favor with some new socks."

"And the occasional little Jewish whore!"

"Could be."

"I get it. . . ."

The inquisitive look the SS man is giving Rudi signals danger. If Latteck reports him, Rudi is gone. He's got to convince him quickly.

"You know, it's only a matter of being a bit friendly to people. That way, they might be friendly toward you, too. There are friendly people who give me cigarettes."

"Cigarettes?"

"Sometimes the odd pack of cigarettes is left in the pockets of the clothes that are sent to the laundry. . . . There's even been the occasional packet of American tobacco."

"American tobacco?"

"Absolutely!" He takes a cigarette out of his pocket. "Just like this one."

"You're a bastard, Rosenberg. A very smart bastard." And the corporal smiles.

"They're not that easy to find, but I might be able to get a few of these for you, sir."

"I love American tobacco," says the corporal, with a greedy glint in his eye.

"It certainly does taste different, sir. Nothing like the dark tobacco."

"No. . . ."

"Light American tobacco is like a blond woman . . . superior quality."

"No question. . . ."

The following day, Rudi heads for his rendezvous with Alice carrying two bundles of pencils in his pocket. He'll have to do a few favors to get the corporal's cigarettes, but he's not too concerned. He knows how to go about it. As he walks toward the boundary fence, his thoughts turn yet again to the existence of the family camp. The Jews have never been allowed to stay together as families before. Why have the Nazis allowed it? The mystery is driving the Resistance mad. He wonders if Fredy Hirsch might know more about it than he's letting on. Is Hirsch keeping something up his sleeve? But then, isn't everyone? Rudi himself doesn't tell Schmulewski about the good relationship he has with some of the SS, which enables him to traffic in small items. The Resistance might not approve, but it suits him. Schmulewski himself is never likely to show all his cards at once. After all, doesn't he revel in the position of assistant to the German *Kapo* in his barrack?

He strides back and forth behind the barracks until he sees Alice approaching, and then he heads for the fence. If the guard on duty in the tower is one of the bad-tempered ones, he'll blow his whistle any moment now and order them to move back. Alice is on the other side of the fence, a few meters away. Rudi has spent two days anticipating this moment, and when he sees her, his happiness makes him forget all the miseries.

"Sit down."

"I'm fine standing up. The ground's muddy."

"But you've got to sit down so the guard knows we're only talking and doesn't suspect us of plotting something close to the fence."

Alice sits down and in the process, her skirt rides up and her underwear—miraculously white in the midst of all the mud—is briefly exposed. Rudi feels an electric current run through his body.

"How's everything going?" asks Alice.

"Now that I'm looking at you, everything's fine."

Alice blushes, but smiles with satisfaction.

"I've got the pencils."

She doesn't seem surprised, and that leaves Rudi feeling a little disappointed. He was hoping the pencils would have a dramatic effect. The girl must have no idea how difficult it is to do deals inside the camp, and the risk he's had to take with an SS guard in order to get them.

Rudi doesn't know about women. Alice really is impressed, as he'd realize if he looked into her eyes. But men always expect to be told everything.

"And how are you going to get the pencils into our camp? A delivery service?"

"You can't trust anyone at the moment."

"So?"

"You'll see."

Rudi has been watching the soldier in the guard tower out of the corner of his eye. He's quite a way off, and Rudi can make out only the outline of a small portion of his upper body and head. But since the guard's gun is slung over his shoulder, Rudi can tell when he's facing toward them and when his back is turned: The tip of the gun sticking up above his right shoulder points away from the camp when he's facing them and toward the camp when he has his back to them. Thanks to this makeshift compass, Rudi has worked out that the guard swivels at a lazy pace. When he sees the muzzle rotate toward him, Rudi takes a few bold steps up to the fence. Alice covers her mouth with her hand, terrified.

"Quick, come closer!"

Rudi removes the two bundles of pencils, each firmly tied together with string, from his pocket and, holding them with the tips of his fingers, carefully passes them through the gaps in the electrified wire fence. Alice rushes to pick them up from the ground. She's never been so close to the fence with its thousands of volts. The two of them step back a few meters just as Rudi sees the muzzle start to swing away and the guard turns to face them.

"Why didn't you warn me?" Alice asks him, her heart still thumping loudly inside her chest. "I would have prepared myself!"

"It's better not to prepare for some things. Sometimes you have to act impulsively."

"I'll give Mr. Hirsch the pencils. We're really grateful."

"We should go now. . . ."

"Yes."

"Alice . . ."

"What?"

"I'd like to see you again."

Alice's smile means so much more than words.

"Same time, same place, tomorrow?" he asks her.

She agrees and begins to walk toward the *Lagerstrasse* of her camp. Rudi waves good-bye, and Alice blows him a kiss from her chapped lips. It flies over the top of the barbed wire fence, and Rudi catches it midair. It never occurred to him before that such a simple gesture could make him so happy.

There is someone else this morning whose head is spinning. Dita is attuned to every gesture, every raised eyebrow and clenched jaw. She wants to find out the truth that words don't reveal. Suspicion is like an itch that is barely felt at the start. But when you become aware of it, you can't stop scratching.

Life doesn't stop, however, and Dita doesn't want anyone to notice that she's worried. So, first thing in the morning, she's already on duty in her library, sitting on a bench with her shoulder propped up against the air intake of the chimney. The books are defiantly displayed on a long bench in front of her. Seppl Lichtenstern has provided her with one of the assistants to help her control the movement of the books during the hourly book exchange, and on this particular morning, there's a young boy with pale skin sitting beside her so quietly that he's yet to open his mouth.

The first person to come by is a young teacher who's in charge of a group of boys nearby. He greets her with a silent nod. She's heard he's a Communist, that he's very educated, and even speaks English. She studies his gestures to work out if he can be trusted, but in the end, she doesn't know what to think. She does notice a sparkle of intelligence under his studied indifference. He casts an eye over the books, and when he comes across the one by H. G. Wells, he nods, as if in approval. Then he pauses over Freud's book of theories and shakes his head disapprovingly. Dita watches him closely, almost frightened by what he's going to say.

Finally, after a moment's thought, he says, "If H. G. Wells were to find out that he's next to Sigmund Freud, he'd be angry with you."

Dita stares at him wide-eyed and blushes.

"I don't understand—"

"Don't pay any attention to me. It's just that it shocks me to see a socialist rationalist like Wells together with a fantasy salesman like Freud."

"Freud writes fantastical tales?"

"Absolutely not. Freud was an Austrian psychiatrist from Moravia and a Jew. He used to examine what people had inside their heads."

"And what did he see?"

"According to him, too many things. In his books, he explains that the mind is a storeroom where memories languish and send people mad. He came up with a way of curing mental illnesses: The patient would lie down on a couch, and Freud would make him talk until he'd exhausted the last of his memories. In this way, Freud probed the patient's most hidden thoughts. He called it psychoanalysis."

"What happened to him?"

"He became famous. That saved his skin in Vienna in 1938. Some Nazis went into his consulting rooms, destroyed everything, and left with two thousand Reichsmarks. When Freud found out, he remarked that he had never charged that much for a consultation. Freud knew a lot of influential people outside Austria, but even so, the Nazis didn't allow him to leave the country and go to London with his wife and daughter until he'd signed a piece of paper where he stated that the Nazi authorities had treated him really well and life in Vienna under the Third Reich was wonderful. He asked if he could add something to the end of the document because he felt the Germans had sold themselves short. Then he wrote, *I strongly recommend the Gestapo to everybody*. The Nazis were delighted."

"They just don't get the Jewish sense of humor."

"As far as the Germans are concerned, humor means tickling your toes."

"And when he reached England?"

"Freud died the following year, in 1939. He was already very old and sick." The young teacher picks up the book by Freud and leafs through it. "Freud's books were among the first to be burned on Hitler's orders in 1933. This book is pure danger. It's not only a clandestine book—it's banned as well."

Dita feels a slight shiver and decides to change the topic.

"And who was H. G. Wells?"

"He was a freethinker and a socialist. But above all, he was a great novelist. Have you heard of *The Invisible Man*?"

"Yes."

"Well, he wrote that novel. And *The War of the Worlds*, in which he talks about Martians landing on Earth. And *The Island of Doctor Moreau*, with that mad scientist who combines human and animal genes. Dr. Mengele would like him. But I think his best book is *The Time Machine*. To go back and forth in time . . ." He sounds pensive as he continues. "Can you picture it? Do you have any idea what it would mean to get inside that machine, fly back in time to 1924, and prevent Adolf Hitler from being released from jail?"

"But all that business of the machine is made up, isn't it?"

"Sadly, yes. Novels add what's missing to life."

"Well, if you think it would be better, I can put Mr. Freud and Mr. Wells at opposite ends of the bench."

"No, leave them where they are. Maybe they can learn something from each other."

And he says it so seriously that Dita can't tell if this young teacher, who has the poise of an experienced man despite his youth, is joking or absolutely serious.

He turns round and returns to his group, and it occurs to Dita that he's a walking encyclopedia. The assistant beside her hasn't spoken a word. It's only when the teacher has gone that he tells Dita in a high-pitched, childish voice—which makes his normal silence understandable—that the teacher's name is Ota Keller, and he's a Communist. Dita nods.

The teachers asked Dita for one of her "living" books for the afternoon—*The Wonderful Adventures of Nils Holgersson*. Mrs. Magda is a fragile-looking woman with snow-white hair and as slight as a sparrow. But when she starts to tell the story, she turns into a giant. Her voice becomes remarkably energetic, and she spreads her arms dramatically to describe the flight of the geese carrying Nils Holgersson through the air. A large group of children of mixed ages climb on board the flock of strong geese, too. They follow every word wide-eyed as they fly, seated on those geese, all over the skies of Sweden.

Almost all the children have heard the story before, in some cases several times, but the ones who enjoy it most are the ones who know it best. They recognize the various stages of the tale and they even laugh in anticipation of events, because they are already part of the adventure. Even Gabriel, the terror of the teachers in Block 31, who is normally incapable of staying still, has turned into a statue.

Nils is a willful boy who plays tricks on the animals on his farm. One day, while his parents are in church and he's alone at home, he has a run-in with a *tomte*, or gnome, who has had enough of the boy's arrogant attitude and shrinks him to the size of a small woodland animal. In an attempt to redeem himself, Nils holds on to the neck of a domestic goose and they join a band of wild geese flying over the Swedish countryside. In the same way that the impertinent Nils, clutching the neck of his goose, begins to mature and to realize that there is more to the world than him, so, too, the group of listeners rise above their harsh reality, full of the egotism of people pushing into the line to get to the soup first or stealing their neighbor's spoon.

Sometimes, when Dita goes in search of Mrs. Magda to tell her that she has a session with Nils Holgersson at a particular time, the woman hesitates.

"But they've all heard the story a dozen times already! When they see that I'm telling it again, they'll get up from their stools and leave."

No one ever leaves. It doesn't matter how many times they listen to the story, they always enjoy it. And not only that, but they always want to hear it from the start. Sometimes Mrs. Magda, worried that she'll bore them, tries to take shortcuts and make the story shorter by skipping sections, but there are immediate protests from her audience.

"No, that's not right!"

And she has to rewind and tell the whole story without leaving anything out. The more times the children hear the story, the more it's a part of them.

The story comes to an end, and the guessing games being played by other groups also finish, along with the craft work. A group of girls has been making puppets out of old socks and wooden sticks. The children leave the hut and return to their families once the deputy director has finished the afternoon roll call.

The assistants finish their tasks quickly. Sweeping the floor with twig brooms is more of a ritual or a way of justifying their positions than an actual necessity. Arranging the stools doesn't take long, either, or cleaning up the nonexistent leftovers from the meal, because nothing is wasted. The bowls are licked clean down to the very last drop of soup; even a crumb is like treasure. As the assistants complete their pretend cleanup, they leave the hut, and a peacefulness descends on Block 31.

The teachers sit down together on stools and discuss the day's events. Dita is in her corner behind the woodpile, where she often goes when classes are over to read for a while, since the books can't be taken from the hut. She notices a stick propped up against a wall in her corner. It has a small net at the top made out of string. It could be a crude butterfly net, although it's so badly strung that if you tried to catch a butterfly, it would escape through one of the many holes. She can't imagine who might be the owner of such a useless item. There aren't any butterflies in Auschwitz anyway. If only!

She spots something in the gap between some planks in the wall, and when she pulls it out, she sees it's a tiny pencil, little more than a stub with a black tip. But a pencil is an extraordinary piece of equipment. She picks up a small origami bird left behind by Professor Morgenstern and carefully unfolds it. She's left with a scrap of paper to draw on. She hasn't drawn anything for so long . . . Not since Terezín.

A very nice art teacher who gave classes to the children in the ghetto used to say that painting was a way of escaping. She was such a cultured and enthusiastic person that Dita never dared contradict her. But unlike books, drawing never took her out of herself or made her climb aboard the carriage of other lives—quite the opposite. Drawing catapulted her inside herself. Her Terezín drawings were dark, with unsettled strokes and dark-gray, stormy skies. Drawing was a way of having a conversation with herself when she was overcome by the idea that her youth, which had barely begun, already seemed to be over.

Dita sketches the barrack: the stools, the straight stone line of the chimney, and the two benches—one for her and the other for the books.

She can't avoid overhearing the teachers' voices, which sound fraught this afternoon. Mrs. Nasty is complaining bitterly that it's impossible for her to teach the children geography over the noise of the yells and orders accompanying the deported prisoners who arrive at the camp and walk past Block 31 on their way to the showers and their death.

"Trains arrive, and we have to pretend that we can't hear anything. We carry on with our lessons, while the children whisper among themselves. We act as if we can't hear a thing, as if we knew nothing about it. . . . Wouldn't it be better to face up to it and talk to the children about the concentration camp? They all know what is going on anyway, so let them talk about their fears."

Fredy Hirsch isn't there today. He tends to shut himself in his cubicle to work and takes part less and less in the social life of the hut. When Dita enters his den to put the books back in their hiding place, she often sees him totally focused on what he's writing on pieces of paper. He explained to her once that it was a report for Berlin; they were really interested in the Block 31 experiment. Dita wonders if those reports are linked to the shadow that Hirsch is trying to hide from the others.

In his absence, it's Miriam Edelstein who has to be uncompromising with the difficult Mrs. Křižková and remind her of the orders of the block management.

"But do you honestly believe that the children aren't concerned?" another teacher interrupts.

"All the more reason, then," answers Miriam Edelstein. "What's the point in endlessly going on about it? Endlessly rubbing salt into the wound? This school has a mission over and above the one of pure education: to convey a certain sense of normalcy to them, prevent them from becoming disheartened, and show them that life goes on."

"For how long?" asks someone, and the conversation gets stirred up again. Comments, both pessimistic and optimistic, erupt everywhere, together with all manner of theories about how to explain the tattoo on the arms of all the children, the tattoo that refers to special treatment after six months. For those in the September transport, that time is edging ever nearer. The conversation descends into chaos.

Dita, the only young assistant allowed to stay in the hut at this hour, is somewhat uncomfortable at witnessing the teachers' discussion, and the word *death* rings in her ears as something almost obscene and sinful, something a young girl shouldn't be overhearing. So she leaves. She hasn't seen Fredy anywhere all day. Apparently, he's busy with something really important. He has to prepare for a ceremonial visit from the high command. Miriam Edelstein has the key to his cubicle. She opens the door so Dita can go in and hide the books. The two exchange a quick look. Dita tries to detect a hint of betrayal or insincerity in the deputy director, but she doesn't know what to think anymore. All she can see in Mrs. Edelstein is a deep sadness.

Dita is lost in thought as she leaves Block 31. She weighs whether she should consult her father, who is a sensible person. Suddenly, she remembers that she has to keep a look out for Mengele and swivels her head around swiftly a few times to check if anyone is following her. The wind has died down, and the snow has begun to fall over the camp. The *Lagerstrasse* is empty apart from a few people walking hurriedly to their huts in search of warmth. There's no trace of any SS. But in one of the side alleys that run between the huts she can see someone leaping about while attempting to defy the cold with a frayed jacket and a handkerchief worn like a scarf. She looks more closely: white stubble, white hair, round glasses . . . It's Professor Morgenstern!

He's vigorously waving a stick up and down with a net tied to it, and Dita recognizes the butterfly net she saw in Block 31. She now knows whose it is. She stands there watching the professor because she can't work out why he's waving the artifact in the air, and then she finally gets it. There's no way she could have imagined that Morgenstern would use it to catch snowflakes.

He sees her watching him and waves a friendly greeting to her. Then he returns to his fanatical pursuit of snowflake-butterflies. Every now and again, he's on the verge of slipping as he pursues a snowflake, but in the end, he catches it and watches it melt in his palm. The elderly professor's stubble is full of sparkling ice crystals and, from where she's standing, Dita thinks she can see a smile of contentment.

10.

WHEN DITA GOES INTO FREDY HIRSCH'S CUBICLE EACH AFTER-
noon to store the books, she tries to leave right away and avoid eye
contact. She doesn't want to risk seeing anything that might break
her trust. She'd rather believe in his goodness. But Dita is stubborn, and no matter how hard she tries, she can't rid her mind of
what she saw.

Dita's sense of curiosity—piqued by the young teacher Ota
Keller—has led her to spend her afternoons curled up in her hidden corner reading H. G. Wells. In the meantime, classes have finished in the hut, and the pupils are playing games, taking part in
guessing competitions, preparing plays, or drawing pictures with the
pencils that have miraculously appeared. She wishes they had some
of those exciting novels the teacher had talked about at their disposal. *A Short History of the World* is the library book borrowed
most frequently because it's the closest thing to a regular school-
book. And there's no question that when she buries herself in its
pages, she feels as if she were back at her school in Prague, and
that if she were to raise her head, she'd see in front of her the black-
board and her teacher's hands covered in chalk.

*The story of our world is a story that is still very imperfectly
known. A couple of hundred years ago, men possessed the
history of little more than the last three thousand years.*

*What happened before that time was a matter of legend and
speculation.*

Wells is more of a novelist than a historian. In the book he
talks about the creation of the Earth, and the bizarre theories about
the moon proposed by scientists at the beginning of the twentieth
century. From there, he takes the reader through all the geological
periods: the Lower Paleozoic with the first algae; the Cambrian
with its trilobites; the Carboniferous with its extraordinary swamps;
and the Mesozoic, when the first reptiles appeared.

Dita wanders in amazement over a planet shaken by volcanic
convulsions and the subsequent marked shifts in climate, alternat-
ing between hot periods and extreme ice ages. The Age of Reptiles
grabs her attention, with its colossally large dinosaurs that became
the masters of the planet.

*This difference between the reptile world and the world of our
human minds is one our sympathies seem unable to pass.
We cannot conceive in ourselves the swift uncomplicated
urgency of a reptile's instinctive motives, its appetites, fears,
and hates.*

She wonders what H. G. Wells would say about the world people
now inhabit, if he would be able to distinguish the reptiles from the
humans.

The book keeps Dita company during the less structured afternoons in Block 31. It guides her safely as she makes her way through
the subterranean passages of the imposing pyramids of Egypt and
the battlefields of Assyria. A map of the dominions of the Persian
Emperor Darius I shows her an enormous expanse of territory, far

greater than any of the empires currently in existence. And the fact that Wells's commentary on "Priests and Prophets in Judea" doesn't match what they taught her as a child about sacred Jewish history leaves her feeling somewhat confused.

That's why she prefers to return to the pages about ancient Egypt, which immerse her in the world of pharaohs with mysterious names and allow her to board the boats that navigate the Nile. H. G. Wells is right. There really is a time machine—books.

When the working day is over, she has to store the books before the final roll call. After standing in line for a torturous ninety minutes while all the prisoners' numbers are checked off, she heads happily for her class with her father. It's geography today.

As she walks past Barrack 14, she sees Margit leaning up against the side wall with Renée. They've just finished their roll call, which is far more unpleasant because it takes place outdoors. They look very concerned, so she stops to talk to them.

"What's up, girls? Is something wrong? You're going to freeze out here."

Margit turns toward Renée, who looks as if she wants to say something. Renée untwists a blond curl on her forehead and chews it nervously. She sighs, and a wisp of breath spirals out of her mouth and disappears into the air.

"That Nazi . . . he's harassing me."

"Has he done anything to you?"

"Not yet. But this morning, he came to my ditch again and planted himself right in front of me. I knew it was him. I didn't lift my head. But he wasn't going anywhere. He touched me on the arm."

"What did you do?"

"I tossed a spadeful of dirt onto the feet of the girl next to me, and she started to screech like a wild animal. There was a bit of a kerfuffle, and the rest of the German patrol came over. He stepped back and didn't say a word. But he was after me. . . . I'm not making it up. Margit saw it yesterday."

"Yes. After roll call. The two of us were chatting before we headed back to our hut to see our parents, and he stopped a few steps away from us. He was looking at Renée—no question."

"Was he looking angrily at her?" asks Dita.

"No. He was just staring. You know . . . that dirty look that men have."

"Dirty?"

"I think he wants to have sex with Renée."

"Are you crazy, Margit?"

"I know what I'm talking about. You can see everything in a man's look. They stare as if they are already imagining you naked."

"I'm frightened," Renée whispers.

Dita hugs her and tells her they're all afraid. She reassures her that they'll keep her company whenever they can.

Renée's eyes are watering and she's trembling, but who knows if it's because of the cold or her fear. Dita picks up a small chip of wood and starts to draw some squares on top of the snow-covered ground.

"What are you doing?" her two friends ask, almost in unison.

"Drawing a game of hopscotch."

"For heaven's sake, Ditiňka! We're sixteen years old. We don't play hopscotch; that's a kids' game."

Dita continues to draw the squares meticulously as if she hasn't heard Margit's comment. And when she's done, she looks up at them as they stand waiting for her reply.

"Everyone's gone inside their huts. No one will see us!"

Renée and Margit frown and shake their heads as Dita searches for something on the ground.

"The woodchip will do," she tells them, and she throws it into one of the squares.

She jumps and lands with a wobble.

"You're clumsy," says Renée, laughing.

"You think you can do any better in this snow?" Dita rebukes her, pretending to be angry.

Renée tucks up her dress, throws the woodchip, and begins to jump with perfect accuracy, to Margit's applause. Margit goes next. She's the worst of the three: She stumbles as she hops and falls spectacularly onto the snow-covered ground. As Dita tries to help her up, she slips on some ice and falls backward.

Renée laughs at the pair of them. From the ground, Margit and Dita throw snowballs at her, which land in her hair and turn it white.

And the three girls laugh. Finally, they are laughing.

Dita, wet but happy, hurries off because it's time for her Wednesday geography class. On Mondays it's math, and on Fridays, Latin. Her teacher is Mr. Adler, her father, and her notebook is her head.

She still remembers the day she came home to the apartment in Josefov and found her father—who no longer had an office to go to—sitting in the living-dining room at the only table they had, twirling the globe with his fingers. Dita walked over with her schoolbag to give him a kiss, as she did every afternoon. Sometimes he would sit her down on his lap and they'd play at naming a country, slowly spinning the globe on its metal stand, and stopping it suddenly using a finger at the spot where they guessed the country might be. He seemed distracted on that particular day. He told her they'd sent a message from her school: holidays. Now, the word *holidays* is music to a child's ear. But the way in which her father had said it, and the sudden appearance of those unexpected school holidays made that music sound off-key. She remembers how her joy turned to distress when she realized that she would never have a school to go to again. Then her father signaled for her to sit on his lap.

"You'll study at home. Uncle Emile, who's a pharmacist, will teach you chemistry, and cousin Ruth will give you art classes. I'll talk to them, you'll see. And I'll give you language classes and math."

"And geography?"

"Of course. You'll get sick of traveling around the world."

And that's what happened.

That was during their time in Prague, until they were deported to Terezín in 1942. And they weren't such bad times when seen from the depths of Auschwitz. Up till the German occupation, her father had worked so hard that he hadn't had much time to spend with his daughter. So Dita was happy that he became her teacher.

Now as Dita walks toward her father's hut, she occasionally looks behind her, just in case Mengele is hot on her heels. Although, if truth be told, she's more concerned at this point with knowing what to expect from the director of Block 31.

Her father is waiting for her by the side of the hut, as he is each Monday, Wednesday, and Friday if it's not raining. They sit down together on a large stone. That's her school. Her father has already traced a map of the world in the mud with a stick. When she was younger, her father would help her to remember places by telling her things like that the Scandinavian peninsula was the head of a giant serpent and Italy was the boot of a very elegant woman. It is hard to recognize the world he's drawn into the mud of Auschwitz.

"Today we're going to study the planet's oceans, Edita."

But she just can't concentrate on her lesson. She thinks about how much her father would enjoy the atlas in Block 31. Removing the books is prohibited, however, and with Mengele breathing down her neck, there's absolutely no way. She's too distracted to listen to her father's explanations, and on top of that, it's freezing cold, and it has started to snow.

So she's delighted when her mother turns up a bit early.

"It's freezing. Leave it for today, or you'll both catch cold."

Here in Auschwitz, where there's no medicine or even enough blankets and food, colds are a killer.

Dita and her father get up, and even though he's the one shivering with cold, he wraps his own jacket around Dita.

"Let's go to the hut; they'll be serving dinner soon."

"Calling a piece of dry bread dinner is really optimistic, Mama."

"It's the war, Edita—"

"I know, I know. It's the war."

Her mother falls silent, and Dita takes advantage of the silence to raise the topic that's been worrying her, though she does so indirectly.

"Papa . . . if you had to confide a secret to somebody here in the camp, whom would you trust absolutely?"

"You and your mother."

"Yes, I know that. I mean, apart from us."

"Mrs. Turnovská is a very good woman. You can confide in her," her mother interjects.

"There's no question you can be confident that if you tell her something, even the head of the latrine cleaning brigade will know about it pretty quickly. That woman is as good as a radio," her husband replies.

"I agree, Papa."

"The most upright person I've met here is Mr. Tomášek. In fact, he came by not long ago to see how we were. He takes an interest in what's happening to other people. There aren't many people like that in here."

"So if you were to ask him for an honest opinion about something, do you think he'd tell you the truth?"

"Absolutely. But why do you ask?"

"Oh, nothing special. Just asking."

Dita makes a mental note of Mr. Tomášek's name. She'll have to go and have a chat with him and see what he thinks about Fredy.

"Your grandmother used to say that the only ones who speak the truth are children and madmen," her mother adds.

Dita thinks of Morgenstern. She can't go to just any adult with her doubts about a person of such high standing as Hirsch. They might accuse her of betrayal, or who knows what, in front of everyone else. But she doesn't run that risk with Morgenstern. If he were to spread her tale, she'd simply say it was another of the old man's crazy inventions. Would he know something about Hirsch?

She tells her parents she's going to see Margit. She knows the retired old architect usually stays in Block 31 until it's soup time, often in that hidden corner behind the woodpile she goes to when she wants to leaf through a book.

The assistants aren't allowed to stay behind after classes are over, but Dita's the librarian, and that gives her certain privileges. That may explain why the other assistants seem to dislike her. Not that it really bothers her. Her head is full of worry and doubt.

A group of teachers are chatting together inside Block 31. They don't notice her when she comes in. She heads to the back and peeps around the woodpile. Professor Morgenstern is refolding an origami bird made out of a well-used piece of paper.

"Good afternoon, Professor."

"Well, well, it's Miss Librarian. What a delightful visit!"

He gets up and bows.

"Can I be of service to you?"

"Oh, I was just walking by—"

"A good idea. A daily half-hour walk extends your life by ten years. A cousin of mine who used to walk for three hours each day lived to a hundred and fourteen. And he died because on one of his walks, he tripped and fell into a ravine."

"It's a pity that this place is so horrible that you really don't feel like going for a walk."

"Well, you can just move your legs. Legs can't see."

"Professor Morgenstern . . . have you known Fredy Hirsch for long?"

"We met on the train bringing us here. That would have been . . ."

"In September."

"Precisely so."

"And what do you think of him?"

"He strikes me as a distinguished young man."

"That's it?"

"You don't think that's enough? It's not easy to find people with class these days. Good manners don't count for anything anymore."

Dita hesitates, but she doesn't have many opportunities to be honest with someone. "Professor . . . do you think Fredy is hiding something?"

"Yes, of course."

"What?"

"Books."

"Damn it, I'm already aware of that!"

"Excuse me, Miss Adler, don't get upset. You asked me, and I'm giving you an answer."

"Yes, of course. Forgive me. What I wanted to ask you, in confidence, is if you think we can trust him."

"You ask some very strange questions."

"Yes. Please forget that I asked."

"I haven't quite understood what you mean by being able to trust Hirsch. Trust in his competence as block chief?"

"Not exactly. What I wanted to ask was if you think he really is who he seems to be."

After a moment's reflection, the professor replies, "No, he isn't."

"He's not who he appears to be?"

"No. Nor am I. Or you. Nobody is. God silenced our thoughts so that only we could hear them. No one else ought to know what we are really thinking. People get angry with me whenever I say what I think."

"Indeed . . ."

"I think what you're asking me is whom can you trust in this hole called Auschwitz?"

"That's it!"

"I must confess that as far as trusting, or what is understood by trusting, is concerned, I personally trust only my best friend."

"And who is your best friend?"

"Me. I am my best friend."

Dita stares as he continues to smooth out the tip of his paper bird. She's not going to get anything useful out of him.

When Dita reaches her hut, she lies down on the bunk. She hasn't seen Mengele for a couple of days. But she mustn't become overconfident; that man sees everything. She wonders if she could talk about Hirsch with Miriam Edelstein, the deputy director. But what if Miriam is his accomplice?

It's all so confusing. She'll try to talk to Mr. Tomášek. As Dita's eyes start to close, an image pops into her head: She and Margit lie flat on the snowy ground, Renée looks on, and the three roar with laughter. As long as they keep on laughing, all is not lost.

11.

TOWARD THE END OF FEBRUARY 1944, A HIGH-LEVEL GERMAN DELEGATION
visited Auschwitz–Birkenau. It was headed by Lieutenant-Colonel
Adolf Eichmann, the *Obersturmbannführer* in charge of the
Gestapo's Jewish Department from 1941 to 1945. Their mission
was to pick up, in person, a report requested from the *Blockältester*
of Block 31, Fredy Hirsch, on the operation of this experimental
barrack, the only one set aside for children in the entire network of
Auschwitz camps.

Hirsch has instructed Lichtenstern to ensure that all the
children, no matter what age, are lined up in a perfect state for inspection. Fredy demands good hygiene. The children get up every
day at seven a.m., and the assistants take them to the washrooms.
In February, morning temperatures can be as low as −25° Celsius,
and there are days when the pipes are frozen.

When Hirsch turns up midmorning, perfectly groomed and
shaved, the lines for roll call have already formed. His manner is
even more military than usual, a sure sign of his stress. There is the
sound of whistles blowing and the thud of boots. A short while
later, a couple of SS soldiers clear the way for a group of officials
whose chests are overloaded with metal insignias and decorations.

Fredy Hirsch comes to attention with a martial click of his
heels. After requesting permission to speak, he starts to describe

the functioning of Block 31. It's clear that Hirsch is comfortable speaking in his native German; he's not a natural in Czech.

Major Rudolf Höss and Eichmann lead the retinue, which includes other members of the SS, among them Schwarzhuber, the *Kommandant* responsible for Auschwitz–Birkenau. Dr. Mengele is farther back, a bit off to the side. As a captain, he's much lower in rank than the lieutenant-colonels heading up the visit, and some might think he's stepped back out of respect for the hierarchy. But Dita watches him and thinks his expression shows an indifference verging on boredom. And she's right. He is bored by this procession of authorities.

Mengele suddenly looks up. He stares at Dita. She pretends she's looking straight ahead, but she feels Mengele watching her. What does he want from her?

Eichmann nods, and his stern expression does not conceal his air of condescension. He's making it clear that he's doing Hirsch an enormous favor by hearing him out. Half a meter is as close as any of the officials will come to the Jewish *Blockältester*. Even though he's wearing a clean shirt and not-too-wrinkled pants, Hirsch looks like a peasant amidst the pressed uniforms and shiny boots. Dita looks at him and, despite all her reservations, she can't help feeling enormous admiration. They may despise him, but they listen. Dita believes in him. She desperately needs to believe in him.

As soon as the delegation moves off, two assistants arrive with the midday soup for the hut, and the normal routine is reestablished. The dented bowls and twisted spoons are pulled out, and the children beg God to let them find at least one small piece of carrot. Once the meal is over, the hut gradually empties. Only a few teachers remain, huddled around the stools at the back and talking about the visit. They would like to know what Hirsch thinks, but he's disappeared into thin air precisely to avoid such questions.

There's a gala lunch in the officers' dining room: tomato soup, chicken, potatoes, red cabbage, oven-baked fish, vanilla ice cream, and beer. The waitresses, prisoners, are Jehovah's Witnesses. Höss prefers them because they never complain. They believe that if this is God's will, they have to comply with it cheerfully.

"Look," he says to his colleagues, getting up from the table without bothering to remove the napkin tucked into his chest.

He signals to one of the waitresses to come forward and pulls out his Luger. He places the barrel against her temple. The other Nazi chiefs have stopped eating and watch expectantly. A hush falls over the dining room. The prisoner, unperturbed, stands stock-still, holding some dirty plates, not looking at the pistol or at the person pointing it. She's not looking anywhere in particular as she prays inaudibly. No complaint, no protest, not even a look of fear.

"She's thanking God," says Höss with a guffaw.

The others laugh politely. Rudolf Höss has recently been re-lieved of his position as commander of Auschwitz because the officers under him have been responsible for certain irregularities in the *Lager*'s accounts. Some members of the Gestapo's high command don't look on him as favorably as in the past. Eichmann returns to his soup without waiting for Höss to resume his seat. These sorts of games seem out of place to him when you're eating. Killing Jews is serious work as far as he's concerned. That's why, when he's asked later on in 1944 by the head of the SS, Heinrich Himmler, to end the Final Solution in light of the inevitable defeat of the Germans,

Eichmann will go on ordering massive exterminations right to the bitter end.

The rumor put out by Mrs. Turnovská—so rightly dubbed Radio Birkenau by Dita—that there'll be a special meal of sausages for the prisoners, has turned out to be false. Yet again.

Dita heads off to see her parents, but as she makes her way through the crowd, she catches a glimpse of Mr. Tomášek and decides it is a perfect opportunity to talk to him. She sets off in his direction, but there's such a crowd on the *Lagerstrasse* that she has trouble making headway. At times, she loses sight of him, but then she spots him again. He's walking toward Block 31 and the hospital hut where there are fewer people. He moves quickly despite being about as old as her father, and Dita can't catch up to him. She sees him skirting past Block 31 and walking on almost to the camp boundary where the clothing hut is located. It's supervised by a regular German prisoner with the rank of *Kapo* rather than by a Jew. Dita has no idea what he's planning to do there since Jewish prisoners aren't allowed to enter that hut without permission. The Germans must think that the rags stored in there are very valuable. Mr. Tomášek is probably trying to get hold of some clothing for a needy prisoner. Her parents have explained to her that kindhearted Mr. Tomášek helps a lot of people, including finding clothes for them.

He strides into the hut before Dita can reach him, so she'll have to wait till he comes out. The wide avenue through which you enter Auschwitz–Birkenau is on the other side of the family camp fence. They're finishing construction of a railway line that will allow the train transports to run under the guard tower, which dominates everything at the main entrance, right to the very heart of the camp. She's not too happy about staying there, in full sight of the guards at the main entrance, so she wanders down the side of the hut until she comes to a crack in the wooden wall. She walks up closer to it and hears Mr. Tomášek's mild voice. He's reciting some names and hut numbers. In German.

Intrigued, Dita sits down beside the wall.

An angry voice interrupts Mr. Tomášek's report.

"We've told you many times already! We don't want the names of retired socialists! We want the names of members of the Resistance."

Dita recognizes the voice and the cold, hard way of speaking. It's the Priest.

"It's not easy. They hide. I try—"

"Try harder."

"Yes, sir."

"Now go."

"Yes, sir."

Dita scurries round to the back of the hut so they won't see her when they come out. She slumps to the ground.

Kindhearted Mr. Tomášek . . . how could he? And whom can she trust now?

She recalls Professor Morgenstern's words: *Trust yourself.*

She's on her own.

Fredy Hirsch has also found himself on his own. He's sitting in his room when there's a knock on the door. Miriam Edelstein comes in, sits down on the wooden floor, and rests her back against the wall. She looks incredibly tired.

"Did Eichmann make any comment about your report?" she asks.

"No, nothing."

"What does he want it for?"

"Who knows. . . ."

"Schwarzhuber was in high spirits. He was smiling at Eichmann the whole time like a little lap dog."

"Or a Doberman."

"True. His face does remind you of a blond Doberman. And what about Mengele? He seemed like a fish out of water."

"He's going it alone."

Miriam falls silent. It would never have occurred to her to speak about Mengele like that—as if he were an acquaintance.

"I don't know how you are able to get along with such a repugnant person."

"He's the one who authorized the delivery to Block Thirty-One of the food parcels sent to dead prisoners. I get along with him because that's my duty. I know some people say that Mengele is my friend. They know nothing. If it were advantageous to our children, I'd get along with the devil himself."

"You already do." And Miriam smiles and gives him an understanding wink as she says it.

"Dealing with Mengele has one advantage. He doesn't hate us. He's too intelligent for that. But that might be why he's the most terrible Nazi of them all."

"If he doesn't hate us, why does he collaborate with this whole aberration?"

"Because it suits him. He's not one of those Nazis who believe that we Jews are a race of inferior, hunchbacked beings from hell. He's told me so. He finds many admirable qualities in Jews—"

"So why does he destroy us, then?"

"Because we are dangerous. We are the race that is capable of confronting the Aryans. We are the ones who can defeat their supremacy. That's why they have to eliminate us. It's nothing personal as far as he's concerned; it's simply a practical matter. Hatred is unknown to him . . . but the awful thing is that he doesn't know compassion, either. There is nothing that moves him."

"I couldn't negotiate with criminals like that."

And pain flashes across her face as she says it.

Fredy stands up, walks over to her, and asks her fondly, "Have you heard anything more about Yakub?"

By the time Miriam and her family had arrived from Terezín six months earlier, the Gestapo already had her husband in custody and transferred him three kilometers away to Auschwitz I, the prison for political prisoners. She has neither seen nor heard anything about him since.

"I was able to talk to Eichmann for a moment this morning. He knows me from some meetings in Prague, but at first he pretended he didn't recognize me. He's despicable, like all the Nazis. The guards were on the point of hitting me, but he did at least stop them, and let me ask him about Yakub. He told me they transferred him to Germany, that he's perfectly fine, and that we'll soon all be reunited. Then he did an about-face and left before I'd finished. I had a letter for Yakub, but I wasn't even able to hand it over. Arieh had written a few lines for his dad. . . ."

"Let me see what I can find out."

"Thanks, Fredy."

"I owe it to you," Fredy adds.

Miriam nods again. She knows he does, but it's something she's not supposed to talk about.

Dita makes her way along the *Lagerstrasse*. She's going after Mr. Tomášek; he disgusts her more than the SS. They wear uniforms, and you know who they are and what they're about. She fears them, she despises them, even hates them . . . but she's never before felt the nausea that the thought of the elegant Mr. Tomášek's Jewish smile provokes in her.

As she rushes to her destination, she tries to form a plan, but she can't come up with anything. She can only tell the truth.

She reaches her father's hut. In front of it she finds the usual group of people gathered around Mr. Tomášek, her parents among them, of course. A woman is talking about something. Mr. Tomášek, eyes half closed, nods in agreement from his spot in the middle of the group and, with a smile, encourages the woman to continue.

Dita bursts in, even splashing mud on some of them.

"My goodness, child!"

Dita blushes, and her voice shakes. But her arm isn't shaking as she raises it and points to the person in the center of the group.

"Mr. Tomášek is a traitor. He's an SS informer."

The muttering can be heard immediately, and people stir nervously. Mr. Tomášek tries to keep his smile in place, but he's not entirely successful. It's skewed to one side.

Liesl Adler is one of the first to stand up.

"Edita! What are you saying?"

"I'll tell you," interjects one of the women. "Your daughter is ill-mannered. How dare she burst in like this to insult an important person like Mr. Tomášek?"

"Mrs. Adler," adds one of the men, "you should give your daughter a good slap. And if you don't, I will."

"Mama, I'm telling the truth," says Dita nervously and with less certainty now. "I heard him speaking with the Priest in the clothing hut. He's an informer!"

"Impossible!" says the woman who spoke earlier, absolutely outraged.

"Either you give your daughter a slap right now to shut her up, or I'll do it for you." The man starts to move toward Dita.

"If anyone is to be punished, then punish me," says Liesl calmly. "I'm her mother, and if my daughter has behaved improperly, then I'm the one you should slap."

At that, Hans Adler speaks up.

"Nobody's going to be slapped," he states firmly. "Edita is telling the truth. I know she is."

A chorus of stunned whispers runs around the group.

"Of course I'm telling the truth," shouts Dita, feeling braver. "I heard the Priest telling him to hand over information about the Resistance. That's why he spends the whole day walking around the camp. That's why he asks so many questions and gets people to talk about their problems."

"Are you going to deny it, Mr. Tomášek?" asks Mr. Adler, firing a look in his direction.

Almost all of them turn their heads toward Tomášek, who's silent. He just stands there, the customary half smile still on his face.

"I . . ." he begins. Everyone prepares to listen. They're sure it's a misunderstanding he can easily clear up. "I . . ."

But that's as far as he gets. He clears a path and hurries off to his hut. Perplexed, they all stand there looking at each other and at the three members of the Adler family. Dita hugs her father.

"Hans," asks Liesl, "how did you know with such certainty that Edita was telling the truth? It seemed so incredible . . . !"

"I didn't know. But it's a trick they use in the courts. You bluff: You pretend you're absolutely certain about something although you aren't really, and the accused is betrayed by his own insecurity. He thinks he's been found out and falls to pieces."

"And if he hadn't been an informer?"

"I would have apologized. But," he adds, winking at his daughter, "I knew I was holding a good hand."

One of the men in the group approaches and places a friendly hand on Hans's shoulder.

"I'd forgotten you were a lawyer."

"Me too."

There's still one thing to do to finish off Mr. Tomášek's career as an informer: activate Radio Birkenau. The Adler family go to see Mrs. Turnovská. The good woman entrusts herself a number of times to God and several biblical patriarchs, and then sets things in motion. Within forty-eight hours, the entire camp has been alerted and Mr. Tomášek has fallen from grace.

12.

RUDI ROSENBERG HEADS AROUND THE BACK OF HIS HUT IN THE
quarantine camp and walks up to the electrified fence. Alice Munk
is waiting for him on the other side. They both stop three paces
from the fence and then, despite the thousands of volts running
through the wires, advance one more step. They slowly sit down so
they won't arouse the guards' suspicion.

It's another of the many afternoons that Rudi gets together
with Alice to talk. Alice tells him about her family of wealthy in-
dustrialists from the north of Prague, and how much she'd like to
go home. Rosenberg talks about his dream of going to America the
day this nightmare of war and camps is over.

"It's the land of opportunity. Business is sacred. It's the only
place in the world where a poor man can become the president of a
nation."

It's freezing cold, and the ground is covered with frost. Rudi is
wearing a cloth jacket, but Alice has only a worn sweater and an old
woolen shawl. When Rudi notices that her lips are turning blue
and she's shivering, he tells her she'd better go back to her hut, but
she refuses.

She's happier sharing this afternoon outdoors in freezing
intimacy than inside a hut full of women who reek of sweat and
illness—and occasionally, of resentment.

When the cold becomes unbearable, they stand up and walk in

step on either side of the fence. The guards have become used to their presence. Rudi gets tobacco for some of them, and sometimes acts as interpreter with the Russian and Czech soldiers, so their afternoon meetings near the fence are tolerated for now.

Rudi talks to Alice about amusing moments in his life as registrar. He doesn't want to tell her about what he sees in the eyes of recent camp arrivals on the other side of his registration table. So now and then, he invents funny anecdotes to make his stories more entertaining. When Alice speaks of the hundreds of people arriving daily, he tells her it's only the terminally ill who are gassed, that she shouldn't be distressed, and immediately changes the topic of conversation.

"I've brought you a present . . ."

He pulls his hand out of his pocket and opens his fist. What's on display is tiny, but Alice's eyes open wide when she recognizes its enormous value. It's a clove of garlic.

Rudi has become something of an expert at keeping an eye on the soldier in the nearest guard tower. When the barrel of his gun suggests he has his back to them, he takes two quick steps to the fence. He mustn't touch the wire, but he can't dither. He's got ten seconds before the guard turns back to face them. He pinches his fingers together and carefully introduces them into the appropriate gap. Five seconds. He releases the garlic clove. Alice reaches out and snaps it up. Four seconds. They both return to their original spots, a few paces from the fence.

There's admiration and fear on Alice's face. Rudi is pleased. There aren't many people willing to insert their fingers in the deadly fences. Some black marketeers toss goods over the tops of the fences that separate the camps, but Rudi believes that sort of action is too visible from a long way off, and there are too many tongues, and too many eyes, in the *Lager*.

"Eat it, Alice. It's got lots of vitamins."

"But then I won't be able to give you a kiss . . ."

"Come on, Alice, it's important. You must eat. You're very thin."

"Don't you like me?" asks Alice, flirting.

Rudi sighs.

"You know I'm mad about you. And your hair is particularly lovely today."

"You noticed!"

"But you have to eat that garlic. It cost me a lot to get it."

"And I'm really, really grateful."

But she hides it in her hand rather than eating it. Rudi swears silently.

"You did the same thing the other day when I brought you a stick of celery."

Then Alice gives him a teasing look and lifts her chin as if she were signaling to him. And Rudi finally notices and claps his hand to his forehead.

"Alice, you're crazy!"

He hasn't realized until this very moment that Alice is wearing a purple hairband. Perhaps a little childish, but a luxury item in this place. It has cost him a celery stick. Alice laughs.

"No, don't do it! Winter isn't over, you've got hardly any warm clothing, and you have to eat. Don't you understand? The person in charge of the corpse cart picks up a dozen people a day in your camp—people who die of exhaustion, malnutrition, or just a simple cold. A cold kills you here, Alice. We're very weak. You've got to eat!" And for the first time, his voice hardens as he speaks to Alice: "I want you to eat that garlic clove right now!"

He had to hand over the names and ranks of the most recently arrived Russian officers to a certain helper in the kitchen in order to get the garlic. Rudi neither knows nor wants to know why he wants the list, but it's valuable information. Favors like that could even cost him his life.

Alice looks at him sadly, and he can see a tear in her eye.

"You don't understand, Rudi."

That's all she says. She's not very talkative. And no, Rudi doesn't understand. Exchanging a celery stalk, so nutritious and hard to get hold of, for a useless piece of wire covered in velvet, made quickly and on the run in one of the camp workshops, seems stupid to him. He doesn't understand that Alice will soon turn sixteen. After spending all her adolescence trapped in the ugliness of war, feeling beautiful for one afternoon makes Alice happy. And that is more nourishing than an entire field of celery.

The face she makes at Rudi seeks his forgiveness, and he shrugs. He doesn't understand her, but it's impossible to be angry with her.

The fate of his garlic clove has already been decided. When the afternoon roll call is over, Alice rushes to Hut 9 in search of Mr. Lada. He's a short little man who works with the group responsible for transporting the dead. It's not a pleasant job, but it does allow him to move throughout the *Lager*, and freedom of movement means making deals. Alice holds a tiny piece of soap and inhales deeply; it smells divine. Lada does the same thing with his garlic clove; it smells divine, too.

Alice is so thrilled with her acquisition that she spends the remaining time before curfew washing her clothes. She puts on a woolen jumper full of holes and a very old plaid skirt she stores under the pillow of her bunk. They are the only items of clothing she can wear when, every two weeks, she washes her underwear, her socks, and her blue dress—now faded to gray.

She has to line up for an hour and a half to get a turn at one of the only three taps that provide a trickle of water. You can't drink the water. It's already killed a few people who either didn't believe it was harmful or couldn't put up with the thirst tormenting them, especially at night when so many hours had passed since their last drop of liquid—their midday soup.

The icy cold tap water burns Alice's hands and leaves them feeling numb and rough. Barely a minute has passed, but the women in the line are already swearing at her to hurry up and finish. Several of them talk unpleasantly about her, loud enough for Alice to hear them. There's no such thing as secrets in the camp; rumors are rife, like the mold that covers the walls from floor to ceiling, and they corrupt everything in their path.

People know about her relationship with that Slovak registrar, and it doesn't please those prisoners who hate the thought of something good happening to anyone else. Eagerness to survive leads many of them into a moral slide that causes them to overcome their fears and pain by being bitterly resentful of their fellow inmates. They believe doing harm to others is a justice of sorts that alleviates their own suffering.

"How unfair, that shameless sluts who open their legs for prisoners with influence have a piece of soap while decent women have to wash with dirty water!" comments one woman.

A mutter of agreement rises from a chorus of women with scarves on their heads.

"Decency has disappeared, and respect has gone, too," says another.

"Disgraceful," adds another voice, speaking loudly to make sure Alice can hear her.

The young girl scrubs furiously, as if hoping the sliver of glycerin soap might remove the resentment. She hurriedly ends her task, even though she hasn't finished. Ashamed and incapable of defending herself, she doesn't dare raise her head; as she leaves, she deposits what's left of the soap on the shelf. Several women launch themselves at it in a huddle of shoves and yells.

Alice is feeling so ashamed and nervous that the last person she wants to see is her mother. So she ends up walking to Block 31. Hut doors must always be ajar, but as Alice pushes the hut door farther open, a metal bowl containing screws falls to the ground. It's one of Fredy Hirsch's tricks so he knows if someone is entering outside the usual hours. The block chief emerges from his cubicle and notices that Alice is trembling.

"What's the matter, child?"

"They hate me, Fredy!"

"Who does?"

"All those women. They insult me because I'm friendly with Rudi!"

Hirsch puts his hands on her shoulders; Alice can't stop crying.

"Those women don't hate you, Alice. They don't even know you."

"They do hate me! They said horrible things to me, and I couldn't even answer them in the way they deserved."

"You did the right thing. When a dog barks fiercely at someone, or even bites them, it does it out of fear, not hate. If you ever have to confront an aggressive dog, don't run or shout, because you'll frighten it and it will bite you. Stand still and talk to it slowly so it becomes less scared. These women are afraid, Alice. They're angry at everything that's happening to us."

Alice begins to calm down.

"You should go and dry your clothes."

She nods and tries to thank him, but Fredy stops her with a wave of his hand. There's nothing to thank him for. He's responsible for all his people. The assistants are his soldiers, and a soldier never says thank you; he stands at attention and gives a salute.

When Alice leaves, Hirsch looks around and then shuts himself inside his cubicle again. But the hut isn't actually empty. There's someone huddled behind the woodpile who's been silently listening.

Dita's father has been unsuccessfully battling a cold for days, and her mother has forced him to abandon their outdoor lessons, so Dita has spent her afternoons keeping guard in her hideout at the back of the hut. She's been waiting for the secret SS contact to reappear, but her surveillance hasn't produced any results so far. If there's no one she can trust, then she'll just have to solve the Hirsch mystery on her own. Fredy has emerged from his cubicle periodically to do push-ups and sit-ups, or lift stools as if they were weights. Miriam Edelstein has dropped in on the odd afternoon, but that's it. Dita misses her conversations with Margit, who she knows sits down for a chat with Renée now and again.

Hirsch, convinced that the hut is empty, has turned out the lights, so it's dark inside. Dita hugs herself tightly to try and keep warm. The shiver reminds her of the patients in the Berghof spa, who would lie down at night facing the Alps so that the cold, dry mountain air would clear their lungs of tuberculosis. These weeks in the *Lager* have made it difficult for her to remember the intensive reading of *The Magic Mountain* she enjoyed in Terezín. The book had such an impact on her that the characters have become part of her store of memories.

The Berghof reminded Dita of the ghetto. Life had been better there than in Auschwitz. It was much less violent and horrific than the factory of pain in which they now struggle to survive, despite the fact that Terezín was a spa where no one was cured.

Hans Castorp arrived for a stay of a few days, which became months and then years. Whenever it looked like he might leave, Dr. Behrens detected a slight problem in his lung and he had to extend his stay. Dita had been in Terezín for a year when she started to read the book, and at that stage she had no idea when she would be able to leave that city-prison. Given the rumors about the world beyond those walls—the Nazis relentlessly advancing through a war-torn Europe with millions already dead and camps where Jews were being sent for extermination—it occurred to her that the walls might be imprisoning her, but they were also protecting her. Much the same could be said of Hans and the Berghof sanatorium he no longer wanted to leave to face his world.

She exchanged her labor in Terezín's perimeter gardens for more comfortable duties in a military garment workshop and, as time passed, while her mother lost energy and her father made ever fewer witty observations, Dita kept reading. The story of Hans fascinated her, and she kept him company until he reached the critical moment of his life. It was carnival night and, taking advantage of the freedom provided by the masks they were all wearing, he dared to speak for the first time to Mme. Chauchat, a very beautiful Russian woman with whom he was hopelessly in love, despite the fact that they had never exchanged more than a few exquisitely polite words of greeting. In the stiflingly ceremonious atmosphere of the Berghof, protected by carnival dispensation, he had dared to address her informally and call her Clawdia. Dita closes her eyes and relives that moment when he prostrates himself so romantically before Clawdia and, in a gallant and impassioned manner, declares his rash love.

Dita likes the incredibly elegant Mme. Chauchat, with her almond eyes, who is usually the last to enter the regal dining room and shuts the door loudly enough to make Hans jump in his seat. The first few times, it irritates him, but then he is swept up by her Tartar beauty. In that moment of freedom offered by carnival, when those speaking are not people trapped within the strict rules of social etiquette but masks, Mme. Chauchat says to Hans, "All Europe knows that you Germans love order more than freedom."

And Dita, tucked up in her hidey-hole of wooden boards, nods in agreement.

Mme. Chauchat is so right.

Dita thinks she'd like to be Mme. Chauchat, such a cultured, refined, and independent woman: When she entered a room, all the boys would steal a look at her. After the undoubtedly daring but charming compliments of the young German, which the Russian lady finds not the least bit offensive, something completely unexpected happens. Mme. Chauchat opts for a change of environment and leaves for Daghestan, or maybe Spain.

If Dita had been Mme. Chauchat, she would have been unable to resist the charm and graciousness of a gentleman like Hans. It's not that she lacks the bravery to roam the world, because when this nightmare war is over, she'd like to go anywhere with her family. Maybe even to that land of Palestine Fredy Hirsch talks about so much.

Just then, she hears the sound of the hut door opening. When she carefully peers out, she sees the same tall figure in boots and a dark cape that she saw the first time. Her heart jumps in her chest.

The much anticipated moment of truth has arrived. But does she really want to confront it? Each time the truth is revealed, something falls apart. She sighs and thinks it would be best if she left the hut; she is racked with uncertainty. But she needs to know the truth.

Dita had once read a piece about spies in one of the magazines her parents kept on the coffee table in the living room. The article suggested you could hear conversations through walls by putting your ear up to the bottom of a glass placed against the wall. She tiptoes up to the wall of the *Blockältester*'s cubicle, breakfast bowl in hand. It's risky. If they catch her spying, who knows what will happen to her.

As she places the metal container against the wall, she realizes she can hear perfectly well just by putting her ear to the wooden divider. There's even a small hole in the panel through which she can see inside.

She spies Hirsch, with a dark expression on his face. She can see only the back of the blond man facing him. He's not wearing an SS uniform, but he's not wearing regular prison garb, either. Then she spots the brown armband worn by barrack *Kapos*.

"This will be the last time, Ludwig."

"Why?"

"I can't go on deceiving my people." Fredy slicks back his hair with one hand. "They believe I'm one thing, when in reality, I'm something quite different."

"And what is that terrible other thing you are?"

Fredy smiles bitterly.

"You already know that. Better than anyone."

"Come on, Fredy, dare to name it. . . ."

"There's nothing more to say."

"Why not?" The words of his interlocutor are loaded with irony and resentment. "The fearless man doesn't dare admit what he is? Do you lack the courage to say the terrible thing that you are?"

The *Blockältester* sighs and his voice drops:

"A . . . homosexual."

"Dammit, call it what it is! The great Fredy Hirsch is a queer!"

Hirsch, beside himself, launches himself at the man and grabs him violently by his lapels. He smashes him up against the wall, and the veins stand out in his neck.

"Shut up! Never ever say that again."

"Come on! Is it so horrible? I'm one, too, and I don't consider myself a monster. Do you think I am? Do you think I deserve to be branded a pariah?" And, as he speaks, he points to the pink triangle sewn onto his shirt.

Hirsch releases him. He closes his eyes and slicks back his hair as he tries to compose himself.

"Forgive me, Ludwig. I didn't mean to hurt you."

"Well, you have." Ludwig fixes his crumpled lapel with the fastidiousness of a dandy. "You say you don't want to deceive the people who follow you. So what will you do when you get out of here? Find a nice Jewish girl who'll cook you kosher meals and marry her? Will you deceive her?"

"I don't want to deceive anyone, Ludwig. That's why we have to stop seeing each other."

"Do whatever you like. Repress your feelings if that makes you feel better. Try making love to some girl. I've tried it: It's like eating a tasteless bowl of soup. But it's not totally bad. And do you think that the deceptions will be over? Absolutely not! There'll still be someone you'll be lying to: yourself."

"I've already told you it's over, Ludwig."

His words leave no room for a response. They look at each sadly without saying a word. The *Kapo* with the pink triangle slowly nods his assent, accepting defeat. He walks up to Hirsch and kisses him on the lips. A silent tear runs down Ludwig's cheek.

On the other side of the wooden wall, Dita almost cries out. It's more than she can bear. She's never seen two men kiss, and she finds it disgusting. Even more so because it's Fredy Hirsch. Her Fredy Hirsch. She runs silently out of the hut, not even noticing the shock of the cold night air. She's so upset she doesn't think to look out for Dr. Mengele. She's stunned on the outside and feels dirty on the inside. She feels an incredible anger toward Fredy Hirsch; she feels defrauded. Tears of rage cloud her sight.

That's why she bumps into someone walking in the opposite direction.

"Careful, young lady!"

"You're the one who's not looking where you're going, dammit!" she replies.

But as she looks up, she sees the face of Professor Morgenstern, and realizes she's been rude. She's almost knocked the poor old man to the ground.

"Please forgive me, Professor. I didn't recognize you."

"It's you, Miss Adler!" And as he says this, he peers at Dita with his myopic eyes. "But are you crying?"

"It's the cold. It's irritating my eyes, dammit!" she answers sharply.

"Is there anything I can do for you?"

"No, nobody can."

The professor puts his hands on his hips.

"Are you sure?"

"I can't explain. It's a secret."

"Then don't tell me. Secrets are for keeping."

The professor bows and marches off to his hut without another word. Dita feels even more bewildered than she was before. Maybe it's her fault. Maybe he's right, and she shouldn't stick her nose into other people's business. She wants to talk with someone; she thinks of Miriam Edelstein. She's the only one who visits Hirsch outside regular hours.

Dita finds Miriam with her son, Arieh, inside Barrack 28. There's not much time left before curfew. It's not the best time for visits, but when the deputy director sees Dita's distress, she can't bring herself to say no.

The darkness and the cold don't lend themselves to long conversations, but Dita tells her everything from the beginning: Mengele's warning, how she accidentally witnessed Hirsch's first encounter with a particular individual, her doubts, and her attempts to resolve them by finding out the truth. Miriam listens without interrupting her, with no sign of surprise when Dita tells her about Hirsch's secret affairs with other men. She even remains silent for a while after Dita has finished her tale.

"So?" asks Dita impatiently.

"You've got your truth now," Miriam replies. "You'll be satisfied."

"What do you mean?"

"You wanted truth, but a truth that suited you. You wanted Fredy Hirsch to be a brave, efficient, incorruptible, charming, flawless man . . . and you feel cheated because he's a homosexual. You could have chosen to be happy at the confirmation that he's not an SS informer, that he really is one of us, and one of the best. But instead, you feel offended because he's not exactly what you'd like him to be."

"No, don't misjudge me. Of course I'm relieved that he's not one of them. It's just that . . . I couldn't imagine him being that way!"

"Edita, you talk about this as if it were a crime. The only thing that's different is that instead of being attracted to women, he likes men. It's no crime."

"In school, they told us it was an illness."

"The real disease is intolerance."

They stop talking for a moment.

"You already knew, didn't you, Mrs. Edelstein?"

The woman nods.

"Please call me Miriam. We share a secret now. But it's not our secret, so we have no right to reveal it."

"You know Fredy well, don't you?"

"He's told me some things and then I've found out others. . . ."

"Who is Fredy Hirsch?"

Miriam gestures that the two of them should walk around the hut. Her feet are freezing.

"Fredy Hirsch's father died when he was very young. He felt lost. And then they signed him up for the JPD, the German organization that gathered together young Jews at that time. He grew up there and found a home. And sport was everything to him. The organization quickly realized that he had talent as a coach and an event organizer."

Dita links arms with Miriam Edelstein to try and stay warm as they walk. Miriam's words blend with the sound of their clogs stamping on the night frost.

"His reputation as a JPD coach grew. But the rise of the Nazi party ruined everything. Fredy told me that Adolf Hitler's supporters were a bunch of mean-spirited barroom troublemakers who used to defy the laws of the German Republic. Later, they were the ones who started to make laws to suit their own purposes."

Hirsch told Miriam he'd never be able to forget the afternoon he arrived at JPD headquarters and was confronted by the words *traitor Jews* painted on one of the walls. He wondered what they had betrayed and couldn't come up with an answer. Some afternoons, stones would hit the windowpanes during a pottery workshop or while the choir was rehearsing. Each blow against the glass shattered something inside Fredy.

One afternoon, his mother asked him to come home straight from school because they had to discuss something important. Fredy had matters to attend to, but he accepted his mother's request because one of the JPD teachings he had absorbed was to respect hierarchies and ranks zealously.

When he got home, he found the family gathered, somber. His mother informed them that their stepfather had lost his job because he was a Jew, and the situation was becoming dangerous. They had decided to leave for South America—Bolivia—to start over.

"Go to Bolivia? You mean run away!" Fredy replied harshly.

His stepfather started to stand up to confront him, but it was Fredy's older brother, Paul, who told Fredy to shut up.

Fredy walked out of the house, stunned. Bewilderment and force of habit led him to the only place where everything was orderly and coherent—JPD headquarters. It was there he found one of the directors checking the water bottles before the next excursion. Normally, Hirsch didn't talk about personal matters, but he couldn't bear the cowardice of running away.

The coordinator of outdoor activities, whose blond hair was

starting to turn white, had watched Fredy grow up in the JPD. He looked at Fredy long and hard, and told him that if he wanted to stay, there'd be a place for him in the JPD.

Fredy was only seventeen, but he already possessed self-confidence. His family left, and he was on his own. Although not entirely: He had the JPD. In 1935 they sent him to the Düsseldorf branch as a youth instructor. He told Miriam that initially he was euphoric over his new job in such a vibrant city, but his euphoria rapidly disappeared in the face of the hostility shown to the Jews. They stopped fixing the windows at the JPD headquarters because the stone-throwing became a daily event. Insults were hurled at them from the street, and each day saw a drop in the number of children who attended. Some mornings, his basketball team consisted of a single player.

One afternoon, from an upstairs window, Fredy spotted some-one painting a yellow X on the large wooden entrance to the build-ing. He raced down the stairs. The boy with the paintbrush looked at him mockingly and went on painting, unconcerned. Fredy grabbed him by the shirtfront so forcefully that he dropped his can of paint.

"Why are you doing this?" asked Fredy, taking in the swas-tika armband with a mix of bewilderment and anger at what was happening in his own country.

"You Jews are a danger to civilization," yelled the adolescent disdainfully.

"Civilization? You and your friends are going to give me les-sons in civilization when you spend your days beating up old people and throwing rocks at houses? What would you know about civili-zation? While you Aryans were living in the north of Europe in wooden cabins, wearing animal skins and roasting meat on two sticks, we Jews were building entire cities."

Fredy grabbed hold of the young Nazi. Various people who saw him do this started to approach.

"There's a Jew hitting a boy!" shouted a woman.

The owner of a fruit shop came toward them with the metal pole used for lowering the shop shutters, followed by about another dozen men. A hand grabbed Fredy's arm and pulled him away.

"Let's go!" the director shouted at him.

They only just had time to run inside the building and slam the main door shut before an avalanche of enraged citizens rushed toward them in what seemed to Fredy to be a display of collective madness.

They closed the JPD branch the next day and sent Fredy off to Bohemia. He continued to work for Maccabi Hatzair, organizing sports activities for the young people of Ostrava, Brno, and then finally, Prague.

He didn't much like the Czech capital and was perplexed by the Czechs, who seemed more carefree and informal than the Germans. But at Hagibor, on the outskirts of Prague, he found a perfect location for sporting activities. They put him in charge of a group of ten- to twelve-year-old boys. The plan was to get them out of Bohemia and lead them through neutral countries all the way to Palestine. They needed to be in excellent physical shape, but they also had to know the history of the Jews and their adversities so that they would feel a sense of pride and be keen to return to the land of their forebears.

Hirsch applied himself to the task with his customary dedication and enthusiasm for the orders he'd been given. Such was his effectiveness and charisma when it came to his charges that the leaders of the Jewish Youth Council in Prague decided to put this responsible and tenacious young man in charge of the groups of children new to the club, who were often a bit disoriented.

Fredy never forgot how difficult it was to cheer up those children. Unlike the children who had been brought up with the *havlagah* principle of self-restraint, whose parents had imbued them with a strong sense of Jewishness and Zionism, and who had arrived mentally prepared and bursting with enthusiasm, this other group consisted of shy, sad, and apathetic children. They weren't interested in games or sports, and none of Fredy's funny stories prompted a smile.

There was one twelve-year-old boy in the group called Karel who had the longest eyelashes Fredy had ever seen. And the saddest eyes. At the end of that first afternoon, when Hirsch was trying to get to know them better, he suggested that each of them say where they would like to be at that particular moment on that particular September day of 1939. Karel gravely replied that he'd like to be in heaven so he could see his parents. The Gestapo had arrested them, and his grandmother had told him he'd never see them again. Then he sat down and didn't say another word. Some of the other boys, who had so far been very serious themselves, laughed in that typically tactless way that children have—laughing at others allowed them to cover up their own fears.

One afternoon, the vice chairman in charge of youth activities at the Jewish Council of Prague asked to see Hirsch. He grimly explained to Fredy that the Nazi grip was closing, the borders were being sealed, and it would soon be impossible to evacuate anyone from Prague. And so the first *havlagah* group must leave immediately, within twenty-four or forty-eight hours maximum. He asked Fredy, as their top instructor, if he would like to be the person to accompany this group.

It was the best offer Fredy had ever had. He could go with the group, leave the horrors of war behind him, and reach Palestine, as he'd always dreamed of doing. However, going would mean leaving behind the groups he'd started to instruct at Hagibor, abandoning a task he knew was critical for those boys who had been choked by the Reich's prohibitions, hardships, and humiliations. Leaving meant abandoning Karel and the rest of them. He remembered what the JPD had meant to him in Aachen after his father died, when he felt lost. It was where he'd found his place in the world.

"Anyone else would have gone," continues Miriam, "but Hirsch wasn't just anybody. He stayed at Hagibor."

Miriam and Dita sit silently as if they are weighing up the consequences of that decision. It is beyond calculation.

"After everything that's happened . . . I feel guilty for doubting him."

Miriam sighs and her breath emerges as a puff of white vapor. Just then, the curfew siren sounds, ordering everyone back to their barracks.

"Edita . . ."

"Yes?"

"Tomorrow you must speak to Fredy about the business with Dr. Mengele. He'll know what to do. As far as the other matter is concerned . . ."

"It's our secret."

Miriam nods, and Dita races off so fast that she's almost flying over the frozen mud. She still feels a sharp pain deep within her. But while it hurts to have lost her white knight, she is relieved. Hirsch is trustworthy.

13.

A FEW HUTS AWAY, IN BLOCK 31, ANOTHER CONVERSATION IS taking place. Fredy Hirsch is addressing the empty stools.

"I've done it. I've done what had to be done."

His own voice echoing in the darkness of the hut sounds strange to him.

He's told that handsome Berliner not to return. He should feel proud of himself, happy even, because his willpower has triumphed. But he doesn't. He'd prefer to find women attractive, but there's something about his basic assembly. Maybe a piece that's been put in the wrong way round, or something like that . . .

He walks out of the hut and sadly gazes at the landscape of mud, huts, and towers. Under the electric lights he can make out two figures standing face-to-face on either side of the fence—Alice Munk and the registrar from the quarantine camp. It must be close to freezing point outside, but they aren't cold; or if they are, they're sharing it, so it's more bearable.

Maybe that's what love is—sharing the cold.

Block 31 seems small and crowded when all the children are there, but huge and soulless when they leave.

In an effort to warm himself, he lies down on the floor of the hut, elbows pinned to his body, and starts punishing his abdominal muscles by doing scissor-kicks with his legs up in the air. Love has been a constant source of problems for Fredy since he was an ado-lescent. Given how disciplined he has been in everything else, he feels a deep frustration at his inability to overcome his deepest in-stincts.

One, two, three, four, five . . .

On JPD excursions, he liked to snuggle up inside his sleeping bag with the other boys, who were always happy to clown around and accepted him. After his father died, he felt so protected and comfort-able with them. . . . There was nothing like that feeling of compan-ionship. A soccer team wasn't just a soccer team; it was family.

Eighteen, nineteen, twenty, twenty-one . . .

The pleasure he felt hanging out with the boys didn't disappear as he grew older. He felt much more removed from the girls; there wasn't that sense of camaraderie he had with the boys. Girls in-timidated him. They kept the boys at a distance and ridiculed them. He felt at ease only with his teammates and the boys who joined him on hikes and at games. He carried that feeling into adulthood. Then he left Aachen for Düsseldorf.

There comes a point when your body decides for you. Clandestine encounters started. Some took place in public bath-rooms with their weak lighting, permanently wet floors, and rusty stains in the washbasins. But now and again, there was a tender glance, a slightly less mechanical caress, a moment of fulfillment, impossible to resist. Love was like walking on a carpet of shattered glass.

Thirty-eight, thirty-nine, forty . . .

Over the years he's tried to keep busy with his tournaments and training, organizing endless events so as to keep his mind busy and his body exhausted. One slip, and it could destroy his reputation.

Keeping busy has also allowed him to disguise the fact that no matter how popular and in demand he is, he always ends up alone.

Fifty-seven, fifty-eight, fifty-nine . . .

That's why he continues to slice through the air with his scissor-kicks, making his abdominal muscles ache, punishing himself for not being what he'd like to be, or what everyone else would like him to be.

Seventy-three, seventy-four, seventy-five . . .

A pool of sweat shows his determination, his capacity for sacrifice . . . his success. He sits up and, feeling more relaxed, allows his memories to fill the night's emptiness.

And those memories take him back to Terezín.

They deported him to the Terezín ghetto in May 1942, as if he were just one more Czech. He was among the first to arrive. The Nazis also sent machine operators, doctors, members of the Jewish Council, and cultural and sports instructors. They were preparing for the transportation of massive numbers of Jews.

When Fredy reached the town, he found the urban design of a military mind: streets drawn up with a set square and quadrant, geometrical buildings, and rectangular garden beds that would probably produce flowers in the spring. He liked that logical city; it matched his sense of discipline. It even occurred to him that it might be the start of a new, better period for the Jews before their return to Palestine.

The first time he stopped to look at Terezín, a breeze ruffled his straight hair. He smoothed it back into place. He wasn't prepared to let anything make him lose his composure. He belonged to a race thousands of years old, a chosen people.

His work with youth groups in Prague had been intense, and he wanted to continue his sports activities and Friday gatherings to encourage the Hebrew spirit. It wouldn't be easy; he'd have to confront the Nazis, as well as the odd member of the Jewish Council who was aware of the stain he tried so zealously to hide and wouldn't forgive him. Luckily, he could always count on the support of the council chairman, Yakub Edelstein.

He successfully put together athletics teams, classes in boxing and jujitsu, and basketball tournaments. He established a soccer league with several teams, even convincing the German guards to form a team to take on the prisoners.

He remembers glorious moments: the roar of the spectators who packed not only the perimeter of the field but the doors and windows of all the buildings overlooking the inner courtyard where the games were played.

He recalls the moments of frailty, too; there were many of them.

He recalls one game in particular, a soccer match he organized between the SS guards and the Jews, where he was the referee. There was absolutely no space in any of the openings onto the patio. Hundreds of eyes followed that game intently from every possible spot. It was more than a game. Especially for Fredy. He spent weeks preparing the team, studying tactics, preparing them mentally, putting together sets of exercises, asking people to donate milk rations for his players.

There were only minutes left in the game and the forward for the SS team intercepted the ball in the center circle. He started to run in a straight line toward the goal area and caught the midfielders on the prisoners' team off guard. There was only one defender left to intercept him. The Nazi ran toward him, and just when he was about to confront him, the prisoner discreetly pulled back his leg so that the Nazi could get past him. The SS guard took a point-blank shot and scored the winning goal. Hirsch will never forget the expressions of complete satisfaction on the faces of the Aryans. They'd beaten the Jews—even on the playing field.

Hirsch blew the final whistle then and there with perfect equanimity, and went to congratulate the forward who had scored the final goal. He shook his hand firmly, and the SS guard greeted him with a smile so full of missing teeth that it looked as if someone had kicked him in the mouth. Fredy headed for the makeshift change rooms, faking an air of impartiality, and then stopped as if to tie one of his shoelaces. He allowed the players to go ahead of him, waiting until one particular player overtook him. Nobody noticed the quick, violent shove that propelled the player into the broom closet. Once inside, he pinned him up against the mop handles.

"What's the matter?" asked the puzzled player.

"You tell me. Why did you allow that Nazi to score a goal and beat us?"

"Look, Hirsch, I know that corporal. He's an absolute bastard, a real sadist. His teeth are broken because of all the bottles he opens with his mouth. He's a brute. No way I was going to trip him and risk my neck."

Fredy remembers every last word he said in reply, remembers his utter contempt.

"You couldn't be more wrong. It's not a game. There were hundreds of people watching, and we've let them down. There were dozens of children—what will they think? How are they going to be proud of being Jews if we grovel like worms? It's your duty to give your all in every game."

"I think you're getting carried away—"

Hirsch stuck his face right up to the player's and noted the look of fear in his eyes, but the man couldn't retreat any farther in that tiny space.

"Now, listen carefully. I'm going to say this only once. Next time you play against the SS, if you don't stick out your leg, I'll cut it off with a handsaw."

The player, white as a sheet, ducked to one side and scurried off.

Fredy gives a sigh of annoyance as he thinks back on it.

That man was useless. Adults are corrupted. That's why young people are so important. You can still shape them, improve them.

On August 24, 1943, a trainload of 1,260 children from Białystok arrived in Terezín. More than fifty thousand Jews had been interned in the ghetto of that Polish city and, over that summer, the SS had systematically exterminated almost all the adults.

The Białystok children were lodged in a separate part of Terezín, a few blocks in the western section of the town, enclosed by barbed wire. The SS guards kept a very close eye on them. Strict orders were sent to the Council of Elders by the *Hauptsturmführer* of Terezín that any contact with this group of children was absolutely forbidden; they were merely passing through, and their final destination was a secret. Permission to have access was limited to fifty-three people, including health personnel. The most severe penalties would be applied to anyone ignoring these orders.

The Nazis hoped that, by prohibiting any contact with the Polish children—both witnesses and victims of the Białystok massacre—they could keep the lowest possible profile for their crimes in a Europe blinded by war.

It was almost dinnertime in Terezín, and the air was starting to cool down. A thoughtful Fredy Hirsch was refereeing a game of soccer involving fifty players. He was actually concentrating harder on the colonnade leading to the street than on the swarm of legs chasing after the ball.

Despite having sent numerous written requests, he had not received permission for the Youth Office to intervene on behalf of the children from Poland. So when he spied the group of health workers returning from the banned section where the Białystok children had been isolated, he handed his whistle over to the nearest boy and rushed off to meet them.

The medical team, their faces reflecting their deep exhaustion, were walking along the sidewalk still wearing their filthy lab coats. Fredy planted himself in their path and asked them what state the children were in, but they simply walked on. They had been ordered to disclose nothing. There was a nurse lagging behind the group, walking slowly by herself as if she was distracted or slightly disoriented. The woman stopped briefly, and Hirsch saw a look of tired outrage in her eyes.

She told him that the children were terrified and that most of them were suffering from acute malnutrition: "When the guards tried to take them to the showers, they became hysterical. They kicked and shouted that they didn't want to go to the gas chambers. They had to be taken to the showers by force. One of the children, whose wound I was disinfecting, told me that he'd found out just before he boarded the train that they had killed his father, his mother, and his older siblings. He was gripping my arm with all his might and telling me in a voice full of terror that he didn't want to go to the gas showers."

The nurse couldn't help feeling disturbed at the sight of these orphans trembling with fright, being guarded by the very murderers who had killed their parents. She told Fredy they clung to her legs, and faked pain and illness, but what they really needed wasn't medicine but affection, protection, shelter, and a hug to relieve their fear.

The next day various workmen, kitchen staff, and health workers walked through the control barrier to the western section where the Białystok children were being kept. The bored SS guards kept an eye on the activities of the personnel.

A squad of workmen carried through construction materials to do repairs on one of the buildings. One of them had his face hidden by the board he was carrying on his shoulder. He had the construction worker's typically straight shoulders and muscular arms, but he was a sports instructor, not a builder. Fredy Hirsch had managed to sneak in.

Once inside, he could move around freely, and he quickly made for the nearest building. He felt a nervous twinge when he saw two SS guards in front of him, but rather than backtracking, he kept on walking even more resolutely toward them. They paid no attention to him as he passed; there were lots of Jewish civilians moving throughout the area working on a range of tasks.

He entered one of the buildings. It had the same layout as all the other buildings in Terezín: an entrance into a hallway with a staircase on either side and, if you kept going straight ahead, access to a large square inner courtyard formed by the four wings of the building. He randomly picked one of the staircases and headed up. He crossed paths with two electricians carrying rolls of cables who greeted him politely. When he reached the first floor, he caught sight of some of the children sitting on bunks, their legs dangling over the edge.

On the landing, he gave a slight nod to a corporal walking past.

The SS man continued on his way. Fredy noted uneasily that it was too quiet for a place with so many children. They were too still. Just then, he heard someone behind him calling his name.

"Mr. Hirsch?"

His first thought was that it was an acquaintance from the ghetto, but when he turned around, he saw it was the SS guard he'd just walked past, who was smiling at him in a friendly manner. A gap-toothed smile. Hirsch recognized him as the player from the guards' soccer team. His smile in return was steady, but a frown immediately started to form on the Nazi's face, making it look like corrugated cardboard. He'd realized that the gym instructor didn't belong here. He raised his arm and pointed at the staircase with his finger, indicating that Hirsch should walk in front of him, as a prisoner would. Fredy, adopting a light tone, tried to invent some excuse for being there, but the guard was adamant.

"To the guard post! Now!"

When they took him to the SS *Obersturmführer* in charge of the guards, Fredy stood to attention in front of him and even clicked his heels together loudly. The officer demanded to see his authorization for being in the precinct. He didn't have one. The Nazi stuck his face right up to Fredy's and, in a fury, asked him what the devil he was doing there.

Hirsch, looking straight ahead, seemed unflustered and answered in his usual, polite way:

"I was just trying to carry out my job as coordinator of activities for the resident children of Terezín to the best of my ability, sir."

"So you aren't aware that all contact with this contingent of children is forbidden?"

"I am, sir. But as the person responsible for the Youth Office,

I thought I was considered part of the group looking after the children's well-being."

Hirsch's composure reassured the officer and raised doubt in his mind. He told Fredy he would write a report to his superiors regarding the incident, and that Fredy would be informed of the outcome.

"Don't rule out a court-martial," he said.

They locked him in the detention area attached to the guard post and told him he'd be released when they had checked out his details for the report. Fredy was undeterred and paced up and down in what could only be described as an empty dog run, irritated because he hadn't been able to see the children, but otherwise calm. No one was going to organize a court-martial; he was well-regarded by the German administrators of the ghetto. Or so he believed.

Rabbi Murmelstein, a member of the leadership triumvirate of the Jewish Council in the ghetto, was walking along the street on the other side of the enclosure fence. He was unpleasantly surprised to see one of the representatives of the Youth Office locked up inside the enclosure. It was clear that Hirsch had violated the order to stay away from the Białystok children's precinct, and so now he was under detention as if he were a common criminal. The stern council leader approached the fence and locked eyes with Hirsch.

"Mr. Hirsch," he said reproachfully, "what are you doing in there?"

"And you, Dr. Murmelstein . . . what are you doing out there?"

There was neither a court-martial nor any punishment, or so it seemed. But one afternoon, the ghetto Council's official messenger, Pavel—known as Bones because of his skinny legs, and who was the fastest sprinter in Terezín—interrupted the long-jump training session to inform Fredy that his presence was required that afternoon without fail at the headquarters of the Jewish Administrative Authority in the Magdeburg block.

It was Yakub Edelstein, the chairman of the council himself, who gave Fredy the news: German Command had included his name on the list for the next transport headed for Poland or, to be more precise, for the Auschwitz camp near Oświęcim.

They'd heard dreadful things about Auschwitz: mass murders, slave labor under conditions that caused the workers to die of exhaustion, all sorts of harassment and humiliation, people whom starvation had turned into walking skeletons, typhoid epidemics that no one treated. . . . But these were just rumors. Nobody had been able to confirm them firsthand. Then again, nobody had returned to give them the lie. Edelstein told Fredy that the SS Command had asked that Fredy identify himself to the camp authorities when he reached Auschwitz, because they were keen for him to continue his work as the leader of the youth groups.

"So I'll continue to work with the teenagers—nothing will change?"

Edelstein, a man with the kindly, chubby face and horn-rimmed glasses of a schoolteacher, grimaced.

"Things will be tough there, very tough. More than tough, Fredy. Many have gone to Auschwitz, but no one has returned. Even so, we have to keep on fighting."

Hirsch recalls with absolute precision the chairman's last words to him that afternoon: "We mustn't lose hope, Fredy. Don't let the flame go out."

That was the last time Fredy saw Yakub Edelstein, standing with his hands behind his back and gazing out of the window, lost in thought. Edelstein surely knew then that it wouldn't be long before he himself would take the same route to the extermination camp. He had just received the order removing him as chairman of the Jewish Council. As the Jewish leader of Terezín, it was his responsibility to oversee the people inside the ghetto. The SS were not particularly vigilant in controlling the entrances, and there had been internees who had slipped out. Edelstein didn't report them and covered for them until the shortfall became too obvious, and the SS realized that at least fifty-five prisoners had escaped from the ghetto.

The die was cast for Edelstein, and he was the loser. That was why, when he arrived at the *Lager*, it wasn't the Auschwitz–Birkenau family camp he was taken to, but the prison of Auschwitz I. Fredy has never told Miriam, but he knows that inside that prison they practice the cruelest methods of torture known to man.

What has become of Yakub Edelstein? And what will become of us all?

14.

AFTER THE CHILDREN HAVE LEFT AND ONLY A FEW TEACHERS CAUGHT UP in conversation remain, Dita gathers her library together. It might be the last time she does it, because she has to tell the truth: She's been marked by Mengele. So, before she takes the books back, she removes the roll of tape from her secret pocket and fixes a rip in the Russian grammar book. She takes out the bottle of gum arabic and glues the edges of the spines of two more books. The book by H. G. Wells has the corner of a page doubled over, and she straightens it. And as her hand passes over the atlas, she smooths—caresses—it, and then all the other books, even the novel with no front cover to which Hirsch objected so forcefully. While she's at it, Dita fixes a torn page using a narrow strip of tape. Then she carefully puts the books inside the cloth bag from Aunt Dudince, settling them in as if she were a nurse putting newborn babies into their cribs. She walks over to the *Blockältester*'s cubicle and knocks at the door.

Hirsch is sitting in his chair writing one of his reports or working out the schedule for some volleyball tournament. She asks for permission to speak, and he turns toward her with his calm face and the smile that no one knows how to interpret.

"Go ahead, Edita."

"You ought to know about this. Dr. Mengele suspects me of something, maybe to do with the library. It happened after the inspection. He stopped me in the *Lagerstrasse*. He'd somehow realized I was hiding something. He threatened that he was going to keep a close eye on me, and I have the feeling he's watching me."

Hirsch gets up from his chair and walks around the cubicle for a few seconds with a look of concentration on his face. Finally, he comes to a halt and, looking straight into Dita's eyes, says to her,

"Mengele watches everyone."

"He told me he'd put me on a dissection table and open me up from top to bottom."

"He likes dissecting people—he gets pleasure from it." After Fredy has spoken, there's an uncomfortable silence.

"You're going to remove me from my position as librarian, aren't you? I understand it's for my own good—"

"Do you want to give it up?"

Fredy's eyes shine. The little lightbulb that he always says glows inside us has just switched on. And Dita's has turned on, too, because Hirsch's electricity is contagious.

"Absolutely not!"

Fredy Hirsch nods, as if to say, *I knew it.*

"Then you'll stay in your position. Of course it's a risk, but we're at war—although there are people here who sometimes forget that. We're soldiers, Edita. Don't believe those who say we're bringing up the rear and then put down their arms. It's war, and each of us has our own front line. This one is ours, and we must fight to the end."

"So what about Mengele?"

"A good soldier has to be careful. And we have to be very careful with Mengele. You can never tell exactly what he's thinking. Sometimes he smiles at you, and it looks as if he really means it, but almost immediately, he becomes serious, and the look he gives you is so cold that it freezes your insides. If Mengele had any solid evidence against you, you'd already be dead. So it would be best if he didn't see you, hear you, smell you. You have to try to avoid any contact with him. If you see him coming, head in another direction. If he crosses your path, look away discreetly. The best thing that could happen is that he forgets you even exist."

"I'll try."

"Good. Is there anything else?"

"Fredy . . . thank you!"

"I'm asking you to remain in the front line of fire, risking your life, and *you're* thanking *me*?"

What Dita wants to say is *I'm sorry—I regret that I doubted you*. But she doesn't know how.

"Well . . . I wanted to thank you for being here."

Hirsch smiles.

"There's no need. I'm where I ought to be."

Dita heads outside. The snow has settled over the camp, and decorated with it, Birkenau somehow seems less terrible, almost sleepy. The cold is intense, but at times that seems preferable to the feverish conversations inside the huts.

She comes across Gabriel, number one recipient of teacher scoldings and punishments. The outrageous ten-year-old redhead is wearing very wide pants that are way too big for him and held up with string, and a grease-spotted shirt that's just as large. He's leading a commando group of half a dozen boys his age.

He's up to no good, Dita thinks to herself.

There's another group of four- and five-year-olds, all holding hands, trailing along a few meters behind the commando group: old clothes, grubby faces, and innocent eyes sparkling like the newly fallen snow.

THE LIBRARIAN OF AUSCHWITZ   169

Gabriel is one of the idols of the little children in Block 31, thanks to his ability to dream up all sorts of mischief. Just this morning he threw a grasshopper at the head of a very pretentious girl called Marta Kováč, and the whole block was brought to a standstill by her hysterical screams. Even Gabriel stopped dead at her over-the-top reaction, which culminated in the girl planting herself in front of him and, in a fit of rage, slapping him so hard she almost wiped the freckles off his face.

The teacher in charge reached the conclusion that Talmudic justice had been served, and classes continued without further punishment for Gabriel beyond the one that had already been delivered by hand.

Usually when the little kids follow to watch his pranks, Gabriel tries to shake them off or scare them away. So Dita is surprised that he seems happy to have such a crowd tagging along behind him. She decides to follow them at a distance.

She sees them heading toward the camp's exit, at which point she realizes where they're going—the kitchen. Gabriel's friends come to a halt a safe distance from the off-limits kitchen building, but Gabriel continues inside. The others gather around the door. What happens next reminds Dita of a scene from a comedy. Gabriel emerges at a run, followed by a very bad-tempered cook called Beata, who's waving her arms like a windmill to scare off the flock of children as if they were birds.

Dita realizes they must have come to ask for potato peelings, one of the children's favorite treats. But it seems the cook is fed up with freeloaders, and she's decided to send them packing. Gabriel and the older children don't retreat; rather, the boys split into two groups, leaving a corridor down which Gabriel and the angry cook make their way. Gabriel dodges to one side, and the cook almost slips and falls on a patch of ice. When she regains her balance, she finds herself confronted by the group of little children who've just arrived. They're all still holding hands and breathing heavily because of the effort they've had to make to keep up with the older boys. Beata can't avoid the sight of their permanently hungry expressions. Caught unawares by a herd of mud-and-snow-covered cherubs with imploring eyes in front of her, she stops waving her arms and puts her hands on her hips.

Dita can't hear her, but she doesn't have to. The cook has a strong personality, rough hands, and a tender heart. Dita smiles when she thinks of Gabriel's cunning. He's led the youngest children to that spot to soften up the cook. Beata is undoubtedly telling them in her strictest voice that she's prohibited from handing over any leftovers without authorization, that if the *Kapo* catches her or any other kitchen hand doing so, they'll lose their jobs and be severely punished, that this and that and blah, blah, blah. . . . The children keep looking at her with their doe eyes, so . . . she'll make an exception this time, but they'd better not think of coming back, or she'll beat them. Some of the children nod their heads in agreement, fully aware that they have her eating out of their hands.

The cook disappears inside the hut and comes back out a few minutes later with a metal bucket full of potato peelings. She puts a halt to the threat of a riot by holding up her large hand, making them come up one by one, starting with the youngest and ending with the oldest. Then they return to Block 31 chewing on their potato skins.

Dita heads back along the *Lagerstrasse* in a good mood, but halfway back, she bumps into her mother, who is looking unusually disheveled for someone who, even inside Auschwitz, has managed to get hold of an old bit of comb. Her mother always has her hair carefully arranged.

So Dita knows something is wrong. She runs to her mother, who gives her an uncharacteristically strong hug and tells Dita that when she went to meet her husband outside his workshop, he wasn't there. A fellow worker, Mr. Brady, told her that he hadn't come to work in the morning because he couldn't get out of his bunk.

"Mr. Brady told me your father has a fever, but the *Kapo* said it was better not to take him to the hospital."

Her mother is confused and doesn't really know what to do.

"Maybe I should insist the *Kapo* send him to hospital."

"Papa said that the *Kapo* in his hut is a German social democrat, not a Jew. He's aloof, but quite fair. Maybe the hospital isn't a good idea. The hospital is in front of Block Thirty-One. . . ."

Dita stops. She's on the point of saying that the sick people she sees hobbling in usually come out on the corpse cart pushed by Mr. Lada and others. But she mustn't speak of death; death must be kept far away from her father.

"We can't even see him," moans Dita's mother. "We can't go into the men's huts. I asked Mr. Brady, who's a very kind gentleman from Bratislava, to do me the favor of going inside to see him while I waited at the entrance, and then coming back out to tell me how he was." She has to pause, overcome with emotion. Dita holds her hand. "Mr. Brady told me he's no different from how he was this morning: semiconscious because of the fever. And that he looked bad. Edita, maybe your father should go to the hospital."

"We'll go and see him."

"What are you saying? We can't go inside the hut! It's forbidden."

"It's also forbidden to lock people up and kill them, but I don't see that stopping anyone around here. Wait for me at the entrance to the hut."

Dita runs off in search of Milan, one of the assistants in Block 31. Although he's good looking, Dita doesn't find him very likeable.

She finds Milan beside Block 31. It's one of those relentlessly cold Polish afternoons, but he and a couple of his friends are sitting outside, propped up against the wooden boards. They're killing time watching the other inmates go by and making comments about the girls. She's not thrilled at the prospect of standing in front of these slightly older boys, who have the hint of a mustache under their noses and a host of pimples, but who behave like a bunch of fighting cocks. She feels uneasy when she's around them; she thinks they make fun of her skinny legs and her somewhat childish woolen leggings. But she parks herself in front of them, knowing that she can't allow herself to be timid.

"Well, well!" screeches Milan, speaking first so it's clear he's the leader. "Look who's here. It's the librarian—"

"You're not supposed to talk about that outside Block Thirty-One," Dita interrupts. And she instantly regrets her gruffness because the boy goes red. He doesn't like being shown up in front of his friends by a younger girl—and Dita has come to ask him a favor. "You see, Milan, I want to ask you something. . . ."

The three friends elbow each other and begin to giggle slyly. Milan, also encouraged, starts to brag.

"Well, girls usually ask me for lots of things," he says smugly, glancing out of the corner of his eye at his two friends to see how they're reacting to his words. They laugh, showing their broken teeth.

"I need you to lend me your big, long jacket for a while."

Milan's face shows his utter astonishment, and his giggles peter out. His jacket? She's asking him for his jacket? He was incredibly lucky to score the jacket when they were handing out the clothing; it's one of the best jackets in BIIb. He's been offered bread rations and even potatoes for it, but he's not prepared to get rid of it at any price. How would he put up with those afternoons when the temperature dips below freezing without his jacket? And anyway, he looks good in it. The girls like him more when he's wearing it.

"Are you nuts? Nobody touches my jacket. And nobody means nobody, do you hear?"

"It won't be for long—"

"Don't be stupid. Not for a minute, not at all! Do you think I'm an idiot? I give you the jacket, you sell it, and I never see it again. You'd better leave before I get really mad!" And as he's saying this, he stands up with a sour expression on his face, and it's obvious that he's at least twenty centimeters taller than Dita.

"I only want it for a short while. You can stay with me the whole time to make sure the jacket doesn't disappear. I'll give you my evening ration of bread."

Dita has mentioned a magic word: *food*. An extra ration for a growing boy who can't remember the last time he was able to satisfy his hunger is a big promise. His stomach growls all the time, the anxiety over food has become an obsession, and the only thing that excites him more than dreaming about a girl's thigh is dreaming about a chicken thigh.

"A whole ration," he repeats as he weighs up the proposal, already imagining the feast. He would even be able to save part of it to accompany his morning slop and have a real breakfast. "You're saying that you'll wear the jacket for a short while, I'll accompany you, and then you'll return it?"

"Right. I'm not going to trick you. We work in the same hut, so if I tricked you and you reported me, they'd fire me from my position in Block Thirty-One. And none of us wants to leave that hut."

"Okay, let me think about it."

The three boys put their heads together, and there's a mix of whispers and the odd laugh. Finally, a smiling Milan lifts his head triumphantly.

"Fine. I give you the jacket for a while in exchange for a ration of bread . . . but we all get to touch your tits!" He glances at his companions, and they nod so enthusiastically their heads look as if they're mounted on springs.

"Don't be an idiot. I hardly have any. . . ."

She notices that the three of them are laughing as if they were having a great time, or as if they needed the sound of their laughter to hide their nervousness and awkwardness when dealing with such matters. Dita snorts. If they weren't so much taller than her, she'd give each of them a slap.

For being so brazen . . . or so stupid.

But she has no choice.

And after all, what does it matter?

"Fine, okay. Now let me try on the damn jacket."

Milan shivers when he finds himself out in the open with only the three-button shirt he's wearing underneath the jacket. Dita puts on the long jacket, which is enormous on her, exactly as she'd hoped. This article of clothing features an item which makes it very valuable to her right now, and which few other such garments in the camp possess—a hood. She marches off with Milan close behind.

"Where are we going?"

"To Barrack Fifteen."

"And your tits?"

"Later."

"Did you say Barrack Fifteen? But that's a men's hut—"

"Right . . ." And Dita puts the hood over her head, leaving it almost completely hidden.

Milan stops.

"Wait. You're not seriously thinking of going in there? Women are forbidden. I have no intention of going in there with you. If they catch you, they'll punish me, too. I think you're a bit mad."

"I'm going inside. With you or without you."

The boy's eyes widen, and he shivers even more with cold.

"If you want, you can wait for me at the door."

Milan has to walk faster because Dita is striding quickly. She sees her mother a few meters away, lurking near the entrance to her father's hut, and she doesn't stop to greet her. Liesl Adler is so upset that she hasn't even recognized her daughter inside the male garment. Dita walks into the hut without hesitating, and nobody takes any notice of her. Milan has stopped by the door cursing, unsure whether the girl has tricked him and he'll never see his jacket again.

Dita makes her way through the rows of bunks. Some men are lying on top of the horizontal stove, which isn't operating, while others are sitting on their bunks and chatting. Some are lying down on their bunks, even though doing so before lights-out is prohibited, all of which suggests they have a benevolent *Kapo*. The smell is really strong, worse than in her women's hut, a nauseating smell of acrid sweat. Dita hasn't removed her hood, and nobody pays any attention to her.

She finds her father at the back of the hut, stretched out on the straw mattress of his bottom bunk. She pulls back her hood and brings her face close to his.

"It's me," she whispers.

His eyes are half closed, but when he hears his daughter, he opens them slightly. Dita puts her hand on his forehead; it's burning. She's not sure if he's recognized her, but she takes one of his hands and continues to talk to him in a whisper. It's usually difficult to talk to someone when you don't know if he's hearing you, but her words flow with surprising ease, and she tells him the things you never stop to say because you think there'll always be time in future to say them.

"Do you remember when you used to teach me geography at home? I remember it really well. . . . You know so many things! I've always been very proud of you, Papa. Always."

And she talks to him about the good times during her childhood in Prague, and the good moments in the Terezín ghetto, and how much she and her mother love him. She tells him over and over again so the words will filter through his fever. And she thinks he moves slightly. Maybe somewhere deep inside, he's listening to her.

Hans Adler is fighting against pneumonia with very few weapons—a lone, malnourished man broken by all the elements of war against a microbial army bursting with energy. Dita recalls Paul de Kruif's book about the microbe hunters she had read just before they left Prague: If you look at germs under a microscope, they look like a miniaturized pack of predators. Too many to take on.

She releases his hand, tucks it under the dirty sheet, and kisses him on his forehead. She pulls up her hood again and turns to leave. And in that moment, she catches sight of Milan, a few steps away. She thinks he must be furious, but the boy is looking at her with unexpected tenderness.

"Your father?" he asks.

Dita nods. She hunts for something under her clothing and pulls out her evening ration of bread. She holds it out to him, but the boy keeps his hands in his pockets and refuses it with a shake of his head. She reaches the door of the hut and removes the jacket. When her mother recognizes her, she looks puzzled.

"Will you lend it to my mother for a moment?" And without waiting for his answer, she says, "Put it on and go inside."

"But, Edita—"

"You'll be disguised. Come on! It's at the back on the right. He's not conscious, but I think he can hear us."

The woman adjusts the hood and, covered up, goes inside stealthily. Milan stands silently beside Dita, unsure what to do or say.

"Thanks, Milan."

The boy nods and hesitates for a moment, as if he is searching for the right words.

"As far as . . . you know what," Dita says to him as she looks down at her almost-flat chest.

"Forget it, please!" Milan replies, blushing and waving his hands dramatically. "I've got to go now; return the jacket tomorrow."

He turns on his heel and rushes off. He wonders how he's going to explain to his friends why he's returning with no jacket and no girl. They'll think he's an idiot. He could tell them that he ate the bread on his way back to them, and that *he* touched her tits on behalf of all of them, since the jacket is his, after all. But he dismisses that with a shake of his head. He knows they'll spot the lie right away. He'll tell them the truth. They'll laugh at him for sure, and tell him he's gullible. But he knows how to fix things like that. He'll hit the first one who says anything so hard he'll have to search for his teeth with a magnifying glass. And then everyone will be friends again.

Margit turns up while Dita is waiting for Liesl to reappear. From the distraught expression on her face, it's clear that Margit has heard about Dita's father. In Auschwitz, news, and bad news in particular, spreads fast. Margit walks up to her and gives her hug.

"How's your father?"

Dita knows that this question hides another more serious one: Will he live?

"He's not well, he has a high fever, and his chest rattles when he breathes."

"You must have faith, Dita. Your father has overcome many things."

"Too many."

"He's a strong man. He'll fight."

"He was strong, Margit. But these past few years have aged him a lot. I've always been an optimist. But I don't know what to think anymore. I don't know anymore if we'll all be able to hold out."

"Of course we will."

"Why are you so sure?"

Her friend remains silent for a few seconds, biting her lip as she searches for an answer.

"Because I want to believe it."

The two girls don't say another word. The age when you think that just wanting something is enough to make it happen is slipping away from them.

The curfew siren goes off, and her mother emerges from the hut like a ghost dragging its feet through the mud.

"We must hurry," says Margit.

"You go—run," Dita replies. "We'll come a bit more slowly."

Her friend says good-bye, and mother and daughter are left by themselves. Her mother looks lost.

"How's Papa?"

"A bit better," Liesl replies. But her voice is so broken it gives the lie to what she's saying. And anyway, Dita knows her all too well. Liesl has spent her entire life trying to make everything right, attempting to ensure that nothing alters the natural order of things.

"Did he recognize you?"

"Yes, of course."

"So did he say anything to you?"

"No . . . he was a bit tired. He'll be better tomorrow."

And they don't say another word until they reach their hut.

He'll be better tomorrow.

Her mother said it with a conviction that left no room for doubt, and mothers know these things. Dita takes her mother's hand, and they walk more quickly.

When they enter the hut, almost all the women are already lying down on their bunks, and they come face-to-face with the *Kapo*, a Hungarian with the orange badge of a common criminal, a superior status. A thief, a swindler, a murderess . . . any one of these is more valuable than a Jew. She's been overseeing the placement of the containers used by the women to relieve themselves during the night, and when she sees Dita and her mother arriving late, she lifts the stick in her hand threateningly.

"I'm sorry, *Kapo*, but my father—"

"Shut up and get on your pallet, idiot."

"Yes, madam."

Dita pulls on her mother's hand, and they walk to their bunks. Liesl slowly climbs up and, before lying down, briefly turns toward Dita. Her lips don't move, but her eyes show her pain.

"Don't worry, Mama," says her daughter encouragingly. "If there's no change in Papa, we'll talk to his *Kapo* in the morning about taking him to the doctor. If need be, I'll speak with the director of Block Thirty-One. Fredy Hirsch will be able to help us."

"He'll be better tomorrow."

The lights go out, and Dita says good night to her bunkmate, who doesn't respond. She's so distressed she can't even close her eyes. She recalls images of her father and tries to sort out the best ones. There's one she especially likes: It's of her parents seated at the piano. Both of them are elegant and handsome—her father in a white shirt with the cuffs rolled up, a dark tie, and suspenders; her mother in a fitted blouse that accentuates her waist. They're laughing, because it's obvious they can't find a way to coordinate their movements to play a four-handed piece. They are happy.

Dita remembers when they left Prague, that moment when they walked out the front door and put their suitcases on the landing. They were getting ready to close a door that they didn't know if they'd ever open again. Her father went back inside the apartment for a moment while mother and daughter watched him from the landing. He walked up to the sideboard in the living-dining room and twirled the world globe one last time.

And Dita finally falls asleep.

But her sleep is restless; something is disturbing her. As dawn is breaking, she wakes up with a start, convinced that someone has called her. Uneasy, she opens her eyes, her heart beating loudly. The only things next to her are the feet of her sleeping bunkmate, and the only sounds disturbing the silence are the snores and muttering of the women talking in their sleep. It was just a nightmare . . . but Dita is filled with a sense of foreboding. She's convinced it was her father who was calling her.

First thing in the morning, the camp fills with guards and *Kapos* for the morning roll call. It's a two-hour roll call, which feels like the longest of her life. She keeps exchanging glances with her mother while they are lined up. Talking is forbidden, although in this instance, it's almost better not to exchange words. When they finally break ranks, they take advantage of the endless lines for breakfast to go to Barrack 15. As they approach it, Mr. Brady steps out of his breakfast line, his shoulders weighed down by his bad news.

"Mrs. . . ."

"My husband? Is he worse?" asks Liesl, her voice breaking.

"He's dead."

How can you sum up a life in just two very short words?

"Will we be able to go inside to see him?" asks Liesl.

"I'm sorry, but they've already taken him away."

Dita and her mother ought to know that. The bodies are picked up at first light, piled onto a cart, and taken away to be incinerated in the ovens.

Dita's mother seems to sway back and forth for a moment, on the verge of breaking down. At first glance, the news of his death hasn't overly unsettled her; she probably knew from the moment she saw him lying on his bunk. Not being able to say good-bye to him has been a blow. Liesl quickly recovers her composure, however, and puts her hand on her daughter's shoulder to console her.

"At least your father didn't suffer."

Dita, who senses her blood is beginning to boil, finds being addressed as a child even more irritating than her mother's words.

"Didn't suffer?" she replies, brusquely shrugging off her mother's hand. "They took away his world, his house, his dignity, his health . . . and finally, they let him die alone, like a dog, on a flea-infested pallet. Isn't that enough suffering?" And she almost shouts those last few words.

"That's what God wanted, Edita. We must resign ourselves."

Dita shakes her head again and again in disagreement.

"I don't feel like resigning myself!" she screams in the middle of the *Lagerstrasse*. But hardly anyone pays any attention to her. "If I had God in front of me, I'd tell him what I thought of him and his twisted sense of compassion."

She feels bad, and even worse when she realizes she's been very rude to her mother just when what her mother most needs is comfort and support, but she can't stop feeling furious at her mother's docility. She's relieved when Mrs. Turnovská arrives, wrapped in her enormous shawl. She must already know what has happened. She squeezes Dita's arm affectionately, and warmly hugs Liesl, who grabs hold of her friend with unexpected feeling. *This is what I should have done*, Dita thinks to herself, *hug my mother*. But she can't; she's too angry to give hugs. She feels the urge to bite and destroy, just as they have destroyed her.

Three more women, whom Dita barely knows by sight, appear and start to cry noisily. Dita, her own eyes dry, looks at them in utter bewilderment. They approach her mother, but Mrs. Turnovská steps in.

"Get away from her! Go!"

"We just want to express our condolences to the lady."

"If you don't leave in the next ten seconds, I'll kick you on your way!"

Liesl is too shocked to understand what's going on, and Dita doesn't have the strength to apologize to the women and ask them to stay.

"What are you doing, Mrs. Turnovská? Has the whole world gone mad?"

"They're scavengers. They know that family members of the

dead lose their appetites when they are upset, so they pretend to cry crocodile tears and then make off with your food ration."

Dita is stunned; she hates the whole world at that moment. She asks Mrs. Turnovská to look after her mother and walks away. It's not that she's having difficulty getting used to the idea that she'll never be with her father again, but rather that she doesn't want to get used to it. She's not prepared to accept it, she's not going to resign herself to it, not now, not ever. She walks off, her hands clenched and her knuckles white. A white-hot rage burns inside her.

He'll never come back from work in his double-breasted suit and felt hat, or glue his ear to the radio as he gazes up at the ceiling; he'll never sit her on his knees again to show her the countries of the world or gently scold her for her crooked writing.

And she can't even cry for him; her eyes are dry. And that makes her even madder. Since she has nowhere else to go, her feet take her to Block 31. The children are busy with breakfast, and she goes to the back of the hut without stopping, heading for her refuge behind the woodpile. She's startled to find a solitary figure seated on the bench in the corner.

Morgenstern greets her with his old-fashioned politeness, but this time Dita doesn't smile, and the old professor stops his theatrical bowing.

"My father . . ." And as she says it, Dita feels her blood start to boil as it runs through her veins. And a single word rises in her throat like bile:

"Murderers!"

She rolls it around her mouth, and repeats it five, ten, fifty times.

"Murderers, murderers, murderers, murderers . . . !"

She kicks a stool and then grabs it and brandishes it like a mace. She wants to smash something, but doesn't know what. She wants to hit someone, but doesn't know who. Her eyes are wild, and her anxiety is making her gasp. Professor Morgenstern stands up with surprising agility for such a frail-looking old man and removes the stool gently but firmly from her hand.

"I'll kill them!" Dita cries out angrily. "I'll get hold of a gun and kill them!"

"No, Edita, no," he says to her, very gently. "Our hatred is a victory for them."

Dita trembles, and the professor puts his arms around her. She buries her head in the old man's arms. Several teachers and a troop of curious boys and girls poke their heads over the top of the woodpile, alarmed by the noise, and the professor puts a finger to his lips to tell them to be quiet, and then signals with his head for them to go away. Amazed to see the professor so serious, they obey, and leave them on their own.

Dita confesses to the professor that she hates herself for running away, for being unable to cry, for failing her father, for not being able to save him. She hates herself for everything. But the old professor tells her that her tears will come when her anger departs.

"How can I not feel anger? My father never hurt anyone, he never showed disrespect toward anyone. . . . They took everything away from him, and now, in this revolting hole, they've even taken away his life."

"Listen very carefully to me, Edita. Those who go no longer suffer."

Those who go no longer suffer. . . . He whispers to her over and over again.

Morgenstern knows that the comfort he's offering is scant—worn-out and old-fashioned—something old people say, but in Auschwitz, it's the medicine that helps people to endure the sadness they feel for those who have died. Dita stops twisting her fingers, nods in agreement, and slowly sits down on the bench. Professor Morgenstern puts his hand in his pocket and pulls out a somewhat wrinkled and faded origami bird. He offers it to Dita.

The girl looks at the battered paper bird, as vulnerable as her father has been recently. As fragile as the mad old professor with his broken glasses. They're all so fragile. . . . And then she feels insignificant and unexpectedly weak. Her rage subsides, and the tears finally flow.

The old architect nods approvingly, and she cries her heart out on old Morgenstern's shoulder.

"Those who go no longer suffer. . . ."

No one knows how much suffering still awaits those left behind.

Dita raises her head and wipes her tears with her sleeve. She thanks the professor and tells him that she has something important to do before breakfast is over. She rushes off to her hut. Her mother needs her. Or maybe she needs her mother.

What difference does it make . . .

Her mother is sitting with Mrs. Turnovská on top of the air intake of the unlit stove. As she approaches the two women, Dita sees her mother sitting very still, lost in thought while Mrs. Turnovská, her own empty bowl on the ground, is drinking the morning tea from Liesl's bowl, and dipping into it a small piece of bread which the just-widowed Liesl must have left uneaten the night before.

The former fruit seller looks embarrassed when she sees Dita staring at her mother's bowl.

"Your mother didn't want it," she says, somewhat taken aback at Dita's unexpected appearance, which has caught her redhanded. "I kept insisting . . . and it was almost time to go off to the workshop. . . . We would have had to throw it away. . . ."

Dita and Mrs. Turnovská look at each other in silence. Her mother is far away; she must be going through a world of memories. Mrs. Turnovská extends the bowl toward Dita so she can have the last few sips, but Dita shakes her head. There's no reproach in her eyes, just a mixture of understanding and sadness.

"Please finish it. We need you to be healthy so you can help Mama."

Her mother's serene face resembles a statue made out of wax. Dita crouches down in front of her, and her mother reacts by moving her eyes. She focuses on her daughter, and her neutral expression finally breaks. Dita hugs her hard, holds her tightly, and at last, her mother cries.

15.

VIKTOR PESTEK IS FROM BESSARABIA, ORIGINALLY A MOLDOVAN
territory which, in the nineteenth century, became part of Romania,
a country that supported the Nazis right from the start. His SS
uniform, the gun at his waist, and his First Officer stripes make
him a very powerful person in Auschwitz. He is a superior being
with thousands of people at his feet who can't even address him
without permission. Those same thousands of people are obliged to do
whatever he tells them or he will order their death without turning
a hair.

Anyone who sees Pestek walking with his proud swagger, his cap
pulled down, and his hands behind his back would think he was
indestructible. But in Auschwitz, little is what it seems. No one must
know, but this SS man is cracking on the inside: For weeks he hasn't
been able to rid himself of the image of a particular woman.

She is, in fact, a very young woman, and he hasn't exchanged a
single word with her; he doesn't even know her name. He saw her
one day when it was his turn to supervise a work group. On the
surface, she looked like any other Jewish girl—shabby clothes, a
kerchief on her head, and a thin face—but she performed a seemingly insignificant gesture that mesmerized him. She took hold of
one of the blond curls falling over her eyes and unrolled it until it
was long enough for her to be able to chew on it. It was a trivial
movement, one she performed unwittingly, but which, without her

being aware of it, made her unique. Viktor Pestek has fallen in love with that gesture.

That day, he examined her more carefully: She had a pleasant face, lovely golden hair, and the vulnerability of a goldfinch in a cage. And then he couldn't stop staring at her the whole time he was in charge of the guard detail. He tried to approach her a couple of times, but couldn't make up his mind about talking to her. She seemed to be afraid of him, which didn't surprise him.

At the time he joined the Romanian Iron Guard, everything seemed fantastic. They gave you an attractive light brown uniform, took you away to camps to sing patriotic songs, and made you feel important. It was even fun, at first, to pull down the disease-ridden huts belonging to the Gypsies who lurked on the outskirts of his village.

Then things started to get complicated. Fistfights became fights with chains, and then came the guns. He knew some of the Gypsies, but more than that, he had Jewish friends—like Ladislaus. He used to go to Ladislaus's house to do homework, or they'd go hunting for chestnuts in the woods. One day, almost without realizing it, he had a torch in his hand and he was setting fire to Ladislaus's house.

He could have pulled back, but he didn't. The SS paid well, and people patted him on the back. His family was proud of him for the first time ever, and when he came home on leave, they even took him to have his photograph taken in his uniform so they could put it on top of the sideboard in the dining room.

And then one day, he was posted to Auschwitz.

Now he's not sure his family would feel so proud if they knew that his work consists of forcing people to work until breaking point, taking children to the gas chambers, and beating their mothers if they resist. It all seems like madness to him, and he worries that this reaction is starting to be noticed. On a couple of occasions, an officer has told him he needs to be tougher with the prisoners.

He hasn't been assigned guard duty, and command headquarters don't allow the SS to roam around the family camp, but the sergeant at the control booth is a friend of his, so he gets through without any difficulty. The guards stand to attention as he goes by. He likes that.

They're just finishing the afternoon roll call. He knows the group to which the Czech girl is assigned, and so, when they are dismissed, he spots her among the flood of women. He walks toward her, but the girl sees him coming and walks more quickly. He quickens his stride, but the only way he can stop her is to grab hold of her wrist. Her bones are thin, and her skin is rough, but he's filled with unusual joy at being so close to her. Finally, she lifts her head and looks at him for the first time: She has brilliant blue eyes and looks terrified. He notices that other inmates have stopped a few paces away. The SS officer turns menacingly, and the group of spectators immediately dissolves. It feels good to inspire fear in others, and it's easy to get used to doing it.

"My name is Viktor."

She remains silent, and he quickly lets go of her wrist.

"Forgive me, I didn't mean to frighten you. I just . . . wanted to know your name."

The girl is trembling, and she almost can't get the words out of her mouth.

"My name is Renée Neumann, sir," she replies. "Have I done something wrong? Are you going to punish me?"

"No, no! Nothing like that! It's just that I saw you. . . ." The SS officer hesitates; he can't find the words. "I just wanted to be your friend."

Renée looks at him in amazement. *Friend? You can obey an SS officer; you can flatter him or become his informer in order to gain some perks, even become his lover. But can you be the friend of someone in the SS? Can you be the friend of your own executioner?*

Since she's still looking at him perplexed and not saying a word, Pestek lowers his head and quietly says to her, "I know what you're thinking. You think I'm another one of those crazy SS people. Well, I am, but I'm not so crazy. I don't like what's happening to you. It makes me sick."

Renée keeps her mouth shut. She has no idea what all this is about, and she's confused. She's heard all too often about guards who pretend to hate the Reich so that they'll gain the trust of the inmates, pretending to be their friends and then pumping them for information about the Resistance. She's frightened.

The officer takes something small out of his pocket and holds it out to her. It's a square box made of lacquered wood. He tries to place it on the palm of her hand, but she steps back.

"It's for you. It's a present."

She looks at the yellow box with suspicion. He lifts the small lid, and a sweet, metallic tune starts to play.

"It's a music box," he tells her with a smile of satisfaction.

Renée studies the object he's holding out to her for a few moments but gives no sign of taking it. He nods his head and grins, waiting for her enthusiastic response.

Renée shows no enthusiasm. Her mouth is a straight line, and her eyes are blank.

"What's the matter? Don't you like it?" he asks, upset.

"You can't eat it," she replies. Her voice is abrasive, even more so than the cold February breeze, which strips everything bare.

Pestek feels ashamed when he realizes his own stupidity. He has spent the past week looking for a music box. He went back and forth; he negotiated with his fellow SS guards and with all sorts of Jewish dealers until he found one. He bribed, begged, and threatened; he searched high and low until he finally got it. And it's only now that he understands it's a useless gift. In a place where the inmates are cold and hungry, the one thing that occurs to him as a present for the girl is a stupid music box.

You can't eat it. . . .

He squeezes his hand shut so tightly you can hear the crunch of the little music box, which he's crushed as if it were a sparrow.

"Forgive me," he says sorrowfully. "I'm a complete idiot. I don't understand anything."

It seems to Renée that the SS officer is genuinely crestfallen, as if his discomfort were not a pretense and what she thought of him really mattered.

"What would you like me to bring you?"

She doesn't answer. She knows there are girls who sell their bodies for a ration of bread. The expression on her face is one of such indignation that Pestek realizes he's made another mistake.

"Don't get me wrong. I don't want anything in return. I just want to do something good in the midst of all the awful things we do here every day."

Renée still doesn't say a word. The SS guard realizes it's not going to be easy to gain her confidence. The girl tugs at one of her curls and pulls it down to her mouth in that movement he adores.

"Would you like me to come back and see you another day?"

She doesn't answer. Her eyes sweep the camp's muddy ground.

He's SS—he can do what he likes; he doesn't have to ask her permission to speak to her. Or to do whatever he wants to do. She doesn't say anything, but Pestek is so excited that he interprets her silence as a discreet yes.

After all, she hasn't said no.

He smiles happily and says good-bye with an awkward wave of his hand.

"I'll see you soon, Renée."

She watches the SS officer walk away and stands motionless for a long time, perplexed. Silver cogs, springs, and golden splinters are left in the mud.

It's not easy for Dita. Her father's absence weighs unbearably on her. How can something that no longer exists be so heavy? How can emptiness have weight?

She could barely get down from her bunk this morning. She did it so slowly that she infuriated her bad-tempered bunkmate, who started to swear in the filthiest language Dita had ever heard. At any other time, Dita would have been terrified by the old woman's fury, but she didn't even have the energy to be frightened. She turned her head and fixed the woman with a stare of such indifference that, to her surprise, the woman stopped swearing and didn't say another word until Dita had finished her slow descent.

Following the afternoon roll call and the order to fall out, the children from Block 31 noisily march off either to play or go and meet their parents. In a vegetative state, Dita slowly begins to gather together her books, and drags herself over to the *Blockältester*'s cubicle to hide them. Fredy is going through some packages.

"I was keeping something for you, for when you have to carry out repairs on your books," says Hirsch.

He holds out a pair of cute blue scissors with rounded ends—the sort young schoolkids use. It can't have been easy for him to get his hands on such an exceptional item in the *Lager*. And he leaves immediately to avoid hearing her thanks.

Dita decides to take advantage of the scissors to cut some stray threads off the old Czech book. She'd rather stay and do any task in Block 31. She knows that Mrs. Turnovská and a few acquaintances from Terezín are keeping her mother company, and she doesn't feel like seeing anyone. She stows all the books in the hidey-hole except for the dilapidated novel, and then retrieves a little velvet bag tied with string in which she keeps her librarian's small first-aid kit. The bag used to hold a whole potato, the prize in a heavily contested crossword puzzle competition. Dita occasionally lifts the bag to her nose and inhales the marvelous smell of that potato.

She goes over to the corner where the hidey-hole is and painstakingly applies herself to her task. First, she cuts off all the dangling threads with her scissors. Then, as if she were suturing an open wound, she uses a rudimentary needle and thread to resew some pages that are on the verge of coming loose. The result isn't beautiful, but the pages are now firmly held together. She also applies strips of tape to the torn pages, and the book stops looking like something that's going to fall apart imminently.

She wants to escape from the loathsome reality of the camp that has killed her father. A book is like a trapdoor that leads to a secret attic: You can open it and go inside. And your world is different.

She hesitates briefly, wondering whether she should or shouldn't read this book with its missing pages, which according to Hirsch, is unsuitable for young ladies and bears the title *The Adventures of the Good Soldier Švejk*. But her hesitation lasts less time than her midday bowl of soup. After all, who says she wants to be a young lady? And anyway, she'd rather be a research scientist investigating microbes or an airline pilot than a prissy young thing who wears frilly dresses and white ribbed stockings.

Jaroslav Hašek, the author of the book, sets the action in Prague during the Great War and describes the protagonist as a chubby chatterbox who, having already escaped once from joining the army—"exempted because of stupidity"—is drafted again. He arrives at the recruitment office in a wheelchair, supposedly suffering from arthritis in the knees. He's a rogue who's keen to eat all the food and drink all the liquor he can lay his hands on, and work as little as possible. His name is Švejk, and he earns a living by catching stray dogs and selling them as if they were purebreds. He speaks very politely to everyone, and his gestures and friendly gaze are always kindly. Whenever he's asked for something, he usually has some anecdote or story to illustrate the matter, although frequently it has no bearing on the case and no one has asked to hear it. And everyone is puzzled by the fact that whenever somebody attacks him or yells at him or insults him, he doesn't answer back, but agrees with them. In this way, he convinces them he's a complete idiot and they let him be.

"You're a complete nitwit!"

"Yes, sir, what you're saying is absolutely true," Švejk replies in his meekest tone.

Dita misses Dr. Manson, whom she had accompanied in her reading through the mining towns of the Welsh mountains, and even Hans Castorp, calmly stretched out on his chaise longue facing the Alps. This book insists on tying her to Bohemia and to war. Her eyes skim over the pages, and she can't quite understand what this Czech author wants to say to her. A furious officer reprimands the soldier-protagonist, a poor potbellied, shabbily dressed soul who's a bit of a fool. She doesn't like it; the situation is almost decadent. She likes books that enlarge life, not the ones that belittle it.

But there's something familiar about this character. And in any case, the world out there is much worse, so she'd rather stay curled up on her stool, concentrating on her reading and hoping the teachers sitting around talking don't pay too much attention to her.

A bit further along in the book, she comes across Švejk dressed awkwardly in his uniform as a soldier of the Austro-Hungarian Empire, despite the fact that the Czechs, at least those of the working classes, were not at all pleased to be under the command of the snooty Germans in the First World War.

And how right they were, thinks Dita to herself.

He's the adjutant to Lieutenant Lukáš, who yells at him, calls him an animal, and gives him a whack on the back of his head whenever Švejk drives him mad. Because there's no question that Švejk has a talent for complicating everything, for misplacing documents entrusted to him, for executing the exact opposite of every order, and for making the officer look ridiculous, even though he always appears to do everything good-naturedly and with the best of intentions, but with minimal brainpower. At this stage in the book, Dita still can't work out if Švejk is acting the fool or actually is a complete idiot.

She's having a hard time understanding what the author is trying to say. The outrageous soldier answers his superior's questions and orders in such a painstaking and detailed manner that his lengthy replies go on forever. They branch out into digressions and little stories about relatives and neighbors whom the soldier, absolutely seriously, introduces into his response in the most absurd way.

I met a certain Paroubek who had a bar in Libeň. On one occasion, a telegraph operator got drunk on gin and, instead of taking the messages of condolence to the relatives of a poor man who had died, he took them the price list of the alcohol being sold at the bar. It caused a huge scandal. And especially because up until then no one had read the price list, and it turned out that good old Paroubek was charging a few cents extra for each drink; although he did later explain that the extra money was for charitable works. . . .

The stories he uses to illustrate his explanations become so long and so surrealistic that the lieutenant ends up yelling at him to disappear: "Get out of my sight, you blockhead!"

And Dita is surprised to find that she's laughing at the thought of the lieutenant's expression. She immediately scolds herself. How can such a stupid character make her laugh? She even briefly questions whether it's legitimate to laugh after everything that's happened, and with everything that's still going on.

How can you laugh while people you love are dying?

And her thoughts turn momentarily to Hirsch, and that permanent, enigmatic smile of his. And suddenly, she understands: Hirsch's smile is his victory. His smile tells whoever is standing in front of him that he's no match for Hirsch. In a place like Auschwitz, where everything is designed to make you cry, a smile is an act of defiance.

And she sets off after that dope of a Švejk and his tricks. And in this dark moment of her life when she doesn't know where to go, she grabs the hand of a rascal, and he tugs on it to encourage her to keep moving forward.

When Dita goes to her hut, darkness is falling and a freezing wind mixed with sleet stings her face. But her spirits have lifted. However, happiness in a place like Auschwitz is fleeting. Someone is coming toward her whistling a few bars of Puccini.

"My God," whispers Dita.

She still has a few huts to go, but in this zone the middle of the road is dimly lit, so she ducks into the first hut she comes to in the hope that he hasn't seen her. She enters so quickly that she bowls over a couple of women and then slams the door shut.

"What are you doing coming in here in such a hurry?"

Dita's eyes are wide open in fear as she points outside.

"Mengele . . ."

And the women's irritation switches to alarm.

"Dr. Mengele," they whisper.

As the message jumps from bunk to bunk, the murmurs and conversations die down.

"Doctor Death . . ."

Some of the women start to pray while others demand silence so they can hear any sound from outside. A faint, high-pitched tune filters through the sound of the rain.

One of the women explains that Mengele has an obsessive fixation with eyes.

"They say that one of the prisoners, a Jewish doctor by the name of Vexler Jancu, has seen a wooden table with samples of eyes in Mengele's office in the Gypsy camp."

"I've heard he pins eyeballs to a piece of cork on the wall as if they were a collection of butterflies."

"They told me he stitched two children together side by side, and they returned to their barrack still sewn together. They were crying with the pain and smelled of gangrene. They died that same night."

"Well, I heard he was investigating ways of sterilizing Jewish women so they wouldn't have any more children. He irradiated their ovaries and then removed them to investigate the effect. That son of Satan didn't even use an anesthetic. The women's screams were deafening."

Someone asks for silence. The music seems to be moving away.

And then the words of an order begin to be heard ricocheting from one throat to another as it is relayed throughout camp BIIb: "Twins to Block 32!" Inmates who are outside are under orders to relay such an order or face the possibility of severe punishment if they don't—execution is an ever-present possibility in Auschwitz. No matter where they might be, the boy twins, Zdeněk and Jirka, and the girl twins, Irene and Renée, must present themselves immediately at the hospital block.

Josef Mengele graduated with a medical degree from the University of Munich and, from 1931, served in units close to the Nazi party. He was a disciple of Dr. Ernst Rüdin, one of the main supporters of the idea that worthless lives should be eradicated. Rüdin was also one of the architects of the law of obligatory sterilization promulgated by Hitler in 1933 for people with deformities, mental disabilities, depression, or alcoholism. Mengele had managed to arrange to have himself assigned to Auschwitz, where he had a human warehouse at his disposal for his genetic experiments.

The mother of the boy twins accompanies them to their destination. She can't rid her mind of the gory stories about Dr. Mengele. She has to bite her lip to stop herself from crying as the children happily walk beside her, jumping from one puddle to the next. She hasn't the courage to tell them to stop splattering themselves with mud. Her lip is bleeding.

At the camp's entry control point, she hands her children over to an SS guard and watches them go through the metal door and head off toward the Nazi doctor's laboratory. She thinks she may never see them again, or that when they return they'll be missing an arm or have their mouths stitched shut or some other deformity provoked by the outrageous ideas of that madman. But there's nothing she can do about it; refusing an officer's order is punishable by death. Sometimes it's Mengele himself who occupies a room in the medical area of Block 32 and other people, whom she fears even more, bring the children to his laboratory.

So far, the children have returned safely from their encounters with the doctor, happy even, after spending a few hours with him and returning with a sausage or a piece of bread that Uncle Josef has given them. They even say he's pleasant and makes them laugh. They explain that he measures their heads and asks them to make the same movements together and individually, and put out their tongues. Sometimes, however, they don't feel like explaining anything and evade their parents' questions about what goes on during those opaque hours in the laboratory. On this occasion, the mother returns to her hut with what feels like a knot of barbed wire in her throat.

Dita heaves a sigh of relief because she wasn't the one he was looking for tonight. The woman who tells the most graphic stories about Mengele has straggly white hair, which escapes from under her kerchief. Dita approaches her.

"Excuse me, I wanted to ask you something."

"Ask away, young lady."

"You see, I have a friend who was cautioned by Mengele—"

"Cautioned?"

"Yes, warned that he'd be watching her."

"Bad . . ."

"What do you mean?"

"When he's hovering around someone, it's like birds of prey flying above their victims."

"But with so many people in here, and so many things on his mind—"

"Mengele never forgets a face. I know that personally."

And as she says it, she becomes very serious and falls silent. Suddenly, she doesn't want to say any more; a memory has silenced her momentarily.

"Run away from him as if he were the plague. Don't put yourself in his path. The Nazi bosses practice dark magic rituals—I know. They go into the woods and celebrate black masses. Himmler, the head of the SS, never makes a decision without consulting his psychic. They're people from the dark side—I know. Heaven help the poor soul who gets in their way. Their evil isn't of this world; it comes from hell. I believe that Mengele is the fallen angel. He's Lucifer himself who's taken over a human body. If he's after someone, may God have mercy on their soul."

Dita nods and walks off without a word. *If God exists, then so does the devil. They're travelers on the same rail line, moving in opposite directions. Good and evil somehow counterbalance each other. You could almost say they need each other: How would we know that we are doing good if evil didn't exist so that we could compare them and see the difference?* she wonders. There's no other place in the world where the devil moves as freely as he does in Auschwitz.

Would Lucifer whistle opera arias?

Night has closed in, and the only thing whistling is the wind. She feels a shiver run through her. She sees someone near the fence, underneath a beam of light. It's a woman, talking to someone on the other side of the fence. She thinks it's one of the assistants from Block 31, the oldest and the prettiest one, Alice. She was one of Dita's assistants on library duty once. She told Dita she knew Rosenberg the registrar, and she insisted several times that they were just friends, as if it really mattered to her.

Dita wonders what they talk about. Is there anything left to say? Maybe they just look at each other and say those pretty words that people in love say to each other. If Rosenberg were Hans Castorp and Alice were Mme. Chauchat, he'd kneel down on his side of the fence and say, *I know who you are*, as Castorp said to Chauchat on carnival night when he was finally honest with her. He told her that falling in love was to see someone and suddenly recognize them for who they were, knowing that this was the person you'd always been waiting for. Dita wonders if she'll ever experience that sort of revelation.

Her thoughts turn back to Alice and Rosenberg. What sort of relationship can you have with someone who's on the other side of a fence? She's not sure. In Auschwitz, the weirdest things are normal. Would she be capable of falling in love with someone on the other side of a fence? More to the point, is it possible to love in this terrible place? The answer seems to be yes, because Alice Munk and Rudi Rosenberg stand there defying the cold.

God has allowed Auschwitz to exist, so maybe he isn't an infallible watchmaker, as they told her. The most beautiful flowers emerge from the foulest dung heap. *So maybe*, thinks Dita, *God isn't a watchmaker but a gardener.*

God sows and the devil reaps with a scythe that cuts down everything.

Who'll win this mad game? she asks herself.

16.

AS OTA KELLER WALKS TOWARD HIS FATHER'S HUT, HE MULLS over which of the various stories in his head he's going to tell the children this afternoon. One day, he'd like to collect and publish in a book all the stories about the land of Palestine he's invented to distract the children in Block 31.

There are so many things to do! But they are trapped by the war.

There was a time when he believed in revolutions and the idea that there could be a just war.

That was so long ago. . . .

He has taken advantage of the meal break to visit his father who is eating his soup in front of the workshop where he rivets the straps from which the German soldiers hang their water bottles. He's elderly, and has been stripped of everything he was before the war, but Mr. Keller hasn't lost his love of life. Just the week before, he'd offered to give a brief concert at the back of the hut before lights-out. And Ota admits that even though his father's voice has declined, he continues to sound like a professional singer. The men happily listened to him. Few of them knew that Richard Keller had been, until very recently, a very important businessman in Prague, owner of a thriving company that made lingerie and employed fifty people.

Although Richard Keller kept a meticulous eye on the company's finances, his real passion has always been opera. Some businessmen furrowed their brows when they learned of Mr. Keller's excessive fondness for warbling. He even took lessons—at his age!

Ota thinks his father is the most serious man in the world, and that's why he never stops singing, either out loud or sotto voce. When the emissary from the Jewish Council informed half the occupants of his section in Terezín that they were being deported to Auschwitz, some shouted, others cried, and the odd one banged his fists against the wall. His father, however, quietly began to sing the aria from *Rigoletto* when they kidnap Gilda, and the Duke of Mantua is overcome with grief: *"Ella mi fu rapita! . . . Parmi veder le lagrime. . . ."* His voice was the deepest, the sweetest, of them all. Maybe that was why, little by little, silence descended until only his voice remained.

Mr. Keller gives Ota a wink when he sees him. The old man has lost his business and his house—both requisitioned by the Nazis— along with his dignity as an upper-class citizen. But he hasn't lost his inner strength or his willingness to crack jokes.

When Ota sees that his father is well and chatting with his fellow workers about that day's deaths, he heads off toward Block 31. He looks around, and what he sees is sad: emaciated people dressed in rags like beggars. He never thought he'd see his people looking like this, but the more broken they seem to him, the more aware he is of his Jewishness.

He's left behind the period of his adolescence when he allowed himself to be bewitched by the teachings of Karl Marx, when he believed that internationalization and Communism were the answers to all of history's problems. There was a moment when he didn't know exactly where he belonged: He was the son of an upper-class family, he flirted with lounge-room Communism, he was Czech, and he was a Jew. When the Nazis entered Prague and began to round up the Jews, Ota finally realized his place in the world: Blood and a thousand-year tradition tied him so much more to the Jews than to any other group. And if he had any doubt about who he was, the Nazis ensured that he wouldn't forget it for a single moment of his life by sewing a yellow star on his chest.

That was why he joined the Zionists and became an active member of the *hachshara* movement, which prepared young people for the *aliyah*, the return to Palestine. He remembers with pleasure and a touch of melancholy those excursions where there was always someone with a guitar and time to sing songs. In that fraternity, there was something of the primitive spirit he had been looking for—a community of musketeers where it was all for one and one for all.

He began to make up his first tales during those nights around the campfire telling horror stories. In those days, he occasionally bumped into Fredy Hirsch. Fredy struck him as one of those people whose convictions had no chinks. That was why he was so proud to be under his command in Block 31.

These are not good times . . .

But Ota is an optimist. He has inherited his father's ironic sense of humor, and he refuses to believe that the Jews aren't going to get out of this rough patch, given their history of constant setbacks. And in order to get rid of such bad thoughts, he returns to the story he's going to tell the children, because there must be no end to stories, so that imagination never stops and children continue to dream.

You are what you dream, Ota says to himself.

Ota Keller is twenty-two years old, but his self-assurance makes him seem older. He is telling the children a story he's told many times before. It's a story of his own invention, so if he forgets any detail, he just replaces it with another. It's about a traveling rogue who sells silent flutes, which have no holes because, he says, in this way the magnificent sound they produce will be heard only in heaven. . . .

"And you wouldn't believe how many people bought his flutes—until one of his customers was a child."

When he gets to the end of the story, his listeners stampede toward the door with that sense of urgency typical of childhood. Each minute is lived intensely because right now is everything. Ota watches them rushing off, and he also sees one of the assistants whizzing toward the exit like a rocket, her shoulder-length hair swinging to the rhythm of her steps. The librarian with the long, skinny legs is always running. . . .

She seems to have the face of an angel, but her energetic way of moving and gesticulating suggests to Ota that if she doesn't get her way, the devil takes over. He's noticed that she doesn't usually speak with the teachers; she hands over the books and picks them up again with a nod of her head, always in a hurry. But then again, he thinks, she might be pretending to be in a hurry in order to cover her shyness.

And Dita has indeed raced out of the hut. She doesn't want to bump into anyone because she's got two books hidden under her dress, and that's highly inflammatory material.

Earlier, when she'd gone to Fredy Hirsch's cubicle to hide the books in her care, the door was locked. Even though she knocked several times, no one answered. She found Miriam Edelstein in the corner of the hut where the teachers gathered with their stools to chat. Miriam told her that Fredy had been called away without warning by Kommandant Schwarzhuber and had forgotten to leave the key to his cubicle with her. She took Dita aside and quietly asked her what she intended to do with the two books that hadn't been picked up when morning classes ended.

"Don't worry, I'll take care of it."

Miriam nodded her agreement and gave her a look that told her to be careful. Dita didn't provide any further information. That was her right as librarian. The two books she was carrying in her secret pockets would sleep with her that night. It was dangerous, but leaving them in the hut didn't strike her as a safe alternative.

Almost all the children had dispersed, while the tutors had taken others out behind the hut for sports training. But there was a group of boys and girls of mixed ages still inside the hut listening attentively to Ota Keller. Dita was impressed by the young teacher who knew so much and had such an ironic way of speaking. She was about to stay and listen to what he was telling them—she thought it was something to do with Palestine—but she had a date with a scoundrel by the name of Švejk. She overheard a few of the teacher's words, however, and was surprised by what he was saying. It wasn't a class in politics or history, which was his usual fare in the mornings, but a story. And she was struck by the passionate way in which he was telling it. She found it intriguing that such an educated and serious young man could tell stories with so much enthusiasm.

Enthusiasm is very important to Dita. She needs to be enthusiastic about things in order to keep going. That's why she puts her heart and soul into the task of distributing the books—paper ones in the morning, and "living" ones in the afternoon when things are more relaxed. In the case of the "living" books, she's organized a roster for the teachers who have become talking books.

If she were prudent, the two books that haven't been placed in the secret hiding spot would remain hidden under her smock until the next morning. But Dita can't resist the temptation to find out what her friend Švejk is up to, so she goes off to read in the la-trines, a barrack with long rows of black, foul-smelling holes.

She makes herself comfortable in an inconspicuous corner. It occurs to her that Švejk and his creator, Jaroslav Hašek, would have found it a most appropriate place in which to read. In the in-troduction to the second part of his book, Hašek observes that

> people who get angry at vulgar expressions are fainthearted, and real life will sneak up on them. In his writings, Eustachius the Monk says of Saint Louis that whenever he heard a man farting loudly, he would start to cry, and prayer was the only thing that would calm him down. There are various people who would like to have transformed the Czech Republic into an enormous salon with parquet floors you could only walk over wearing tails and gloves—a place where the exquisite traditions of the upper crust world would be maintained and where, protected, the wolves of the elite could give themselves over to their worst vices and excesses.

In here, with hundreds of holes fully occupied every morning, poor Saint Louis would be praying nonstop.

When Dita leaves the latrines, she has to walk carefully because the ground is icy.

After she reaches her hut, Dita searches out her mother. Usu-ally she's a chatterbox, and she tells her mother stories about Block 31 or about the children's pranks, but this evening she says nothing. Liesl feels the hard outline of the books under Dita's dress when she hugs her, but she doesn't say a word, either. Mothers always know more than their children think they do. And in this closed world, news leaps from one bunk to the next like the bedbugs.

Dita thinks she's protecting her mother by not telling her what she does in Block 31. She doesn't know that it's actually the reverse. Liesl understands that, by pretending to be ignorant about Edita's activities, she allows her daughter to worry less about causing her pain and to feel more tranquil. She won't be a burden to her teenage daughter.

When Dita asks if she's been tuning in to Radio Birkenau, Liesl pretends to be angry. "Don't make fun of Mrs. Turnovská," she tells Dita. In fact, she's pleased that Dita is making jokes again. "We were talking about cake recipes. She didn't know the one with blueberries and grated lemon peel! We've had a very pleasant afternoon."

A very pleasant afternoon in Auschwitz?

Dita wonders if her mother is starting to lose her mind. Maybe that might not be such a bad thing. They've been through some very hard days in this horrible month of February.

"There's still an hour before curfew. Go and visit Margit in her hut!"

Liesl does this often in the evening: throws Dita out of their hut, tells her to go and see her friends, makes sure she doesn't stay inside surrounded by widows.

As Dita walks toward Barrack 8, she feels the books swaying slightly under her dress. She thinks her mother has shown amazing strength since the death of her husband.

She finds Margit sitting at the foot of a bunk with her mother and her sister Helga, who is two years younger than Margit. She greets the family. Then Margit's mother, who knows that the teenagers are happier talking about things on their own, says she's going to find one of her neighbors. Helga stays where she is, but her eyes are drooping and she's almost asleep. She's mentally and physically exhausted because she was very unlucky with the job she was given sorting mountains of clothes of the dead people.

Undertaking such hard physical labor with just a liquid drink in the morning, soup at midday, and a piece of bread at night would leave anyone exhausted. Dita, with her habit of giving everyone a nickname, secretly calls Helga Sleeping Beauty, but hasn't called her that out loud since she realized that Margit didn't find the nickname the least bit amusing. But in fact it is exactly what she is: an extremely thin, almost emaciated adolescent who falls asleep from exhaustion as soon as she sits down anywhere.

"Your mother has left us on our own. . . . How considerate she is!" Dita says.

"Mothers know what they have to do," Margit replies.

"I was thinking about my mother as I was coming over here. You know her. She seems so fainthearted, but she's so much stronger than I could ever have imagined. Since my father's death, she's continued to work in that stinking workshop without a single word of complaint; she hasn't even caught a cold in that wooden icebox we sleep in."

"That's a relief."

"I once overheard a couple of young women who sleep near us . . . Do you know what they call my mother and her friends?"

"What?"

"The Old Hens Club."

"That's terrible."

"But they're right. Sometimes they all begin to speak at once from their bunks and they make a racket like hens in a farmyard."

Margit smiles. She's very discreet, and she doesn't think it's a good idea to make fun of older people, but she's also pleased to hear Dita joking again. It's a good sign.

"And what have you heard about Renée?" Dita asks.

Margit becomes serious. "She's been avoiding me for days."

"Meaning what?"

"Well, not just me. As soon as she finishes work, she goes off with her mother and doesn't speak to anyone."

"But why?"

"People are gossiping."

"What do you mean, gossiping? About Renée? Why?"

Margit feels a bit uncomfortable because she can't find the right words to tell her friend.

"She's on good terms with an SS officer."

There are certain lines that can't be crossed in Auschwitz–Birkenau, and that's one of them.

"Are you sure it's not just a rumor? You know people invent all sorts of things."

"No, Dita. I've seen her talking to him. They stand beside the entry guard post because people usually don't go there. But you can see them perfectly from Barracks One and Three."

"Do they kiss?"

"Good God, I hope not. I get the shivers just thinking about that."

"I'd rather kiss a pig."

Margit doubles over with laughter, and Dita realizes she's starting to speak like the good soldier Švejk. What's even worse is that she quite likes the idea.

At that very moment, a few huts away, Renée is removing nits from her mother's hair. It keeps her hands and her eyes busy but otherwise leaves her free to think.

She already knows that the other women criticize her. She doesn't think it's a good thing to accept the friendship of a member of the SS, either, even someone as well-mannered and attentive as Viktor.

Viktor?

Friendly or otherwise, he is a prison guard. Even worse, an executioner. But he behaves himself with her. He gave her the fine-toothed comb with which she's freeing her mother of the lice. He also brought her a small jar of red currant jam. She and her mother had spread it on their nightly pieces of lumpy bread and enjoyed their dinner for the first time in months. They hadn't tasted that flavor for such a long time! Vitamin contributions like that can prevent illness and save your life.

Should she be unfriendly to this young SS man who has never asked her for anything in return? Should she reject his gifts and tell him she wants nothing to do with him?

She knows that many of the women who criticize her would take what they could if they were in the same position. They'd take it for their husbands or their children or whoever, but they'd take it. It's easy to be honorable when people don't put an open bottle of red currant jam and a slice of bread in front of you.

Viktor says he'd like them to get engaged when all this is over. She never replies. He talks to her of Romania, describes his village and how they celebrate their main feast day with sack races and an enormous sweet-and-sour stew in the square. Renée would like to hate him; she knows it's her duty to hate him. But hate is too much like love: Neither of them is a matter of choice.

Night falls in Auschwitz. Trains continue to arrive in the darkness, depositing more disoriented innocents who tremble like leaves, and the red glow of the chimneys marks out the ovens that never stop.

The inmates of the family camp try to sleep on their flea-infested mattresses and to overcome their fear-inspired insomnia. Every night gained is a small victory.

In the morning, another round of face-washing in the metal troughs, and the immodest lowering of underwear and hiking of dresses to perform bodily functions along with three hundred other people. Then the painfully slow head count on another freezing day. The cold ground turns their clogs into shoes of ice. The guards leave the camp, their lists dotted with crosses beside the names of those who have not survived the night. Finally, Fredy Hirsch closes the barrack door and raises an eyebrow. The children raucously break ranks and go to their stools, a few teachers stop by the library, and a new day begins in Block 31.

What Dita craves is the lunchtime soup. It's comforting. And more to the point, it marks the start of the afternoon when she can share again the adventures of that spendthrift soldier who's always putting his foot in it and who has become her friend. One of the Austrian officers in charge of Švejk's battalion is a brute called Dauerling. His superiors value him because he treats his soldiers severely, even hitting them at times.

Reading is a pleasure.

But there are always people ready to spoil any party. Busybody Mrs. Nasty, unmistakable with her dirty bun and display of wobbling skin, leans into Dita's refuge. She's with another teacher who has tiny, almost microscopic eyes.

The two women plant themselves in front of Dita, scowl, and order her to show them what she is reading. She holds out the sheets of paper and one of them grabs the book. The pages come loose and the worn threads that hold them to the spine are on the verge of breaking. Dita makes a face, but she bites her tongue.

As the teacher reads, her eyes widen more and more. The loose skin under her chin wobbles with indignation. Dita fights the urge to smile at the thought that Mrs. Nasty's expression is no different from that of some of the officers in Švejk's regiment at some of his witty remarks.

"This is unacceptable and indecent! No girl your age should read this perverse material. There are inadmissible blasphemies in here."

Just then, the two deputy directors and the teachers' immediate superiors, Lichtenstern and Miriam Edelstein, emerge from of Hirsch's cubicle. Mrs. Křižková gives a satisfied smile at this display of authority and signals them to come over to her immediately.

"Look here, this is supposed to be a school, no matter how dirty it is. As deputy directors, you can't allow our young people to read vulgar pulp novels like this. The worst blasphemies I've heard in my life are contained in this book."

To emphasize her comments, she asks them to listen to an example of lack of respect for the church hierarchy and the foul things said about a priest and a minister of God:

> He's as drunk as a skunk. But he has the rank of captain.
> No matter what their rank, God has given all these military
> chaplains the gift of always being able to fill themselves with
> drink to the point of bursting. I was once with a priest called
> Katz who was almost prepared to sell his soul for a drink. As it
> was, he sold a sacred container and we drank every last cent he
> got for it; and if someone had given us a little something for
> the Church, we would have spent that on drink as well.

Mrs. Křižková slams the book shut when she realizes that Lichtenstern is making a huge effort to stop himself from laughing.

Dita keeps an eye on the harm being done to the book's pages, which are on the verge of coming away from the spine. Křižková asserts that this is a very serious matter and demands that the book be banned. She continues to wave the pages in the air and again questions what sort of values they are inculcating in their youth if they allow them to read such books.

Dita, tired of seeing her wave the book back and forth like a fly swatter, jumps up, plants herself in front of the teacher even though she is fifteen centimeters shorter, and asks her most politely, but with steel in her voice, if she would let her have the book for a moment ". . . please." And she emphasizes the *please* so forcefully that it sounds as if she's hitting the older woman over the head with it. The teacher, caught unawares, holds out the mistreated pages with an offended look.

Dita takes the book with care, adjusts the loose sheets, and re-inserts the dangling pages. She takes her time, and the others, intrigued, watch how she smooths the sheets and mends the book as if she were dealing with a war wound. Her hands and gaze show so such respect and care for the old book that not even the indignant teacher dares say a word.

Eventually, when everything is back in its place, Dita carefully opens the book and addresses herself to the circumspect Lichtenstern and Miriam Edelstein, who has a neutral look on her face. She says that it's true this book contains tales like the ones the teacher has read. But it also tells stories like the following one. And then it's her turn to read:

> The last resort for those who didn't want to go to the front line
> was military prison. I met a teacher who, as a mathematician,
> didn't want to go and shoot in an artillery regiment. He stole an

officer's watch so they'd put him in prison. It was entirely
premeditated. War neither impressed nor fascinated him. He
believed that shooting at the enemy, and firing projectiles and
grenades to kill the math teachers on the other side who were just
as unfortunate as him, was colossal stupidity, an act of brutality.

"These are some of the bad ideas this foolish book teaches: that war is stupid and bestial. Do you disagree with this, too?"

Silence.

Lichtenstern wishes he had a cigarette to put between his lips. He scratches his left ear to gain time, and finally decides to speak so he won't have to pass judgment.

"Forgive me, but I have to go and see the medics urgently about a matter to do with the children's visits."

Too many women at the same time. Lichtenstern opts to remove himself, and quickly.

Without wishing to, Miriam Edelstein has become the referee in the battle over reading matter.

"What Edita just read seems very sensible to me. Moreover," she adds looking straight at Mrs. Křižková, "we can't say that this is a sacrilegious book that treats religion disrespectfully when all it says, in the end, is that some Catholic priests are drunkards. Nowhere is the scrupulous integrity of our rabbis questioned."

The two women teachers, offended and angered by the sarcasm, turn around as they mutter who knows what complaints and reproaches. When they are a safe distance away, Miriam Edelstein whispers to Dita that she'd like to borrow the novel one afternoon when Dita has finished it.

17.

DITA SPREADS OUT HER LIBRARY FOR ANOTHER MORNING. WHEN she went to Hirsch's cubicle, she found him sketching out tactics for his volleyball team, which is going head-to-head with another teacher's team in an important game behind the hut this afternoon after lunch. Dita is not as cheerful as her boss; she has pins and needles in her legs after the lengthy morning head count.

"How's it going, Edita? It's a lovely morning—the sun's going to come out for a while today, you'll see."

"My feet are killing me, thanks to these wretched head counts. They're never ending. I hate them."

"Edita, Edita . . . *Blessed* head count! Do you know why it takes so long?"

"Well . . ."

"Because we're all still here. We haven't lost a single child since September. Do you understand? More than five thousand people in the family camp have died from disease, starvation, or exhaustion since September." Dita sadly nods her head. "But not a single child from Block Thirty-One! We're succeeding, Edita. We're doing it."

Dita gives him a sad smile of victory. If only her father were there so she could tell him.

She unobtrusively moves the bench with the books a few meters, so she can follow Ota Keller's classes more closely. Now that her father has gone, she has to keep up her studies on her own; Keller always has something interesting to say. She studies him—his thick woolen sweater and round face, which suggests he was probably a chubby little boy.

He's talking to the children about volcanoes.

"Many meters underground, the Earth is on fire. Sometimes, the internal pressure creates cracks from which white-hot material rises to form volcanoes. This material is molten rock, which becomes a really hot sort of paste called lava. At the bottom of the sea, volcanic eruptions create lava cones, which end up forming islands. That's how the islands of Hawaii, for example, were formed."

Dita listens to the sounds of the lessons rising from the little groups; it's like steam heating up the inhospitable stable in which they are located and converting it into a school. And she asks herself yet again why they are all still alive.

Why have they allowed five-year-olds to run around here? It's the question they all ask themselves.

If Dita could place her metal bowl against the wall of the *Lager* officers' mess hall and listen, she would have the answer she's looked for so many times.

SS Camp Kommandant Schwarzhuber, in charge of Birkenau, and Dr. Mengele, the SS captain with "special" responsibilities, are the only two left in the mess hall. The *Kommandant* has a bottle of apple schnapps in front of him while the medical captain has a cup of coffee.

Mengele studies the *Kommandant* with detachment—his long face and fanatical look. The medical captain does not consider himself an extremist; he's a scientist. Perhaps he doesn't want to admit to being envious of Schwarzhuber's incredibly blue eyes, so unmistakably Aryan compared to his own, which are brown, and which, together with his darker skin, give him a disconcertingly southern Mediterranean appearance. At school, some children made fun of him, calling him a Gypsy. He'd love to lay them down on his dissection table and ask them to repeat their comments to him now.

Vivisection is an extraordinary experience. It's like the view a watchmaker has of a watch, but of life . . .

He observes Schwarzhuber drinking. It's deplorable that an SS *Kommandant* with dozens of assistants at his disposal is incapable of appearing with perfectly polished boots or properly ironed shirt collars. It's a sign of slackness, and that's unforgiveable. He despises country bumpkins like Schwarzhuber who cut themselves when they shave. And on top of that, Schwarzhuber does something that utterly annoys Mengele: He repeats conversations they've already had, using the exact same words and the same stupid arguments.

Yet again Schwarzhuber asks Mengele why his superiors have such an interest in this absurd family camp, expecting the doctor to give him the usual answer. Mengele musters his patience and puts on a show of affability while deliberately speaking as if to a small child or the mentally handicapped.

"You are already aware, *Herr Kommandant*, that this camp is strategically very important to Berlin."

"Dammit, *Herr Doktor*, yes, I do already know that! But I don't know why it's shown such consideration. Are we now going to set up a child care center for them as well? Have they gone mad? Do they think Auschwitz is a resort?"

"That's what we would like a few countries that are keeping a close eye on us to think. Rumors are rife. When the International Red Cross started to request more information about our camps and asked to send inspectors, our commander in chief, SS Reichsführer Heinrich Himmler, was brilliant, as always. Rather than banning the visit, he encouraged them to come. We will show them what they want to see: Jewish families living together and children running around Auschwitz."

"Too many complications—"

"All the work that was done in Theresienstadt will have been use-less if, when we receive inspectors of the International Red Cross who have tracked the inhabitants of that ghetto to here, they see what we don't want them to see. We'll invite them to see the house, but we won't show them the kitchen, just the playroom. And they'll return to Geneva satisfied."

"To hell with the Red Cross! Who do these cowardly Swiss, who don't even have an army, think they are, telling the Third Reich what it should do? Why aren't they shown the door as soon as they get here? Or even better, have them sent to me, and I'll stick them in the ovens without first stopping off in the kitchen."

Mengele smiles condescendingly as he watches Schwarzhuber becoming more and more red in the face. He has to restrain himself from grabbing his riding crop and bringing it down on Schwarz-huber's head. No, not his crop, that's too valuable. Better yet, he would have enjoyed pulling out his gun and blowing Schwarzhuber's brains out. But Schwarzhuber is the *Kommandant* of Birkenau, even if he is a complete idiot.

"My dear *Herr Kommandant*, don't underestimate the impor-tance of the image we offer to the world and our project. We must be careful. Do you know which executive office our beloved Führer first held within the Nazi party?"

Mengele pauses theatrically; he knows he's going to answer his own question, but he enjoys humiliating Schwarzhuber. "Head of propaganda. He talks about it in his book, *Mein Kampf*—have you read it?" He relishes the *Kommandant*'s worried expression. "Many people, both within Germany and outside our borders, have still not understood the need to cleanse humanity genetically by eliminating racial degeneration. There are still countries that would go on alert and open up new war fronts. And we absolutely don't want that right now. We want to be the ones who decide where and when fronts are opened. It's the same as performing an operation, my dear *Kommandant*. You can't cut just anywhere; you have to choose the appropriate place for an incision. The war is our scalpel, and we have to handle it with precision. If you handle it like a madman, you might end up sticking it into yourself."

Schwarzhuber can't stand Mengele's patronizing tone—the same one a teacher might use with a hopeless pupil.

"Dammit, Mengele, you talk like a politician! I'm a soldier. I have my orders and I'll carry them out. If SS Reichsführer Himmler says we have to keep the family camp, so be it. But this business of a child care center . . . where does that fit in?"

"Propaganda, *Herr Kommandant* . . . pro-pa-gan-da. We're going to get these inmates to write home and tell their Jewish relatives how well they're being treated in Auschwitz."

"And what the devil do we care what those Jewish pigs think about how we treat them?"

Mengele breathes in and mentally counts to three.

"My dear *Herr Kommandant*, there are still many Jews out there who'll have to be brought here progressively. An animal that doesn't know it's going to the slaughterhouse allows itself to be led there much more docilely than one that knows it's going to be sacrificed and thus puts up all kinds of resistance. As someone from a village, Schwarzhuber, you ought to know that."

Mengele's final comment irritates Schwarzhuber.

"How dare you call Tutzing a village? For your information, Tutzing is considered the most beautiful town in Bavaria, in all of Germany, even . . . which means we could say in the whole world."

"Of course, *Herr Kommandant*. I completely agree: Tutzing is a marvelous town."

Schwarzhuber is about to reply, but he realizes that this pedantic, middle-class doctor is deliberately provoking him, and he's not going to play along.

"Very well, *Herr Doktor*, a child care center, whatever is necessary," he roars. "But I'm not going to let it cause the slightest problem or disturbance in the camp. It will be closed at the first sign of lack of discipline. Do you think that Jew who's in charge will be able to maintain discipline?"

"Why not? He's German."

"Captain Mengele! How dare you say that a repugnant Jewish dog like him belongs to our glorious German nation?"

"Well, call him what you will, but Hirsch's file says he was born in Aachen in North Rhine–Westphalia. As far as I know, that's in Germany."

Schwarzhuber gives Mengele a fiery look. Mengele can read his thoughts—his superior finds his impertinence intolerable—but Mengele's not worried, because he can also detect his superior's mistrust. Schwarzhuber knows that he has to tread carefully, because Mengele has powerful friends in Berlin. There's a flash of malice in his eyes, as if he's licking his lips in anticipation of the moment when Mengele's lucky star will fade and Schwarzhuber can allow himself the pleasure of crushing him. But Mengele smiles affably; he knows that moment will never arrive. He's always a step ahead of these military men who, in reality, have understood nothing and have no idea why they are at war. Mengele does know. He's fighting to turn himself into a celebrity. First, he'll head up the DFG, the German Research Foundation, and then he'll change the course of medical history. The course of humanity, ultimately. Josef Mengele knows he's not a humble man; he leaves that to the weak.

History will teach Mengele a lesson. That the greatest weakness of all is precisely that of the strong: They end up believing they are invincible. So the strength of the Third Reich is also its fragility. Believing it is indestructible, it will open so many battlefronts that it will end up collapsing. The planes of the Allies are already starting to circle over Auschwitz, and the first bombardments can be heard in the distance.

Nobody avoids weakness. Not even the invincible Fredy Hirsch.

It happens a few days later. When the last activities of the afternoon are over and the hut starts to empty, Dita hurries to gather her books. She wraps them up in a piece of material to protect them from the soil in the hidey-hole and walks over to Hirsch's cubicle to stow them away. She wants to get back to her mother quickly, to keep her company.

She knocks on Hirsch's door and hears him giving her permission to come in. She finds him, as usual, sitting in the cubicle's only chair, but this time he isn't working on a report. His arms are crossed, and he's staring blankly into space. Something inside him has changed.

She accesses the wooden trapdoor hidden under a pile of folded blankets and fits the books into the space. She works speedily so she can leave quickly without disturbing Hirsch too much. But as she turns around to leave, she hears his voice behind her.

"Edita . . ."

Hirsch sounds unhurried, perhaps a little tired, and lacking that energy which inspires his young listeners when he gives his pep talks. When she faces the athlete, what she sees is a man who is unexpectedly exhausted.

"You know something? Maybe, when all this is over, I won't go to the Promised Land."

Dita looks at him, mystified, and Fredy smiles benevolently at her reaction. It's logical, he thinks, that she wouldn't understand. He's spent years putting all his effort into explaining to young people that they should feel proud to be Jews and should prepare themselves to return to the land of Zion, where they can use the Golan Heights as a springboard to be closer to God.

"Look, the people here . . . what are they? Zionists? Anti-Zionists? Atheists? Communists?" A sigh blurs his words momentarily. "And who cares? If you look more carefully, all you can see is people, nothing more. Fragile, corruptible people. Capable of the best and the worst."

And Dita struggles to hear some of his words, which, like the earlier ones, Hirsch is addressing to himself rather than to her:

"Everything that was important now strikes me as insignificant."

He falls silent again and gazes into space—which is what we do when we want to look inside ourselves. Dita doesn't understand a thing. She doesn't understand why a man who has fought so hard to return to the Promised Land has suddenly lost all interest in going there. She'd like to ask him, but he's no longer looking at her; he's not there anymore. She decides to leave him alone in his labyrinth and depart without making a sound.

She'll understand later, but right at that moment, she's incapable of seeing in his change of heart that rare moment of clarity that comes to people when they find themselves on a cliff-edge of life. From the top of the precipice, everything looks incredibly small.

Dita glances at the table. The papers lying on it are in Hirsch's hand, but when she looks at them more carefully, she realizes they aren't reports or administrative notes, but poems. Lying on top of them, like a rock that has come loose and crushed everything, is a sheet of paper bearing the letterhead of the camp's command head-quarters. She only has time to read one word on it written in bold: *Transfer.*

News of the transfer has already reached the office of the registrar in the quarantine camp, Rudi Rosenberg. The six-month deadline for the September transport has been reached and, as forecast on the file, the Germans are setting in motion the "special treatment."

That's why, as he waits anxiously for Alice to meet him at the fence, he buttons the jacket he acquired on the black market all the way to the top. He can't stop moving.

The day before, he'd asked Alice for her help in carrying out the assignment Schmulewski has given him, to find out exactly how many people there are in the family camp's Resistance cell. The Resistance operates so secretly that the collaborators themselves often don't know one another. This afternoon, Rudi has learned that even Alice herself is linked to the Resistance through a friend.

Schmulewski says little, rarely more than half a dozen words. It's part of his technique for survival. Whenever he's asked for further explanation or someone reproaches him for his lack of speech, he replies that a criminal lawyer friend once told him that mute people reach old age. But Rudi had found him especially bleak and, moved by his anguish, couldn't avoid asking him if the signs were bad. His words—always few, always veiled—were "Things are going badly."

By "things," he means the family camp.

As on so many other occasions, what the guards in the towers see is the quarantine camp registrar and his Jewish girlfriend from the family camp walking toward the fence—a routine to which they no longer pay any attention. The Germans don't distinguish between one scrawny Jewish woman dressed in rags and another. That's why they don't notice that the woman approaching the fence on this particular occasion isn't Alice Munk, but her close friend Helena Rezková, one of the coordinators of the family camp Resistance. She's come to the fence to give Rudi the confidential information the head of the Resistance has asked for: there are thirty-three secret members divided into two groups. Helena asks Rudi if he knows anything more about the transfer, but there's not much news to add. He's heard a rumor about a possible move to Heydebreck camp, but there are no details. The authorities are not giving anything away.

They stand looking at each other for a while without speaking. The girl might have been pretty under other circumstances, but her dirty, tangled hair, sunken cheeks, chapped lips, and filthy clothes have turned her into a twenty-two-year-old beggar. Rosenberg, normally so chatty, has no idea what to say to this girl who has a battered present and a dark future.

He receives permission that afternoon to go to camp BIId, supposedly to take over some lists, but in reality, to meet Schmulewski. He finds him sitting on a wooden bench in front of his hut, chewing on a twig in the absence of any tobacco. Rudi, who always works things out so he's well stocked with everything, offers him a cigarette.

He passes on Helena's information about the number and basic occupations of the insurgents in the family camp, which Schmulewski acknowledges solely with a nod of his head. Rudi hopes to get some sort of explanation of the situation, but he gets nothing. Pretending that Schmulewski doesn't already know, he tells him that it's March 6, and so they're getting close to the six-month deadline since the arrival of Alice's September contingent, when the "special treatment" kicks in. "I'd prefer it if that moment never arrived."

Schmulewski smokes his cigarette without saying a word. Rosenberg gathers that the meeting is over and mumbles an awkward good-bye. He returns to his camp, not sure if the Pole's silence is because he has crucial information to hide or because he has absolutely no idea what is going on.

The afternoon roll call takes longer than usual. Various SS soldiers notify all the *Kapos* that the inmates should line up at the entrance to the camp. Waiting there for them are the camp *Kapo*— the civilian responsible for BIIb, an ordinary German prisoner called Willy—and the noncommissioned officer they call the Priest, flanked by two guards with machine guns at the ready. The inmates watch as the heads of all the barracks start walking toward the noncommissioned SS officer and form a half circle around him.

Fredy Hirsch strides energetically across the *Lagerstrasse*, overtaking other *Kapos* who are less keen to get to the meeting. Night is falling, but it's easy to distinguish Hirsch's proud and self-assured figure making his way there.

The Priest is waiting for them with his hands tucked inside the sleeves of his greatcoat. He watches them arriving with a cynical smile; it's obvious he's in a good mood. It's good news for the sergeant that he's getting rid of many of the inmates: half the prisoners means half the problems. An assistant hands the *Kapos* lists with the numbers of the people in their huts from the September transport. The *Kapos* must inform them that they are to line up separately next morning and bring with them their belongings—their spoon and bowl—in order to proceed with the transfer to another camp. Only one person sleeps in Block 31, the *Blockäl-tester* himself, and he accepts the shortest list of all. It has just one number on it, his own. In the midst of the silence, inter-rupted only by the rustle of paper lists, he is the only one who dares to make his way forward and stand at attention in front of the sergeant.

"Permission to speak, *Herr Oberscharführer*. Would we be able to know to which camp we're being transferred?"

The Priest stares at Hirsch for a few seconds without blinking. Asking a question without being asked to speak first is an act of contempt that the NCO normally doesn't tolerate. On this occa-sion, however, he limits himself to giving a sharp reply.

"You'll be informed when it happens. Dismissed."

The *Kapos* stand in front of their huts and start to yell out the numbers of the people who will be transferred the next day. There's bewildered muttering: People don't know whether or not to be happy about leaving Auschwitz. The same question is asked again and again:

"Where are they taking us?"

But there's no response, or there are so many different replies that none of them is any use. Everyone has heard of the special treat-ment after six months. What will it be?

Dita has been chatting with Margit, trying to come up with an answer in the midst of so many questions. As members of the December transport, they aren't going anywhere yet. Mentally ex-hausted with so much speculation, Dita makes her way back to her hut. She's so distressed at the news that she doesn't carry out her usual precautions of checking behind her and walking right beside the huts in case she has to rush inside one of them. She hears a German voice, and feels a hand on her arm.

"Dita . . ."

She jumps. It's Fredy Hirsch, returning to his hut. There's a feverish glint in his dark eyes, and Dita can see that he's back to being his usual energetic and irresistible self.

"What are we going to do?"

"Keep going. This is a labyrinth in which you might get lost, but retracing your steps is worse. Don't pay attention to anyone, listen to the voice inside your own head, and keep going forward."

"But where are they taking you?"

"We'll be going to work somewhere else. But that's not what matters. What is important is that there's a mission to complete here."

"Block Thirty-One—"

"We have to finish what we started."

"We'll carry on with the school."

"That's it. But there's another important thing still to do."

Dita looks at him with a puzzled expression.

"Listen to me: Not everything is as it seems in Auschwitz. But there'll come a moment when a small gap will open up for the truth, you'll see. The Germans believe that lying favors them, but we'll score a goal at the last second because they'll be overconfident. They think we're broken, but we aren't." He becomes thoughtful as he's speaking. "I can't be here to help you win the game. But you must have faith, Dita, really believe. Everything will work out well, you'll see. Trust Miriam. And above all else"—he looks into her eyes while giving her his most seductive smile—"you must never give up."

"Never!"

He smiles enigmatically and walks off with his athletic stride while Dita stands there quietly, not entirely sure what he meant by scoring a goal in the last second.

It's a night of little sleep in the huts, with rumors whispered among the bunks, along with more and less absurd theories and prayers.

"What does it matter where they take us? We can't go to a worse place," some protest. It's a comfort amid the distress.

The oversized woman who shares her bunk with Dita is part of the September transport, so she'll be one of the transferees. She says little apart from the rude jokes she shares with her neighbors. She never says anything to Dita, good or bad. Dita says good night to her when she lies down next to her feet, as she always does. And as always, the woman doesn't answer—not even the noise she usually mutters by way of reply. She pretends to be asleep, but her eyes are shut too tightly for that. Even the toughest of the tough can't fall asleep during this long night that could be her last.

The day dawns cloudy and cold. The wind gusts bring snowflakes with them. Pretty much like any other day. There's some confusion when it comes to lining up, since the usual order has changed: The September people are on one side, and the December ones on the other. The *Kapos* are fully employed in forming the groups, and the SS guards are more nervous than usual, too. They even let loose with an occasional blow from a rifle butt, a rare occurrence during morning roll calls. The atmosphere is tense, and faces are long. Roll call is exasperatingly slow as the *Kapos*' assistants mark the lists. After so many hours standing on her feet, Dita has the feeling that she's slowly sinking into the mud and that if the roll call takes much longer, she'll end up being swallowed whole.

Finally, almost three hours after roll call began, the nearly four thousand people who make up the September group begin to move. For now, their destination is the quarantine camp next to the family camp, and they drag their weary feet in that direction. Rudi Rosenberg, the registrar, stands in the quarantine camp, his face serious as he watches all the activity attentively, as if, in the posture and the gesticulations of the guards, there might be some clue that will reveal the fate of these people, among whom is his Alice.

Dita and her mother stand watching in silence, along with all the others from their transport. They remain in their lines at the entrances to their huts while the guards lead the September veterans toward the exit of camp BIIb in an orderly manner. The procession is not at all festive, although some of the inmates smile, convinced there's a better place waiting for them. Some heads turn for a last farewell. Hands wave in both groups—those who are staying and those who are going. Dita grabs her mother's hand and squeezes it firmly. She doesn't know if the sharp feeling in her stomach is due to the cold or fear for those who are leaving.

She sees mischievous Gabriel marching past, laughing loudly; he's deliberately walking out of step to trip up a slender girl who's walking behind him and cursing. An adult hand stretches out from even farther back and pulls Gabriel's ear hard; Mrs. Křižková is so good at handing out punishment that she can do it without losing step. Acquaintances and teachers from Block 31 walk past Dita on their way to the quarantine camp along with many faces she's never noticed before—most of them are gaunt and grave. Some of them greet the children from the December transport who are staying behind and who wave back to them tirelessly, entertained by an event which breaks up the monotonous camp routine.

Professor Morgenstern walks past in his patched jacket and broken glasses, dispensing his ridiculous little bows. When he reaches Dita, without stopping or breaking step so as not to annoy those behind him, he suddenly becomes serious and gives her a wink. Then he continues on his way and goes back to performing his bowing routine with that little crazy-old-man laugh of his. It was only a matter of seconds, but as she was looking at him, Dita saw the professor's expression change, and his face was different as if, just for a moment, he'd raised his mask and allowed her to see his real self. It wasn't the faraway look of a crazy old man, but the composed expression of a completely serene person. And then Dita is left in no doubt.

"Professor Morgenstern!"

She throws him a kiss and he turns to thank her with a clumsy bow that makes the children laugh. He bows to them, too. He's an actor leaving the stage at the end of the show and bidding farewell to his audience.

She would have liked to give him a hug and to tell him that she knows now—in fact, she has always known—that he's not mad. If they lock you up in a lunatic asylum, the worst thing that can happen to you is that you're sane. His fake absentmindedness at just the right moment during the inspection of the Priest and Mengele saved her. He probably saved her life, hers and everyone else's. She knows that now. It's just as Fredy said: Not everything is as it seems to be. She would have liked to give the professor a big farewell kiss, but she won't be able to. Morgenstern, still playing the fool, is moving off, swallowed up in the departing crowd.

"Good luck, Professor."

A troop of women goes by. One of them—one of the few who isn't wearing a scarf on her head, contravenes the strict orders and, stepping firmly out of line, walks toward her. At first Dita doesn't recognize the woman, but it's her oversized bunkmate. Her loose, tangled hair is covering up the scar that splits her face. She plants herself directly in front of Dita with her toadlike eyes, and they briefly look at each other face-to-face.

"My name's Lida!" she says in her gravelly voice.

The *Kapo* gallops up, starts to yell at her to return to her group immediately, and waves her club menacingly. As the woman hurriedly rejoins her group, she looks back momentarily, and Dita waves good-bye to her.

"Good luck, Lida! I love your name," she shouts.

She thinks her bunkmate smiles proudly.

One of the last people to walk past those waving good-bye is Fredy Hirsch. He's wearing his jacket, and his silver whistle swings slightly on top of it. He walks with martial precision, head high and eyes fixed firmly in front of him, focused on his own thoughts and paying no attention to any of the waves or farewells, even from those who call his name.

His state of mind and the doubts that torment him are not important. It's a new exodus of the Jews, now expelled from their own prison, and they must face it with the utmost dignity. There can be no sign of frailty or weakness. That's why he doesn't respond to any greeting or wave, though his attitude is interpreted by some as arrogance.

It's true that he feels proud of what he has achieved: In the whole time Block 31 has existed, not one of the pupils has died. To keep 521 children alive for months is a record that no one has probably achieved in Auschwitz. He looks forward, not at the back of the neck of the person in front of him but much, much farther, toward the row of poplars in the distance, and even farther than that, toward the horizon.

As the September inmates file past, a rumor that they're going to be transferred to the Heydebreck camp runs through the ranks. Most of them think there'll be a drastic selection process and that many of them won't get there. Some think that not one of the transferees will make it.

18.

March 7, 1944

RUDI ROSENBERG WATCHES AS THE 3,800 SEPTEMBER TRANSPORT prisoners from the family camp arrive at the quarantine camp, BIIa. The news Schmulewski has given him is horrifying. Anyone would be deeply depressed by it. But Rudi is searching for one thing among the columns of prisoners: the slender figure of his girl-friend, Alice. Finally, their eyes meet and their smiles of satisfaction rise above the anguish. Once all the prisoners have been assigned to huts, the Nazis allow the inmates to move freely about the camp. In his room, Rudi gets together with Alice and her two Resistance friends, Vera and Helena.

Helena tells him that most of the prisoners seem to have accepted the official story—that they'll be transferred to a more northerly camp located close to Warsaw.

Vera has a shrill voice that makes her emaciated face seem even more birdlike.

"Some of the important representatives of the camp's Jewish community think that the Germans won't dare exterminate the children because they're scared that word would spread."

Rosenberg has no alternative but to pass on Schmulewski's impressions from this morning, which are grimmer and more to the point than ever:

"He told me there wasn't much time left, and he believed they could all die tomorrow."

Rudi's words are met with complete silence. The women understand that the head of the Resistance knows the facts better than anyone because he has an extensive network of spies throughout Auschwitz. Nervousness gives rise to all sorts of rumors, half rumors, wishes, ideas, fantasies. . . .

"And if the war were to end tonight?"

Helena momentarily recovers her cheerfulness.

"If the war ended tonight and I returned to Prague, the first thing I'd do is go to my mother's house and eat a bowl of goulash the size of a barrel."

"I'd climb into the saucepan with a loaf of bread and leave it so clean that I could then use it as a mirror to pluck my eyebrows."

They start to sniff the aroma of the spicy stew and sigh with happiness. And then they return to reality and the smell of fear. They try to reorder their thoughts again in an attempt come up with something positive in such a densely black outlook, some tiny detail they've overlooked that would provide a satisfactory explanation for everything. A nail on which they can hang their hopes—and their lives.

The only additional information Rudi can provide, because as registrar he's seen the transport lists, is that nine people in total from the September transport will be left behind in the family camp: the two sets of twins whom Dr. Mengele has reserved for his experiments; three doctors and a pharmacist who have accompanied the transferees to the quarantine camp, whom Mengele has also claimed; and the mistress of Mr. Willy, the camp *Kapo*. All the others will receive the special treatment specified in the Nazi plan laid out when they arrived in September.

Rudi's information is, in fact, incorrect. There are more people on the "not to be transferred" list, but things are too confusing at this stage, although all will be revealed in due course. After an hour of exhaustive reflection that leads nowhere, they're so weary they fall silent.

Vera and Helena leave, and Rudi and Alice find themselves alone. For the first time, no barbed wire comes between them, no guards in towers with guns at their shoulders watch them, and no chimneys remind them of the degradation that surrounds them. They look at each other for a moment, shyly and with some awkwardness at first, and then more and more intensely. They're young and they're beautiful, full of life and plans and desires and an urgency to drink their fill of the present moment. And as they gaze again at each other, with the spark of desire well alight in their eyes, they feel that their happiness insulates them, that it takes them to another place and that nothing can snatch this moment from them.

For the time this dream lasts, as he hugs Alice's body, Rudi believes that his happiness is so complete nothing can destroy it. He falls asleep thinking that when he wakes up, all evil will have been erased and that life will flow again as it did before the war— roosters will crow at dawn, and there'll be a smell of freshly baked bread and the sound of the milkman's cheerful bicycle bell. But the next day dawns, and nothing has been erased; Birkenau's menacing landscape remains intact. He's still too young to know that happiness cannot conquer anything—it's too fragile.

Rudi is woken abruptly by an agitated voice, and it feels as if a window inside his head has exploded into a million pieces. It's Helena, and she's extremely worried. She tells him Schmulewski is looking for him urgently; the whole camp is overrun with SS soldiers, and something really serious is about to happen. Rudi tries to put on his boots as Helena, almost hysterical, tugs at his arm and practically drags him from his bed, while Alice dozes on between the sheets, desperately clinging a little longer to her dreams.

"For God's sake, Rudi, hurry up! There's no time, there's no time!"

As soon as Rudi steps outside, he too senses that something's not right. There are lots of SS guards—he's never seen so many before—which suggests they've asked for special reinforcements from other detachments. It doesn't look like the routine procedure for escorting a contingent of prisoners to a train for a regular transfer. He's got to see Schmulewski right away. There's no question that he'd prefer not to see him, not to listen to what he has to say, but he must go and meet him in camp BIId. Given his rank, he has no difficulty in exiting the quarantine camp on the pretext that he has to pick up some bread rations that are missing.

The Resistance leader's face isn't a face anymore—it's a confusion of wrinkles and bags under his eyes. He doesn't beat around the bush anymore. His words aren't discreet or cautious anymore: They're razor-sharp.

"The people transferred from the family camp die today," he says with no hesitation.

"You mean there'll be a selection? You mean they want to get rid of the old people, the sick, and the children?"

"No, Rudi. Everybody! The young Jewish male prisoners forced to help with the disposal of gas chamber victims have received orders to prepare the ovens tonight for four thousand people."

And almost without pausing, he adds, "There's no time for regret, Rudi. It's time to rebel."

Schmulewski is under a great deal of strain, but his words are absolutely precise, perhaps because he's rehearsed and repeated them dozens of times throughout his long night of insomnia.

"If the Czechs organize an uprising, if they force a confrontation and fight, they won't be on their own. Hundreds, or maybe thousands of us will be beside them and, with a bit of luck, this could work out well. Go and talk to them. Tell them they have nothing to lose: They fight or they die—there's no other option. But they haven't got a chance in hell without someone to lead them."

And in response to Rudi's look of incomprehension, Schmulewski points out that there are at least half a dozen distinct political organizations in the camp: Communists, Socialists, Zionists, anti-Zionists, social democrats, Czech nationalists. . . . "If one of these groups takes the initiative, it's likely to create discussions, differences of opinion, and confrontations with the others, which would make it impossible to achieve a united uprising. That's why we need someone whom the majority respects. Someone with a great deal of courage, who won't hesitate, who'll speak out, and whom the rest of them are prepared to follow."

"But who could that be?" Rudi asks incredulously.

"Hirsch."

The registrar slowly nods in agreement, conscious that events have assumed an enormous significance.

"You have to speak to him, inform him of the situation and convince him to lead the uprising. Time is running out, Rudi. There's a lot at stake. Hirsch has to rebel and take everyone with him."

Uprising . . . an exciting, magnificent word, worthy of history books. A word that nevertheless falters when Rudi raises his eyes and looks around: men, women, and children dressed in rags, unarmed and starving, confronting machine guns mounted in towers, trained dogs, armored vehicles. Schmulewski knows that. He knows that many, if not all of them, will die . . . but a breach might be opened and a few of them—dozens, maybe, or hundreds—might escape into the forest and get away.

Maybe the rebellion will take off, and they'll blow up vital camp installations. In that way, they might be able to disable the machine of death, even if only momentarily, and save many lives. Or it might achieve nothing more than people being mowed down by rounds of machine-gun fire. There are many unknowns lined up against the certainty of the overwhelming power of the SS, but Schmulewski keeps repeating the same thing again and again:

"Tell him, Rudi. Tell him he's got nothing to lose."

Rudi Rosenberg entertains no doubts as he returns to the quarantine camp—their death sentence is sealed, but they can fight for their destiny. Fredy Hirsch holds the key around his neck, that silver whistle. One blast to announce the unanimous, violent uprising of almost four thousand souls.

As he's walking, he thinks of Alice. So far, he's acted as if Alice weren't part of the September contingent condemned to death, as if none of this had anything to do with her. She is one of the condemned, but Rudi keeps telling himself that she isn't, that it's not possible that Alice's youth and beauty, her body full of delights, and her doelike eyes could turn into inert flesh in a few hours' time. *It isn't possible*, he tells himself. *It's against all the laws of nature. How could someone want to see a young woman like Alice die?* Rudi quickens his pace and clenches his fists, overcome by a rage that is turning his despondency into fury.

He arrives back at the camp, his cheeks burning with anger. Helena is nervously waiting for him at the camp entrance.

"Tell Fredy Hirsch to come to my room for an urgent meeting," he says to her. "Tell him it's a matter of the utmost importance."

It's all or nothing.

Helena is back in a flash, accompanied by Hirsch, the idol of the young people, the apostle of Zionism, the man who's capable of speaking as an equal with Josef Mengele. Rudi looks him over quickly: sinewy, his wet hair impeccably combed back, a serene, slightly severe gaze, as if he is irritated at being roused from his thoughts.

When Rudi explains that the leader of the Resistance in Birkenau has gathered definitive proof that the September transport from Terezín is going to be exterminated in its entirety in the gas ovens that very night, Hirsch's expression doesn't change. There's no surprise, no response. He remains silent, almost standing at attention like a soldier. Rudi fixes his eyes on the whistle hanging from Fredy's neck like an amulet.

"You are our only chance, Fredy. Only you can speak to the leaders in the camp and convince them to stir up their followers. To launch themselves as one against the guards and start an uprising. You have to talk to all the leaders, and that whistle around your neck has to give the signal that the uprising has begun."

Still no response from the German. His expression is impenetrable, and his eyes are fixed on the Slovak registrar. Rudi has already said all he has to say and falls silent, too, as he waits for Hirsch's reaction to this desperate proposal in the midst of a totally hopeless situation.

And Hirsch finally speaks. But the person who is speaking isn't the social leader or the intransigent Zionist or the proud athlete. Rather, it's the children's educator. And he speaks in a murmur.

"And what about the children, Rudi?"

Rosenberg would have preferred to leave this discussion until later. The children are the weakest link in the chain. In a violent uprising, they're the ones with the least chance of surviving. But Rudi has an answer to this, too.

"Fredy, the children are going to die no matter what—no question. We have a possibility, maybe just a small one, but a possibility nevertheless, of getting thousands of prisoners to rise up and destroy the camp, thereby saving the lives of many deportees who will no longer be sent here."

Fredy's lips remain tightly sealed, but his eyes speak for him. In an uprising involving hand-to-hand combat, the children will be the first ones they slaughter. If a breach is opened in the fence and there's a stampede to escape, they'll be the last ones to fight their way through. If the prisoners have to run hundreds of meters cross-country under a hail of bullets to reach the forest, the children will be the last to get there and the first to be cut down. And, if any of them reach the forest, what will they do, alone and disoriented?

"They trust me, Rudi. How can I abandon them now? How can I fight to save myself and leave them to be killed? And what if you are mistaken and there is a transfer to another camp?"

"There won't be. You're doomed. You can't save the children, Fredy. Think about the others. Think about the thousands of children all over Europe, and all the children who'll come to Auschwitz to die if we don't rebel now."

Fredy Hirsch closes his eyes and lifts one of his hands to his forehead as if he had a fever.

"Give me an hour. I need an hour to think about it."

Fredy leaves the room with his customary upright posture. No one who sees him walking across the camp could know that he's carrying the unbearable weight of four thousand lives on his shoulders. As he walks, he strokes his whistle obsessively.

Several members of the Resistance, who are already aware of the situation, come into Rudi's room to find out what's happened, and Rosenberg tells them the outcome of his conversation with the head of Block 31.

"He's asked for a while to think it over."

One of them, a Czech with a steely look, says Hirsch is buying time. They all look at him, asking him to explain what he means.

"They're not going to destroy him. He's useful to the Nazis. He's prepared valuable reports for them and anyway, he's German. Hirsch is waiting for Mengele to claim him, to remove him from here any moment; that's what he's waiting for."

A tense silence hangs briefly in the air.

"That's a low comment typical of Communists like you! Fredy has taken risks for the sake of the children hundreds of times more often than you!" Renata Bubeník yells at him.

The Czech starts to shout, too, calling her a stupid Zionist and saying that they've heard Hirsch asking the *Kapo* in his current hut if there's been any message for him.

Rudi stands up and tries to make peace. He now realizes why it's so important to find a leader, a single voice, someone capable of bringing such a mixed group of people together and convincing them to rise up as one.

When everyone else leaves, Alice comes to sit beside Rudi and share the wait, because that's all they can do now, wait for Hirsch's reply. Alice's presence is a relief in the midst of chaos and uncertainty. She finds it hard to believe that the Nazis will kill all of them, even the children. Death is something terrible but foreign to her, as though it could happen to others but not to her. Rudi tells her it's horrible, but Schmulewski can't be wrong about something like this. Then he asks her to change the topic. They talk about life after Auschwitz, about how much she likes country houses, about her favorite foods, the names she'd like to give her children one day . . . about real life, and not this nightmare in which they are trapped. For a short while, a future seems possible.

The minutes pass. And the weight of tension is almost unbearable. Rudi thinks about Hirsch's burden. Alice is talking to him, but he's no longer listening. There's a stifling heaviness in the air. There's a clock inside his head with an infernal tick-tock that's driving him mad.

An hour goes by, and there's no news from Hirsch.

Minutes pass; another hour. No sign of Hirsch.

Alice fell silent some time ago, and her head is resting in Rudi's lap. Rudi starts to become aware that death is very near.

Meanwhile, in the family camp next door, classes have been suspended in Block 31. The teachers from the December transport, who are now in charge of the school, are too concerned. Some try to organize games for the children, but the children themselves are restless. They want to know where their classmates are going, and they aren't at all interested in guessing games or songs. It's an afternoon of lethargy and tense calmness. There's no fuel for the fire, and it's colder than ever. One of the assistants arrives and tells everyone that new *Kapos* have been named to replace the Jewish barrack heads of the September transport.

Dita sticks her head outside every now and again to see what's happening in camp BIIa, where half her former companions are now located. She can see people walking along the main street in the quarantine camp; some even walk up to the fence, but security is tight and the soldiers immediately move them on.

The atmosphere is so charged that Dita thinks it would be foolish to move the books, which remain carefully hidden in what was, until yesterday, Hirsch's den, and is now occupied by Lichtenstern. The new head has exchanged his meal ration for half a dozen cigarettes. He's smoked them one after another, and continues to pace up and down the hut like a caged lion.

Everyone is concerned about what's going to happen to the September transport people. Out of solidarity and compassion, no doubt, but also because whatever happens to those people might be a preview of what lies in wait for them three months from now, when their six months in the camp are over.

19.

IN BIIA, RUDI CAN'T WAIT A MOMENT LONGER.

He springs up energetically and looks at Alice without saying a word. He cracks his knuckles and decides to go over to Hirsch's hut and force him to make a decision. And he won't accept any answer but yes. The uprising has to explode without further delay.

He leaves the hut feeling very anxious, but the farther along the busy main street of the camp he gets, the bolder he becomes, and the more decisive his stride. He's prepared to resolve Hirsch's doubts and objections forcefully. He walks purposefully, inhaling deeply so he'll be able to confront any obstacle the leader of the family camp might offer him: He's ready to overcome them all so that the whistle sounds and the rebellion breaks out. While he was waiting, he went through an exhaustive replay of any objections Hirsch might put in front of him, and he's prepared a definitive answer for each one. Rudi has a lofty view of himself—he is convinced he's anticipated every possibility and can overcome them all.

It's true that Rudi has answers to all the questions. He hasn't left anything out, and there's no way they can be rebutted. But what he hasn't prepared for is that there won't be an objection. There's no way he could have anticipated the scene that awaits him when he reaches the hut in which Hirsch has a tiny room of his own.

The determined registrar walks energetically into the hut, knocks on Hirsch's door, and when there's no answer, resolutely walks in. He sees Fredy stretched out on his bunk. When he approaches the bunk to wake him, he notices with alarm that Fredy is breathing with great difficulty, his face blue. Hirsch is dying.

Rudi races from the hut, shouting for help like a madman. He returns with two doctors who were already gathering their few instruments in preparation for their return to the family camp before nightfall, as Mengele had ordered. Their examination of Rudi is short. They repeat it two more times and consult each other in whispers with grave expressions on their faces.

"It's a serious case of poisoning; an overdose of sedatives. There's nothing we can do for him."

Alfred Hirsch's life is expiring.

Rudi Rosenberg feels his heart skip a beat and almost faints. He has to lean against the wooden wall to remain upright. He looks over, undoubtedly for the last time, at the great athlete. The metal whistle on Hirsch's chest is still. He realizes with horror that, in the end, the great man has been unable to bear the thought of taking his young charges to certain death. He has decided to depart first.

Rosenberg, overwhelmed with anxiety, thinks there might just be time to find another leader, that Schmulewski will find some other way of starting the revolt. He rushes off, but when he tries to leave the camp to go and talk to the head of the Resistance, things have changed: He encounters a swarm of SS guards. The quarantine camp has been sealed. Nobody can enter or leave, under any circumstances.

Rudi walks up to the fence separating him from camp BIIb and signals to a member of the Resistance, who is permanently wandering up and down on his own side of the fence, that he wants to have a word. He tells the Resistance member that he has to get some crucial information to Schmulewski right away.

"Fredy Hirsch has committed suicide. For the love of God, tell Schmulewski!"

The man says it's impossible; they've just been given orders that no one can leave the family camp. Rudi turns back and makes his way along the quarantine camp's *Lagerstrasse* with difficulty. It has become a nervous anthill teeming with inmates and armed guards, all on edge.

Alice, Helena, and Vera come to meet him. He hurriedly explains the situation: Fredy Hirsch will never ever lead anything again, and Schmulewski is out of reach. The separation of the three camps has now become an abyss.

"But the uprising can start anyway," the girls say to him. "You give the order, and we'll get things going."

He tries to explain to them that it's not that simple, that things don't work like that, that he's not authorized to make a decision of such magnitude without an order from Schmulewski. They don't quite understand what he's telling them. Rudi is worn out.

"I can't make that decision; I'm a nobody. . . ."

Right now, proud Rosenberg feels that he's the most insignificant man on earth. Not only does he feel that everything is falling down around him, but that he's going to pieces, too.

Inside the family camp, the news is bouncing from one mouth to the next. It's as brief as a telegram announcing a death. The shortest sentences are the most devastating; there's no chance for a reply. The news continues on its way around the camp like a bulldozer, leaving a trail of destruction in its path.

Fredy Hirsch is dead.

The rumor grows, and the word *suicide* begins to be heard. And the word *Luminal*, a sleeping pill that is deadly if taken in large quantities.

Rozsi Krausz, a Block 31 assistant from Hungary, rushes into the barrack looking shaken. Her eyes are bright with fear. She can barely say the words in Czech, but rather than sounding comical, her strange Hungarian accent adds a mournful note to the news: Fredy Hirsch is dead.

She can't say more; there's nothing more to add. She collapses onto a stool and starts to sob.

Some people don't want to believe her. Others don't know what to think. More assistants begin to arrive, their faces ashen, and the children's smiles gradually disappear as they stop singing and playing games. Their faces reflect more fear than sadness. A shiver runs down hundreds of spines. Death had not managed to enter Block 31 even once in the past six months. They had managed miraculously to keep all the children alive. And now the miracle worker himself is dead. Everyone wants to know how, why—although at heart, what they really want to ask is, *What's going to happen to them without Fredy?* Whistles blow, and sharp commands are shouted in German ordering everybody to return to their huts immediately for the evening roll call.

Liesl is already waiting for Dita. She gives her a hug. They all know that Hirsch is dead. Mother and daughter don't need to say anything; they simply stand cheek to cheek for a moment and close their eyes tightly.

Their new *Blockältester* climbs up on top of the horizontal chimney that runs across the floor and calls for silence so angrily that all the muttering stops. She's Jewish, not much older than eighteen, but she's now the one with the power. She's going to hand out the soup and bread rations. She won't go hungry anymore, and she won't have to wear those wooden clogs that smell foul, because she'll be able to buy some boots on the black market with the pieces of bread she hides away. That's why she won't allow herself to waver. If the camp *Kapo* or the SS order her to shout, shout she will; and if they ask her to hit the inmates, that's what she'll do. In fact, she'll shout and hit them before the SS order her to do it. And double what they ask, so she lives up to their expectations. First off, she shouts rudely that they are forbidden to go outside the hut until the wake-up call the next morning. The guards will shoot to kill anyone who does.

Dita has spent so much time longing to have a bunk to herself, but now that she's finally got it, she can't sleep. Night has fallen on Birkenau, the camps are silent, and the only sounds outside are the wind and the monotonous hum of the electrified barbed wire fences. So much time wanting to sleep by herself, and now she doesn't know how—she can't. Eventually, she jumps from her bunk and walks over to her mother, who also has a bunk to herself. She snuggles up beside her mother as she used to do when she was a little girl having nightmares. When that happened, she'd climb into her parents' bed, because nothing bad could happen to her there.

Rudi tries again to access camp BIId to inform Schmulewski. His excuse is that he has to hand over some important papers, but permission is denied. He insists, saying that they have to transfer Hirsch's body, but permission is again denied. He returns to the fence to talk to his contact in BIIb, but he's not there; everyone is inside the huts, and contact is impossible.

Rudi returns to his tiny cubicle and, a short while later, goes out again, hoping that they'll have changed the guard on the gate and that this time, he'll be able to persuade the NCO to allow him into camp BIId. Just then, a horde of *Kapos* brought in from other camps swarm into the quarantine camp. They're armed with clubs,

and they start to hit people and shout at them to gather into two
groups quickly, men on one side and women on the other. Beatings
follow, and the sound of whistles, and howls of pain and panic.

Alice runs toward Rudi and grabs hold of his arm. A guard
yells viciously that the men and women must separate: *"Männer
hier, und Frauen hier!"*

Blows from the clubs rain down around Rudi and Alice, and
blood splatters the mud. Alice separates herself from Rudi without
taking her eyes off him, without abandoning her sad smile. They
push her in the direction of a group of women prisoners and hurriedly lead them to a truck parked at the entrance to the camp.
Vehicles keep arriving until there's a row of trucks waiting with
their engines idling.

Rudi is momentarily paralyzed, and the crowd begins to drag
him along toward a group of men huddled together to protect
themselves from the blows. Suddenly he realizes that he's being
absorbed into the group of men they're shoving toward the death
trucks.

He tries to walk against the flow before the mob swallows him
up. The *Kapos* with their clubs, and the SS guards with their machine guns are making sure that no one escapes: They kick and shove
anyone who tries. Rudi puts a cigarette in his mouth, faking a
calmness he doesn't feel, and forcefully pushes other prisoners out
of his way so he can reach a *Kapo* he knows by sight who's standing
on the edge of the group.

Before the *Kapo* can bring his club down on Rudi to force him
back into the group, Rudi yells out that he's the secretary of Hut 14—

"The block chief has ordered me to report to him immediately."

The *Kapo* is a German with the badge of the common prisoners.
He gives Rudi a quick look in the midst of the surrounding

maelstrom, recognizes him, and stops his club in midflight. He gestures at a soldier with a submachine gun, and they let him leave. A man who grabs hold of Rudi's jacket and tries to leave with him is hit in the ribs with the submachine gun. Rudi hears him pleading, but he doesn't turn around. He walks away, trying to feign indifference, but his legs almost collapse under him.

As he walks to his hut, he hears the noise of the shouts, the orders, the sobs, the truck doors slamming shut, the engines moving off. He thinks about Alice. He remembers her doe eyes looking at him for the last time, and shakes his head as if he wants to shake off the memory so that it won't weigh him down. He continues on his way, walking quickly, and finally reaches his room and shuts himself inside.

There's no documentary evidence to indicate if Rudi Rosenberg cried.

Dita is still awake in her bunk, as are all the women. It's so quiet you can even hear the sound of brakes squealing again and again on the damp ground and trucks coming to a halt with their engines still running. More and more trucks.

And then the night explodes. Shouts, whistles, sobs, pleas, cries to an absent God erupt in the camp next door. And then the sound of truck doors being slammed is heard again, immediately followed by the screech of metal bolts. Cries of panic have given way to the sound of sobs and pitiful moans, the sound of hundreds of voices intermingling in a confused storm of screams.

Nobody sleeps in the family camp. Nobody speaks; nobody moves. In Dita's hut, when someone anxiously asks, "What's happening? What will happen to them?" in a loud voice, the other women, irritated, quickly tell her to be quiet and demand total silence. They have to keep listening so they know exactly what's happening, or maybe they want complete silence so the SS officers won't hear them, won't notice them, and will let them stay alive on their filthy bunks—at least for a little longer.

The metallic bang of truck doors rings out and the sound of the voices dies down. The rumble of the engines suggests that the first lot of loaded trucks is moving off. And then Dita, her mother, and all the other occupants of the hut think they can hear music—perhaps a hallucination produced by their own distress. But then the sound grows in volume.

"Is that voices singing?"

The chorus is drowning out the growl of the trucks. A perplexed voice says it out loud, and other voices repeat it, as if they find it so hard to believe that they have to tell everyone else, or themselves, about it—"They are singing! The male and female prisoners being taken away in the trucks to die are singing!"

They can make out the Czech national anthem, "Kde Domov Můj?"—Where Is My Home?—and as another truck goes by, it carries the notes of the Jewish anthem, "Hatikvah," while from yet another truck, "The Internationale" can be heard. The music inevitably sounds broken, like a fugue, and diminishes as the trucks move away. The voices shrink until they disappear. On this night, thousands of voices are switched off forever.

During the night of March 8, 1944, 3,792 prisoners from the family camp BIIb were gassed and then incinerated in Crematorium III of Auschwitz–Birkenau.

20.

THE NEXT MORNING, DITA DOESN'T NEED TO WAIT FOR THE YELLS
of the *Kapo* to wake her, because she hasn't managed to get to
sleep. Her mother gives her a kiss, and then Dita jumps off her
bunk and sets off to Block 31 for roll call, as she does every day.
Except this isn't a day like all the others; half the people who used
to be with her have gone and won't return.

Despite the risk of attracting the attention of some *Kapo* or
guard, Dita turns off the *Lagerstrasse* and heads for the rear of the
huts closest to the fence. She looks over into the quarantine camp
with the remote hope of finding someone alive. But there's nothing
moving among the huts of camp BIIa, except for the odd scrap of
material torn from some piece of clothing fluttering on the ground.

Nothing remains of the shouts from the previous night; just a
thick silence. The camp is deserted. It's as quiet as a cemetery. The
ground is strewn with trampled hats, an abandoned coat, and
empty bowls. The head from one of the clay dolls the children
made in Block 31 peeps out from among the other objects. Dita
spies something white lying on top of the mud: a wrinkled scrap of
paper. She closes her eyes to stop herself from looking at it any
longer. It's one of Professor Morgenstern's origami birds, trampled
and crushed in the mud.

And that's exactly how Dita feels.

Seppl Lichtenstern has been charged with carrying out the roll call this morning under the impassive gaze of an SS guard, but once the guard leaves the hut, everyone relaxes a little. The children have spent the whole time looking from side to side for those who are missing. No matter how much the daily roll call normally irritates the children, its brevity this morning has shattered them.

Dita heads outside to escape the feeling of oppression in the barrack. But although dawn broke a short time ago, something is darkening the atmosphere. The breeze is carrying a dry rain that is making everything dirty. Ash. A black snowfall the likes of which has never been seen before.

The people working in the ditches look skyward. Those hauling stones leave them on the ground and come to a standstill. The people in the workshops stop laboring, despite the yells of the *Kapos*, and go outside to look, in what could be their first act of rebellion—looking up at the black sky, indifferent to orders and threats.

Night seems suddenly to have returned.

"My God! What is it?" someone asks.

"It's God's curse!" cries another.

Dita looks up, and her face, hands, and dress are spotted with tiny gray flakes that disintegrate between her fingers. The inhabitants of Block 31 come outside to see what's going on.

"What's happening?" asks a frightened little girl.

"Don't be afraid," says Miriam Edelstein to the children. "It's our friends from the September transport. They're returning."

Children and teachers crowd together in silence. Many of them quietly pray. Dita cups her hands so she can catch some of that rain of souls, unable to hold back her tears, which form white furrows down her blackened face. Miriam Edelstein is hugging her son, Arieh, and Dita joins them.

"They've come back, Dita. They've come back."

They'll never leave Auschwitz again.

Some teachers have stood their ground and say they won't teach any classes. For some, it's a way of protesting, while others simply find themselves incapable of carrying on. Lichtenstern tries to raise their morale, but he lacks the charisma and the self-confidence of Fredy Hirsch. And he can't cover up the fact that he, too, is demoralized.

One of the teachers asks what happened to Hirsch. Others gather around crestfallen, as if they were at a funeral. Someone says he was told that Hirsch was loaded into one of the trucks on a stretcher, either dying or already dead.

"I think he killed himself out of pride. He was too proud to allow himself to be killed by the Nazis. He wasn't going to give them that pleasure."

"I think that when he saw his own German compatriots had tricked and betrayed him, he couldn't bear it."

"Children suffering is what he couldn't bear."

Dita listens, and something stirs inside her, as if she senses that there is something about Hirsch's death that doesn't lend itself to a conventional explanation. She feels not only devastated but confused. *What will happen to the school if Hirsch isn't here to fix everything?* She's found a spot on a stool as far away as possible from all the others, but she can see Lichtenstern, thin and clumsy, coming her way. He's nervous, and he'd give ten years of his life for a cigarette.

"The children are frightened, Edita. Look at them, they're not moving; they're not talking."

"We're all angry, Seppl."

"We have to do something."

"Do? What can we do?"

"The only thing we can do is carry on. We have to make these children respond. Read something to them."

Dita looks around and sees that the children have gradually sat down on the ground in silent groups, biting their nails and gazing up at the ceiling. They've never been so depressed or so quiet. Dita feels weak, and she has a bitter taste in her mouth. What she'd really like to do is stay on her stool without moving or speaking or having someone talk to her, and never get up again.

"And what am I going to read to them?"

Seppl Lichtenstern opens his mouth, but no words come out, so he closes it again and, somewhat embarrassed, looks down. He admits that he doesn't know about books, and they can't ask Miriam Edelstein because she's too overcome. She's sitting at the back with her head in her hands, refusing to speak to anyone.

"You're the librarian of Block Thirty-One," Lichtenstern reminds her sharply.

Dita nods in agreement. She must assume her responsibility. No one has to remind her of that.

As she makes her way to the *Blockältester*'s cubicle, she wishes she could ask Mr. Utitz, the chief librarian at Terezín, which would be the most appropriate book for her to read to the children under these tragic circumstances. She has a serious novel, some math books, and some books about understanding the world. But before she has even lifted the pile of rags which hide the trapdoor to the hidey-hole, she's already made up her mind.

She takes out the messiest of the books—little more than a bundle of unbound sheets. It may be the least suitable, the least pedagogic, and the most irreverent of them all. There are even teachers who disapprove of it, finding it indecent and in poor taste.

But those who believe that flowers grow in vases don't understand anything about literature. The library has now become her first-aid kit, and she's going to give the children a little of the medicine that helped her recover her smile when she thought she'd lost it forever.

Lichtenstern gestures to one of the assistants to go and stand guard at the door, and Dita sits on a stool in the middle of the hut. The odd child looks at her with halfhearted curiosity, but most of them continue to examine the tips of their clogs. She opens the book, finds a page and starts to read. Maybe they can hear her, but no one is listening. The children are listless; many of them are lying on the floor. The teachers continue to whisper among themselves, chewing over what they know about the deaths of the September group. Even Lichtenstern is sitting on a stool, his eyes closed in an attempt to distance himself.

Dita is reading for nobody.

She begins with a scene in which the Czech soldiers, under orders from the Austrian high command, are traveling by train to the front, and Švejk's outrageous opinions manage to irritate an arrogant lieutenant called Dub, who inspects the troops when they reach their destination. He paces back and forth accompanied by his habitual refrain. "Do you know me?" he says. "Well, I'm telling you that you don't really know me! But when you do know me I'll reduce you to tears, you idiots!" The lieutenant asks them if they have any brothers, and when they say they do, he shouts that their brothers must be just as stupid as they are.

The sad-faced children are still sitting in their corners, although the odd one has stopped chewing his nails and a few others have even stopped staring at the ceiling and are watching Dita as she continues to toss words into the air. A few of the teachers have also turned their heads toward her, although they haven't entirely abandoned their conversations. They can't quite work out what Dita is doing on her stool. Dita goes on reading until the grim-faced lieutenant comes across Švejk, who's criticizing a propaganda poster in which an Austrian soldier is using his bayonet to skewer a Russian Cossack to a wall.

> *"What is it about the poster that you don't like?" Lieutenant Dub asks him rudely.*
>
> *"What I don't like is the careless way in which the soldier is handling his regulation weapon, sir. The bayonet could snap when it hits the wall. Moreover, it's a fairly useless action, because the Russian already has his hands in the air, so he's surrendered. He's now a prisoner, and you have to treat prisoners properly, because they're people, too."*
>
> *"Are you insinuating that you feel sorry for that Russian enemy soldier?" the lieutenant asks maliciously.*
>
> *"I feel sorry for both of them, sir. The Russian because he's been bayoneted, and the soldier because they'll lock him up for what he's done. He must have broken his bayonet, sir, since the wall is stone and steel is not as strong. While I was finishing my military service, before the war, we had a sublieutenant who used more swear words than a veteran. On the parade ground, he used to shout at us: 'When I say "attention," you have to stare straight in front of you the way a cat does when it's relieving itself.' But other than that, he was a very sensible person. One time, at Christmas, he went crazy and bought a cartload of coconuts for the whole company. Ever since that day, I know how fragile bayonets are: Half the company snapped their bayonets, one after another, when they tried to open the*

coconuts, and the sublieutenant had us locked up for three days."

Some of the children are now paying attention while others who were farther away have moved closer so they can hear better. Some of the teachers are still talking, but others are telling them to be quiet. Dita reads on with gentle determination. The sound of the words and Švejk's wisecracks have gradually silenced the muttering.

"They arrested our sublieutenant as well, and I was really sorry because he was a good person apart from his fixation with coconuts . . ."

Lieutenant Dub glares furiously at the childlike face of the good soldier Švejk and angrily asks him:

"Do you know me?"

"Yes, sir, I know you."

Lieutenant Dub's eyes are popping out of his head. He starts to stamp his feet and roar:

"No, you don't know me yet."

And Švejk answers in his sweet, deliberate way:

"Yes, I know you, sir. You belong to our battalion."

"I'm telling you that you still don't know me!" the lieutenant yells again, beside himself. "You may know my good side, but when you get to know my bad side you'll shake with fright: I'm tough and I make people cry. So, do you, or do you not, know me?"

"Of course I know you, sir."

"I'm telling you for the last time that you don't know me, you ass. Do you have any brothers?"

"At your service, sir; I have one."

*At the sight of Švejk's guileless face and good-natured
expression, the lieutenant becomes furious and shouts even
louder:*

*"So your brother will be an animal just like you; he must
be a complete idiot."*

"Yes, sir, a complete idiot."

"And what does your complete idiot of a brother do?"

*"He was a teacher, and when he was called up because of
the war, they made him a lieutenant."*

*Lieutenant Dub looks daggers at Švejk, who's watching
him with a kindhearted look on his face. Red with rage, Dub
yells at him to get lost.*

Some children laugh. From the back of the hut, Miriam Edelstein peeks out through her fingers. Dita continues to read more
unexpected events and adventures of that soldier who, by pretending to be a fool, ridicules war, any war. Miriam looks up at her librarian. That small book with its stories has managed to bring the
whole hut together.

When Dita shuts her book, the children stand up and move
about again, even running around the hut. Life has been recon-
nected. Dita caresses the old spine of the book which has been
sewn back together with thread, and she feels happy because she
knows that Fredy would be proud of her. She has fulfilled the
promise she made to him: to keep going and never give up. A veil
of sadness nevertheless falls over her. *Why did he give up?*

21.

MENGELE WALKS THROUGH THE ENTRANCE TO THE FAMILY CAMP
accompanied by the sound of Wagner's Valkyries and a blast of cold.
He studies everything that moves around him. He appears to have
X-ray eyes. He looks as if he's searching for something, or someone,
but Dita is inside Block 31. She's safe there . . . at least for now.

They say that one of the deeds most celebrated by Rudolf
Höss, the former *Kommandant* of Auschwitz, was the way in which,
toward the end of 1943, Mengele put a stop to a serious outbreak of
typhus that was already affecting seven thousand women. The fever
was out of control because the huts were infested with lice. But
Mengele came up with a solution. He ordered an entire hut of six
hundred women to be sent to the gas chamber and then had their
hut disinfected from top to bottom. Bathtubs with disinfection kits
were placed outdoors and all the women from the next hut were ordered to go through disinfection before being sent into the clean
hut. Then the hut *they* had been occupying was disinfected, and
this procedure was followed with all the women in the camp. And that
was how Mengele succeeded in putting an end to the epidemic.

High command congratulated the doctor. They even wanted to
give him a medal. This was the criterion that governed his behavior: Global results and scientific advancement were fundamental;
the human lives abandoned in his wake were unimportant.

A senior sergeant brings him his twins. The children approach somewhat timidly and greet him in chorus with, "Good day, Uncle Pepi." He smiles at them, ruffles little Irene's hair, and they all head off to his quarters in Camp F, which the SS guards refer to as the Zoo when Mengele isn't around.

Several pathologists work there under Mengele's orders. The children have good food, clean sheets, and even toys and treats. But whenever they go inside that place with the doctor, their parents' hearts seem to stop beating until they return. So far, these children have always returned happy, with a bun in their pocket as a reward, and tales of being measured all over, having their blood tested, and being given the occasional injection, after which the doctor always gives them a candy bar.

Other children haven't been so lucky. Mengele has been researching the effects of illness on twins; in the Gypsy camp, he injected various sets of twins with typhus to see how they reacted, and then he killed them so he could carry out autopsies to study the evolution of the organism in each twin.

But this time, Mengele strokes the heads of his twins and even smiles affectionately at them as he says good-bye.

"Don't forget Uncle Pepi!" he tells them, because he has no intention of forgetting them.

Forgetting is not a choice. Days of funereal routine have gone by in Auschwitz, but Dita can't forget. Actually, she doesn't want to forget. Fredy Hirsch suddenly turned off the tap of his life, but a question persistently drips onto her head and bores into her brain: *Why?*

She continues to perform her duties as librarian—managing her books at the end of each lesson—but she has withdrawn into herself. She's pleased to see how Block 31 keeps going despite everything. Nevertheless, perhaps because there are fewer of them, everything seems smaller, more commonplace even, since Hirsch has gone.

Dita's assistant today is a very likeable boy who's even handsome, with a sprinkling of cinnamon-colored freckles over his face. She might have tried to be friendlier toward him on another occasion, as there aren't too many good-looking boys around, but she barely responds when he tries to start a conversation. Her mind is somewhere else.

She continues to work over in her head the question of why Hirsch took his own life.

It's not like him.

Given everything he'd put up with and how disciplined he was—his personality was a combination of German and Jewish traits—running away from his responsibilities seems abnormal. Dita shakes her head, and the sway of her hair back and forth duplicates that *no*—there's a piece missing from the puzzle. Fredy told her they were soldiers and they had to fight to the end. How is it possible that he would abandon his post? No, it doesn't fit with Fredy Hirsch's logic. He was a soldier. He had a mission. It's true he was more melancholy than usual when she saw him that last afternoon, more fragile, maybe. He probably knew that the transfer bore all the signs of ending badly. But she doesn't understand why he committed suicide. And Dita can't bear not being able to understand something. She's stubborn, as her mother always tells her. And her mother is right: Dita is one of those people who never leave a jigsaw puzzle unfinished.

That's why, when her work is done in Block 31, she goes straight to her barrack. She takes advantage of her mother being on her own with Mrs. Turnovská.

"Excuse me for interrupting, Mrs. Turnovská, but there's something I'd like to ask you."

"Edita, must you always be so abrupt?" says her mother reproachfully.

Mrs. Turnovská smiles. She's delighted when young women consult her about things.

"Let her be. Talking with young people keeps me young, my dear Liesl." And she giggles.

"It's to do with Fredy Hirsch. You know who he was, right?"

Mrs. Turnovská gives a slight huffy nod. She finds Dita's question almost insulting.

"I'd like to know what they're saying about his death."

"He poisoned himself with those dreadful pills. They say pills cure everything, but I don't believe it. If the doctor recommends pills for my cold, I never take them. I've always preferred to inhale eucalyptus oil vapor."

"How right you are; I used to do the same. Have you tried to boil mint leaves?" asks Dita's mother.

"Actually, no I haven't—on their own or mixed with eucalyptus?" Dita grunts.

"I already know about the pills, but I want to know why he did it! What are they saying out there, Mrs. Turnovská?"

"Oh, my dear, they're saying so many things! That man's death has generated a lot of talk."

"Edita always said he was a good man," Dita's mother responds.

"Of course. Although being a good person in life isn't enough. My poor husband, may he rest in peace, was a really good person, but he was also so timid that there was no way we could make a go of the fruit shop. The farmers all fobbed off on him the overripe fruit that no one else would accept."

"Fine," interrupted Dita, on the point of exploding, "but what are they saying about Hirsch?"

"I've heard all sorts of things, child. Some say he was scared of being gassed; others that he was addicted to pills and overdid it. Someone commented that he did it out of sadness when he saw they were going to kill the children. One woman explained to me—as if it was a secret—that they had cast the evil eye on him, because there are Nazis who practice black magic."

"I think I know who you're talking about—"

"I also heard something beautiful. . . . Somebody said it was an act of rebellion. He killed himself so that the Nazis couldn't do it."

"And who do you think is right?"

"I can assure you that each theory sounded right at the time the person was presenting it."

Dita nods and says good-bye to the two women. Discovering the truth in Auschwitz is like catching snowflakes with Professor Morgenstern's butterfly net. Truth is the first casualty of war. But Dita is determined to find it, no matter how deeply buried in the mud it is.

And that's why that same night, when her mother has already climbed into her bunk, Dita scurries off to Radio Birkenau's bunk.

"Mrs. Turnovská . . ."

"What is it, Edita?"

"There's something I want to ask you . . . and I'm sure you have the answer."

"That's possible," she replies with a hint of vanity. "You can ask me about anything you like. I have no secrets from you."

"Can you give me the name of someone in the Resistance I could contact?"

"But, my dear girl . . ." Mrs. Turnovská already regrets having said that there are no secrets between them. "That's not a matter for young girls. It's very dangerous. Your mother would never speak to me if I led you to the Resistance."

"I don't want to enlist; although now that you mention it, that might not be such a bad idea. But given my age, I'm sure they wouldn't want me. I just want to ask one of them about Fredy Hirsch. They must know better than anyone what happened to him."

"You already know that the last person to see him was the registrar of the quarantine camp, Rosenberg—"

"I know, but it's really difficult to get hold of him. If I could talk to someone from this camp . . . please."

Mrs. Turnovská grumbles a little longer.

"All right, but don't tell him I sent you. There's a man from Prague called Alter. He's assigned to workshop three, and he's easy to recognize because his head is as smooth as a billiard ball and his enormous nose looks like a potato. But I know nothing."

"Thank you. I owe you."

"You don't owe me anything, my dear. You don't owe anyone anything. In here, we've all more than paid our debts."

Dita spends the next day in Block 31.

The following day, classes are somewhat less rowdy, but with the usual feeling of hunger and fear that it might be the last day ever. Once the day is done, she'll see if she can find that Alter person.

It's one of those days when she has to help Miriam Edelstein improvise a handwriting lesson for a group of seven-year-old girls. It's raining, so this afternoon there are no outdoor games or sports. The children are grumpy because they haven't been able to play Steal the Bacon or hopscotch, and Dita is disgruntled because it's been raining for a few days and people have taken shelter in their huts. That's why she hasn't been able to find the bald-headed man.

Miriam Edelstein hides her anguish from the children, but Hirsch's death has left her feeling abandoned. On top of that, she's heard nothing more about her husband, Yakub, since Eichmann's visit to the family camp, when he told her that her husband had been transferred to Germany and that he was perfectly fine.

But what she doesn't know is that Eichmann lied. The truth is quite different: Yakub continues to be a prisoner in the horrendous prison in Auschwitz I, just three kilometers from Birkenau. There are cells in that prison that are cement cupboards in which the prisoners can't even sit down, and they have to sleep standing up; their legs fuse together. The torture is methodical: electric shocks, whippings, injections. One of the tortures the guards find most entertaining is fake executions. They take the prisoners out to the courtyard, blindfold them, cock their rifles, and then, when the prisoners start to shake or lose control of their bodily functions, there's the sound of a metallic click from the unloaded guns. Then the guards take the prisoners back inside. Executions are, in fact, so frequent that they don't even clean the wall where the prisoners stand, and a reddish line of hair and brains snakes along the wall marking the average height of the victims.

Dita makes an effort to help file down the tips of the girls' spoons on a stone. Those whose spoons are done use them to sharpen the ends of splinters of wood into points. Sometimes the splinters have knots in them and can't be used; at other times, the point snaps off and the process begins again. After a tiring hour's work, the girls have splinters with sharp tips. Then Miriam carefully sets fire to some wood shavings in a saucepan, and scorches the ends of the splinters. Each splinter becomes a crude, sooty pencil with which the children can write three or four words. Paper is a scarce commodity, too, and Lichtenstern acquires it, a scrap at a time, by telling the Nazis he has to prepare lists.

Miriam dictates a few words to the girls, which they painstakingly write down. Dita stands to one side to watch them kneeling on the floor and using the stools as desks. It might all be very basic, but the girls work hard at their handwriting. The librarian picks up one of the pencil-splinters and a piece of paper. She hasn't drawn for a long time, and her fingers fly over the paper, but the sooty tip wears out very quickly. Miriam Edelstein leans over Dita's shoulder to have a look. She sees some vertical lines and a circle— that's all the pencil was good for—but despite that, her eyes open wide in recognition.

"Prague's astronomical clock," she says wistfully.

"You recognized it. . . ."

"I'd recognize it even if it were at the bottom of the sea. For me, it represents the Prague of clockmakers and artisans."

"Everyday life."

"Life, yes."

Dita feels the deputy director's hand putting something inside the top of her woolen sock, and then, as if nothing had happened, they go back to correcting the girls' work. When Dita touches her leg, she notices a small bump. It's a real lead pencil. It's the best present she's been given in years. And it's because of acts like this that everyone now calls Miriam Edelstein Aunt Miriam.

Dita spends the rest of the afternoon working busily on her drawing of Prague's astronomical clock, with its skeleton, its rooster, its zodiac spheres, its patriarchs, and its leaning gargoyles. Several children have discovered that she's drawing and come over to watch. Not all of them are from Prague, and some of those who were born there don't even remember their city. Dita patiently explains that a skeleton rings a bell on the hour and then the figures begin to file out of one door and into another.

When her drawing is done, she carefully folds it and goes over to Arieh, Miriam's son, who's holding hands with some other boys and playing a game of semaphores. She puts the piece of paper in his pocket and tells him it's a present for his mother.

Since she needs to keep herself occupied with something, she takes time to reglue Freud's essay, which was out on loan and has returned with some of the spine unstuck. She also runs her hands over the pages, smoothing them down one by one after the hard day they've had.

SS First Officer Viktor Pestek is also happy as he brushes and then messes up Renée Neumann's curls.

Renée lets him do it. She doesn't allow him to kiss her or come any closer. But when Viktor begged her to let him brush her hair, she either couldn't or didn't know how to refuse him, or maybe she didn't want to.

He's a Nazi, a repressor, a criminal . . . but he treats her with a respect that's hard to find among her own companions in the camp. At night, Renée has to sleep with her bowl under her arm or tied to her foot because robberies are frequent. There are women who sell their own bodies, and informers. There are also some very upright, staid, religious people who insult her and call her a slut for giving her mother a piece of fruit that was a present from an SS officer.

By contrast, the time she spends with Viktor is a moment of calm. Viktor—who does most of the talking while she listens—has told her that he worked on a farm before the war. She pictures him carrying bales of hay. If this damned war hadn't broken out, he'd probably be an ordinary, honest, hardworking boy like any other. Who knows, she might even have fallen in love with him.

But this particular afternoon, Viktor is much more nervous than usual. He brings her a present each time they meet. He's learned his lesson—this time he brings her a sausage wrapped up in paper. But the present he wants to offer her is something else.

"A plan, Renée."

She looks at him.

"I have a plan for us to get away from here, get married, and start a new life together."

She doesn't say a word.

"I have it all worked out. We'll walk out through the gate without raising any suspicions."

"You're mad . . ."

"No, no. You'll be wearing an SS uniform. It will be after night has fallen. I'll give the password, and we'll calmly walk out. You mustn't say a word, of course. We'll catch a train and go to Prague. I've got a contact in that city. I've made some friends among the prisoners; they know I'm not like the other SS guards. We'll get some forged documents and head to Romania. And we'll wait there for the war to end."

Renée looks carefully at this thin, rather short, somewhat awkward guard with his black hair and blue eyes.

"You'd do that for me?"

"I'd do anything for you, Renée. Will you come with me?"

There's no doubt that love and madness have some common features.

Renée sighs. To get out of Auschwitz is the dream of each and every one of the thousands of prisoners caught between the fences and the crematoriums. She looks up, tugs on one of her curls and nibbles at it.

"No."

"But you mustn't be scared. It will work. It will be one of the days when some of my friends are on duty. There'll be no hitch—it will be easy. . . . Staying here is just waiting for your turn to die."

"I can't leave my mother here by herself."

"But Renée, we're young—she'll understand. We have a life in front of us."

"I'm not going to leave my mother. There's nothing more to discuss. Don't insist."

"Renée—"

"I've told you there's nothing more to discuss. It doesn't matter what you say, I won't change my mind."

Pestek thinks for a moment. He's never been a pessimist.

"Then we'll get your mother out as well."

Renée starts to get annoyed. It all sounds like a lot of hot air, something entertaining that she doesn't find the least bit amusing. There's no risk for Pestek, but there certainly is for herself and her mother. They're in no position to go around playing games about getting out of Auschwitz, as if it were a cinema where, if you got tired of the movie, you could just get up from your seat and leave.

"For us, being in here isn't a game, Viktor. My father died of typhus, and my cousin and his wife were killed with the rest of the September transport. Forget it. This escape game isn't funny."

"Do you think I'm joking? You still don't know me. If I say I'm going to get you and your mother out of here, then that's what I'm going to do."

"That's impossible, and you know it. She's a tiny fifty-two-year-old woman with rheumatism. Are you going to dress her up as an SS guard?"

"We'll modify the plan. Let me work on it."

Renée looks at him and doesn't know what to think. Is there even the remotest possibility that Viktor is capable of getting the two women out of there alive? And if they got out, what would happen after that? Would two Jewish women escapees from Auschwitz and a traitor be able to hide themselves from the Nazis? And even if they could . . . would she link her life to that of a Nazi, even if he was a deserter? Does she want to spend the rest of her life with someone who, up till now, has not been troubled when it's time to take hundreds of innocent people to their death?

Too many questions.

Once again, she falls silent. She limits herself to not saying anything, and Pestek understands her silence as acceptance, because that's what he wants to believe.

It finally stopped raining, so Dita took advantage of the soup break to try and find the man from the Resistance. But the earth, which had become a sticky, muddy quagmire, seemed to have swallowed him up. She was circling the workshop when the prisoners had their break, but she didn't come across him.

Now, sitting on her bench, she carefully smooths out the wrinkles in the French novel, which is missing its front and back covers, and applies some glue to its spine. The glue comes from Margit, who secretly removed it from the workshop to which she's assigned, where they make military boots. Dita wants to do a thorough repair job on the book before she lends it to the only person who ever asks for it, a teacher with a somewhat sour disposition called

Markéta. She has straight hair that is too gray for her age, and her arms are like sticks. They say she was governess to the children of a government minister before the war. She teaches one of the groups of nine-year-old girls, and Dita occasionally overhears her teaching a few words of French to her pupils, who are very attentive because she's always telling them that it's the language spoken by elegant young ladies. To Dita, the musical words sound like a language invented by troubadours.

Although Dita found Markéta somewhat distant and not interested in conversation, the teacher had asked Dita for the novel so many times that one day, Dita asked her if she knew the book. Markéta looked her up and down in utter amazement.

Thanks to Markéta, Dita was able to catalogue the book formally by its title and author, *The Count of Monte Cristo* by Alexandre Dumas. The teacher also told her that it was a famous book in France.

Today, Markéta asked her if she could have the book for a while, so once Dita has finished fixing it, she goes over to the stool where the teacher is sitting by herself, sunk in her thoughts. Markéta rarely talks to anyone, but Dita has given some consideration as to how she can approach her, and now is the time. The hut is quiet because Avi Fischer's choir is having a rehearsal down the back, and they've driven everyone else away with their warbling. Without waiting to be invited, Dita plonks herself down on the neighboring stool.

"I'd like to know what this book is about. Would you tell me?"

If the teacher tells her to get lost, she'll get up and walk away. But Markéta gives her a look and, against all the odds, doesn't send her away. Rather, she seems glad of Dita's company. And what's even more surprising is that this woman of few words begins to tell her the story with unexpected warmth.

"The Count of Monte Cristo . . ."

She talks to Dita about a young man called Edmond Dantès, whose name she pronounces the French way, with very open and striking vowels, thereby instantly granting him a literary pedigree. She says that Edmond is an honest, strapping, young man, who's sailing back to Marseilles in command of the *Pharaon*, and looking forward to seeing his father and his Catalan fiancée.

"He had to take command of the ship after the death of the captain at sea. The captain's dying wish was that Edmond take a letter on his behalf to an address in Paris. Life is treating Edmond well at that stage: The ship owner wants to make him captain, and his fiancée, the lovely Mercédès, loves him madly. They're going to get married right away. But a cousin of Mercédès, who is also wooing her and is an officer on the ship, is angry because he hasn't been named the new captain. He denounces Dantès for treason, and the dead captain's letter incriminates him. It's terrible. So on his wedding day, Dantès plummets from the heights of happiness to the depths of despair when he's arrested during the wedding ceremony and taken as a prisoner to the horrific penal island of If."

"Where's that?"

"It's a small island facing the port of Marseilles. There he'll spend many years locked up in a cell. But Dantès finds a companion in misfortune in a nearby cell, the Abbé Faria. He's an abbot whom all consider mad because he constantly shouts at the warders that if they release him, he'll share a fabulous treasure with them. The abbot has spent years patiently digging a tunnel with tools he himself has made, but he has miscalculated the direction the tunnel should take and, instead of exiting outside the prison wall, he turns up in Dantès's cell. Thanks to the tunnel, about which the warders know nothing, the two cells are now connected, and the two men keep each other company and ease the burden of their imprisonment."

Dita listens carefully. She identifies with Edmond Dantès, an innocent man whom malice has caused to be most unjustly imprisoned, just as has happened to herself and her family.

"What's Dantès like?"

"Strong and handsome, very handsome. And above all else, he is kindhearted, good, and generous."

"And what happens to him? Does he get the liberty he deserves so much?"

"He and Faria plan their escape. They spend years digging a tunnel, and in the meantime, Abbé Faria becomes Dantès's mentor, almost like his father, teaching him history, philosophy, and many other subjects during their hours of imprisonment. But when the tunnel is almost complete, Abbé Faria dies. Their plan falls apart. Just as Dantès thinks freedom is centimeters away, his friend's death wrecks everything."

As if her own misfortune weren't enough for her to worry about, Dita now purses her lips and laments poor Dantès's bad luck. Markéta smiles.

"Dantès is a very resourceful and brave man. After the warders have ascertained that the abbot is dead and have left his cell, Dantès goes through the secret tunnel to Faria's cell, transfers the body of his good friend into his own cell, and lays him down on the bunk. Then he returns to Faria's cell and sews himself inside the dead abbot's body bag. When the people charged with burying the body arrive, they take away Dantès, whose plan is to get out of the bag and escape the moment he's left unattended in the morgue."

"Good plan!"

"Not so good. What he doesn't know is that there is no morgue in the sinister If prison, or burials, because the bodies of the prisoners are thrown into the sea. They throw Dantès, still inside the sack, into the sea from a great height, and so when they discover they've been tricked, they assume that Dantès will have drowned anyway."

"And does he die?" asks Dita anxiously.

"No, there's still a long way to go in the novel. He manages to escape from the bag and, although he's exhausted, he successfully swims to shore. But do you know the best part? Abbé Faria wasn't mad; he really had found treasure. Edmond Dantès goes in search of it, and the riches he finds enable him to adopt a new identity: He becomes the Count of Monte Cristo."

"And does he spend his life living happily ever after?" asks Dita naïvely.

Markéta gives her that look of utter amazement and slight reproach.

"No! How can he go on as if nothing had happened? He does what he has to do. He takes revenge on all those people who betrayed him."

"And is he successful?"

Markéta nods so enthusiastically that there's no question that Dantès ruthlessly exacts revenge. She summarizes the astute and intricate schemes whereby Dantès, now the Count of Monte Cristo, imposes devastating punishment on the people who ruined his life. It's a complex and Machiavellian plan from which there is no escape, even for Mercédès, who when she thought Dantès was dead, finally married her cousin, unaware of his trickery. He shows her no mercy, either. He gets close to all of them, gains their confidence in his role as the rich and worldly count, and then crushes them."

When Markéta finishes her story of the relentless revenge of the Count of Monte Cristo, the two of them fall silent. Dita gets up to go, but before she does so, she turns to the teacher and says, "Markéta . . . you've told the story so well it's almost as if I'd read it. Would you like to be one of our 'living' books? That way we'd have *The Wonderful Adventures of Nils Holgersson*, the stories of the American Indians, the history of the Jews, and now *The Count of Monte Cristo*."

Markéta averts her eyes and looks down at the floor of rammed earth. She's gone back to being the timid and unsociable woman she usually is.

"I'm sorry; that's not possible. I'm fine teaching my girls, but for me to stand up in the middle of the hut . . . definitely not."

Dita sees that just the thought of doing it has made the woman blush. But they can't afford to lose a book, and so Dita quickly thinks about what Fredy Hirsch would have said in a situation like this.

"I know it's a huge effort for you, but . . . for the time the story lasts, the children stop being in a stable full of fleas, they stop smelling burned flesh, they stop being afraid. During those minutes, they're happy. We can't deny this to these children."

The woman agrees a bit reluctantly. "We can't. . . ."

"If we look at our reality, we feel anger and disgust. All we have is our imagination, Markéta."

The teacher finally stops looking at the floor and raises her angular face.

"Add me to the list."

"Thank you, Markéta. Thank you. Welcome to the library."

The teacher tells Dita that it's too late for her to read the book now, and so she'll ask her for it again tomorrow morning.

"I have to go over a few passages."

It strikes Dita that there's a touch of joy in her voice and that there's a new spring in her step as she walks away. Maybe she's coming round to the idea of being a "living" book. Dita sits there quietly a while longer, leafing through the book, whispering the name of Edmond Dantès, and trying to make it sound French. She wonders if she'll manage to get away from where she is, as the protagonist of the novel did. She doesn't think she's as brave as him, although if she had an opportunity to run toward the woods, she wouldn't hesitate.

She also wonders if, were she successful, she'd dedicate her life to taking revenge on all the SS guards and officers, and if she'd do it in the same methodical, implacable, and yes, even merciless, manner as the Count of Monte Cristo. Of course she'd be delighted if they suffered the same pain they inflicted on so many innocent people. But nevertheless, she can't avoid feeling some sadness at the thought that she liked the happy and confident Edmond Dantès of the beginning of the story much more than the calculating, hate-filled man he became. She asks herself, *Can you really choose, or do the blows dealt to you by fate change you no matter what, in the same way that the blow of an ax converts a living tree into firewood?*

The memory pops into her head of her father's last days, when he was dying in the dirty bunk without any medicine to give him relief, slowly being killed by the illness with which the Nazis have allied themselves in their obsession with death. And as she thinks about this, she feels her temples throb with rage and an insatiable hunger for violence. But then she remembers what Professor Morgenstern taught her: *Our hatred is a victory for them.* And she nods in agreement.

If Professor Morgenstern was mad, then lock me up with him.

22.

TWO COMPOUNDS AWAY FROM THE FAMILY CAMP, A SCENE TAKES place that no prisoner wants to witness. But they are given no choice. Rudi Rosenberg, who has come to BIId with some lists, is walking along the *Lagerstrasse* when an SS patrol enters the camp. They are escorting four thin Russians who are still feisty, despite their bruised faces, scraggly beards, and torn clothes. It was Rudi's friend Wetzler, an inmate assigned to the camp morgue, who told him that the Russian prisoners of war were working on the extension to Birkenau on the other side of the camp perimeter. They spent exhausting days stacking up metal sheets and piles of wood.

One of those mornings, when the *Kapo* supervising the Russians disappeared for a few hours to make out with the woman in charge of the group of female prisoners clearing the adjacent land, the four Russian prisoners managed to build a small hideout. They placed four thick planks edgewise to form the walls, with another board on top to form a roof. Then they piled more wooden planks all around, leaving the little hideout buried underneath. Their plan was to wait until the *Kapo* was distracted and then pull aside the board that served as the roof and climb inside the hideout. When it was time for roll call, their absence would be noticed. Assuming they had escaped, the Germans would start to look for them in the forest and surrounding area, because they wouldn't suspect that they were, in fact, hiding outside the electrified perimeter of the camp complex, just a few meters from their own camp fence.

The Germans were methodical. Any escape activated a state of alert that instantly mobilized SS soldiers into search parties and heightened security at the checkpoints in nearby towns for precisely three days. At the end of this time, these special measures came to an end and the SS returned to their normal guard duties. So the Russians would have had to wait inside their hideout for exactly three days and then take advantage of the fourth night to reach the edge of the forest and begin their flight without the added pressure of the special search and capture forces.

The idea of escaping has taken hold of the registrar himself, to the point where it has become an obsession. Some of the camp veterans talk about escape fever as an illness that attacks people in the same way as a contagious disease. There comes a moment when the victim suddenly starts to feel the urgent and unstoppable need to escape. At first, you think about it now and again, then more and more often, and in the end, you're incapable of concentrating on anything else. You spend all day and night planning how to do it.

It has been only a few days since the Russians left their hideout and tried to escape, and Rosenberg watches with a heavy heart as a group of SS soldiers escorts the chained fugitives into the camp with the *Kommandant*, Major Schwarzhuber, bringing up the rear. The prisoners have difficulty walking, with their clothes in shreds and their eyes so swollen there's scarcely a slit to look through. The camp guards use whistles to order all the prisoners out of their huts. Together with those who are already out and about, they are forced to watch the spectacle. The Germans beat anyone who tries to avoid it. They want everyone to see, because punishment and executions are pure teaching tools for the Nazis. There is no better and more practical way of demonstrating to the inmates why they shouldn't escape than to show them live and direct what happens to those who attempt to do so.

The *Kommandant* orders the patrol to stop in front of a barrack that has a pulley near the roof. People might assume it's there to hoist bales of straw or sacks of grain, but it's actually used to hang people. Schwarzhuber, enjoying the moment, gives a long, unhurried speech in which he praises the efficient way in which the Reich deals with those who disobey orders, and gleefully announces the merciless punishment that awaits them.

Before executing the fugitives, as if by way of a macabre service charge, they are given fifty lashes. Then, one by one, a rope is put around their necks. A lieutenant points to half a dozen men who are watching and tells them to start pulling on the rope. When they hesitate momentarily, he makes as if to draw his gun from its holster, and the six quickly set to work. As they pull on the rope, the body of the first fugitive, kicking and choking, begins to detach from the ground and from life.

Rudi gazes in horror at the man's contorted face: his eyes— looking like hard-boiled eggs—forcing their way through his swollen eyelids, his enormous tongue, the soundless cries emerging from his twisted mouth, the end of the frantic kicking, the leakage of every conceivable fluid onto the ground. When he turns away, Rudi's eyes catch sight of the faces of the other fugitives, who are barely upright and lean against each other as they wait their turn to be executed. They already see death as liberation. That's why they accept the noose around their necks so meekly—to put an end to it all as quickly as possible.

Although the scene leaves Rosenberg deeply shaken, it doesn't lessen his determination to escape from Auschwitz II one way or another. Alice has left him with a blurred, bittersweet memory, and above all, she has proved to him that nothing beautiful can blossom in this hell. Suddenly, the camp is suffocating him, and he finds it unbearable to be in such close proximity to death. He has to try to get away, even if he ends up dangling and kicking with a rope around his neck.

He's made some initial contacts in camp BIId, where he is in touch with people who know their way around every chink in the *Lager*. One afternoon, he comes across František, the secretary of one of the huts he deals with and a prominent member of the Resistance. Many barrack *Kapos* have secretaries who act as their assistants and whom they protect. Rudi talks to him about his keen desire leave, and František tells him to come by his room the next day for a coffee.

Coffee?

Coffee is a luxury available only to those who have good connections with the black market, because you don't just need coffee, but also a grinder, a coffee pot, water, and the means of heating it. Rudi keeps the appointment, naturally! He loves coffee, and even more than coffee, he loves being on good terms with well-connected people. He enters the hut—empty at this hour because everyone in this camp is outside working on the extension of Auschwitz—and heads for František's room. He goes inside without knocking, but he's the one who gets a surprise. His heart skips a beat when he sees that, apart from the secretary, there's a uniformed member of the SS. The word *betrayal* hits him instantly.

"Come in, Rudi. It's all right. You're among friends."

He hesitates briefly in the doorway, but František is trustworthy, or so he believes. The SS man hurries over to introduce himself, holding out his hand in a friendly manner.

"My name is Viktor, Viktor Pestek."

Rudi has heard many things in his work as registrar, but he's never heard anything as astonishing as the proposal the SS guard proceeds to put to him.

"Would you like to escape with me?"

Viktor explains his plan in great detail, and if truth be told, it's not so harebrained, or at least not the first part: leaving through the main gate dressed in an SS uniform, without raising any suspicion, and catching the train to Prague. By the time the Germans realized the next morning that they were missing, they'd be arriving in Prague. The second part of the plan seems more insane to Rudi: getting papers for themselves and for two women, and then returning to Auschwitz to get the women out.

Rudi listens very carefully, and there's no question he would be hard put to find a better way of escaping than leaving in the company of an SS officer, but something tells him it wouldn't work. Perhaps it's his heartfelt distrust of the SS that causes this instinctive negative reaction. But whatever the reason, he decides to decline politely, assuring the two men of his absolute discretion.

It turns out that František doesn't have a coffeepot, only a sock filled with coffee that he submerges in an ordinary pot and boils on top of the stove. But the cooking pot coffee tastes wonderful. Rudi leaves the room thinking that the SS man talks too freely about his plans.

It is true that Viktor Pestek is starting to spread word in a dangerous manner that an SS officer is looking for others to escape with him. While it could be that many of those who hear the rumor won't believe it and will think it's a myth like the pot of gold at the end of the rainbow, Pestek really does exist, and he perseveres with his undertaking. He could go alone, but he needs someone who is acquainted with the clandestine groups within Prague, so that he can acquire the false papers he needs to get Renée and her mother out of Auschwitz as quickly as possible.

He persists, and eventually, he comes across someone prepared to take part in his scheme. His name is Siegfried Lederer. He's one of the inmates of the family camp and a member of the Resistance. He's another person infected by the obsession to escape; he'll do whatever it takes to get out of Auschwitz.

That afternoon, Pestek meets with Renée. She arrives as she always does, very serious, a bit ashamed, her hands clasped in front of her, and her head bowed.

"This is our last time together in Auschwitz."

Viktor has spent days talking to her about the escape, but she couldn't bring herself to believe him.

"The great day has arrived," he tells her. "Well, part one of it, anyway. First I'll get out of here, and then I'll come back for you and your mother."

"But how?"

"It's better you don't know the details. Any slipup could be fatal, and it might even be that I have to change my plans on the run if things don't turn out as I anticipate. But don't you worry about a thing. One day, you'll walk out of the entrance to the camp and we'll be free."

Renée looks at him with her pale blue eyes, and she coquettishly pulls one of her curls down to her mouth in the way he loves so much.

"I have to go now."

Renée nods.

At the last moment, she grabs him by the sleeve of his jacket, holding him back. "Viktor . . ."

"What?"

"Be careful."

And he sighs happily. There'll be no stopping him now.

And nothing will stop Dita's eagerness to discover what happened to Hirsch that caused him to commit suicide. She has spent several days hanging around the workshop in search of Alter, all to no avail.

But sometimes you have to grab luck by the throat.

She cautiously approaches what seems to her to be the last group of men leaving the workshop at the end of the day.

"Excuse me . . ."

The tired men give her a friendly look.

"I'm looking for a man . . . without any hair."

The men exchange looks that suggest that at this late stage in the day their brains are working slowly. They don't seem to understand what this young girl is after.

"Without hair?"

"Yes. I mean, bald. Completely bald."

"Completely bald?"

"Of course!" says one of them. "She means Kurt, for sure."

"I guess so," Dita replies. "And where might I find him?"

"In there," they reply, pointing inside the workshop. "He's always the last to leave. It's his job to sweep, clean, and put everything in order."

"A tough task," comments one of the men.

"Yes, that's what happens when, on top of being a Jew, you're a Communist as well."

"And bald, to boot," points out another of the men sarcastically.

"It's an advantage to be bald. The lice slide off your head."

"And on days when it snows, they skate on top of your head," adds the sarcastic man.

They walk away, laughing as if Dita weren't there. She waits outside for a long time and finally, the man with no hair emerges. And indeed, Mrs. Turnovská was right when she said that he'd be recognizable by his nose.

Dita starts to walk beside him.

"Excuse me, but I need some specific information."

The man gives her a dirty look and quickens his pace. Dita accelerates to a trot and catches up.

"You see, I need to find out something about Fredy Hirsch."

"Why are you following me? I don't know anything—leave me in peace."

"I don't want to bother you, but I have to know—"

"Why are you talking to me? I'm just a workshop sweeper."

"I've been told you're something more—"

The man brakes and gives her an angry look. He checks this way and that, and Dita suddenly realizes that if Mengele comes across her right now, it will be the end.

"They gave you the wrong information."

The man starts walking again.

"Wait!" shouts Dita, annoyed. "I want to talk to you! Would you rather that we shouted at each other?"

A few heads turn toward them out of curiosity, and the man swears softly under his breath. He grabs Dita's arm and takes her into the narrow space between two huts, where there is less light.

"Who are you? And what do you want?"

"I'm one of the assistants from Block Thirty-One. I'm trustworthy. You can ask Miriam Edelstein about me."

"Fine, fine . . . talk."

"I'm trying to understand why Fredy Hirsch killed himself."

"Why? That's simple—he got scared."

"What do you mean?"

"Exactly what you're hearing. He chickened out. He was asked
to lead an uprising, and he didn't have the guts. End of story."

"I don't believe you."

"I don't care if you believe me or not. That's what happened."

"You didn't know Fredy Hirsch, did you?"

The man comes to a complete stop at Dita's comment, as if
he'd been caught doing something wrong. Dita tries hard to prevent her anger from turning into tears as she speaks.

"You didn't know him. You know nothing about him. He
never walked away from anything. You think you know a lot, that
the Resistance knows everything . . . but you don't understand a
thing."

"Look, kid, what I do know is that the order was transmitted to
him from the leaders of the Resistance, and what he did after that
was take all those pills in order to wipe himself off the map," answers Alter, annoyed. "I don't know why there's so much interest
in him. The whole business of Block Thirty-One is a pantomime.
The whole family camp is a pantomime. Hirsch and the rest of us
have played the Nazis' game. We've been their helpers."

"What do you mean?"

"This camp is a front, a cover-up. Its only purpose is to cover
up the truth in the face of international observers who may come
here to discover if there's any basis to the rumors that have reached
some countries that the German camps are slaughterhouses. The

family camp and Block Thirty-One are a stage set, and we are actors in the play."

Dita falls silent. The bald man shakes his head.

"Stop brooding over it. Your friend Hirsch became frightened. That's only human."

Fear . . .

Dita suddenly sees fear as a type of rust that undermines even the strongest convictions. It corrodes everything; it destroys all.

The bald man walks off, nervously glancing to his left and right.

Dita stays in the side street. The words boom inside her head and block out everything around her.

A set decoration? Actors in a play? Nazi puppets? Their entire effort in Block 31 has been to benefit the Germans?

She has to put her hand against the side of the hut to steady herself because she feels dizzy. *The entire family camp is a lie? None of it is real?*

She begins to think that maybe it has to be so. Truth is put together by destiny; it's nothing more than a whim of fate. A lie, on the other hand, is more human; it's created by mankind and tailor-made to purpose.

Dita heads off in search of Miriam Edelstein. She finds her in her hut, sitting on her bunk. Her son, Arieh, is saying good-bye as he heads off to walk along the *Lagerstrasse* with some other boys before the evening crust of bread is handed out.

"Am I bothering you, Aunt Miriam?"

"Of course not."

"You see . . ." Dita's voice hesitates; Dita herself hesitates. Her legs are shaking again like pistons. "I've been talking to a man from the Resistance. He told me an incredible story: that the family camp is a cover-up for the Nazis in case observers from other countries come to investigate. . . ."

Miriam nods silently.

"So it's true! You knew it!" whispers Dita. "So the only thing we've done all this time has been to serve the Nazis."

"Not at all! They had a plan, but we've carried out our own plan. They wanted the children to be abandoned like junk in a warehouse, but we opened a school. They wanted them to be like cattle in a stable, but we've made them feel like people."

"And what use has that been? All the children in the September transport have died."

"It *was* worth it. Nothing has been in vain. Do you remember how they used to laugh? Do you remember how wide-eyed they were when they were singing 'Alouette' or listening to the stories of the living books? Do you remember how they jumped for joy when we put half a biscuit in their bowls? And the excitement with which they prepared their plays? They were happy, Edita."

"But it lasted such a short time—"

"Life, any life, is very short. But if you've managed to be happy for at least an instant, it will have been worth living."

"An instant! How short is that?"

"Very short. It's enough to be happy for as long as it takes a match to be lit and go out."

Dita is silent as she weighs up how many matches have been lit and gone out in her life—and there have been lots. Many brief moments in which a flame has shone, even in the midst of the deepest darkness. Some of those moments have occurred when, in the middle of some huge disaster, she has opened a book and buried herself in it. Her small library is a box of matches. As she thinks this, she smiles with a hint of sadness.

"And what will become of the children now? What will happen to all of us now? I'm scared, Aunt Miriam."

"The Nazis can strip us of our homes, our belongings, our clothes, and even our hair, but no matter how much they take away from us, they can't remove our hope. It's ours. We can't lose it. You hear more and more Allied air raids. The war won't last forever, and we have to prepare ourselves for peace. The children have to keep learning, because they're going to find a country and a world in ruins, and it will be they, and you, the teenagers, who will have to rebuild it."

"But the fact that the children's camp is a Nazi trick is awful. The international observers will come, the Germans will show this to them, they'll hide the gas chambers, and the observers will see that children survive in Auschwitz, and they'll go away deceived."

"Or not."

"What do you mean?"

"That will be our moment. We won't let them leave without knowing the truth."

Then Dita begins to recall the afternoon before the September transport left, when she came across Fredy on the *Lagerstrasse*.

"I've just been reminded of something Fredy said the last time I spoke with him. He made some comment about a moment when a crack would open. It would be the moment of truth, he said. And we had to take the risk. He said you had to shoot a goal in the final second when they were least expecting it, to earn the win."

Miriam nods in agreement.

"That was the plan. He gave me some papers before he left. He was writing much more than reports for the camp command. He'd put together facts, dates, names, a complete dossier of what's going on in Auschwitz, which he'd prepared to hand over to a neutral observer."

"Fredy won't be able to hand it over anymore."

"No, he's no longer here. But we're not going to give up, are we?"

"Quit? No way. Count on me, for anything. No matter the cost."

The deputy director of Block 31 smiles.

"But then why did he surrender at the last minute and commit suicide?" Dita persists. "The Resistance people say he got scared."

Miriam Edelstein's smile suddenly freezes.

"The man from the Resistance said that they asked him to lead a revolt, and he got cold feet. I told the man he had no idea what he was talking about, but he seemed so sure of himself. . . ."

"It's true that they suggested he lead a revolt when they were already certain that the entire September transport was going to be sent to the gas chambers. I've been told that by a source I trust."

"And he rejected the offer?"

"A revolt consisting of a contingent of families that included old people and children facing armed SS soldiers wasn't exactly a terrific plan. He asked them for time to think it over."

"And then he committed suicide."

"Yes."

"Why?"

Miriam Edelstein's sigh leaves Dita feeling empty inside.

"We don't always have an answer for everything."

The woman takes Dita by the shoulder and draws her close. They remain together for a long moment, during which their silence unites them far more than any words they could say. Then they exchange a warm good-bye and Dita leaves the hut. She walks along, thinking that maybe there isn't an answer for everything.

But Fredy said to her, *Don't ever give up*, and she'll never give up on her desire to find that answer.

The murmur of the classes in Block 31 drags her away from her thoughts. Ota Keller's group is just a few meters away. The children are following his explanations very attentively, and Dita pricks up her ears so she won't lose the thread the Nazis have cut. She misses school. She would have liked to go on with her studies and maybe become a pilot like the woman she had seen in one of her mother's illustrated magazines. The woman was called Amelia Earhart, and she appeared in photos getting down from a plane in a man's leather jacket, with a pair of flying goggles on her forehead and a dreamy look in her eyes. Dita thinks you would have to study hard to become an aviator. The mixed murmurs of several teachers reach the spot where she's sitting, and she isn't able to pick out the lessons of any individual one of them.

She watches Ota Keller teaching. They say he's a Communist. Ota is talking to his group about the speed of light and how there is nothing faster in the universe; the stars they see shining in the sky are the result of the light photons they emit reaching our pupils after traveling millions of kilometers at breakneck speed. He hypnotizes the children with his contagious enthusiasm, his eyebrows move constantly, and his index finger wiggles like the needle on a compass.

It suddenly occurs to Dita that compasses, like the ones in aircraft, are difficult to understand. Maybe she'd prefer to be an artist rather than a pilot. It sounds like a good idea. It would be a way of flying without having to rely on so much equipment. She'd paint the world as if she were flying over it.

Margit is waiting for her when she leaves Block 31; she's with her sister Helga, who is even thinner than before. Margit whispers to Dita that she's a bit concerned about how gaunt her sister looks. Helga has had the misfortune to be assigned to a drainage ditch brigade and, thanks to the constant spring rains, they spend all day removing the mud that accumulates.

There are lots of inmates like Helga, who seem to be so much thinner than others. It's as if the piece of bread and soup went in and straight through their bodies without leaving any trace. Maybe they are just as thin as the others, but there is something in their downcast expressions and the defeat in their eyes that makes them seem more fragile. There's constant talk of typhus and tuberculosis and pneumonia, but not so much is said about the depression sweeping through the *Lager* like a plague. It happened to Dita's father, too: People suddenly begin to switch off. They are the ones who have given up.

Dita and Margit try to cheer up Helga by joking around.

"So, Helga, have you found any good-looking boys around here?"

Helga stands there with no idea how to answer, so Dita tosses the question to her sister.

"Well, Margit, have you found nothing worth a second look in the camp, either? We'll have to ask camp command for a transfer."

"Wait . . . I have seen one boy in Hut 12. He's gorgeous!"

"Gorgeous? Did you hear that, Helga? What a prissy way of speaking."

The three girls laugh.

"And have you said anything to this cute boy?" asks Dita, continuing the game.

"Not yet. He must be at least twenty-five."

"Heavens. Far too old. If you went out with him, people would think you were his granddaughter."

"And what about you, Dita?" Margit counterattacks. "Is there no assistant in this entire hut who's worth the effort?"

"Assistants? Nooo. Who would be interested in a boy with a face full of pimples?"

"Well, there's got to be some interesting boy!"

"Nooo."

"Not one?"

"There is someone who's different."

"Different how?"

"He hasn't got three legs, that's for sure." And then Dita stops joking. "He's one of those people who seem very serious, but he knows how to tell stories. His name is Ota Keller."

"One of those boring types, then."

"Not at all!"

"Hmmm. What do you think, Helga? The scene as far as boys are concerned is pretty disastrous, isn't it?"

Helga smiles in agreement. She's embarrassed to talk about boys with her sister, who's normally very serious. But when Dita is around, she makes everything seem less important.

That night, while Helga, Margit, Dita, and the rest of the camp sleep, a first officer of the SS enters the family camp without anyone noticing. He's carrying a backpack.

He heads to the back of one of the huts and slides out the piece of wood that bars the door. Siegfried Lederer immediately emerges from the shadowy interior and silently changes his clothes. The beggar transforms into a sparkling SS officer. Pestek feels it's preferable to wear a uniform with the insignia of a lieutenant because it's less likely that anyone will dare to address the wearer.

They leave by the security checkpoint, where the two guards in the booth give them a respectful raised-arm salute. They walk toward the main entrance of the camp situated under the enormous guard tower, which looks like a sinister castle. Because it's dark, the upper part of the tower, which contains the enclosed observation deck from which the guards keep watch, is lit up. Lederer is sweating inside his lieutenant's uniform, but Pestek is walking confidently—he's convinced they are going to pass through the control point without any difficulty.

They approach the checkpoint under the imposing tower. When the guards see the two soldiers coming, they—and their machine guns—swivel to face them. Pestek quietly tells Lederer to slow down so that he can go first, but to keep moving and, most importantly, to do so without hesitation. If Lederer looks assured, the guards won't have any doubts. They won't dare tell a lieutenant to stop.

With total self-confidence, Pestek walks a few steps ahead. He approaches the guards and, as if he were among friends and sharing a confidence, he lowers his voice and tells them that he's going to take an officer recently transferred to Auschwitz for a stroll down to the brothel in Auschwitz I.

The guards don't even have time to share a complicit laugh because the lieutenant, back ramrod straight, is already walking past. They all stand to attention, and the fake officer responds with a lazy nod of his head. Pestek joins his superior officer, and the two of them disappear into the night. The checkpoint guards think the two officers are lucky guys. And they are.

Pestek and Lederer head for Oświęcim station. From there, they are to catch the train for Krakow that is due to leave in a few minutes. If all goes well, in Krakow they'll take another train to Prague. They walk in silence, trying to ensure that they don't look as if they're in a hurry. Freedom is scratching Siegfried on the back, or maybe it's the officer's uniform.

23.

THE MORNING ROLL CALL IS NEVER ENDING. WHEN IT'S DONE, there are SS whistles and shouts in German. A guard arrives and gives the order for the roll call to be repeated. Many of the Czech Jews speak German, so the order produces a murmur of frustration in the hut. Another hour on their feet. . . . They don't know what's going on, but something's happening, because the guards are noticeably nervous. One word is muttered from one row to the next: *escape*.

Later that morning, a thunderous rendition of "Alouette" sounds throughout Block 31. Avi Fischer conducts the choir with his habitual cheerfulness, and the children, no matter their age, delight in singing the song that has become Block 31's anthem. Dita joins the chorus. They are all caught up in the acoustic vibration of the music. Practically all of the 360 children in the hut empty their lungs to form a single voice of many parts.

When they have finished, Seppl Lichtenstern announces that it will soon be the Passover Seder meal and that the leaders of the children's barrack are working hard to make it a momentous occasion. The children clap, and some even whistle enthusiastically. Rumors have been rife that the block chief has spent days trying to get hold of enough ingredients on the black market for the celebration. It's the sort of news that makes the day-to-day more cheerful and provides an air of normality for the children. Another rumor that has spread through the camp with the speed of light is

about the escape of an inmate called Lederer. That was why they
had to have the second roll call and why they'd ordered that the
heads of all male prisoners, including boys, be shaved. The *Kapos*
kept yelling out the word *hygiene*, but it was all about spite. Luckily for Dita's thick head of hair, the women were spared.

But what does it matter?

The Germans are particularly irritated by this escape because
they say Lederer got away thanks to the collaboration of an SS
guard who has deserted. Nothing could rile them more. Any rope,
no matter how crude, will do to hang him. Margit told Dita that the
guard in question is the one who used to meet Renée, but Renée's
not talking to anyone. Not about this, not about anything.

And at this stage, thank God, they haven't been caught.

Fate is fate. Dita is walking along the *Lagerstrasse*, eyes and
ears alert for any sign of Mengele. But the person she spies is a
high-ranking prisoner whom she'd occasionally seen on the other
side of the fence. Dita has spent weeks racking her brains, trying
to find a way to meet him, and now here he is, walking by himself
with his hands in his pockets. He's wearing trousers that look like
jodhpurs, as if he were a *Kapo*. But it is the registrar of the quarantine camp, Rudi Rosenberg.

"Excuse me . . ."

Rudi slows down but doesn't stop. He's very focused on his
own plan. There's no going back anymore. The itch has become
unbearable. Dead or alive, he has to get out of here. He can't wait
any longer. The day is set, and there are only a few loose ends to tie
up to do with supplies. The ball is rolling, and he can't allow himself any distractions.

"What do you want?" he answers grumpily. "I don't have any
food to give you."

"That's not what I'm after. I worked in Block Thirty-One with Fredy Hirsch."

Rosenberg nods but keeps on walking, and Dita has to quicken her pace in order to keep up with him.

"I knew him—"

"Don't kid yourself. Nobody knew that man. He didn't allow it."

"But he was brave. Did he say anything to you that would explain why he killed himself?"

Rosenberg pauses briefly and looks at her with a tired expression on his face.

"He was human. You all thought he was a biblical patriarch, a legendary Golem, or something like that." He sighs dismissively. "He had created this aura of a hero. But he wasn't up to it. I saw him; he was a man like any other. To put it plainly, he couldn't take it anymore. He snapped, just like anyone else would have. Is that so hard to understand? Forget him. His moment is gone. Just focus on how you're going to get out of here alive."

Rudi, visibly out of sorts, brings the conversation to a close and walks off. Dita thinks about what he has said, and his hostile tone. Of course Hirsch was human; he had his weaknesses, as she well knows. He never said he wasn't afraid; of course he was. What he did say was that you had to swallow your fear. Rosenberg is one of those people who knows many things—everyone says so. He has given her sound advice: Just think about yourself. But Dita doesn't want to be sensible.

April has brought warmer temperatures, and the biting cold of winter has eased. The rain has turned the *Lagerstrasse* into a quagmire full of puddles, and respiratory illnesses have increased with the damp. The cart that picks up the dead in the camp each morning is full of bodies overcome by pneumonia. Cholera takes many of them, too, and even typhus. It's not a sudden overall increase in deaths like in an epidemic, but a steady trickle.

April has brought not only a flood of water to Birkenau, but a flood of transports, too. There are days when up to three trains crammed with Jews arrive, spilling water and people onto the new platforms inside the camp. The children in Block 31 become unsettled; they want to go outside to see the trains arriving and wonder at the mountains of suitcases and packages piled up on the ground. Boxes and boxes of food, which they stare at greedily, their mouths watering.

"Look, a huge cheese," shouts a ten-year-old boy called Wiki.

"And scattered over the ground . . . is that cucumbers?"

"My God, a box of chestnuts!"

"Oh, you're right. It's chestnuts!"

"If only the wind would blow just one chestnut over here! I'm not asking for much—just one chestnut!" And Wiki starts to pray quietly: "God in heaven, just one chestnut. Nothing more!"

A little girl of five with a grubby face and hair like a scrubbing brush takes a few steps forward, and an adult hand grabs her by the shoulder so she won't go any farther.

"What are chestnuts?"

The older children laugh as they look at her, but then they grow serious. The little girl has never seen a chestnut. She's never tasted a roasted chestnut or the typical November chestnut cake. Wiki decides that if God hears him and the wind blows over a chestnut, he'll give half of it to the little girl. You haven't lived if you don't know what a chestnut tastes like.

The teachers don't look at the packages of food, but at the bundles of broken people whom the guards are beating into formation so they can be put through the typical macabre routine of every transport: separating those who will be shaved, tattooed, and thrown into the quagmire where they'll work till they drop from those who'll be killed then and there. The six- and seven-year-olds in the family camp on the other side of the fence sometimes joke about the new arrivals. It's hard to tell if they really are making fun of them and don't care about the suffering of these strangers, or if pretending to their companions that they don't care is their way of seeming to be strong and overcoming their own anxiety.

On the first night of Passover, families usually gather around the table and read the Haggadah, which tells of the exodus of the Israelites from Egypt. It's customary for four glasses of wine to be drunk in God's honor. The *keara* is prepared, a traditional plate on which the following foods are placed: *zeroah* (usually a lamb bone); *beitzah* (a brown egg, which symbolizes Pharaoh's hard heart); *maror* (bitter herbs or horseradish, which symbolize the harshness of Jewish slavery in Egypt); *charoset* (a sweet mixture of apple, honey, and dried fruits, which represents the mortar used by the Jews to build their houses in Egypt); and *karpas* (a small amount of parsley in a cup of salted water to symbolize the life of the Israelites, always bathed in tears). And the most important element, *matzah*, the unleavened bread, of which each person around the table takes a piece. The last supper Jesus shared with his disciples was a celebration of Seder, and the Christian Eucharist arose from this Jewish rite. Ota Keller explains all this to his group of children and not one of them misses a word: Religious traditions and the traditional meal are sacred to them.

Lichtenstern has got his way—they'll be able to celebrate Passover. Although they don't have all the ingredients to allow for the celebration in the Orthodox manner, all the children are waiting expectantly when the block chief comes out of his cubicle carrying a piece of wood that serves as the special plate. Laid out on it in precise order are a bone of something that could be chicken, an egg, a slice of radish, and a pot full of salted water with some herbs floating in it.

Aunt Miriam has put beetroot jam into the morning tea to create pretend wine. She is also the one charged with kneading the bread dough. Valtr, one of the men who regularly helps with the hut's maintenance tasks, has got hold of a thick piece of wire and bent it to form a metal grill on which to bake the bread. The children watch the entire process, mesmerized. In a place where food is such a scarce commodity, they observe in amazement how a handful of flour and a little water give rise to a delicious bread with a mouthwatering aroma. Finally, a miracle.

The youngest ones, who have been chasing each other noisily at the back of the barrack, are soon told to be quiet, and a respectful silence charged with mysticism floats in the air.

Finally, six pancakes of bread are ready and are placed in the middle of the board. It's not much for more than three hundred children, but Lichtenstern orders each person to take a tiny piece, just enough to be able to taste the *matzah*.

"It's the unleavened bread that our forefathers ate during their escape from slavery to freedom," Lichtenstern tells the children.

And they all start to pass in front of him in an orderly manner to receive their sacred little piece.

The children return to their groups, sit down, and listen to their teachers explaining the story of the exodus of the Jews while they eat their ritual bread and drink fake wine. Dita bounces her way between the groups, listening to the different voices telling their versions of the same extraordinary deeds that make up the long march through the desert under the leadership of the prophet Moses.

The children are fascinated by these stories, and they listen attentively as Moses climbs up the steep slopes of Mount Sinai to get closer to that thunderous God, then the Red Sea parts to allow the Jews passage to the other side. It is probably the most unorthodox celebration of Passover night in history—it's not even night, but midday. And of course they can't eat the traditional lamb; there's nothing of the Seder that they can eat. But, as a special treat, each child will receive half a cookie. The effort itself, however, and the faith with which they celebrate the festive day, despite all their deprivations, turns it into a moving ceremony.

Avi Fischer gathers together the choir and they begin to sing Beethoven's *Ode to Joy*, at first timidly and then with style. Since it's hard to rehearse anything in secret in this hut, most of those present know the words by heart from hearing it so often, and they launch into song as well, until there is a single, giant chorus of hundreds of voices.

The power of their music passes through the walls and filters through the barbed wire fences. The prisoners working in the camp's drainage ditches stop briefly and lean on their shovels to hear better.

"Listen! It's the children—they're singing. . . ."

In the clothing hut and in the mica hut, where they make condensers for electric machines, they also slow down their work for a moment and turn their faces toward the happy melody filtering through from some place that seems foreign to the *Lager*.

"No, no," someone replies, "it's angels from heaven."

In the ditches into which ash never stops falling, and which the *Kapos* pressure the inmates to dig until their hands bleed, that music and those voices carried by the wind are a miracle. The words speak of a time when millions will embrace each other, the whole world will exchange kisses, and all mankind will be brothers and sisters. A cry for peace shouted as loudly as possible in the biggest factory of death of all time.

The *Ode* rings out so loudly it even reaches the desk of a notable music lover. He lifts his head as if he smells the aroma of a delicious tart so strongly that it must be tracked to the oven in which it is baking. He quickly abandons his papers, crosses the *Lagerstrasse* of the family camp, and plants himself on the threshold of Block 31.

The children have already repeated several times the strains of the first verse, which is the one they all know by heart, and they have just reached the end of the chorus when the figure wearing the peaked cap with its silver death's head insignia appears in the doorway, projecting an excessively large and menacing shadow. Lichtenstern feels icy cold, as if winter had suddenly returned.

Dr. Mengele . . .

He continues to sing, but his voice weakens. They aren't authorized to celebrate any Jewish feasts. Dita becomes momentarily mute, but then she immediately picks up the words again because, even though the adults have fallen silent, the children have continued to sing with all their might as if nothing has happened.

Mengele stands there listening for a few moments, his expression neutral, impassive, impenetrable. He turns his head toward Lichtenstern, who has stopped singing and is looking at him, terrified. Mengele nods his head in approval, as if he likes what he's hearing, and waves his white-gloved hand to encourage them to go on singing. The officer turns around, and the block finishes the *Ode* with everyone singing as loudly as they can to send a message of strength to Mengele. Then they burst into applause, some of it directed at themselves, their energy, and their daring.

Shortly after the celebration of Passover has come to an end, when everyone is getting ready for the evening roll call and the sounds of *Ode to Joy* are still vibrating in their ears, a different kind of music is heard outside. Sharper, more compelling, monotonous, with no trace of joy, even though some people smile when they hear it. It's the alarm sirens blaring throughout the *Lager*.

Members of the SS run in all directions. Two soldiers who were in the *Lagerstrasse* rush to their guard posts. The sirens are signaling an escape. Escapes are an all-or-nothing situation—freedom or death.

It's the second time the escape siren has gone off in the past few days. First, it was that man Lederer, who is rumored to be a member of the Resistance and who they say escaped with an SS deserter. There has been no further news of them, and that's the best possible news. Word is that the Nazi got Lederer out dressed as a member of the SS, that they calmly walked through the main gate, that the guards on watch were so stupid they even invited them to share a few shots of vodka.

Now the siren rings out again. Escapes upset the Nazis. They are a contempt of their authority, but in particular, they are a breach of the order the Germans have so obsessively established. For Schwarzhuber, two escapes so close together in time constitute an offense. And so it proves: When they inform him of the news, he begins to kick his subordinates and demand that heads roll. Any heads.

The prisoners know it's going to be a long night, and they're not wrong. The Germans make everyone, including the children, line up outdoors on the main street of the camp. Roll call is repeated several times—three hours pass, and they are all still standing there. It's one way of checking that no one else is missing, but it's also a form of revenge, because the Nazis can't direct their rage at the fugitives. Or at least not right now.

While the guards race around and tension rises, Rudi Rosenberg the registrar and his comrade, Fred Wetzler, maintain total silence a few hundred meters away, in pitch-darkness. They are in a tiny hideout somewhat like a vault, and only their frantic breathing adds life to the thick darkness. In his mind's eye Rudi projects an image from a few days ago, when the Russian fugitives were hanged in the middle of the camp—their blue, swollen tongues, their eyes crying tears of blood as they burst from their sockets.

A drop of sweat rolls down his forehead, and he doesn't dare wipe it away for fear of moving even one millimeter. Now he's the one in the bunker built by the Russians, together with his friend Fred. They've decided to go for broke—all or nothing.

The camp sirens wail. He extends his hand toward Fred and touches his leg. Fred puts his hand on top of Rudi's. There's no going back now. They waited a few days to see if the Nazis would dismantle the Russians' hideout, and when they didn't, the two of them reached the conclusion that it was secure. They'll soon know whether that's the case.

Back in the family camp, after an exhausting day and with only a few minutes before lights-out, Dita is helping her mother get rid of her nits before they turn into lice. This requires running the little piece of comb through her hair again and again. Her mother can't bear lack of hygiene, or at least she couldn't before, when she used to scold Dita, always telling her to wash her hands with soap before touching anything. Now she has no choice but to put up with the dirt. Dita thinks back to her mother before the war; she was a beautiful woman—much more so than her daughter—and very elegant.

Some of the other inmates are also taking advantage of the time before they go to sleep to kill the undesirable tenants who live in their hair. And while they do this without pause, comments on the day's events are passed from one bunk to the next.

"I don't understand why someone working as a registrar, who never feels hungry, who doesn't have a particularly tough job, and who is never put up for selection because he's highly regarded by the Nazis, risks his life in this way."

"No one understands it."

"Escape is suicide. Almost all of them end up back here and hanged."

"And anyway, we'll be out of here soon," notes another of the women. "They say the Russians are forcing the Germans to retreat. The war could end this very week."

This comment gives rise to a host of lively murmurings, optimistic theories strengthened by the desire to see an end to this interminable war.

"On top of that," adds one of the women who's calling the shots, "whenever there's an escape, there are reprisals for rest of us: more restrictions, punishments. . . . In some of the camps they've sent people to the gas chambers in retaliation. Who knows what might happen to us? It's incredible that some people are such egotists that they don't care about putting the rest of us in danger."

Everyone nods in agreement.

Liesl Adler rarely takes part in these discussions. She doesn't like to call attention to herself, and she's always telling off her daughter for not being discreet enough. It seems astonishing that a woman who speaks several languages would opt so frequently for the language of silence. But on this occasion, she speaks.

"A sensible voice, at last." The sea of heads nods again. "Someone finally speaking the truth."

Approving murmurs can be heard. Liesl continues.

"Finally, someone has spoken about what is really important: We're not the least bit concerned about whether or not this man escapes with his life. What concerns us is how it might affect us, that they might give us one less spoonful of soup at mealtime or keep us standing outdoors for several hours doing roll calls. That's what's important."

Some of the women mutter in bewilderment, but Liesl keeps talking.

"You say there's no point in escaping. The Germans are going to have dozens of patrols searching for the fugitives, and that forces them to keep more and more troops on the home front rather than sending them to fight against the Allies who are going to rescue us. Is it pointless for us to fight here in order to distract the German troops? Does it serve any purpose for us to stay here obeying whatever the SS tell us to do until they decide to kill us?"

Astonishment has stifled all the muttering and given rise to differences of opinion. Dita is frozen on the spot in amazement, still holding the comb. Liesl Adler's is the only voice to be heard in the hut.

"I once heard a young girl refer to us as 'old hens.' She was right. We spend the whole day clucking and not doing much else."

"And you, who are talking so much, why don't you escape if it's such a good thing?" screeched the woman who had been speaking earlier. "It's fine to talk, but—"

"I'm too old, and I'm not strong enough. Or brave enough. I'm an old hen. That's why I respect those who are brave enough to do what I wouldn't do."

The women around her have not only stopped murmuring; they've stopped saying anything. Even that friendly chatterbox, Mrs. Turnovská, who always takes a leading role in any conversation, looks at her friend quizzically.

Dita puts the comb down on the mattress and looks at her mother as if she were studying her under a microscope, surprised to have discovered someone quite different from the person she's always lived with. She has thought her mother was living in isolation in her own world since the death of her husband, quite removed from everything that was going on around her.

"Mama, I haven't heard you say so much in years."

"Do you think I said more than I ought to have, Edita?"

"Absolutely not."

A few hundred meters away, silence reigns. And darkness. If either fugitive raises his hand to his face, he can't even see his fingers. In this wooden cubicle, where they either have to sit or lie down, the passage of time is agonizingly slow, and they feel a bit sick from breathing in the overused air inside the cubicle. A veteran advised them to soak tobacco with kerosene to throw the dogs off their scent.

Rudi notices Fred Wetzler's agitated breathing. They have the time to go over the same list of things a million times in their heads. It's impossible for Rudi to avoid thinking how crazy he is to have left his advantageous position in the camp, where he could have waited out the war getting by as he has so far. But escape fever took hold of him, and there was no way to get rid of it. He couldn't rid his mind of Alice Munk's final look at him or of Hirsch's blue face. After seeing an indestructible being like Fredy Hirsch fall apart in front of his eyes, there's no way he believes in any sort of resistance to the fever.

And what is there to say about the death of Alice? How can he accept that her beauty and her youth were not enough to halt the steamroller of hate? There are no barriers for the Nazis; their determination to kill even the last Jew hiding at the ends of the earth is methodical and unrelenting. He and Wetzler have to escape. But that isn't enough. They must also tell the world—particularly the slow-moving West, which believes the front is in Russia or France—that the real slaughter is taking place in the heart of Poland, in the places they refer to as concentration camps, which only truly concentrate on perpetrating the most heinous criminal operation in history.

And so, despite the anguish that is adding to the cold on this dark, freezing night, Rudi ultimately decides he is where he ought to be.

Time ticks on, although the minuscule crack doesn't allow them to see if it's day or night. They must spend three days submerged in the total darkness of night. Even so, they know that the day has already dawned outside because of the sound of activity.

Waiting is difficult. They manage to doze off from time to time, but on awakening, they react with a nervous start because when they open their eyes, the world has disappeared, swallowed by blackness. And then almost immediately they remember that they are in this bunker and they calm down, but only a little, because they are hidden just a few meters from the guard towers. Their heads spin.

They've imposed complete silence, because for all they know, someone could be wandering around outside and might hear them. They also have no idea if the tiny crack in the lacework of wooden planks will be enough to prevent them from suffocating. But despite all this, there comes a moment when one of them can't take it any longer and, in a whisper, asks what would happen if one morning more planks were placed on top of their pile, and they weighed so much that they couldn't move them. They both know the answer—the hideout would turn into a sealed coffin in which they would slowly die an agonizing death from asphyxiation or hunger and thirst. It's inevitable that during this long and stressful wait, they will become delirious, inevitable that they will ask themselves which of the two of them will die first, should they become trapped.

They hear the barking of dogs, their worst enemies, but luckily they're quite far off. But then they start to hear another sound coming ever closer: footsteps and voices approaching until they sound worryingly defined.

The guards' boots thud on the ground. The two fugitives hold their breath. They couldn't breathe even if they wanted to, because fear seals their lungs. They hear the muffled sound of planks being moved aside. Some of the SS soldiers are removing boards in the area where they are hiding. Bad news. The soldiers are so close now that they can even catch snippets of conversation, angry words from troops who have had their leave canceled because they have to tramp around the perimeter of the *Lager*. Their words are full of hatred directed at the fugitives. They're saying that when they find the men, if Schwarzhuber doesn't execute them, they'll happily smash in their skulls themselves. And their words are so clear that Rudi feels his body grow cold, as if he were dead already. His life depends solely upon the thickness of the board that covers them. A mere four or five centimeters is all that separates them from death.

The drumming of boots around him and the movement of boards next to his hideout signal the end. He feels such anguish that he just wants them to remove the top of his little cubicle, peer inside, and bring all this to a conclusion as quickly as possible.

He'd rather the guards shot them right here. He hopes their fury will save the two of them the humiliation and pain of being hanged in public. A moment ago, Rudi was aiming for freedom; now, all he wants is to die quickly. His heart is beating so strongly that he starts to shake.

Boots thud, planks are moved with a scraping sound like that of a gravestone. Rudi has already started to give in, and relaxes his frozen position; there's nothing to do now. During the days preceding their escape, he thought obsessively about the distress he'd feel when they caught him, when he realized with absolute certainty that he was going to die. But he now knows that's not the case, that the anguish happens before. When the Nazi points his Luger at you and tells you to raise your arms, what hits you is a cold calmness, a letting yourself go, because there's nothing more you can do and nothing worse to fear. He listens to the sound of the wood being moved and instinctively starts to lift his arms. He even closes his eyes to avoid the explosion of light after days of darkness.

But the burst of light doesn't come. It seems to him that the thud of the boots is somewhat more muffled and the scrape of the wood is less loud. He's not dreaming. . . . When he pricks up his ears, he realizes that the conversations and the noises are moving away. And with each passing second—each as long as an hour— the sniffer dogs are also heading away. Eventually, silence returns, with only the occasional sound of a distant truck or whistle. Other than those noises, the only sound to be heard is an out-of-control thudding, and Rudi doesn't know if it's his heart, or Fred's, or their two hearts together.

They're safe . . . for now.

To celebrate, Rudi allows himself the luxury of a huge sigh and a slight shift in position. Then it's Fred who stretches out his sweaty hand in search of Rudi, and Rudi who takes it. They shiver together.

When several minutes have gone by and the danger is over, Rudi whispers in Fred's ear, "We're leaving tonight, Fred—we're leaving forever."

And that fact brooks no argument: They're leaving forever. When they pull aside the board that serves as a ceiling and crawl to the forest protected by the dark, no matter what happens, they'll never again be prisoners in Auschwitz. They'll either be free men or they'll die.

24.

WHILE BIRKENAU CAMP SPENDS A RESTLESS NIGHT SLEEPING inside its electrified fence, a wooden cover slides open on the other side of the barbed wire. It slides open slowly like the top on a box of chess pieces. From below, four hands move it until the cold night air floods into the tiny cubicle. Two heads peer out cautiously. Rudi and Fred gobble up the fresh air. It's like a banquet.

Rudi looks around carefully. He sees there are no guards nearby and that they are protected by the darkness. The closest tower is no more than forty or fifty meters away, but the guard is watching the inside of the camp and doesn't notice that outside the perimeter, among the planks piled up in preparation for the new huts to extend the *Lager*, two figures are crawling toward the forest.

Reaching the trees and filling their lungs with the forest's damp smell is such a new sensation for the two men that they feel reborn. But the euphoria produced by their first taste of freedom is short-lived. The forest, which from a distance is so beautiful and welcoming, is an inhospitable place for humans at night. They soon realize that blindly walking cross-country is not an easy task. The ground is full of traps: shrubs that scratch them, branches that whack them, foliage that drenches them. They try as best they can to walk in a straight line and put as much distance as possible between themselves and the *Lager*.

Their plan is to reach the Slovakian border in the Beskidy Mountains, 120 kilometers away, walking by night and hiding during the day. And praying. They know they can't hope for help from the Polish civilian population because the Germans shoot any locals who provide refuge to fugitives.

They walk in the dark, tripping, falling, getting up, and walking on again. After a few hours of slow walking, uncertain if they're heading in the right direction, the two men notice that the forest thins out, the trees start to disappear, and they find themselves in scrubland. They even make out the light of a house a few hundred meters away. They finally emerge onto a dirt road. It's riskier, but as the road isn't paved, they figure it will be little used. They decide to continue along it, keeping as close to the ditch as they can, alert to any sound. Owl hoots add an eerie note to the darkness, and the breeze is so cold it leaves them breathless. Whenever they come close to a house, they head back into the forest and skirt round it at a safe distance. On one occasion, dogs bark nervously, trying to betray their presence; the runaways quicken their step.

When the sky begins to lighten, they decide in whispers to make their way into the densest part of the forest and find a tall tree to climb so they can spend the day hidden. They can now see the outline of their surroundings better and make headway more easily. Thirty minutes later, there is enough light for them to see clearly. They stare at each other for a moment. They are unrecognizable. They've spent three days in the pitch-dark, and their beards are longer than usual. There's a different expression on their faces—a mixture of unease and delight at being outside the camp. They actually don't recognize each other because they are different now—they are free men. They smile.

They climb a tree and try to make themselves comfortable among the branches, but it's hard to find a stable position. They take a piece of bread as hard as a log out of their bag and drain the last few drops of water from their small flask. They wait expectantly for the sun to appear, and then Fred knows their position: He points toward a low line of hills.

"We're well on track for the Slovakian border, Rudi."

Come what may, no one will take this moment of freedom away from them, as they each chew their bread free of armed Nazis, sirens, and orders. It's not easy to keep their balance without falling or to avoid sharp branches poking into their bodies, but they're so tired they manage to reach a state of drowsiness that allows them to rest a little.

Sometime later, they hear voices and the sound of hurried footsteps over the dead foliage. Alarmed, they open their eyes and see a horde of children rushing past a short distance from their tree. They have armbands with swastikas and they're singing German songs. The fugitives exchange a look of alarm: It's a Hitler Youth group on an outing. Bad luck would have it that the young leader in charge of the twenty or so children decides to stop for lunch in the clearing a few meters from their tree. The two men freeze and don't move a muscle. The children laugh, shout, run, fight, sing. . . . From their perch, the fugitives can make out their khaki uniforms and short pants. The rowdiness and energy of the children, and their occasional appearances dangerously close to the base of the tree searching for berries to throw at their companions are unsettling. Snack time ends, and the instructor orders the children to set off again. The noisy troop moves away, and there are sighs of relief from the top of the tree, as hands open and close in an attempt to get the circulation going again after being rigid for so long.

They're both anxiously counting the hours till nightfall. They take advantage of the last rays of the sun to get close to the road again and use the sunset to accurately locate the west.

Their second night is much more grueling than the first. They have to stop frequently to rest; they're worn out. The adrenaline rush brought on by their escape, which gave them strength the previous day, has tailed off. But even so, they continue on their way until the sky begins to lighten and they can't go any farther. Their road has offered them many crossings and junctions, and they've made their choices intuitively, but they really don't know where they are.

They've left the dense forest behind and reached a much less overgrown area, with scatterings of trees, cultivated fields, and scrubland. They know it's a populated area, but they're too tired to fuss. It's still very dark, but on one side of the road, they make out a clearing surrounded by shrubs. They head toward it, feel around for some leafy branches to pick up, and build an improvised shelter so they can sleep for a few hours. If the shelter is inconspicuous, they might even be able to spend the whole day in it. They climb into their hideout and close off the entrance with a couple of bushy branches. Daybreaks in Poland are very cold, so they huddle together to keep warm, and finally manage to fall into a sleep of sorts.

They sleep so deeply that when the sound of voices wakes them up, the sun is high in the sky, and they feel a stab of panic in their stomachs. Their refuge is nowhere near as dense as they had thought; the branches they used to close off the entrance leave obvious gaps, and they're astonished at what they see through these holes. They haven't stopped to rest in the clearing of a wood, as they believed. In the dark of night, without realizing it, they had reached the edge of a town, and what they had actually done was go to sleep in a public park. What they see, a few meters from what they thought was an unobtrusive clearing, are benches and swings.

The two exchange a petrified look, not daring to move a muscle, because they can hear footsteps approaching. When they were preparing their escape, they devised ways to avoid SS patrols, checkpoints, and dogs, but it is children who have become their worst nightmare.

Before fear has had time to overcome them, two children, a boy and a girl with blond hair and blue eyes, have already planted themselves in front of the entrance to their shelter and are staring at them with Aryan curiosity. They see a pair of black boots approaching a few steps behind the children, who turn around and run off, shouting in German,

"Papa, Papa, come! There are some strange men!"

The cap of an SS sergeant appears, and the Nazi stands there looking at them. Rudi and Fred are paralyzed, huddled together, completely vulnerable. The *Oberscharführer*'s head looks disproportionally large as it leans in among the branches, like the head of an ogre. The skull on the cap's peak looks at them as if it recognizes them. In that moment, the two fugitives see their entire lives flash before their eyes. They want to say something, but fear has taken away their voices and frozen any movement. The Nazi sergeant studies them, and a malicious smile appears on his face. They see his wife's high heels approaching and don't quite catch what her husband whispers to her.

All they hear is the scandalized German woman's loud reply:

"You can't bring children to a public park anymore without finding two men embracing each other among the plants! It's a disgrace!"

The woman storms off indignantly, and the sergeant, the little smile still on his face, collects his children and walks off after her.

Rudi and Fred look at each other lying on the weeds. They hadn't noticed that they were still hugging each other, as they were when they fell asleep. And so now they hug each other even more firmly and are eternally grateful that fear left them speechless. Anything they might have said, even a single word, would have betrayed them as foreigners. Silence is usually golden.

Rudi Rosenberg and Fred Wetzler believe they are not far from the Slovak border, though they don't know exactly the right road to the Beskidy mountain range. But that's their second problem. Their first is that they are not invisible. On a sharp corner of a lane, they almost run headfirst into a woman. They are in a populated area with open fields: It's inevitable that they'll come across people like this Polish peasant with a heavily wrinkled face, who is looking at them apprehensively.

The two men decide they have no other option but to risk everything—they were going to bump into someone sooner or later. And anyway, they need help. They've been without food for more than twenty-four hours, they haven't slept for days, and they don't even know if they're on the right track to Slovakia. They exchange a quick glance and instantly agree to tell the truth to this woman. In uncertain Polish, mixed with Czech phrases, much hand waving, and even interruptions to what the other is saying in an attempt to produce a convincing explanation, they tell the old woman that they are fugitives from Auschwitz. They are peaceful and just need to know how to get to the border so they can go back home.

The suspicious expression on the peasant woman's face hasn't altered: She even steps back when they try to come closer. Fred and Rudi fall silent. She peers at them with tiny eyes like peppercorns.

They are tired, hungry, disoriented—and frightened. They beg her for help with gestures, and she looks down. The two men exchange glances, and Fred motions with his head that they have to leave before the woman starts to shout for help and gives them away. But they are afraid that she'll sound the alarm the minute they turn around and stop eye contact with her.

They don't have time to launch into their retreat. The woman looks up, takes a step toward them as if she has reached a sudden decision, and grabs Rudi by the sleeve of his sweater. They realize that she wants to look at them more closely. She examines them in detail, just as she would a horse or a calf. She wants to see what sort of men they are: Their unshaven faces and dirty clothes aren't enough to convince her that they've told her the truth, but she also notices their haggard eyes, swollen from lack of sleep and sunken into their thin, almost cadaverous faces. She notices how their bones protrude everywhere and almost poke out through their skin. And then finally, she gives a nod. She gestures for them to stay where they are and indicates with another hand motion that she'll bring them something to eat; they even think they understand a bit of what she says to them in Polish—"person" and "border." After taking a few steps, the woman turns around and insists that they wait, that they stay right where they are.

Rudi whispers that she might go and report them to the German authorities, and that it might be an SS patrol that appears. Fred points out that they can go and hide but, if she raises the alarm that two fugitives from Auschwitz are here, the Germans will cordon off the area and search it. It would be very difficult for them to escape.

They decide to wait. They go over to the other side of the wooden bridge across the little stream from which they had taken a drink that very morning, so that if the SS do come, they'll see them early enough to be able to head into the forest and gain a minute's advantage. An hour goes by, and the old peasant woman hasn't reappeared. Their stomachs begin to demand something more than air.

"The sensible thing would be to return to the forest," mutters Rudi.

Fred agrees, but neither of them makes a move. They can't; they've used up all their energy. They've got nothing left to burn.

After two hours, they give up expecting anyone to come and huddle together to get some protection from the cold. They even doze off. The calm is broken by the sound of hurried footsteps. They aren't going to bother even trying to escape, no matter who it is. They open their eyes and see that the source of the footsteps is a twelve-year-old boy in a sackcloth jacket and a pair of pants held up with string. He is carrying a parcel. They manage to understand that the boy's grandmother has sent him. When they open the little wooden box he's carrying, they discover two steaming hot boiled potatoes on top of two thick fried fillets of veal. They wouldn't exchange them for all the gold in the world.

Before the boy leaves, they try to ask him about the Slovak border. The boy tells them to wait. So, somewhat calmer after the friendly gesture of food and invigorated by the meal, which they devoured with speedy delight, they stay where they are. Night falls almost immediately, and the temperature drops. They decide to go on short circular walks to keep stiffness and some of the cold at bay.

Finally, they hear the sound of feet again, more cautious this time, and hidden in the darkness. They only make out the man in the moonlight when he's almost on top of them: He's dressed in peasant clothing, but he's got a gun in his hand. Weapons are synonymous with bad news. The man stops in front of them and lights a match, which briefly illuminates their three faces. He has a thick, light brown mustache, which looks like a brush for polishing shoes. He lowers his hand with the gun and stretches out the other one for a handshake.

"Resistance."

That's all he says, but it's enough. Rudi and Wetzler jump with joy, they start to dance and hug until they fall to the ground. The Pole looks at them, perplexed. He wonders if they're drunk. And they are drunk—with freedom.

The partisan introduces himself as Stanis, although they suspect it isn't his real name. He explains to them in Czech that the reason the woman who found them was suspicious was that she thought they might be Gestapo agents in disguise, on the hunt for Poles collaborating with the Resistance. He tells them they're very close to the border, and they'll have to be careful about patrols of German soldiers, but he knows their timetable, and they are so precise that they go past the same spot at the exact same time every night, so the two fugitives will have no trouble avoiding them.

Stanis tells them to follow him. They walk silently in the dark along deserted paths for quite some time until they reach an abandoned stone hut with a collapsed straw roof. The wooden door gives way easily with a push. Inside, the vegetation and dampness have overgrown the four-sided stone space. The Pole squats down, lights a match, removes a few pieces of rotten wood, and grabs hold of a metal ring. He pulls on it and reveals a trapdoor. He takes a candle from his pocket and lights it. With help of the light, they go down a staircase into an old storeroom for hay built underneath the hut, but now containing some mattresses, blankets, and provisions. The three of them dine on cans of soup heated over a little gas camping stove. Then, for the first time in ages, Fred and Rudi sleep peacefully.

The Pole is a man of few words but extraordinary efficiency. They leave early the next morning, and he proves to know the forest tracks with the accuracy of a wild boar. After an entire day walking through the forests with barely a stop, they spend the night in a cave. The next day, they don't even stop. They go up and down the mountains, avoiding the patrols with ease, searching out rocks to hide in until the danger has passed and they can continue on their way. And at dawn the day after, they finally stand on Slovakian soil.

"You're free," says the Pole by way of farewell.

"No, we're not," answers Rudi. "We still have one duty to fulfill. The world must know what's happening."

The Pole nods, and his bushy mustache moves up and down in agreement.

"Thank you, thank you very much—you've saved our lives," Rudi and Fred tell him.

Stanis shrugs; there is nothing to say in reply.

The second part of the two men's journey will consist of trying to ensure that the world knows what's really going on inside the Third Reich, what Europe doesn't know or doesn't want to know: that it's a question of something more than a war about borders— it's the extermination of an entire race.

On April 25, 1944, Rudolf Rosenberg and Alfred Wetzler appeared before Dr. Oscar Neumann, the representative of the Slovakian Jews, in the headquarters of the Jewish Council in Zilina. Given his position as registrar in Auschwitz, Rudi was able to dictate a report full of chilling statistics. For the first time, the report described the mechanics of murder on a massive, organized scale, the physical exploitation of slave labor, the appropriation of belongings, the utilization of human hair for the production of cloth, and the extraction of gold and silver teeth and fillings with the objective of melting them down and converting them into coins for the Reich. Rudi calculated the number of Jews liquidated in Auschwitz at 1.76 million.

Rudi also spoke about lines of pregnant women with children clinging to their skirts being led to showers that spewed out poisonous gas; about punishment cells the size of concrete coffins, within which the prisoners couldn't even sit; about the long workdays spent outdoors by prisoners with snow up to their knees, dressed only in a summer shirt, and with only a bowl of watery soup for the entire day. He talked and talked, and from time to time, tears came to his eyes, but he didn't stop talking. He was possessed by a feverish desire to shout at a world deafened by the bombs of war that an even dirtier and more terrible war was happening within Europe's borders behind closed doors. And it had to be stopped, no matter the cost.

When Rudi finished dictating his report, he felt exhausted but satisfied, and at peace with himself for the first time in years. The report was sent immediately to Hungary. The Nazis had taken that country and were organizing the transportation of Jews to concentration camps, which the whole world believed were merely gathering places, not realizing that in reality they were factories of death.

But war not only destroys bodies with machine guns and explosions; it also wipes out sanity and kills souls. Rudi and Fred's warnings reached the Jewish Council in Hungary, but nobody took any notice of them. The Jewish leaders preferred to believe certain promises made to them by the Nazis and went ahead with the allocation of Jews to transports heading to Poland. This led to a massive increase in the number of arrivals of Hungarians in Auschwitz. After all the pain and suffering, after the joy of freedom, Rudi had to swallow the bitter pill of disillusionment. The report didn't save the Hungarian lives he believed they'd be able to save. War is like an overflowing river: It's hard to control and, if you put up a small barrier, it only gets swept along in its path.

Rudi Rosenberg and Fred Wetzler were evacuated to England, where they presented their report. They were listened to in the British Isles, although there was little that could be done from there except, perhaps, to fight with greater daring to put an end to the madness devastating Europe.

25.

ON MAY 15, 1944, ANOTHER TRANSPORT ARRIVED IN THE FAMILY CAMP
from Terezín with 2,503 new deportees. The next day a second train
arrived with another 2,500. And on the eighteenth, a third contingent arrived. All in all, there were an additional 7,500 people, of
whom almost half were German Jews (3,125); the rest were 2,543
Czechs, 1,276 Austrians, and 559 Dutch.

It's been chaotic this first morning—shouts, whistles, confusion.
Dita and her mother have not only been forced to sleep together in
the same bunk, but have had to share it with a third prisoner. She's
a very frightened Dutch woman who hasn't even been capable of
saying "good morning." She spent the night trembling.

Dita hurries toward Block 31, where Seppl Lichtenstern and
his team are overwhelmed trying to reorganize their barrack
school. The situation is anarchic because, on top of everything
else, there are now German and Dutch children in the hut along
with the Czech speakers, and it's difficult for them to understand
each other. Three hundred additional children arrived in the May
transport, and Dita has received orders from Lichtenstern and
Miriam Edelstein to suspend the library service temporarily until
new class groups have been organized and the situation becomes
clearer.

The little ones are nervous, and there are quarrels, shoving,
fights, arguments, tears, and an air of confusion that seems to keep

growing. They can't keep still; they're upset by the bites from bed-bugs, fleas, lice, and all manner of mites that live in the wet straw. Good weather encourages not only flowers but all sorts of bugs as well.

Miriam makes a drastic decision: She decides to use the last bit of coal that was being kept for an emergency to heat up buckets of water to wash the children's underwear. There's a huge kerfuffle, and there's no time to dry them fully on the chimney, so the children have to put them on again still damp, but it looks as if most of the insects have been drowned and as the day progresses, calm is gradually restored.

When those who have been assigned to work in Block 31 reach the row of huts where it is located, they think they have arrived at a bog. But discovering a clandestine school has left them stunned—and hopeful.

Lichtenstern calls them all together at the end of the day, when groups have been more or less organized and a certain school routine has been put in place. He introduces them to a young teenage girl with the legs of a ballerina and woolen socks, who is nervously rocking back and forth on her wooden clogs. Anyone who doesn't look at her carefully would think she's slight, maybe even fragile, but if they study her, they'll see the fire in her eyes. She seems to move about shyly, but at the same time she shamelessly observes everything around her. She tells them she's the block librarian.

Some people ask her to repeat what she's just said because they can't believe what they're hearing: "Is there a library as well? But books are forbidden!" They don't understand how such a dangerous and delicate matter can be in the hands of a young girl. So Miriam asks her to climb onto a stool so that everyone will listen to her.

"Good afternoon. I'm Edita Adler. We have a library of eight paper books and six 'living' books."

The look of puzzlement on the faces of some of the recent arrivals is so obvious that even Dita, who started speaking in a serious voice in order to convey her responsibility properly to so many adults, can't keep back a small laugh.

"Don't worry. We haven't gone mad. Obviously, the books aren't alive. It's the people who tell the stories who are alive; you'll be able to borrow them for your afternoon activities."

Dita continues to explain how the library works in Czech and amazingly fluent German. The newly appointed teachers standing in front of her are still bewildered by the inherent contradiction that arises in the discussion of the normal operation of a school inside the most abnormal place in the world. When she is done, Dita bows her head in the slightly exaggerated manner of Professor Morgenstern and barely manages to stop herself from laughing at her own formality. She finds even funnier the openmouthed amazement with which some of them look at her as she makes her way back through them to her more secluded spot.

"She's the librarian of Block Thirty-One," they whisper.

There's such a racket in the afternoon that it's impossible for Dita to hide away and read. She goes to her usual hiding spot and finds half a dozen boys gathered there torturing ants.

Poor ants, she thinks. *They must already have a tough enough time finding crumbs in Auschwitz.*

So she puts *A Short History of the World* under her clothes, scurries off to the latrines, and hides down the back behind some containers. Clearly it's hard to see, and the smell is awful—but it's so bad that the SS guards rarely stick their heads inside. What

Dita doesn't know is that for precisely that reason, the latrines are the preferred spot for black market deals.

It's almost soup time and hence the time to do business. Arkadiusz, a Polish man who does repair jobs around the camps, is one of the most active black marketeers: tobacco, a comb, a mirror, a pair of boots. . . .

He's Santa Claus with a prisoner's face, who can be asked for anything as long as you're prepared to give him something in return. Dita hears voices in the hut and turns over the pages of her book even more quietly. The conversation filters into her ears. One of the people talking is a woman.

Dita can't see her, but Bohumila Kleinová has a pointed nose that turns up, making her look somewhat haughty, but her soft, swollen bruised eyelids spoil that impression.

"I have a client. I'll need a woman the day after tomorrow, in the afternoon, before the evening count."

"Aunt Bohumila can arrange it, but the *Kapo* in charge of our hut is a bit nervous, and we'll have to give her more."

"Don't overdo it, Bohumila."

And then the tone of voice gets louder.

"I'm not asking for me, stupid! I'm telling you that it's the *Kapo*. If she doesn't turn a blind eye and doesn't let us use her cubicle, you'll be left without your tasty morsel."

Arkadiusz lowers his voice but he still sounds angry and menacing:

"We agreed on a ration of bread and ten cigarettes. You won't get a crumb more from me. Split it up among you however you want."

Even Dita hears the woman's grumble.

"Everything would be settled with fifteen cigarettes."

"I said that's not possible."

"Damned Polish moneylender! Fine, I'll give the *Kapo* two more cigarettes from my commission. But if I lose my income and I can't buy food on the black market, I'll get sick. And who's going to get you pretty young Jewish women? Then you'll come crying to Aunt Bohumila, yes, indeed, and you'll be sorry you were so pigheaded with me."

And then there's silence. When the exchanges are being finalized, there's always a moment's silence, as if the two parties need to concentrate in their own particular way. Arkadiusz takes out five cigarettes; Bohumila always asks for half in advance. The other part of the payment, the ration of bread, will be paid to the woman at the time of the rendezvous.

"I want to see the goods."

"Wait."

There's silence again for a few minutes and then Dita hears the woman's nasal voice again.

"Here it is."

Dita can't resist craning her neck and leaning forward a little, taking advantage of the shadows. She can make out the taller figure of the Pole and the bulky one of Bohumila, who doesn't look the slightest bit undernourished. There's also another woman, thinner, her head lowered and her hands in her lap.

The Pole lifts her skirt and gropes her intimate parts. Then he separates her arms and fondles her breasts, slowly kneading them while she stands motionless.

"She's not very young . . ."

"Better—that way she knows what she has to do."

Many of the women Bohumila recruits are mothers. They want the extra ration of bread because they can't bear the sight of their children going hungry.

The Pole nods and leaves.

"Bohumila," the woman whispers shyly, "this is a sin."

The other woman looks at her with a fake look of seriousness.

"You shouldn't worry about that, my dear. It's God's design—you have to earn your bread."

And she bursts into obscene laughter. She leaves the latrines still laughing, with the woman trailing along behind her, head bowed.

Dita feels a bitter taste in her mouth. She can't even escape back into the French Revolution and continue reading. She returns to her hut pale-faced, and as soon as her mother sees her come in, she abandons her conversation group while one of the women is midsentence and goes over to hug Dita. Just then, Dita is feeling small and vulnerable again. She'd like to spend the rest of her life in her mother's arms.

The flood of trains into the *Lager* loaded with Hungarian Jews—147 freight trains in total, carrying 435,000 people—adds even more nervousness to the camp these days. There are always hordes of children close to the camp fence absorbed in the train arrival spectacle: disoriented people being yelled at, pushed around, stripped, beaten.

"Das ist Auschwitz–Birkenau!"

Their bewildered faces demonstrate that the name means nothing to them. Many won't even learn where they are going to die.

Dita has no idea when the international observers will arrive and the window that Hirsch and Aunt Miriam talked about will open so that the truth can be shouted out. Nor does she know what hoops they'll have to go through. If she closes her eyes, she sees Dr. Mengele and his blank expression waiting for her in his white lab coat next to a marble slab.

And yet despite this worry, Dita still can't get Hirsch's death out of her mind. They've told her he decided to give up, but despite the evidence, she refuses to believe it. No explanation has satisfied her, no doubt because none has been what she wants to hear. They tell her she's stubborn—and they are right. The moment to give up may come, but she doesn't want to, so she goes to Block 32, the medical block, prepared to play her last remaining card. They were the last people to see Fredy Hirsch still breathing; they heard his final words.

There's a nurse folding sheets marked with repulsive-looking black rings at the entrance to the hospital.

"I wanted to see the doctors."

"All of them, child?"

"One of them . . ."

"Are you ill? Have you informed your *Kapo*?"

"No, I don't want them to treat me. I just want to consult them about something."

"Tell me what's wrong. I know by now how to treat everything that needs to be treated here."

"It's a question about something that happened with the September transport."

The woman tenses and looks at her suspiciously.

"And what do you want to ask?"

"It's about a person."

"A member of your family?"

"Yes, my uncle. I think the September transport doctors who were in the quarantine camp attended to him before he died."

The woman stares at her. Just then one of the doctors heads toward them; he's wearing a white coat covered with yellow rings.

"Doctor, here's a girl asking after someone from the September transport who she says was treated in the quarantine camp."

The doctor has bags under his eyes and looks tired, but even so, he attempts a friendly smile.

"Who was it you say we treated in the quarantine camp?"

"His name was Hirsch. Fredy Hirsch."

The smile disappears from his face as if a curtain had been closed. Suddenly, he becomes hostile.

"I've already repeated it a thousand times! There was nothing we could have done to save his life!"

"But what I wanted to—"

"We're not gods! He turned blue; nobody could have done anything. We did what we had to do."

Dita wants to ask him what Fredy said, but the doctor angrily turns and, clearly irritated, marches off without a good-bye.

"If you don't mind, sweetheart, we have work to do." And the nurse points to the door.

As she is leaving, Dita notices that someone is watching her. It's a slim, long-legged boy she's occasionally seen going in and out of the hospital block; he works as a messenger. She marches off angrily in search of Margit. She finds her delousing Helga at the back of the hut, so she sits down on a stone nearby.

"How are things, girls?"

"There are more lice since the May transports arrived."

"It's not their fault, Helga. There are more people, so there's more of everything," Margit replies in a conciliatory tone.

"More chaos, more racket . . ."

"Yes, but with God's help, we'll get through it," says Margit in an attempt to cheer her up.

"I can't take any more," sobs Helga. "I want to leave. I want to go home." Her sister begins to stroke her head rather than looking for lice.

"Soon, Helga, very soon."

In Auschwitz, everyone is obsessed with leaving, getting out of there and leaving that place behind forever. The only dreams, the only demands of God are to go home.

There is someone, however, who is moving in the reverse direction, someone who is returning to Auschwitz. Against all logic, against all wisdom, against all good sense, Viktor Pestek is traveling in a train *toward* Oświęcim, at the edge of which the biggest extermination camp in history has been built.

On May 25, 1944, Viktor Pestek reverses his journey of six weeks earlier: After he and Lederer had walked out of the *Lager* gate, they had caught a train in Oświęcim, according to their plan. The Czech, dressed as a lieutenant, had pretended to fall asleep as soon as they took their seats, and none of the patrols that swept through the train had dared even think about bothering an SS officer who was peacefully sleeping on the way to Krakow.

Once they had reached their destination, and without even leaving the station, they immediately caught a train to Prague. Viktor remembers that moment of hesitation when it came time to get off at Prague's huge main station. He particularly recalls the look he and Lederer exchanged. It was the moment to abandon the relative safety of the train compartment and launch themselves without any defenses into a place full of watchful eyes. Pestek's instructions had been clear: head high, eyes front, a disagreeable expression, and no stopping.

The waiting room in the station had been overrun with Wehrmacht soldiers who looked at their black SS uniforms with a mixture of respect and distrust. The civilians hadn't even dared raise their heads to give them a glance. No one had dared to address them. Lederer had suggested that they head for Plzen, where he had friends. Once there, they hid their SS clothes and found refuge in an abandoned cabin in the woods on the outskirts of the town. Lederer had cautiously started to reach out to his contacts so they could get false documents for the two of them and for Renée and her mother. That had taken several weeks. What they didn't know was that the Gestapo was hot on their heels.

For this return to Auschwitz, Pestek is wearing civilian clothes and carries a duffel bag, his SS uniform perfectly folded inside so he can put it on for one last time.

From his window seat, Viktor goes over the plan he has executed thousands of times already in his head. He took a sheet of paper from the camp office with the Katowice Command Headquarters stamp on it and prepared an authorization to collect Renée and her mother. It was common for the Gestapo to order prisoners to the Katowice detention center for interrogation. A pickup was organized, the prisoners were taken to the guardhouse at the camp's entrance, and a car from Katowice Headquarters collected them. Many never returned.

Viktor knows the procedure well. He knows which code words are used. He will make the call requesting that the two prisoners be made available for the Gestapo. And a member of the SS will go in a car to collect them up from Auschwitz–Birkenau. It will be Lederer, with the stamped authorization Viktor prepared before their escape. His fellow fugitive speaks perfect German. He'll pick up the women, collect Viktor in a spot nearby and then—freedom.

Lederer left one day earlier to meet with his Resistance contacts, who will provide them with a car. It must be dark and discreet. And German, of course.

Viktor's only doubt occurs when he tries to imagine Renée's reaction once they are free. He won't be an SS officer, and she won't be a prisoner. She'll be free to love him or reject him because of his previous life. She has said so little during their meetings that he realizes he knows very little about her. But that's not important to Viktor: They have their entire lives in front of them.

The train draws into the Oświęcim station very slowly. It's a gloomy afternoon. He'd forgotten the dirty color of the sky above Auschwitz. There aren't many people on the platform, but he spies Lederer sitting on a bench reading a newspaper. He was afraid the Czech would pull out at the last minute, but Lederer told him Viktor could count on him, and there he is. Nothing can go wrong now.

He gets out, happy to be so close to Renée. He pictures her smiling at him and tugging at one of those curls until it reaches her mouth. Lederer gets up from his bench to walk over to him. But two columns of SS guards beat him to it, almost bowling him over as they run onto the platform, machine guns at the ready.

Victor knows they've come for him.

The officer in charge blows stridently on his whistle and shouts. Pestek calmly sets his bag on the ground. SS soldiers yell at him to put his hands in the air; others shout at him to keep still or they'll kill him right there. It seems chaotic, but it's precisely executed. Contradictory orders are shouted out to confuse and paralyze the suspect. He smiles to himself sadly. He knows the procedure for an arrest by heart; he's carried it out himself many times.

On the platform, Lederer slowly retreats. They haven't noticed him, and he takes advantage of the commotion caused by the arrest to slip away. As he walks off, trying to stay calm, he curses the heavens: The Resistance is riddled with informers. Someone has betrayed them. He finds an unchained motorbike in town, gets on it, and doesn't look back.

Viktor Pestek is taken to the central quarters of the SS. They will torture him for days. They want to know why he came back to Auschwitz; they want information about the Resistance, but he knows nothing about them, and he says nothing about his relationship with Renée Neumann. He will remain in jail until he is executed on October 8, 1944.

26.

MARGIT AND DITA ARE SITTING AT THE BACK OF THE HUT. THE
afternoons have grown longer, and it's even starting to get a bit hot.
It's a sticky heat in Auschwitz, stained with swirls of ash. The girls'
conversation has tapered off. Their friendship has reached a point
where moments of silence don't bother them. An old friend suddenly appears.

"Renée! It's been a long time!"

The blond girl gives a faint smile at the reception. She tugs
down a curl and chews it. Hardly anyone has treated her kindly in
recent times.

"Did you hear about Lederer's escape with a first officer of the
SS who didn't want to be a Nazi anymore?"

"Yes. It was that Nazi you used to tell us about, the one who
used to look at you. . . ."

Renée nods her head very slowly.

"It turns out he wasn't a bad person," she tells them. "He really
didn't like what was going on in here. That's why he deserted."

Dita and Margit don't say a word. To a Jew, a Nazi SS officer
who acts as an executioner in an extermination camp . . . can it
really be that he's not a bad person? It's hard to accept. And yet,
every one of them has stood watching one of those immature young
men dressed in his black uniform and high boots. And when they

look into his eyes, they don't see an executioner or a guard; they see a young man.

"Two patrol guards approached me this afternoon. They pointed at me and laughed. They told me that two days ago they arrested— well, those two pigs said he was my lover, but that's a dirty lie. Anyway, they arrested him at Oświęcim station."

"Three kilometers from here! But he escaped almost two months ago! Why didn't he hide farther away?"

Renée looks thoughtful for a moment. "I know why he was so close."

"Was he hiding in the town all this time?"

"No, I'm sure he was coming from Prague. He came back to get me out of here—and my mother, of course, I'd never have gone without her. But they caught him. . . ."

The other two girls remain silent. Renée looks down. She regrets having been so honest with them. She turns and starts to walk back to her hut.

"Renée," Dita calls after her. "That Viktor, maybe he wasn't a bad person, after all."

Renée takes her time in agreeing. In any event, she'll no longer be able to find out.

Margit heads off to spend some time with her family, and Dita is left on her own. Today, there aren't any inmates in the quarantine camp, and the neighboring camp on the other side, camp BIIc, is also temporarily empty, its occupants evacuated to where no one knows. It's unusual for these two neighboring camps to be empty. And because of the unusually hot afternoon, people in the family camp are inside their huts. Dita pauses to take in the rare moment of silence.

Then she notices that someone is looking at her. A solitary

figure in camp BIIc waves and gestures at her. It's a prisoner, a teenager who must be carrying out some repairs. As she walks toward the fence on her side, taking a proper look, she sees that he's wearing a newer striped suit than usually worn by the prisoners in the camps, and his beret is a sign that he belongs to the maintenance crew, a privileged group. She recalls Arkadiusz, the Pole who takes advantage of his assigned task of covering the barrack roofs with asphalt sheets to do deals in the latrines. His talent for carrying out all sorts of repairs gives him access to all the camps and, what's even better, to improved food rations. That's why the maintenance people are instantly recognizable, just like this one, by their healthy look.

Dita makes as if she's leaving, but he gesticulates wildly, waving her closer. He seems pleasant enough and, between laughs, says a few words in Polish that Dita doesn't understand. She only manages to decipher the word *jabko*, which means "apple" in Czech—a magic word. Anything that suggests food is magic.

"*Jabko?*"

He smiles and signals no with his finger.

"Not *jabko . . . jajko!*"

Dita feels a little disillusioned. It's been so long since she tasted an apple that she's almost forgotten what it's like. She thinks they are sweet but a little tart, but what she remembers best is the crunch of their flesh. Her mouth waters. She has no idea what the boy is trying to saying to her. Maybe it's nothing in particular and he just wants to flirt with her, but she's determined to find out. It makes her a bit uncomfortable, but she's not really bothered that older boys now notice her.

She's frightened of the electric fence. She's already seen several inmates walking with feverish resolve until they hit the fence and receive a lethal electric shock. After the first time, whenever Dita has seen someone heading toward the fence with that mad look in their eyes, she's walked away as quickly as she can, away from the horrific cries. She's never been able to forget that first spark, the frizzy hair of that sickly woman, her body suddenly turning black, the disagreeable smell of singed flesh, the wisps of smoke rising from the charred body.

She really dislikes approaching the fence, but hunger is like a worm that never stops gnawing your innards. It can barely be soothed at night with a piece of bread and a hint of margarine and, if she's not lucky enough to catch something floating in her soup, it has to wait another twenty-four hours before something solid hits her stomach. Dita isn't prepared to miss any chance of putting something in her belly, even if she doesn't understand what the Polish boy is saying.

To avoid attracting the attention of the soldiers in the towers, Dita gestures for the boy to wait and goes into the latrine barrack. She races through the revolting hut and comes out the back door. She's now at the back of the building, close to the fence. She's scared she'll find bodies on the ground, because that's where they usually bring the people who have died during the night, but the area is clear. The Polish boy has a hooked nose, and his ears stick out like fans. He's not very handsome, but he has such a cheerful smile that Dita finds him cute. He, in turn, signals to her to wait a moment and goes back inside the rear of his hut as if he were in search of something.

The only person visible in that back part of BIIb is a gaunt prisoner who has lit a fire a few huts away and is burning bundles of ragged clothes. Dita doesn't know if he has been ordered to burn them because they are infested with lice or because they belonged to someone who died of a contagious disease. Either way, handling infected rags isn't a great job, but it's better than many others. From a distance he looks like an old man, but he's probably not even forty yet.

While she waits for the carpenter boy to return, she keeps herself entertained by watching the ragged clothes burn, shrinking and twisting in the flames before they disintegrate in a puff of smoke. And at that very moment, she senses a presence behind her. When she turns around, the tall black figure of Dr. Mengele is standing two paces away from her. He's not whistling; he's not making any sound or movement. He's just looking at her. Maybe he followed her here. Maybe he thinks the Polish boy is a contact from the Resistance. The man burning the clothes rises and scurries off. At last, she's on her own with Mengele.

She wonders how she'll explain the pockets on the inside of her dress when they do a body search. Or if it's really worth justifying anything. Mengele doesn't interrogate his prisoners; he's interested only in their internal organs.

The medical captain says nothing. Dita feels compelled to apologize for her presence at the fence:

"Ich wollte mit dem Mann dort sprechen—" I wanted to speak with the man who's over there.

She speaks without much conviction. The man is no longer by the fire.

Mengele stares at her intently, and Dita realizes that his eyes are half closed, and he has the expression of someone who's trying to recall something he's on the verge of remembering. She recalls what the seamstress said to her: *You're a bad liar.* Right then she is absolutely convinced that Dr. Mengele hasn't believed her, and she feels her body suddenly grow cold, as if it's already on that chilly marble slab on which he'll slit her open.

Mengele gives a brief nod. It's true, he was trying to remember something—it had slipped his mind—but now he's got it. He almost smiles, reaching for his belt, his hand just a few centimeters from his gun. Dita tries not to shake. At this very moment Dita asks for something very small, a tiny concession—she begs that she won't shake in her last moment, or wet herself. A last shred of dignity. That's all.

Mengele continues to nod, then starts to whistle. And Dita realizes that he's not exactly looking at her; his gaze is passing through her. She is so insignificant to him that he hasn't even noticed her. He turns on his heel and marches off whistling contentedly.

Bach occasionally eludes him.

Dita watches his tall, black, horrible figure move away. And then it comes to her: *He doesn't remember me at all. He has no idea who I am. He was never pursuing me. . . .*

He never waited for her at the door of the hut, or took note of her in his little book; the way he looked at her was no different from the way he looked at everyone else. It was all just the routine, macabre joke of someone who told the children to call him Uncle Pepi, who smiled as he stroked their hair and then plunged an injection of hydrochloric acid into them to study its deadly impact.

Dita gives a sigh of relief, unburdened. Although she's still in danger, of course. That's Auschwitz. . . .

It would be wise to go quickly to her hut; Mengele might return. But she's curious to find out why the Polish carpenter boy was calling her so urgently.

Would it simply be some promise of love? Dita's not interested in romance, especially not with some Pole she can't understand, whose ears look like bowls. She doesn't want anyone to tell her what to do.

But despite all this, she stands obstinately rooted to the spot.

The Polish boy saw Mengele coming and stayed hidden in the empty hut. When he sees that Mengele has gone, he reappears on the other side of the fence. Dita doesn't see anything in his hands and feels tricked. The boy looks to one side and the other and then takes a few hurried steps to the fence. He's still smiling. Dita doesn't find his ears so big anymore; his smile wipes out everything else.

Her heart stops beating when the young carpenter puts his closed fist through a gap in the barbed wire fence. When he opens his fist, something white drops out and rolls to Dita's feet. At first sight, it looks to her like a huge pearl. It is a pearl: a boiled egg. She hasn't eaten an egg in two years. She can hardly even remember what they taste like. She takes it in both hands as if it were delicate, and looks up at the boy who has pulled his hand back through the thousands of volts that snake through the wires.

They can't understand each other; he speaks only Polish. But the way in which Dita leans over, the way her eyes sparkle with happiness, he understands better than any speech. He lowers his head in a ceremonial bow as if they had met at a reception in a palace.

Dita thanks him in all the languages she knows. He winks at her and slowly enunciates "*jajko*." She blows him a kiss with one hand before starting to run back to her hut. Still smiling, the Pole pretends to jump and catch the kiss in the air.

As she runs back with her white treasure to find her mother and have a feast, she thinks this language lesson will accompany her for the rest of her life; in Polish, an egg is a *jajko*. Words are important.

This will become especially clear the next day. During morning roll call, the prisoners are informed that after the evening's roll call, each adult will be given a postcard so they can write to their loved ones. The camp *Kapo*, a German with the triangle of a regular convict on his jacket, goes up and down the rows repeating that no defeatist or defamatory messages about the Third Reich are allowed; in such cases, the postcards will be destroyed and their authors severely punished. And he stresses the word *severely* with an ill will that foreshadows the punishment.

The block *Kapos* are given even more concrete instructions: Words like *hunger, death, execution* are forbidden. Also out are any words that cast doubt on the great truth: They are privileged to work for the glorious Führer and his Reich. During the meal break, Lichtenstern explains that the camp *Kapo* has insisted that each block chief order their respective huts to write cheerful messages. The director of Block 31, his face ever skinnier on his diet of cigarettes and turnip soup, tells them to write whatever they please.

All sorts of comments are heard throughout the day. Some people are surprised by this humanitarian gesture on the part of the Nazis, allowing them to contact their families and ask them to send food packages. But the veterans quickly explain to them that the Nazis are, first and foremost, pragmatic. It suits them to have packages sent to the camp; they'll help themselves to the best items. And Jews outside the camps will receive comforting messages from family members, generating doubt about what's happening in Auschwitz.

There is reason for concern: The members of the September transport were given postcards to write just before they were sent to the gas chambers. The December transport is now about to complete its six-month stay in the camp.

But postcards are also distributed to the recent May arrivals. A contagious uncertainty is added to the habitual hunger and fear in Block 31. No one can focus on the afternoon games and songs.

The postcards are finally handed out—to adults only—after the evening roll call. Many of the inhabitants of other huts have gone to line up in front of Arkadiusz, the black marketeer, who has delivered the packets of postcards and discreetly made it known that he has several pencils for loan in return for a piece of bread. Others have gone to find Lichtenstern, who has a few pencils for the school and has reluctantly allowed them to be used.

Dita sits down outside the door of her hut with her mother and watches people nervously pacing, holding their postcards. Her mother wants Dita to write to her aunt; it's been almost two years with no news. Dita wonders what will have happened to her cousins, what will have happened in the world out there.

By her estimation, there's room for thirty words. If the gas chamber awaits them after they've written their postcards, then those thirty words will be the last ones she'll leave behind, her only legacy. And she can't even put down what she really feels, because if the letter is gloomy, they won't send it and they'll punish her mother. *Are the Germans really going to read more than four thousand postcards?* she thinks to herself.

The Nazis are disgustingly methodical.

And she keeps turning over those thirty words. She overhears one of the women teachers say that she will mention in her card that she was reading a book by Knut Hamsun, to signal to her relatives *Hunger*, the title of his most famous novel. Dita finds that somewhat obscure. Others try subterfuges, too—some ingenious, others so metaphorical that no one will understand them—to hide their forbidden messages of genocide. Some want to ask for the maximum allowable amount of food; others want news of the outside world, but many simply want to say that they were alive. In the afternoon, the teachers organize a competition to see who was best able to disguise the secret messages.

Dita tells her mother they should write the truth.

"The truth . . ."

Her mother, somewhat scandalized, mutters the word *truth* as if it were blasphemy. Telling the truth implies talking about terrible sins and writing about aberrations. How could you consider telling even a small part of something so abominable?

Liesl Adler feels ashamed of her own fate, as if anyone who receives such luck has to be guilty of something. She regrets the fact that her daughter is so impulsive and so flighty, that she isn't more discreet in weighing up the significance of things. In the end, she takes the card and decides that she herself will write a note in which she'll say that the two of them are fine, thanks be to God; that her beloved Hans, may he be with God, didn't overcome an infectious disease; and that they are really looking forward to seeing all of them again. Dita looks at her mother defiantly for a moment, and Liesl tells her that they know this postcard will reach its destination and keep them in touch with their family.

"This way, they'll have some news about us."

Despite her caution, Dita's mother won't achieve her objective: When her postcard reaches its destination, nobody is there to receive it.

The Allied aerial bombings are becoming more frequent and rumor has it that the Germans are losing ground at the front, that the war has changed direction, and the end of the Third Reich could be close. If they pass the six-month mark and are still alive, then maybe they *will* see the end of the war and be able to return home. But nobody is very optimistic: There's been talk of the end for years.

The next morning, Dita displays her library on the wooden bench yet again, and while the groups are getting settled on their stools, Miriam Edelstein comes over and puts her mouth close to Dita's ear.

"They're not going to come," she whispers.

Dita gestures that she doesn't understand.

"Schmulewski has found out. It seems that the international observers were in Terezín and the Nazis organized everything to perfection. So they didn't ask to see anything else. The International Red Cross observers won't be coming to Auschwitz."

"So . . . what about our moment?"

"I don't know, Edita. I want to believe that there's always a moment for truth. We'll have to be attentive and patient. If the Red Cross isn't going to come, the family camp probably stops being useful to Himmler."

Dita feels cheated. And if their lives have been worth very little up to this point, now they are worth nothing.

"Bad, bad," Dita mutters.

Events don't take long to unfold. On a morning seemingly like all the others, Lichtenstern calls classes to an end five minutes early, although no one else realizes it—he's the only one in the entire camp who has a watch. He climbs with some difficulty onto the horizontal ledge of the stove. The children, who think morning classes are over before soup time, race around laughing and happily playing jokes on each other. No one expects it when the block chief raises the whistle to his lips, calling for attention.

Just for an instant, the sound reminds the old hands of the much-missed Fredy Hirsch, and they fall silent; they know that something serious must have occurred if Lichtenstern is using Hirsch's whistle.

Lichtenstern says that he has important news. He looks tired, but his voice is decisive.

"Teachers, students, assistants, I have to tell you that Birkenau–Auschwitz Command Headquarters has informed us that this block has to be vacated by tomorrow. That's all I know."

By the afternoon, Block 31 is empty, only a warehouse again. Dita knocks on the door several times, and when Lichtenstern doesn't answer, she uses the key they gave her weeks ago.

She takes advantage of the fact that Lichtenstern is absent, and that there's still a bit of time before curfew, to take out the library books one by one.

She hasn't leafed through the atlas for days and feels immense pleasure as she retraces the sinuous outline of the coastlines, climbs up and down mountain ranges, whispers the names of cities like London, Montevideo, Ottawa, Lisbon, Peking. . . . And as she does this, she feels she can hear her father's voice again as he turns the globe. She removes the yellowing cover of *The Count of Monte Cristo*, a book whose secrets she was able to discover even though they were in French, thanks to Markéta. She whispers aloud the name of Edmond Dantès and works on imitating a French accent until she feels satisfied. The moment to abandon the prison on If has arrived.

She also places H. G. Wells, her private professor of history, on top of the table. And the Russian grammar, Freud's book, and the geometry treatise, as well as the Russian novel with no front or back cover that contains the mysterious Cyrillic script she failed to decipher. Very carefully, she takes the last book out of the hidey-hole—*The Adventures of the Good Soldier Švejk* with its missing pages. She can't resist the temptation to read a few lines to assure herself that the rogue Švejk is still there, lurking among its pages. And there he is, in full flight, trying to soothe Lieutenant Lukáš after his most recent blunder.

> *"Half the consommé soup in this bowl you've brought me from the kitchen is missing."*
>
> *"Yes, Lieutenant. It was so hot that it was evaporating as I came over here."*
>
> *"It's evaporated into your belly, you shameless parasite."*
>
> *"Lieutenant, sir, I can assure you that it was all caused by evaporation; these things happen. There was a mule driver transporting some casks of hot wine to Karlovy Vary who . . ."*
>
> *"Out of my sight, you animal!"*

Dita hugs the pile of pages as if it were an old friend.

She devotes time to gluing some of the loose spines carefully with gum arabic and to using a bit of saliva on a cloth to clean the odd cover stained with dirt from the hidey-hole. She mends their wounds, no doubt for the last time. When she can do no more to fix them, she runs her hand back and forth over the pages like an iron to remove some of the creases. She's not just smoothing them; she's caressing them.

When they're lined up, the books form a tiny row, a modest display of veterans. But over these past few months, they've enabled hundreds of children to walk through the geography of the world, get close to history, and learn math. And also to become drawn into the intricacies of fiction and amplify their lives many times over. Not bad for a handful of old books.

27.

THE WORKSHOPS AND BLOCK 31 HAVE ALREADY BEEN SHUT DOWN. HER mother is taking part in a conversation of the women led by Mrs. Turnovská. Dita sits at back of the hut, her back propped up against the wall. There are so many women that it's hard to find a spot to lean against. Margit comes over to join her and settles herself as best she can on the tiny piece of blanket provided by Dita. She chews her lower lip, a sure sign she's agitated.

"Do you really think they're going to transfer us somewhere else?"

"You can count on it. I just hope it's not to the other world."

Margit fidgets nervously beside her. They hold hands.

"I'm frightened, Ditiňka."

"We're all frightened."

"No, you are so calm. You even joke about the transfer. I'd like to be as brave as you, but I'm really afraid. I'm shaking all over. It's hot, and I feel cold."

"Once, when my legs were really shaking, Fredy Hirsch told me that the truly brave people are the ones who are afraid."

"How can that be?"

"Because you have to be brave to feel fear and keep going. If you're not frightened, what's the advantage of choosing one thing over another?"

"I saw Mr. Hirsch going past along the *Lagerstrasse* a few times. He was really handsome! I would like to have known him."

"He wasn't someone you could get to know easily. He spent his life inside his cubicle. He did the Friday chats, organized sports activities, resolved problems if they came up—he was very friendly toward everyone . . . but then he would disappear into his cubicle. It was almost as if he wanted to keep himself apart."

"Do you think he was happy?"

Dita turns toward her friend with a look of incredulity.

"What a question, Margit! Who would know that? I don't know . . . but I think so. It wasn't easy for him, but I suspect he liked challenges. And he never got cold feet."

"You admired him, didn't you?"

"How can you not admire someone who teaches you to be brave?"

"But . . ." Margit hunts for the right words, because she knows she's going to say something that might offend. "But in the end, Hirsch did get cold feet. He didn't hold up right to the end."

Dita gives a deep sigh.

"I've thought a great deal about his death. They've told me this and that. But I still think there's something missing, that there's something in all of this that doesn't fit. Hirsch giving up? No."

"But the registrar, Rosenberg, saw him die."

"Indeed."

"Although I've also heard that you can't always trust what Rosenberg says."

"They say so many things. But I believe that on that afternoon of the eighth of March something happened that changed everything. The unfortunate thing is that we'll never be able to ask him what it was."

Dita stops talking, and Margit respects her silence for a few moments.

"And what will happen to us now, Ditiňka?"

"Who knows? There's no point in worrying too much. You and I can't do anything. If someone decides to organize a revolt, we'll hear about it."

"Do you think there'll be a revolt?"

"No. If there wasn't one with Fredy, without him it's impossible."

"Then we'll have to pray."

"Pray? To whom?"

"To God. Who else? You should pray, too."

"Hundreds of thousands of Jews have been praying to him since 1939, and he hasn't listened to them."

"Maybe we haven't prayed enough, or loudly enough so he'll hear us."

"Come on, Margit. God is capable of knowing that you've sewn a button on a shirt on the Sabbath and punishing you, but he hasn't discovered that thousands of innocents are being killed and many other thousands are being held captive and being treated worse than dogs? Do you really believe he hasn't found out?"

"I don't know, Dita. It's a sin to question why God does what he does."

"Well then, I'm a sinner."

"Don't talk like that. God will punish you!"

"More?"

"You'll go to hell."

"Don't be naïve, Margit. We're already in hell."

Rumors continue to slither through the camp. There are those who say that the Germans are going to kill everyone. Others believe that they'll set apart those suitable for work and kill the rest.

The Priest comes into the camp without warning, accompanied by two armed guards. People pretend they're not watching him, but they don't take their eyes off him. The three Germans come to a halt at the entrance to one of the huts, and the *Kapo* instantly appears.

She strolls anxiously around the immediate area and then points to a prisoner sitting along the side of the hut, a woman with a child resting his head in her lap. It's Aunt Miriam and her son, Arieh. The sergeant informs her that he has direct orders from Kommandant Schwarzhuber: They're going to transfer her and her son to be with her husband.

Eichmann had told her they'd soon be together. In this instance, he was telling the truth. But Eichmann's truths are even worse than his lies.

They take Miriam and her son by jeep to Auschwitz I and escort them into a room where two guards are holding the handcuffed Yakub by the arms with a vise-like grip. Miriam has a hard time recognizing him inside his dirty striped suit and, even worse, inside the shredded skin barely sticking to his bones. It probably takes him a moment to recognize her, because he isn't wearing his round glasses with their tortoiseshell frames. No doubt he lost them when he first arrived, and everything after that must have been a blur.

Miriam and Yakub Edelstein have sharp minds. They immediately understand why they have been reunited. No one can begin to imagine what must pass through their minds in this instant.

An SS corporal takes out his gun, points it at little Arieh, and shoots him on the spot. Then he shoots Miriam. By the time he shoots Yakub, he is surely already dead inside.

When the process to close camp BIIb is set in motion on July 11, 1944, it holds twelve thousand prisoners. Dr. Mengele organizes the selection, which takes three days. Out of all the huts, he chooses Block 31 for the process since, as it contains no bunks, it offers a brighter workspace. Mengele comments to his assistants that it is the only hut where the smell isn't nauseating. Although he is a great fan of autopsies, Mengele is also a refined person who can't stand bad smells.

The family camp has come to the end of its life. Dita Adler and her mother get ready to pass through the filter of Dr. Mengele, who will decide if they live or die. They've been ordered to line up according to their huts after their breakfast slop. All the inhabitants of the camp are agitated: People move about on edge and go back and forth, using up what might be their last few moments. Husbands and wives run to each other to say good-bye. Many couples meet in the middle of the *Lagerstrasse*, halfway between their respective huts. There are hugs, kisses, tears, and even reproaches. There is still the odd person who says, "If we'd gone to North America when I told you. . . ." They all spend what could be their final moments in their own way. Before the indifferent gaze of the SS soldiers who have arrived in the camp, the *Kapos* angrily blow their whistles to order everyone back to their own barracks.

Mrs. Turnovská comes over to wish Liesl good luck.

"Luck, Mrs. Turnovská?" says another of the women from their group of bunks. "What we need is a miracle!"

Dita walks a few steps away from the bustle of people nervously wandering up and down. She senses that someone has stopped right behind her; she can even feel his breath on the back of her neck.

"Don't turn around," comes the order.

Dita, so accustomed to orders, stands rooted to the spot without looking behind her.

"You've been asking about Hirsch's death, right?"

"Yes."

"Well, I know things . . . but don't turn around!"

"The only thing they've told me so far is that he was afraid, but I know that the fear of dying wouldn't have given him cold feet."

"You're right about that. I saw the list of inmates the SS were going to reclaim and remove from the quarantine camp to be brought back to the family camp. Hirsch was on that list. He wasn't going to die."

"Then why did he commit suicide?"

"You're wrong about that," comes the reply, but there's hesitation in his voice for the first time, as if he doesn't know how much to tell. "Hirsch didn't commit suicide."

Dita wants to know the full story, and she turns toward her enigmatic speaker. But as she does, he breaks into a quick run through the crowd of people. Dita recognizes him: It's the errand boy from the hospital block.

She's about to set off in pursuit when her mother grabs her by the shoulder.

"We have to line up!"

Their *Kapo* has started to lay about with her stick, and the guards are doing the same with their guns. There's no time. Dita reluctantly gets in line next to her mother.

What does it mean that Fredy Hirsch didn't commit suicide?

So then what? He didn't die in the way they told her? She thinks maybe the boy has invented his story. *But why would he do that? It was all a joke, and that's why he ran off when she turned around? It's possible.* But something tells her that's not the case: There was no smile in his eyes in that instant when she looked at him. She's now more convinced than ever that what happened in the quarantine camp that afternoon bears no resemblance to what people in the Resistance are saying. *So why would they lie? Maybe even they didn't know the ultimate truth of what actually happened.*

Too many questions at a time when the answers might come too late. There are thousands of people in the family camp, but they all have to pass in front of the compass-needle eye of the mad Dr. Mengele, which points toward life or death.

Groups have been going into and out of Block 31 for hours, and nobody knows for sure what's happening. They've been given their lunchtime soup, and they've been allowed to sit on the ground, but tiredness and nervousness caused by the wait have left their mark on the women in Dita's group. And rumors are rife, of course. The healthier inmates are being separated from the ill and the unproductive ones. Some of the women comment that Dr. Mengele is deciding who lives and who dies with his customary indifference. The male and female prisoners have to enter the hut naked so that the captain can examine them. Someone says that Mengele has at least had the decency to have the men and the women go in separately. They say he doesn't even look at the naked women in a lustful way, that he looks at everyone with absolute indifference, that he occasionally yawns, tired and bored with his task as examiner of human beings.

A cordon of SS soldiers controls access to Block 31. The groups who won't go through selection that day stroll tensely around the camp. The teachers try to keep the children occupied until the last minute. Some groups sit behind the huts and try to organize guessing games or whatever else they can come up with. Even snooty Markéta is playing Drop the Handkerchief with some of her girls. Each time she picks up the handkerchief, she furtively lifts it to her face to wipe away her tears. Her eleven-year-old girls, who are running around full of life, arguing and fighting over who managed to touch the hanky first . . . will the Germans consider any of them old enough to be part of the workforce, or will they kill them all?

Finally, Dita is lined up with the women from her hut in front of Block 31. They make them undress and put their clothes on top of huge piles, which are starting to form a mountain range of rags on the surface of the mud.

She feels more concern for the nude body of her mother on public display than for her own. She turns away so she won't see Liesl's wrinkled breasts, her exposed sex, the bones sticking out from under her skin. Some women have their arms crossed in an attempt to hide their intimate parts as best they can, but most don't care anymore. There are small groups of SS soldiers on either side of the lines. They are at ease and off duty, and they spend the morning eyeing the naked women maliciously and making loud comments about the ones they fancy. The bodies are squalid, their ribs are more curved than their hips, and there are girls who have barely a wisp of pubic hair between their legs, but the soldiers are desperate for some distraction, and they are so used to seeing the skeletal thinness of the inmates that they cheer on the women as if they were luscious beauties.

Dita tries to peer over the wall of soldiers to see what's

happening inside the hut by getting up on her tiptoes. Despite the fact that both her own life and her mother's are at risk, she can't stop thinking sadly about her library. The books are still in the hidey-hole, stored underground and sleeping deeply until someone finds them by chance and opens them, thereby restoring them to life, just like the Prague legend of the Golem, who lies inert in a secret place waiting for someone to resuscitate him. She now regrets not having left a message with the books in case some other prisoner trapped inside Auschwitz finds them. She would like to have said, *Take care of them, and they'll take care of you.*

They have to wait naked for several more hours. Their legs hurt, and they become weak. One woman sits down because she can't take any more, and she refuses to stand up despite the shouts and threats of a young *Kapo*. Two guards haul her off to the hut as if they were carrying a sack of potatoes. The rest of the women suspect that they'll have thrown her directly onto the reject pile.

Dita's turn finally comes, and enveloped by murmurs and prayers, she and her mother walk through the entrance of Block 31. The woman just in front of them is sobbing.

"Don't cry, Edita," whispers her mother. "Now's the time to show that you're strong."

Dita nods. Inside the hut, despite the tension in the air, the armed SS soldiers, and the table in front of the chimney where Mengele pronounces his sentence, she somehow feels protected. The Germans haven't removed the children's pictures from the walls. There are various versions of Snow White and her dwarves, princesses, jungle animals, and ships drawn in many colors from the early days when there were still some drawing classes. She realizes how much she misses being able to draw in Auschwitz as she used to in Terezín, to turn the chaos of her emotions into a picture.

However, though the drawings and stools are still there, Block 31 no longer exists. It is no longer a school. It is no longer a refuge. Now, just inside the door, they come up against an office table with Dr. Mengele seated behind it, together with a registrar and two guards with submachine guns. Two groups of those already selected are forming at the back of the hut. The one on the left will stay in Auschwitz, and the one on the right will be sent to work at another camp. The young women and the middle-aged women who look healthy—in other words, those who can still work—are in the group on the right. The other, much bigger group consists of small children, old women, and women who look sick.

When they say that the group on the left is going to stay in Auschwitz, they are telling the truth: Their ashes will settle on top of the forest slime and mix forever with the mud of Birkenau.

The impassive Nazi doctor waves his white-gloved hand to the left and to the right, and channels people to one side of life or the other. He does it with remarkable ease. And without hesitation.

The line in front of Dita is dwindling. The woman who was crying has been sent to the left with those whom the Reich deems weak and expendable.

Dita takes a deep breath: It's her turn.

She takes a few steps and stops in front of the medical captain's table. Dr. Mengele looks at her. Dita wonders if he really will recognize her as a member of Block 31, but it's impossible to know what he's thinking. What she sees in the doctor's eyes, however, sends shivers up her spine: nothing. No emotion whatsoever. The look is frighteningly empty and terrifyingly neutral.

He recites the questions he's spent hours routinely asking each inmate:

"Name, number, age, and profession."

Dita knows that the instructions given to everyone are to name any profession that might be useful to the Germans—carpenter, farmer, mechanic, cook—and the instructions given to minors is to bump up their age and say they are older so that they're more likely to make the cut. Dita knows all that, and she has to be careful, but her character demands something different.

Standing in front of the all-powerful Dr. Josef Mengele, owner of life and death like an Olympian god, she recites her name, Edita Adler; her number, 73305; her age, sixteen (she's added a year). When it comes time to provide her profession, she hesitates briefly and then, instead of saying something useful and convenient that will please the SS man with the iron cross on his chest, she finally says, "Painter."

Mengele, bored, tired by what for him must be mere routine, looks her in the eye more attentively, in the same way that snakes lift their heads when prey comes within reach.

"Painter? Do you paint walls or portraits?"

Dita feels her heart beating repeatedly in her throat, but she answers in her impeccable German and with a composure that smacks of rebellion:

"I paint portraits, sir."

Screwing up his eyes a little, Mengele looks at her with the faint hint of an ironic smile.

"Could you paint me?"

Dita has never been so scared. She couldn't be in a more vulnerable position: fifteen years old, alone and naked in front of men with submachine guns who are going to decide right now if they will kill her or let her live a little longer. Sweat runs down her naked skin, and the drops fall to the ground. But she answers with surprising vigor.

"Yes, sir!"

Mengele studies her slowly. It's not a good sign if the medical captain pauses to think. Any veteran would say that nothing good can come out of that mind. Everyone is waiting for the outcome. There's not a sound in the hut; you can't even hear people breathing. Even the SS guards with the submachine guns don't dare disturb the doctor's moment of reflection. Finally, Mengele gives an amused smile and, gesturing with his gloved hand, sends her to the right—to the fit group.

But there's no sigh of relief from Dita yet: Her mother is next in line. Dita walks more slowly and turns her head to look back.

Liesl is a woman with a sad face and a sad body, and her shoulders are hunched, all of which emphasize her sickly appearance. She's convinced she won't make the cut and is defeated before she even starts to fight. She hasn't a chance, and the doctor doesn't waste a second.

"Links!"

Left. The bigger group, the one for the useless women.

Nevertheless, with no attempt at rebellion of any kind, simply because of her mother's total bewilderment—or so it seems to Dita—Liesl heads toward the right behind her daughter and stands in a line where she shouldn't be. It takes her daughter's breath away: What's her mother doing here? They'll drag her away, and there'll be a terrible scene. She'll chain herself to her mother, come what may. Let the guards drag both of them out.

But fate, which has behaved so badly toward them, determines that just at this very moment, not one of the guards, tired of the docile manner of the prisoners and more concerned with eyeing the younger girls than with being vigilant, actually notices. Nor does Mengele, distracted just then by the registrar, who apparently has not heard one of the numbers dictated to him and asks the doctor for his assistance. Some of the women sent to the left have shrieked and begged and thrown themselves on the ground, and the guards have had to drag them away. But Liesl didn't complain or protest. She has calmly walked nude in front of Death's eyes with a naturalness and a lack of haste that would have unnerved even the bravest of the brave.

Dita has to grab her chest to stop her heart from leaping out. She glances at her mother, who is standing behind her and looking at her absentmindedly, seemingly unaware of what she has done. She's not brave enough to do something like that in a premeditated way . . . although Dita doesn't know what to think. Without saying a word, they hold hands tightly and squeeze as hard as they can. And they look at each other and say everything with that glance. Another woman joins the line and places herself behind Liesl to hide from the guards' line of sight.

The Germans send them to the quarantine camp. Once there, there are joyous hugs among those who find themselves in this group, which has been saved for now, and dejected faces near the entrance waiting for relatives and friends who never arrive. Mrs. Turnovská isn't in the quarantine camp group, nor are any of the woman who were part of her mother's conversation group. The children don't arrive, either. And Dita has heard nothing more of Miriam Edelstein, although it is true that there's a great deal of confusion. They begin to evacuate the first groups of people toward the station platform before the final selections of BIIb have been completed. Margit isn't in Dita's group, either.

It is a fact that they have momentarily dodged death. But survival is a minuscule consolation when so many innocent people are left behind to die.

28.

ANOTHER TRAIN. EIGHT MONTHS HAVE PASSED SINCE THE LIQUIDATION OF the family camp, and once again they are inside a stock car traveling to who knows where. Her very first trip was from Prague to Terezín. Then it was from Terezín to Auschwitz. Next, it was from Auschwitz to Hamburg. And now Dita no longer knows where this diaspora by train, which has derailed her youth, is taking her.

On the Auschwitz platform, the Germans had shoved them into a freight train and sent them with a group of women to Germany. It was a voyage of hunger, of thirst, of mothers separated from their children, of daughters without mothers. When they opened the stock car in Hamburg, the SS found a container full of broken dolls.

Exchanging Poland for Germany hadn't made things any better. There, the members of the SS had more news of the war, and nervousness spread. Germany was retreating on all fronts, and the feverish dream of the Third Reich was starting to crack. The guards vented their rage and frustration on the Jews, whom they blamed for the inevitable defeat.

They'd sent their prisoners to a camp where the working day was so long that it seemed as if the days had far more than twenty-four hours. When they got back to their huts, they didn't even have the strength to complain. They only managed to eat their soup in silence and stretch out on their bunks to try and recover for the next day.

Dita has one image drilled into her head from the months they spent in Hamburg: her mother in front of a brick-packing machine, sweat dripping from under the kerchief on her head. Liesl was sweating, but her expression was as impassive, focused, and serene as if she were preparing a potato salad.

Dita was suffering because of her mother, who was so fragile that not even the slight improvement in rations compared with Auschwitz had led to her putting on any weight at all. It was forbidden to talk while they worked, but whenever Dita passed with a load of some material near the conveyor belt at which her mother was working, she would wordlessly ask how she was doing, and Liesl would nod and smile. She was always fine.

Dita admits that sometimes her mother drives her mad—no matter how she's feeling, Liesl always says she's fine. How can Dita know the truth?

But Mrs. Adler is always feeling fine for Dita.

Right now, in this train, Liesl, her head resting against the wall of the carriage, is pretending to be asleep. She knows that Edita wants her to sleep, although in actual fact, for months now, she's only been able to sleep off and on during the night. But she's not going to tell that to her daughter, who's too young to understand how tragic it is for a mother not to be able to give her daughter a happy childhood.

The only thing that Liesl can do for her daughter—who is already stronger, braver, and more perceptive than she ever was—is to worry her as little as possible, and always to say she's perfectly well, although since the death of her husband, she feels a wound inside her that is continually bleeding.

Work in the brick factory in Hamburg hadn't lasted long. The nervousness in the Nazis' top leadership group had produced contradictory orders. A few weeks later, Dita and her mother were transferred to another factory, where they recycled military material. Defective bombs that hadn't exploded were being repaired in one of the workshops. Nobody particularly seemed to mind working there, and that included Dita and Liesl: You worked under cover, so when it rained, you didn't get wet.

One afternoon as she was heading back to her hut after she'd finished her working day, Dita spotted Renée Neumann coming out of a workshop, chatting animatedly with some girls. Dita was really pleased to see her. Renée gave her a friendly smile and a brief wave from a distance, but kept on walking without stopping, utterly absorbed in the conversation with her companions. *She's made new friends*, thought Dita, *people who don't know she once had a friend in the SS and to whom she doesn't owe any explanations. She doesn't want to stop and talk with her past.*

And now the Germans have mobilized the prisoners yet again, without telling them where they're going, turning them once more into livestock that has to be transported.

"They treat us like lambs being taken to the slaughterhouse," complains a woman with a Sudeten accent.

"If only! They *feed* sheep being taken to the slaughterhouse."

The stock car sways with the sound of a sewing machine. It's like a metallic oven for baking sweat. Dita and her mother are sitting on the floor together with a contingent of women of various nationalities, but many of them German Jews. Of the thousand women who left the family camp at Auschwitz behind eight months ago, only half now remain. They're exhausted. Dita examines her hands; they are the hands of an old woman.

Although perhaps it's a different type of exhaustion. They've spent years being shoved from one place to another and threatened with death, sleeping poorly and eating badly, without knowing if there's a purpose to it all, if they really are going to see the end of this war.

The worst thing is that Dita is beginning not to care. Apathy is the worst possible symptom.

No, no, no . . . I won't give in.

She pinches her arm until it hurts. Then she pinches herself even harder until she almost draws blood. She needs life to hurt. When something pains you, it's because that something is important to you.

She remembers Fredy Hirsch. She's been thinking less about him these past months, because memories end up being filed away. But she still continues to wonder what happened to him that afternoon. The messenger boy with the long legs said he didn't commit suicide, but he asked the doctor for tranquilizers, so . . . did he overdo the tranquilizers? She wants to believe he didn't intend to wipe himself out. But she knows that Hirsch was very methodical, very German. How could he have taken too many pills by mistake?

Dita sighs. Maybe none of this matters anymore: He's not here any longer, and he's not coming back. What difference does it make?

There's a rumor going around the train that they are being sent to a place called Bergen-Belsen. They listen to conversations where they're speculating about the new camp. Some people have heard that it's a labor camp, that it's nothing like Auschwitz or Mauthausen, where the only industry is killing people. So they're not taking them to a slaughterhouse. The news sounds reassuring, but most of them keep quiet because hope has acquired a razor-thin edge, and each time you put your hand on it, it cuts you.

"I'm from Auschwitz," says one woman. "Nothing can be worse than that."

The other women don't say a word. She doesn't convince them. They've discovered over the years that horror is bottomless. They don't trust anyone—once bitten, twice shy. But the worst of it is that they're going to be proven correct.

It's a short trip from Hamburg to Bergen-Belsen, but the train takes several hours before it finally stops with a grinding of gears. They have to walk from the platform to the entrance of the women's camp. They are escorted by several guards from the women's section of the SS, who shove them violently and shout swear words at them. There's a steely meanness in their eyes. One of the prisoners stares at a guard, and the guard spits in her face so she'll turn away.

"Pig," mutters Dita under her breath. Her mother gives her a pinch to stop her talking.

Dita wonders why the guards are so angry with the prisoners, given that they are the ones who have been humiliated and deprived of everything, given that they've barely set foot in the camp and haven't done anyone any harm, given that all they're going to do is obey and work feverishly for the Reich without asking for anything in return. But these robust, well-fed, and well-dressed guards prove to be furious. They taunt the prisoners, hit them in the ribs with their clubs, insult them with obscene phrases, and generally show themselves to be irascible toward these docile new arrivals. Dita is surprised by the irritation of their aggressors, their display of indignation toward people who have done them no harm.

When the prisoners have lined up in formation, the supervisor appears. She's tall, blond, and has broad shoulders and a square jaw. She moves with the assurance of a person used to being in charge and instantly obeyed. She informs them in her booming voice that they are forbidden to leave their huts after the seven o'clock curfew under pain of death. She pauses and eagerly searches out a glance from any of the inmates. Their eyes are all fixed straight in front of them. Then one young woman makes the mistake of returning her glance. The supervisor takes two strides and plants herself in front of the girl. She grabs her violently by her hair, drags her out of the line, and throws her to the ground in front of the group. Although it appears as if no one is looking directly, they all see. She hits the girl once with her club. Then again, and again. The girl doesn't cry out; she only sobs. After the fifth stroke, she's not even sobbing, and barely moaning. They don't hear what the supervisor says when she puts her mouth to the girl's ear, but the prisoner gets up, dripping blood, and stumbles back to her place in the line.

The name of the supervisor in charge of the guards at Bergen-Belsen is Elisabeth Volkenrath. After training as a warden at Ravensbrück, she moved on to Auschwitz, where she forged a solid reputation for the ease with which she ordered executions by hanging for the slightest misdemeanor. She was posted to Bergen-Belsen at the start of 1945.

The path they take goes past several fenced-off areas that enclose a range of compounds about which they'll learn more later on. They include a camp for the male prisoners; the "star" camp, for inmates destined to be exchanged for German prisoners of war; the "neutral" camp, for several hundred Jews who hold passports from neutral countries; the quarantine camp to isolate prisoners with typhus; a camp for Hungarians; and the feared prison camp, which in reality is an extermination compound where sick prisoners from other labor camps are interned, forced to work under extreme conditions, and exploited until they die a few days later.

Eventually Dita's group reaches the small women's camp, which the Germans have had to set up in a hurry on some barren land next to the main camp because of the huge number of female detainees who have arrived at Bergen-Belsen over the past few months. It's a temporary camp with prefabricated barracks, no plumbing, and no waste pipes, just four thin, wooden walls.

In the barrack to which Dita, her mother, and about fifty other women have been assigned, there's no dinner, no beds, and the blankets smell of urine. They have to sleep on the wooden floor, and there's barely any room for them, not even on the floor.

Bergen-Belsen was originally a camp for prisoners of war under the supervision of the regular army, the Wehrmacht, but the pressure from the Russian troops in Poland has caused prisoners to be rerouted there from Polish camps, so the SS has taken control. New transports arrive constantly, and the installations are overflowing. Overcrowding, lack of food, and poor sanitary conditions have caused prisoner deaths to skyrocket.

Mother and daughter exchange looks. Liesl grimaces bleakly at the sight of their new hut companions, all so emaciated and sickly. But even worse is the fixed expression of many of them, the absent look—most of them are so listless that you'd think they'd already given up on life. Dita doesn't know if her mother's expression is a reaction to the starving prisoners or to themselves, because this is exactly how they will look very soon. The veterans hardly respond to the disturbance caused by the latest arrivals. Many don't get up from their improvised beds made out of piles of old blankets. Some couldn't, even if they wanted to.

Dita stretches out her mother's blanket on the floor and tells her to lie down. Mrs. Adler does as she's told and curls up. She puts her face on the blanket and encounters an army of jumping fleas, but she's unfazed. It doesn't even matter anymore. One of the new arrivals asks a veteran what sort of work is done in the camp.

"You don't work here anymore," the woman on the floor answers reluctantly. "You just survive for as long as you can."

They've heard the sound of explosions from Allied planes throughout the day, and at night they can see the glow of detonating bombs. The front is already very close; they can almost touch it. It spreads a certain euphoria among the prisoners. The noise from the Allied bombs sounds like an ever-approaching storm. Some of the women discuss what they'll do when the war is over. One woman without any teeth says she'll replant her entire garden with tulips.

"Don't be stupid," replies a bitter voice. "If I had a garden, I'd plant potatoes so I never spend another day of my life feeling hungry."

In the morning Dita and her mother understand what the internee meant when she said that you don't work in Bergen-Belsen, you just survive. A pair of SS guards wakes them up with kicks and shouts, and they rush outside to line up. The guards disappear, however, and the new inmates stand at the door for a long time awaiting instructions that never arrive. Some of the old hands haven't even got up from their blankets and stoically put up with the kicks without moving.

More than an hour later, a guard appears and shouts at them to line up for roll call, but immediately notices that there is no list of names. So the guard asks for the hut *Kapo*. Nobody answers. She asks three more times, getting angrier with each one.

"You damned bitches! Where the devil is the *Kapo* of this fucking hut?"

Nobody answers. Red with rage, the guard furiously grabs a prisoner by the neck and asks her where the *Kapo* is. The victim is a new arrival and tells her she doesn't know. Then the guard turns to a veteran, who's easily recognizable because she's almost a walking skeleton, and repeats her question while aiming at her with her club.

"Well?"

"She died two days ago."

"And the new *Kapo*?"

The inmate shrugs her shoulders.

"There isn't one."

The guard thinks this over and doesn't know what to do. She could name any one of these women *Kapo*, but there isn't a single regular prisoner among them. They're all Jews in this hut, and she could be looking for trouble. Eventually, she turns around and leaves. The veteran prisoners break ranks of their own accord and go back inside the hut. The newcomers, still standing by the entrance to the hut, exchange looks. Dita almost prefers to remain outside, as she's constantly bombarded by fleas and lice inside and she feels an intense itchiness over her entire body. But her mother is tired and gestures inside with her head.

Once there, they ask a veteran what time breakfast appears. The huge grimace, which hides a bitter smile, is eloquent.

"Breakfast time?" says another woman. "Let's pray we have a dinnertime today."

They spend the whole morning doing nothing until someone shouts a harsh "*Achtung*," which makes everyone quickly stand. The supervisor comes into the hut, followed by a couple of assistants. She points her club at one of the veterans and asks if there are any deaths. The prisoner points to the back of the hut, and another inmate in the area points to the ground. A woman hasn't gotten up at the sound of the shout. She's dead.

Volkenrath looks around quickly and signals to four prisoners, two veterans and two newcomers. She doesn't say a word, but the old hands already know what has to be done. They hurry over to the corpse with unexpected enthusiasm, and each of them grabs a leg. They know they have to get hold of the right part: The legs of a corpse weigh less, and that end is sometimes less unpleasant. Rigor mortis has already dislocated the jaw, and the woman's mouth and eyes are open excessively wide. With a nod of their heads, they indicate that the other two prisoners should grab the shoulders. Between the four of them, they make their way to the door, carrying the dead woman.

The guards disappear again, and nobody else comes into the hut until evening. Then a guard looks inside and signals to four inmates to go to the kitchen to get the pot with the soup. That causes a stir, and there are shouts of joy.

"Dinner's on!"

"Thank you, God!"

The inmates reappear carrying the pot with the help of two long planks so they won't burn themselves, and that night they dine on soup.

"This cook studied at the same school as the one in Birkenau," says Dita between sips.

And Liesl ruffles her daughter's shoulder-length hair, which is starting to turn up at the ends.

In the days that follow, anarchy will increase. There'll be days when they eat a bowl of soup at lunchtime, but there'll be no breakfast or dinner; on the odd day they'll have lunch and dinner, but at other times they won't get any food at all. Hunger becomes a form of torture and a source of anxiety that blocks the mind and doesn't allow for thought; there's just the agonized wait for the next meal. All that free time, combined with the anxiety caused by hunger, turns the mind into mush, and everything starts to fall apart.

29.

MORE PRISONERS ARRIVE IN THE WEEKS THAT FOLLOW, AND THE
gaps between meals becomes longer. The mortality rate grows expo-
nentially. Even without gas chambers, Bergen-Belsen becomes a
killing machine. Half a dozen bodies have to be removed from
Dita's hut every day. The deaths are officially listed as due to natural causes.

Whenever the guards arrive to pick the prisoners assigned to
remove the dead, all the women freeze and hope it's not their day to
win the lottery. Dita tries to blend in with the others.

But today is her lucky day.

The SS guard unmistakably points at her with the club. She's the
last one selected, so when she reaches the corpse, the positions at the
feet are already taken. She and a very dark woman who looks like a
Gypsy pick up the dead woman by her shoulders. Dita has seen many
dead bodies over these years, but she has never touched one. She
can't avoid brushing against this woman's hand, and its marble-like
coldness makes her shiver.

Dita and the Gypsy woman support the bulk of the weight. But
she worries about the dead woman's arms, how to keep them from
swinging.

One of the women carrying the feet of the corpse leads the way
and they come to an area that's fenced off with barbed wire. Two

guards armed with submachine guns accompany them. They reach a piece of waste ground where a German officer in shirtsleeves meets them and orders them to halt. They stop, still holding the dead woman, and the officer gives her a quick look. He jots something down in a notebook and signals for them to go on. One of the veterans whispers that it's Dr. Klein, and it's his job to control outbreaks of typhus. If the disease is detected in a hut, the Germans send the infected women to a quarantine camp to die.

As the four women advance, the stench becomes more nauseating. There are several sinewy men working a few meters farther on; the dirty handkerchiefs they use to cover their noses make them look like bandits. Another group of women is standing in front of them, in the process of depositing a corpse next to several other bodies. One of the men signals to Dita's group that they should leave their body on the ground. The men throw the bodies into an enormous pit, as if they were sacks of potatoes. Dita leans over the edge for an instant, and what she sees makes her so queasy she has to grab hold of one of her companions.

"My God . . ."

It's a huge trench crammed with corpses. The ones on the bottom look singed; the ones on top are piled up in a jumble, a tangle of arms, heads, and yellowish skin.

Dita's stomach churns, but it's her most deeply held convictions that are stirred more than anything.

That's all we are? Bits of decomposing matter? A few atoms, like those of a willow tree or a shoe?

Even the veteran who has been here several times is upset. No one speaks on the return journey. Seen like this, life appears to have no value.

When Dita gets back, her mother gives her a look asking how it went. Dita hides her face in her hands. She'd like to be left alone, but her mother hugs her and shares her pain.

The chaos increases. Although there are no organized work groups anymore, they're given the order to stay close to the hut all day in case they are needed. Occasionally, one of the SS guards appears, her arms swinging energetically as she displays her healthy-looking, well-fed legs. She calls out some names in a shrill voice and tells them to go with her to work on the drainage ditches or in some shop. A couple of times, Dita is recruited for a workshop where they punch holes in belts and tabs for uniforms. The machines are very old, and you have to use a lot of force to make the puncher strike the strips of leather with sufficient pressure.

After roll call one morning, the supervisor appears in front of the assembled group. Volkenrath is easily recognizable because of the ostentatious bun of hair on top of her head from which blond strands are always escaping. She has the appearance of someone who's been to an expensive salon and then rolled around in a barn. Dita has heard that when she was a civilian, she was a hairdresser, which explains the hairstyle she sports amid the filth, lice, and typhus of Bergen-Belsen.

Volkenrath is her usual angry self, which scares even her assistants. It occurs to Dita that if Hitler hadn't come to power and war hadn't broken out, this unscrupulous woman now standing in front of them with a killer's glint in her eye would be yet another of those slightly plump, pleasant hairdressers who give the girls ringlets and cheerfully comment about the neighborhood gossip. Their clients, including German-Jewish women, would lower their heads, and she would cut their hair with her scissors, and none of them would be the least bit worried about placing their necks in the hands of this oversized woman who is addicted to somewhat fanciful, upswept hairstyles. If anyone had insinuated that, some years down the track, Elisabeth Volkenrath might be a murderer, the entire community would have been outraged. *Good old Beth? That woman wouldn't hurt a fly!* they'd say indignantly. They'd demand that the author of the calumny retract it immediately. And they might have been right. But things have turned out otherwise. Now if any of the women who arrive at her establishment don't behave in the way she wants, the inoffensive girl from the hairdressing salon puts a rope around their neck and hangs them.

Dita is absorbed in these thoughts when a sound penetrates her brain like the metal puncher piercing the leather in the workshop:

"Elisabeth Adler!"

The administrative mess is so bad that the Germans have gone back to calling the prisoners by their names, not their numbers. The voice of the SS supervisor (authoritarian, strong, aggressive, military-sounding, impatient) rings out again calling for . . . "Elisabeth Adler!"

Her mother had been distracted. She now makes a move to step out of the line, but Dita is much faster and decisively steps forward.

"Adler, here!"

Adler, here! Liesl's eyes open wide, and she's so taken aback by her daughter's audacity that, for a few seconds, she doesn't know what to do. Just as she decides to step forward and sort out the mixup with the guards, there's a shout of "Break ranks!" The sea of women energetically surging around her blocks Liesl's path, and by the time the knot of people has untangled itself, her daughter has disappeared inside the hut to transfer that day's corpses. Liesl stands stock-still, getting in the way of her companions, who are in a pointless hurry, as if they'd forgotten they have nowhere to go. Dita emerges a short while later carrying a body with three other inmates. Her mother, still rooted to the same spot, and now on her own in the middle of the avenue of mud, angrily watches her daughter heading off.

Another trip to mankind's final frontier.

Dita again leans over the edge of the pit and comes back pale with queasiness. They all say it's the stench that makes them ill, but what really upsets them is the sight of those lives thrown on a dump site.

Dita hopes she never gets used to it.

When she gets back to the hut, her mother is still standing near the door, as if she hadn't broken ranks after the roll call. Her expression is one of deep anger, even rage.

"Are you stupid? Have you forgotten that assuming the identity of another prisoner is punished by death?" Liesl shouts at her.

Dita can't remember the last time her mother shouted at her. An inmate walking by turns to stare, and Dita feels herself blushing. It seems unfair, and she feels tears flooding her eyes, even though she doesn't want to cry. Only her pride prevents them from spilling out. She nods and turns around.

She can't stand it when her mother treats her like a child. It's not right. Dita did it because she knows her mother is weak and doesn't have the strength to carry a corpse. But Dita hasn't been given a chance to explain. She thinks her mother should be proud of her, but instead she's earned the worst reprimand since the slap Liesl gave her in Prague.

She doesn't value anything I do. . . .

She feels misunderstood. She may be in a concentration camp, but she's no different from the millions of other teenagers the world over who are about to turn sixteen.

Dita is mistaken, however: Liesl is immensely proud of her daughter. She's not going to tell her so. She's been tortured with doubts about the sort of person her daughter would become growing up under military repression, with inadequate schooling, in places infected by hatred and violence. Her daughter's generous act confirms all her intuitions and hopes—she knows that if Dita survives, she'll be a fine woman.

But she can't say all this to Dita. If she showed satisfaction at such reckless behavior, it would encourage Dita and spur her on to putting her life in danger again and again to save her mother from punishment. In any event, as a mother, she wants to avoid such things for her daughter. Because life isn't either better or worse for Liesl anymore. Life has become unimportant to her. Her only happiness is the one that she sees in her daughter's eyes. Her daughter is still too young to understand all this.

The next day, a guard, whom Dita has christened Crowface, turns up at the hut and orders them all to line up outside.

"Everybody out! And I mean everybody. I'll finish off anyone who doesn't get up with a bullet!"

Grumbling, taking their time, the women start to mobilize.

"Take your blankets!"

The women exchange looks, but the mystery is soon revealed. The Germans are moving them to the main women's camp to make room for a new contingent that has just arrived. Inside the main camp, the inmates are just as emaciated and water is very scarce, so it's only used for rationed drinking water. Nothing can be washed. The chaos has reached such heights that some prisoners don't even wear their striped uniforms, while others put a vest or another piece of clothing over their prison tops. Grime blackens the women's skin to the point where it's hard to know if they are wearing strips of clothing or strips of blackened, peeling flesh. An SS guard is supervising a group of women gritting their teeth as they work in a drainage ditch; it's hard to distinguish between their arms and the handles of the hoes.

The hut is crammed but has the small advantage of containing bunks like the ones in Auschwitz, which means they have dirty straw mattresses—they're packed with bedbugs, but at least they stop their bones from digging into themselves. A lot of women are lying down. Most of them are ill and have stopped getting up. Others pretend they are ill so they'll be left alone. The guards don't approach them because they're terrified of catching typhus.

Dita and her mother sit down on the empty bunk they'll be sharing. Her mother is very tired, but Dita feels restless and gets up to explore the camp. There's not really much to see: huts and fences. There are groups of women still able to chat animatedly, the ones from the most recent transports who still have some energy stored in their bodies, but there are others who don't have the strength even to talk: You look at them, and they don't look back.

They've given in.

Then she notices a girl along the side of the one of the huts. She's wearing the striped dress of a prisoner and a white kerchief on her head—astonishingly white in the middle of this gigantic dunghill. Dita looks at her and then shuts her eyes because she thinks she's mistaken in what she's seeing. But when she opens them again, it's not a mirage. She's right there.

"Margit . . ."

Her friend suddenly raises her head and starts to stand up but finds herself bowled over by Dita, who throws herself on top of Margit, and the two of them fall over and roll around, laughing, on the ground. They grab hold of each other by the arms and stare at one another. If happiness is possible in these sorts of circumstances, then at this very moment, they are happy.

They hold hands and go off to see Dita's mother. As soon as she sees Liesl, Margit approaches her and, although she's never done it before, hugs her. In fact, she clings to her shoulders; she's needed a safe haven where she can cry, for a long time.

After she's eased some of her pain, Margit tells them that the selection in the family camp was awful; her mother and sister were both assigned to the group that had been condemned. With the precision of someone who has relived the same scene many times over in her mind, she explains how they were sent to the ranks of the feeble.

"I could see them the whole time we were inside the hut, until they finished the selection. They were very calm and holding hands. Then the smaller group of fit women, which I was part of, was ordered to leave. I didn't want to go, but a tide of women was pushing me toward the door. I could see Helga and my mother on the other side of the hut's chimney, getting smaller and smaller, and surrounded by old women and children. They were watching me go. And do you know what, Ditiňka? As they were watching me leave . . . they were smiling! Can you believe it? They were doomed to die, and they were smiling."

Margit remembers that moment, which has been burned into her memory, and shakes her head as if she can't believe it.

"Did they know that being in that group of old people, sick people, and children was almost certainly a death sentence? Maybe they did, and were just happy for me, because I was part of the group of those who might be able to save themselves."

Dita shrugs, and Liesl strokes Margit's head. They picture Margit's mother and sister at that moment when they are already on the other side, when the fight for survival is over and there's no longer any fear.

"They were smiling," whispers Margit.

They ask about her father; she hasn't seen him since that same morning in BIIb.

"I'm almost glad I don't know what has become of him."

Maybe he died; maybe he didn't; either way, the uncertainty keeps her company.

Margit may already be sixteen, but Mrs. Adler orders her to transfer her blanket to their hut. There is so little control that nobody will notice, and the three of them will sleep together on the bunk.

"You'll be uncomfortable," Margit replies.

"But we'll be together." And Liesl's answer brooks no response.

Liesl Adler takes charge of Margit as if she were her second daughter. For Dita, Margit is that big sister she has always wanted. As they are both dark-haired and have a sweet smile and gap teeth, many people in the family camp were convinced that they were sisters anyway, and the misunderstanding pleased both of them.

The two girls examine each other. They are thinner and somewhat the worse for wear, but neither one says so to the other. They cheer each other on. They talk, although there's not much to tell. Chaos and hunger, total indifference, infections and sickness. Nothing new.

A few rows from their bunk, two actual sisters ill with typhus are already losing the game of life. The younger sister, Anne, is shaking with fever in her bunk. The elder, Margot, is even worse. She's lying immobile in the lower bunk, connected to the world by a wisp of breath that is fading.

If Dita had gone over to look at the girl who was still alive, she would have discovered that they were very similar: teenagers with a sweet smile, dark hair, and the eyes of dreamers. Like Dita, Anne was an energetic and talkative girl, a bit of a rebel and with an imagination. She was also a girl who, apart from her unruly and self-assured appearance, had a reflexive and melancholy inner voice, but that was her secret. The two sisters had arrived in Bergen-Belsen in October 1944, after they'd been deported from Amsterdam to Auschwitz. Their crime: being Jewish. Five months have been too many to avoid death in this wet hole. Typhus has no respect for youth.

Anne dies alone in her bunk the day after her sister. Her remains will stay buried forever in Bergen-Belsen's mass graves. But Anne has done something that will end up being a small miracle: Her memory and her sister's memory will bring them back to life many years later. In the secret place in Amsterdam where the two girls and their family hid, she spent two years writing notes about her life in the "house at the back"—some rooms attached to her father's office, which were closed off and converted into a hiding place. For two years, with the help of family friends who supplied provisions, the family lived there, together with the van Pels family and Fritz Pfeffer. Shortly after they moved into their hideout, they celebrated Anne's birthday, and among the presents was a small notebook. Since she couldn't have a close friend in the hideout with whom she could share her feelings, she shared them with that notebook, which she christened Kitty. It didn't occur to her to give a title to this outline of her life in the "house at the back," but posterity took care of that. It has become part of history as *The Diary of a Young Girl*.

30.

FOOD HAS BECOME A RARITY. THE GERMANS GIVE THEM ONLY A few pieces of bread for the entire day. Every now and again, a pot of soup appears. Dita and her mother have lost even more weight than they did in Auschwitz. The inmates who have been there the longest and know this situation well are no longer skinny or emaciated— they're just wooden puppets with stick arms and legs. Water is scarce and you have to wait in line for hours to fill a bowl from any tap that's still dripping.

And yet another transport with women arrives at this jam-packed camp where there's nothing but infections and sickness. They are Hungarian Jews. One of them asks for the latrines. What an innocent.

"We have bathrooms with gold taps. And be sure to ask Volkenrath to bring you some bath salts."

Some of the women laugh uproariously.

There aren't any latrines. They made holes in the ground, but these are already full.

Another woman from the transport, furious, turns to one of the guards who have just arrived and tells her that they are workers. They must be sent to a factory and taken out of this dunghill. She's had the misfortune to say it to the least appropriate person. One of the veterans tells her it's Volkenrath, the supervisor of the guards but the warning comes too late.

Volkenrath calmly adjusts her partially collapsed blond top-knot, takes her Luger out of her belt, and rams the barrel against the woman's forehead. She also gives the woman a look as rabid as a dog foaming at the mouth—the foam Pasteur dedicated himself to studying. The prisoner raises her arms, and her legs shake so much she looks as if she's dancing. Volkenrath laughs.

She's the only one laughing now.

The gun is like a rod of ice against the prisoner's head, and warm urine begins to trickle down her legs. It's not very respectful to wet yourself in front of a supervisor. They all grit their teeth and prepare themselves for the sound of the gunshot. Some women look down so they won't see the head exploding into little pieces. Volkenrath has a heavy vertical wrinkle between her eyebrows running right up to her hairline. It is so noticeable and deep that it looks like a black scar. The knuckles clutching the gun are white from the fury with which she's holding it. She's angrily pushing the weapon against the woman's forehead, and the woman is crying and peeing at the same time. Finally, the supervisor removes the gun; the prisoner has a reddish circle on her forehead. With a movement of her chin, Volkenrath sends her back to her place.

"I'm not going to do you the favor, Jewish bitch. No, it's not your lucky day."

And she lets loose a demented guffaw that sounds just like a saw.

A white-haired woman spends much of the night crying over the death of her daughter. She doesn't even know what caused the death. In the morning, she kneels behind the hut and starts to dig a grave for the girl with her bare hands. She manages only to make a small hole a sparrow might fit into. The woman flops onto the muddy ground, and her bunkmate comes over to console her.

"Is no one going to help me bury my daughter?" the woman shouts from the ground.

There's not much energy left, and no one sees the sense in wasting what little there is on something that can't be fixed. Even so, various women offer to help her and start to dig. But the ground is hard, and their weak hands start to bleed. Exhausted and in pain, the women stop, although they've removed only a few fistfuls of earth.

Her friend tries to persuade her to take her daughter to the pit.

"The pit . . . I've seen it. No, please, not there. It offends God."

"She'll be with all the other innocents. That way, she won't be by herself."

The woman agrees very reluctantly. Nothing can console her.

The camp stinks. It's filled with the excretions of those who have dysentery. They lean against the wooden walls of the huts and collapse onto the ground on top of their own excrement, and nobody lends them a hand. If a dead person has family or friends, they take the body to the pit. If they don't, the body lies on the ground in the camp until some SS guard takes out her gun and forces prisoners to drag the body away.

Dita, Margit, and Liesl walk slowly around the camp, and the sight is equally devastating no matter where they look. Dita holds Margit's hand on one side, and her mother's on the other. Her mother is shaking, either with fever or horror, but it's impossible to distinguish disease from degradation.

They go back to their hut, and it's even worse: the sour smell of disease, the moans, the monotonous murmur of prayers. Many of the ill are unable to get down from their bunks; many of them perform their bodily functions right where they are, and the smell is unbearable.

Dita looks at the devastatingly gloomy bunks. Family and friends are gathered around, trying to give relief to the sick, but in many cases, the sick are suffering alone, fading alone, dying alone.

Dita and her mother decide to leave the hut. April has arrived, but it continues to be intensely cold in Germany—a cold that hurts your teeth, numbs your fingers, and freezes your nose. Anyone who stays outdoors starts to shake.

"It's better to die of cold than of disgust," Dita says to her mother.

"Edita, don't be vulgar."

Many other prisoners have opted, like them, to move outside. Liesl and the two girls have found a bit of space by the hut where they can lean against the wall, and that's where they stay, wrapped up in blankets they prefer not to examine too closely. The camp is closed, nobody goes in or out anymore, and there are only a few guards in the towers with machine guns. They should try to escape—if they are caught, at least they'll die more quickly—but they don't even have the strength to try. There's nothing left.

As the days go by, everything collapses. The SS guards have stopped patrolling the camp, which has turned into a cesspit. There hasn't been any food for days, and the water has definitely been cut off. Some prisoners drink from the puddles, but they soon writhe on the ground with stomach cramps and die of cholera. The weather is getting warmer, and the corpses are decomposing more quickly. No one remains to remove them.

Hardly anyone gets up from where they are. Many will never get up again; some try, but their legs, thin as wire, are too weak, and they collapse on the ground, which is covered with excrement. Others fall spectacularly on top of corpses. It's hard to distinguish between the living and the dead.

Explosions from the battles are getting closer. The shots are louder, the impact of the bombs sends vibrations up their legs, and the only hope they have left is that this hell will end in time. But death seems to advance much more quickly and resolutely on its own front.

Dita hugs her mother. She looks at Margit, whose eyes are closed, and decides that she's not going to fight any longer. She shuts her eyes, too; the curtain lowers. She promised Fredy Hirsch she'd hold out. She hasn't given up, but her body has. And anyway, Hirsch himself also let go in the end. Or not? But what does it matter now?

When she closes her eyes, the horror that is Bergen-Belsen disappears and she shifts to the Berghof sanatorium of *The Magic Mountain*. She even thinks she feels a burst of that cold, clear air from the Alps.

Dita's feebleness extends to her mind. Moments, places, and people she has known in real life get mixed up with others she has met in books, and Dita is unable to distinguish the real from the imagined.

She doesn't know if the arrogant Dr. Behrens from the Berghof—who looked after Hans Castorp—is more real than Dr. Mengele; at one point she can see them strolling together through the gardens of the sanatorium. Suddenly, she walks into a dining room and finds the gentlemanly Dr. Manson from *The Citadel* sitting at a table set with a magnificent banquet, together with the handsome Edmond Dantès in his unbuttoned sailor shirt and the elegant and seductive Mme. Chauchat. She looks more carefully and sees that the person at the head of the table is Dr. Pasteur, who instead of carving the juicy turkey fresh from the oven so they can eat it, is dissecting it with a scalpel. Mrs. Křižková walks past, the woman she always called Mrs. Nasty, and she's scolding a waiter who tries to give her the slip; the waiter's face is that of Mr. Lichtenstern. A fatter waiter approaches carrying a tray with a delicious meat pie, but with unheard of clumsiness, he trips, and the pie sails speedily through the air onto the table, splattering grease over the dinner guests, who look at him with disapproval. The waiter apologizes, full of remorse for his blunder, and lowers his head in a submissive bow several times as he hurries to pick up the remains of the destroyed pie. That's when Dita recognizes him: It's that rascal Švejk doing his thing! She's sure he'll mount a feast for the kitchen hands with those destroyed pieces of pie.

Her sanity is already as slippery as butter. It's better that way. She knows she's disconnecting from reality. And she doesn't mind. She feels happy, just as she did when she was little. When she closed her bedroom door, the world remained outside and nothing could harm her. She feels dizzy, and the world clouds over and begins to fall apart. She sees the mouth of the tunnel.

She hears outlandish voices inside her head from another world. She feels she has already crossed the border and is on the other side, in a place where there are strong male voices speaking an incomprehensible language, an enigmatic gibberish that only the chosen ones know how to decipher. She'd never asked herself what language was spoken in heaven. Or in purgatory. Or in hell. It's a language she doesn't understand.

She also hears hysterical shouts. But those high-pitched shrieks . . . they are too laden with emotion. It can't be the afterlife. They are from this world. She's not dead yet. She opens her eyes and sees prisoners shouting like madwomen. There's lots of noise, whistles are blowing, and she can hear the sound of footsteps. She's so stunned that she doesn't understand a thing.

"They've all gone mad," she whispers. "The camp is a lunatic asylum."

Margit opens her eyes and gives her a frightened look, as if they could still be afraid of anything. She touches her mother's arm, and Liesl opens her eyes as well.

And then they see it—soldiers are entering the camp. They're armed, but they're not Germans. They are wearing light brown uniforms, totally different from the black uniforms they've seen till now. The soldiers first point their weapons in all directions but then they immediately lower them, some put them over their shoulders, and then they put their hands to their heads: *"Oh my God!"*

"Who are they, Mama?"

"They're English, Edita."

Dita's and Margit's mouths are as wide open as their eyes.

"English?"

A young NCO climbs onto an empty wooden box and shapes his hands into a megaphone. He speaks in rudimentary German:

"This camp has been liberated in the name of the United Kingdom of Great Britain and her allies. You are free!"

Dita elbows Margit. Her friend is paralyzed; she can't speak. Although she has no strength left in her, Dita manages to get up on her feet and rests one hand on Margit's shoulder and the other on her mother's. And finally, Dita utters the sentence she's spent her entire childhood waiting to be able to say.

"The war is over."

The librarian of Block 31 begins to cry. She cries for all those people who couldn't survive to see this: her grandfather, her father, Fredy Hirsch, Miriam Edelstein, Professor Morgenstern. . . .

A soldier walks toward the survivors in her area, and he's

shouting at them in strangely accented German, saying that the camp has been liberated and they are free.

"Free! Free!"

A woman drags herself along the ground until she can embrace the soldier's foot. He bends down smiling, ready to receive the thanks of the liberated. But the gaunt woman says to him with bitter reproach,

"Why have you taken so long?"

The British troops were expecting to be received by a euphoric populace. They were expecting smiles and cheers. They weren't expecting to be met with complaints, sighs, and death rattles, people crying with a mixture of joy for having been saved and deep sorrow for husbands, brothers, uncles, friends, neighbors—so many people who haven't been liberated.

There are some soldiers whose faces show compassion; others, incredulity; and many, disgust. They never thought an internment camp for Jews could be this quagmire of bodies. The living are even more skeletal than the dead. The English thought they were going to liberate a camp full of prisoners, but what they've found is a cemetery.

There are voices still capable of giving a modest cheer at the news, although most of the women who are alive have only the strength to stare incredulously. And they stare even harder when they see a party of prisoners walk past them. Dita has to look twice before she believes it. For the first time in her life, those under arrest are not Jews. At the front, guarded by armed British soldiers and walking with her head held high, is Elisabeth Volkenrath, her topknot spilling over her face.

31.

THE FIRST DAYS OF FREEDOM HAVE BEEN STRANGE. THERE HAVE been scenes that Dita, even in her wildest dreams, could never have imagined: Nazi guards dragging the dead with their own hands; Volkenrath, always so impeccable, carrying corpses in her arms to the pit in a muddy uniform and with greasy hair. The British have put Dr. Klein to work lowering the bodies that the SS guards, now prisoners sentenced to hard labor, are passing to him.

Freedom has arrived, but nobody in Bergen-Belsen is happy. The number of deaths is devastating. The British soon realize that they can't be as respectful toward the dead as they would like; the spread of diseases is too rapid. In the end, they order the SS guards to pile up the bodies, and a bulldozer pushes them as far as the pit. Peace is very demanding: It has to wipe out the effects of war as quickly as possible.

Margit is in line waiting for the midday ration when she feels a hand on her shoulder. It's an insignificant gesture. But there's something in it that suddenly makes her life expand. Before she turns around, she knows the hand belongs to her father.

Dita and Liesl are really happy for Margit. Seeing her happy makes them happy. When she tells them that the English have already assigned her father a place on the train for Prague and he has made arrangements for her to accompany him, they wish her luck in her new life. Everything is changing at dizzying speed.

Margit becomes very serious and gives them an intense look.

"My home will be your home."

She not just being polite. Dita knows that it's a sister's declaration of love. Margit's father jots down the address of some Czech friends who are not Jewish on a scrap of paper. He hopes they're still all right, and that he and Margit can stay with them.

"We'll see each other in Prague!" Dita tells him as they hold hands and say good-bye.

This time it's a more hopeful farewell. A farewell where it finally makes sense to say, "See you soon!"

Confusion reigns for the first few days. The British were trained to fight, not to look after hundreds of thousands of disoriented people with no personal documentation, many of them sick or malnourished. The English battalion has an office to deal with the repatriation of the prisoners, but it's overwhelmed and the assignment of provisional papers is unbearably slow. At least the inmates have received food rations and clean blankets again, and field hospitals have been set up for the thousands of sick people.

Dita didn't want to spoil Margit's day by telling her that she was worried about Liesl: She isn't well. Although she's eating, she's not gaining weight and has the beginning of a fever. There's no other option but to admit her to the field hospital, which means Dita and her mother will have to delay their transfer to Prague. In the field hospital, set up by the Allies in the former camp hospital to look after the survivors of Bergen-Belsen, there is little evidence that the war has ended. The German army has surrendered. Hitler has committed suicide in his own bunker, and the SS officers have either become prisoners awaiting summary trial or they've gone into hiding. But in the hospital, war is stubbornly refusing to give in. The armistice doesn't make the amputated limbs of the mutilated

grow back; it doesn't cure the pain of the wounded; it doesn't erad-
icate typhus; it doesn't rescue the dying from their decline; it doesn't
return those who have marched on. Peace doesn't cure everything,
at least not that quickly.

Liesl Adler, who has resisted all the deprivations, tragedies,
and miseries of these years, becomes gravely ill with the arrival of
peace. Dita can't believe that after all she has overcome, she isn't
going to live in peace. It's not fair.

Liesl is lying on a field bed, but at least the sheets are clean
compared to the last few years. Dita takes her mother's hand and
whispers words of encouragement in her ear. The medication keeps
Liesl sedated.

As the days pass, the nurses become accustomed to the presence of the Czech girl with the face of a mischievous angel, who
doesn't leave her mother's bedside. To the extent that it's possible,
they try to look after Dita as well: They make sure she eats her
food ration and periodically gets out of the hospital, that she doesn't
stay with her mother for too many hours at a time, and that she
wears a mask when she's sitting beside her.

One afternoon, Dita spots one of the nurses—a round-faced
young man with freckles called Francis—reading a novel. She
walks over and stares avidly at the title. It's a Western, and the
front cover has a picture of an Indian chief with a striking feather
headdress, war paint on his cheeks, and a gun in his hand. Feeling
himself under intense scrutiny, the nurse looks up from the book
and asks Dita if she likes Westerns. Dita has read a novel by Karl
May, and she really likes Old Shatterhand and his Apache friend
Winnetou, whom she imagined experiencing amazing adventures
on the never-ending plains of North America. Dita touches the book
as if she were stroking it, and then runs a finger very slowly up and

down the spine. Puzzled, the soldier watches her. He thinks the girl might be a little disturbed. After living in that hell, it wouldn't surprise anyone.

"Francis . . ."

Dita points to the book and then at herself. He understands that she wants to borrow it. He gives her a smile and gets up. From the back pocket of his pants, he removes two more novels with similar features: small, flexible, with yellowish paper and brilliantly colored front covers. One is a Western and the other a crime novel. He gives them to Dita, and she walks off with them. And then something suddenly clicks in his mind, and he calls out to her,

"Hey, sweetie! They're in English!" And then he translates what he's said into clumsy German: *"Mädchen! Sind auf Englisch!"*

Dita turns around and without stopping, gives him a smile. She doesn't care. While her mother sleeps, she sits down on an empty bed and inhales the smell of paper, fans the pages quickly with her thumb, and smiles at the way it sounds like a deck of cards being shuffled. She opens a page, and the paper rustles. She runs her hand up and down the spine again and notices the blobs of glue on the covers. She likes the names of the authors—English names that sound exotic to her. As she holds the books in her hands, her life begins to fall into place again. Doing this helps her slowly put the pieces of the puzzle back where they belong.

But there is one piece that doesn't fit: Her mother isn't improving. The days pass by, and Liesl keeps getting worse. The fever is taking its toll, and her body is becoming more and more transparent. The doctor in attendance doesn't speak German, but he gesticulates in such a way that Dita knows perfectly how things are going—not very well.

One night, Liesl deteriorates: Her breathing is intermittent, and she flails around in the bed. Dita decides to give it one last go, to play her final hand. She goes outside and walks until she's well away from the blinking lights powered by the hospital generators. She is looking for darkness and discovers it in an area of level ground a few hundred meters from the hospital. When she finds herself totally alone, she lifts her face to the cloudy night sky in which there is no moon and there are no stars. She falls on her knees and asks God to save her mother. After everything that's happened, he can't let her die without even being able to return to Prague. He can't do this to her. He owes it to her. This woman has never hurt anyone, never offended or annoyed anyone, never stolen even a crumb of bread. Why punish her like this? Dita reproaches God, she begs him, she humbly implores him not to let her mother die. She makes all sorts of promises in exchange: becoming the most devoted of the devout, making a pilgrimage to Jerusalem, dedicating her entire life to praising God's infinite glory and generosity.

As she's returning, she sees a tall, thin figure standing in the illuminated doorway of the hospital, looking out into the night. It's Francis. He's waiting for her. Looking very serious, he takes a step toward her and puts an affectionate hand on her shoulder. A heavy hand. He looks at Dita and shakes his head slowly to tell her that no, it wasn't possible.

Dita runs to her mother's bed, and the doctor is there closing his bag. Her mother has gone. All that remains is her tiny human form, the body of a little bird. Nothing else.

Broken, Dita sits down on a bed. The freckle-faced nurse comes over.

"Are you okay?" And he raises his thumb so she understands that he's asking if she's all right.

How can she be all right? Destiny, or God, or the devil, or

whatever it might be, hasn't relieved her mother of a single minute of suffering during six years of war, and at the same time, hasn't allowed her to enjoy even one day of peace. The nurse continues to look at her as if he is waiting for an answer.

"*Scheisse,*" she replies.

The nurse makes that funny face the English make when there's something they don't understand—he stretches his neck and raises his eyebrows as high as they'll go.

"Shit . . . *Scheisse,*" says Dita, who has learned the English word over the past few days.

And then the nurse agrees.

"Shit," he repeats, and sits down beside her in silence.

Dita is left with the consolation that her mother took her last breath as a free woman—though it seems very small for such a lot of pain. But she turns to the nurse, who is watching her with some concern, and gives him the thumbs-up to tell him she's fine. The young health worker feels somewhat relieved and gets up to give some water to a patient in another bed who's asking for it.

Why did I tell him I'm fine if I'm feeling dreadful, if I couldn't be worse? Dita asks herself. And she knows the answer before she finishes the question: Because he's my friend, and I don't want him to be worried.

I'm starting to behave like my mother. . . .

It's as if she's taken over that role.

Next day, the doctor tells her that they're going to speed up her paperwork so she can go home right away. He hopes this will cheer her up, but Dita listens to him as if she were sleepwalking.

Go home? she asks herself. *To where?*

She has no parents, no home, no ID. Is there any place to go back to?

32.

THE WINDOW OF THE HEDVA DEPARTMENT STORE IN NA PŘÍKOPĚ
reflects a stranger: a young woman wearing a long blue dress and a
modest gray felt hat with a ribbon. Dita examines her carefully but
still doesn't recognize her. She can't accept that she is the stranger,
her reflection in the glass.

The day the Germans entered Prague, she was a nine-year-old
girl walking along the street holding her mother's hand; now she's
a woman of sixteen on her own. She still shakes when she remembers the shudder of the tanks crossing the city. It's all over, but in
her head, nothing has finished. It will never end.

After the jubilation of victory and the celebrations marking the
end of the war, after the dances organized by the Allied forces and
the pompous speeches, postwar reality shows itself for what it is:
mute, harsh, and without fanfare. The bands have gone, the parades
are over, and the grand speeches have been reduced to silence. The
reality behind peace is that in front of her is a country in ruins.
She has no parents or siblings, no home, no studies, no belongings
apart from the clothes they gave her in the Civilian Assistance
Society, and no way to survive beyond the little ration card she was
able to get after a great deal of cumbersome paperwork. On this, her
first night in Prague, she'll sleep in a hostel set up for the repatriated.

The only thing she has is a scrap of paper with an address scrib-
bled on it. She's has looked at it so many times she knows it by heart.

War changes everything. So does peace. What will be left of the sisterly relationship she shared with Margit in the concentration camps now that the war is over? Margit and her father thought Dita and her mother would take a transport train a couple of days after them, but her mother's illness delayed her return by several weeks. During that time, Margit could have made new friends. She might want to forget everything that happened in the past, like Renée, who greeted her from afar without stopping.

The address jotted down by Margit's father belongs to some non-Jewish friends with whom he'd been out of touch for years. In fact, when they left Bergen-Belsen, Margit and her father didn't know where they'd go to live or what they would do with their new lives. They didn't even know if those friends of theirs would still be at that address after all those years of war, or if they'd want to have anything to do with them. The piece of paper is getting wrinkled in the palm of her hand, and the writing is becoming illegible.

She wanders through the northern part of the city, looking for the address, asking people and trying to follow their instructions along streets she's never been in. She no longer knows her way around Prague. The city seems enormous and like a labyrinth. The world appears colossal when you feel small.

Finally, she reaches the square with the three broken benches they told her to look for; number 16 of the street on the piece of paper is close by. She goes inside the main entrance and rings the bell of apartment 1B. A somewhat overweight blond woman opens the door. She's not Jewish; fat Jews are an extinct species.

"Excuse me, but do Mr. Barnai and his daughter Margit live here?"

"No, they don't live here. They've gone to live some distance from Prague."

Dita nods her head. She doesn't reproach them. Maybe they waited, but it's taken her so long to return to Prague that it's too late. After everything that's happened, it's not enough just to turn to a new page. You have to close that book and open another.

"Don't stand on the doorstep," the woman says to her. "Come in and have a piece of freshly made cake."

"No, thank you, please don't bother. Someone's waiting for me, in fact. A family commitment, you know. I'm off. Some other time . . ."

Dita turns around to leave as quickly as she can and makes to walk away. But the woman calls out to her.

"You're Edita, Edita Adler."

And Dita stops. She already has one foot on the stairs.

"You know my name?"

The woman nods.

"I was expecting you. I have something for you."

The woman introduces Dita to her husband, a man with white hair and blue eyes who is still handsome at his advanced age. The woman brings her an enormous piece of hazelnut cake and an envelope with her name on it.

They are such kind people that Dita doesn't hesitate to open the envelope in front of them. Inside are two train tickets and a note from Margit written in her schoolgirl hand:

Dear Ditiňka, we're waiting for you in Teplice. Come right away. A huge kiss from your sister, Margit.

A person waiting for you somewhere is like a match you strike at night in the countryside. It may not be able to light up everything, but it does show you the way back home.

While they are all eating, the couple explains to Dita that Mr. Barnai found work in Teplice, and he's living there with

Margit. They tell her that Margit spent entire afternoons talking about her.

Before she leaves for Teplice, Dita has to fix up her papers, just as they told her in the Jewish Council office. So, first thing the next morning, she stands in the very long line of the office that issues identity papers.

Hours of waiting in line, again. But it's not like the lines in Auschwitz, because here people are making plans as they wait. There are also angry people, even more irate than those who waited in half a meter of snow for a watery bowl of soup or a piece of bread. Now those who wait are irritated by the delay or because they've been misinformed or because of the number of papers they need. Dita smiles to herself. Life is back to normal when it's small things that annoy people.

Someone joins the line right behind her. When she sneaks a look, she realizes it's a familiar face—one of the young teachers from the family camp. He also seems surprised to meet her here.

"The librarian with the skinny legs!" he exclaims.

It's Ota Keller, the young man who people said was a Communist, and who used to make up stories about Galilee for his pupils. Dita immediately recognizes that ironic look of intelligence that used to intimidate her a little.

Now, though, she sees something special in the young teacher's eyes, a special warmth. He doesn't just remember that she was a companion in the camp at a critical moment in their lives, but he discovers a thread that unites them. They hardly spoke in Block 31. In fact, nobody ever introduced them; they are two people who seemingly have never met. But when they bump into each other in Prague, it's as if they are two old friends meeting again.

Ota looks at her and smiles. His lively, somewhat roguish eyes are telling the girl, *I'm happy you are alive; I'm happy to have found you again.* Dita smiles at him, too, without really knowing why.

She is immediately infected by his good humor.

"I've found work doing the accounts in a factory, and I've found modest accommodation. . . . Though if you think about where we've come from, you'd have to say it's a palace!"

Dita smiles.

"But I hope to find something even better. They've offered me a job as an English translator."

The line is long, but it seems short to Dita. They talk without pause, without any embarrassing silences, and with the confidence shared by old comrades. Ota talks about his father, the serious businessman who always wanted to be a singer.

"He had an extraordinary voice," Ota explains with a proud smile. "They took away his factory in 1941; they even put him in jail. Then they sent us all to Terezín. And from there to the family camp. In the selection of July 1944, when they broke up camp BIIb, he didn't make the cut."

Ota, so resolute and talkative, notices that he's choking on his words, but it doesn't embarrass him if Dita sees that his eyes are moist.

"Sometimes, at night, I think I can hear him singing."

And when one of them looks away to remember a difficult or painful moment from those years, the other one also turns their eyes toward that same point to which we only allow people we trust completely to accompany us, those who have seen us both laugh and cry. Together, they visit those moments that have marked them forever. They're so young that telling each other about those years amounts to telling each other about their whole lives.

"What will have happened to Mengele? Have they hanged him?" Dita wonders.

"Not yet, but they're looking for him."

"Will they find him?"

"Of course they will. Half a dozen armies are looking for him. They'll catch him and put him on trial."

"I hope they hang him straightaway. He's a criminal."

"No, Dita. They have to give him a trial."

"Why waste time on procedures?"

"We are better than them."

"Fredy Hirsch used to say that, too!"

"Hirsch . . ."

"How I miss him."

It's her turn at the window—time to resolve all her issues. That's it. They are still two strangers. It's the moment to wish each other luck and say good-bye. But Ota asks her where she's going next. She tells him she's off to the Jewish Community Office and asks if what they've told her is true: that she can request a small orphan pension.

Ota asks her if she'd mind if he accompanied her there.

"It's on my way," he says, so seriously that she doesn't know whether to believe him or not.

It's an excuse to stay with her, but it isn't a lie. Dita's way is already part of his path.

A few days later, in Teplice, some kilometers from Prague, Margit Barnai is sweeping the entrance to her building. As she sweeps, she daydreams about a young man who does deliveries on his bicycle and rings his bell merrily each time he cycles past her. She thinks that perhaps it's time to start paying more attention to her hair in the mornings and putting a new ribbon in it. Suddenly, out of the corner of her eye she glimpses the shadow of someone coming through the entrance.

"You're very fat, girl!" the person shouts.

Her first impulse is to give a rude response to her rude neighbor. But then the broom almost falls out of her hand.

It's Dita's voice.

Margit is the older of the two girls, but she's always felt like the younger sister. She throws herself into Dita's arms in the way little children do—not worrying about the speed, not holding back.

"We're going to fall!" says Dita, laughing.

"And what does that matter, as long as we're together!"

It was true. Finally, something good was true. They *were* waiting for her.

EPILOGUE

OTA BECAME A SPECIAL FRIEND WHO USED TO COME ON THE
train to see her on afternoons she had off from the occasional work
she found. She combined the work with classes she attended in the
school in Teplice, where she and Margit were making up for some
of the time they had lost in schooling. If that were possible.

Teplice is an old spa city renowned for its waters. Dita had finally found her Berghof. There were no Alps as in *The Magic
Mountain*, but the high country of Bohemia was close by. She liked
to stroll along the streets with their geometric stone pavements,
despite the fact that the war had severely punished this beautiful
city with its stately buildings. She occasionally wondered what had
become of the enigmatic Mme. Chauchat, who left the spa resort in
search of new horizons. She would like to have asked her advice
about what to do with her life.

The beautiful synagogue had burned down, and its scorched
ruins were a reminder of those burned-out years. On Saturdays, Ota
accompanied her on her walks. He talked to her about a thousand
things. He was a young man with a voracious curiosity; everything
interested him. He sometimes complained a little of having to take
various combinations of trains and buses to travel the eighty kilometers between Prague and Teplice. But his complaints were more
like the satisfied purr of a cat.

There were months of pleasant strolls through those squares, which little by little, regained their flowerpots and began to give Teplice back its charming air of a town of hot springs. During those walks, Ota and Dita gradually became entwined. A year after their meeting in the line at the documents office, Ota said something to Dita that changed everything:

"Why don't you come to Prague? I can't love you from a distance!"

They had already told each other their entire lives. It was the moment to start from scratch, to begin again.

Ota and Dita were married in Prague.

After a great amount of paperwork, Ota managed to take back his father's business and get it going again. It was an exciting project, because in a way, Ota was able to recover the past. He couldn't bring back those who were absent or erase the scars, but at least it was a way of returning to the Prague of 1939, even though Ota wasn't sure if he wanted to be a businessman. He, like his father, preferred opera scores to balance sheets, and the language of poets to the language of lawyers.

But he didn't have the time to be disillusioned. The footprints of the Nazi boots on the streets of Prague had not yet disappeared when the boots of the Soviets made their mark. With that delightful obstinacy history has of repeating itself, the factory was again confiscated. This time, it wasn't in the name of the Third Reich but of the Communist Party.

Ota didn't give in; neither did Dita. They were born to swim against the tide. Thanks to his mastery of English and knowledge of literature, Ota found work in the Ministry of Culture, choosing which new English-language publications were interesting enough to be translated into Czech. He was the only employee at his level who was not a Communist Party member. Many in that period

spouted Leninist slogans, but no one was going to teach him anything. He knew more about Marxism than any of them; he had read
more than any of them. He knew better than anyone that Communism was a beautiful path that ended at a precipice.

They accused him of being an enemy of the Party, and things
started to get difficult. In 1949, the year their first child was born,
Ota and Dita decided to emigrate to Israel, where they ran into
another old inmate from Block 31, Avi Fischer, now called Avi
Ofir, the man who had converted a modest barrack full of child
prisoners into a cheerful glee club. He helped them find work at
the Hadassim School near Netanya. There, Ota and Dita worked as
English teachers at one of the most renowned schools in Israel. The
school accepted many children who came in the wave of immi-
grants after the end of World War II. Later, the school took care of
children from families with problems and students at risk of social
exclusion. They always employed teachers who were particularly
involved in those sorts of issues, but it was hard to find people
more sensitive to the suffering of others than Ota and Dita.

The couple had three children and four grandchildren. Ota, the
great storyteller from Block 31, wrote various books. One of them,
The Painted Wall, fictionalized the lives of a series of people in the
family camp, BIIb. Dita and Ota experienced life's ups and downs
together for fifty-five years. They never stopped loving and support-
ing each other. They shared books, an indestructible sense of humor,
life in general.

They grew old together. Only death could break the iron bond
forged in the most terrible times anyone could experience.

POSTSCRIPT

THERE ARE STILL SOME IMPORTANT THINGS TO TELL ABOUT THE librarian of Block 31, and about Fredy Hirsch.

The bricks used to construct this story are facts, and they are held together in these pages with a mortar of fiction. The real name of the librarian of Block 31, whose life has inspired these pages, was Dita Poláchová. Ota Keller, the young teacher in the novel, is based on the person who would become Dita's husband, the teacher Ota Kraus.

A brief mention of the existence of a minuscule library in a concentration camp made by Alberto Manguel in his book *The Library at Night* was the point of departure for my journalistic investigation, which gave rise to this book.

There are those who don't share my fascination for discovering why certain people risked their lives to run a secret school and clandestine library in Auschwitz–Birkenau. There are those who might think that this was an act of useless bravery in an extermination camp when there were other, more pressing concerns—books don't cure illnesses; they can't be used as weapons to defeat an army of executioners; they don't fill your stomach or quench your thirst. It's true: Culture isn't necessary for the survival of mankind; for that, you only need bread and water. It's also true that with bread to eat and water to drink, humans survive; but with only this, humanity dies. If human beings aren't deeply moved by beauty, if they don't close their eyes and activate their imaginations, if they aren't capable of asking themselves questions and discerning the limits of their ignorance, then they are men or women, but they are not complete persons: Nothing significant distinguishes them from a salmon or a zebra or a musk ox.

There's a great deal of information about Auschwitz on the internet, but it only talks about the place. If you want a place to speak to you, you have to go there and stay long enough to hear what it has tell you. In order to find some trace of the family camp or some track to follow, I traveled to Auschwitz. I needed not only quantitative data and dates, but to feel the vibration of that accursed place.

I flew to Kraków, and from there I took a train to Oświęcim (Auschwitz). Nothing in that small, peaceful city hints at the horror experienced on its outskirts. Everything is so normal, and you can even get to the camp entrance by bus.

Auschwitz I has a parking lot for buses and a museum-like entrance. It used to be a Polish army barracks, and the pleasant, rectangular brick buildings separated by wide, paved avenues—complete with pecking birds—give no indication, at first sight, of the horror. But there are various pavilions you can go into. One of them has been designed like an aquarium: You walk along a dark corridor lined with huge illuminated fish tanks. They contain worn-out shoes, mountains—thousands—of them. Two tons of human hair form a dark sea. Dirty prostheses resemble broken toys. And there are thousands of pairs of broken glasses, almost all of them with round frames like the ones Morgenstern wore.

The family camp, BIIb, is three kilometers away, at Auschwitz–Birkenau. The phantasmagorical watchtower at the entrance to the *Lager* still stands, with a tunnel at its base that was used from 1944 onward to allow the railway line to run right into the camp. The original huts were burned after the war. There are a few recon-structed ones you can go inside: They are horse stables, which seem gloomy even when they are clean and well-ventilated. Behind this first line of huts, which are in what would have been the quarantine camp, BIIa, there is an immense expanse of waste ground that origi-nally contained the rest of the camps. To see the spot that BIIb occupied in its day, you have to abandon the route of the guided tour, which doesn't go beyond the first row of replica huts, and skirt the entire perimeter. You have to be on your own. Walking through Auschwitz–Birkenau in solitude means enduring a very cold wind that carries echoes of the voices of those who remained there forever and became part of the mud present-day visitors walk on. All that's left of BIIb is the metal door at the entrance to the camp and an intensely solitary space where even bushes barely grow. Only cobblestones, wind, and silence remain. A tranquil or ghostly place—it depends how much the eyes looking at it know.

I returned from that trip with many questions and almost no answers; some sense of what the Holocaust was that no history book could teach me; and, completely by chance, a copy of an important book: *Je me suis évadé d'Auschwitz*, the French translation of Rudolf Rosenberg's memoir, *I Cannot Forgive*, which I found in the bookstore at the Shoah (Holocaust) Museum in Kraków.

There was another book that particularly interested me and which I started to track down as soon as I got home. It was a novel set in the family camp, with the title *The Painted Wall*, written by someone called Ota Kraus. There was a website where the book could be purchased and sent to you, cash-on-delivery. It wasn't a very professional website: You couldn't pay with a credit card, but there was a contact address. I wrote to the address, expressing my inter-est in the book and asking how payment should be made. And then

I received one of those emails that prove to be a crossroads in your life. The reply, very polite, was that I could send the money via Western Union; there was an address in Netanya, Israel, and the message was signed D. Kraus.

With all the tact I could muster, I asked if she was Dita Kraus, the girl who had been in the family camp at Auschwitz–Birkenau. She was. The librarian of Block 31 was alive and was writing an email to me! Life is full of surprises, but sometimes, it can be truly extraordinary.

Dita was not so young anymore—at that stage she was eighty— but she was still the same passionate and tenacious person she had always been, who was now battling to ensure that her husband's books were not forgotten.

From that moment, we began to correspond. Her incredible kindness helped us to understand each other despite my poor English. Eventually, we agreed to meet in Prague, where she spent a few weeks every year, and she took me to visit the Terezín ghetto. Dita is not one of those old-style, placid grandmothers. She's a friendly whirlwind, who immediately found accommodation for me close to her apartment and organized everything. When I arrived at the Hotel Tříska's reception desk, she was already waiting for me on one of the sofas in the lobby. She was exactly as I had imagined her: thin, restless, active, at once serious and cheerful, totally charming.

Dita's life wasn't easy during the war years, nor has it been easy since. She and Ota were very close until his death in 2000. They had two sons and a daughter; their daughter died before she turned twenty, after a long illness. But Dita hasn't allowed herself to be broken by fate's blows—she didn't allow it back then; she won't allow it ever.

It is remarkable how someone who carries so much accumulated pain manages to keep on smiling. "It's all I have left," Dita tells me. But she has many other things left—her energy, her dignity as a battler against everything and everyone—and this makes her an upright eighty-year-old woman with fire in her eyes. As we travel around Terezín, she refuses to take a taxi, and I don't dare contradict her thriftiness, typical of anyone who has lived through bad times. We take the subway, and she stands. There are free seats but she doesn't sit down. No one can vanquish a woman like that. The entire Third Reich failed to do it.

Indefatigable or tired but never resigned to giving up, Dita asks me to give her a hand because she's going to take fifty copies of *The Painted Wall* to the Terezín Memorial store, which has run out. We don't rent a car; she insists that we go by coach. We make the same trip she made almost sixty years earlier, although now she's dragging along a suitcase full of books. I'm scared she might find herself affected by this trip back in time, but she's a strong woman. Right now, her greatest concern is to restock the ghetto library with these books.

Terezín turns out to be a peaceful place full of square buildings, dotted with lawns and trees and bathed in brilliant May light. Dita not only drops off the books but, being her normal feisty self, gets me free entry into the permanent exhibition.

The day is full of emotionally charged moments. Among the pictures by the ghetto internees on the wall is one by Dita herself, a dark and gloomy picture that shows a much less dazzling town than the one we're walking around now. There's also a room with the names of the children who were sent to Terezín. Dita runs through the list and smiles as she remembers some of them. They are almost all now dead.

Four video screens show the testimony of survivors talking about their experiences in Terezín. An older man with a deep voice appears on one of them. It's Ota Kraus, Dita's husband. He speaks in Czech, and although there are English subtitles, I don't pay attention to them because I'm too hypnotized by his voice. It conveys such composure that you can't help but listen to it. Dita silently pays attention. She's looks grave but doesn't shed a single tear. We leave and she tells me we're going to see where she lived. She's made of steel, or gives that appearance. I ask her if it isn't difficult for her. "It is," she replies, but she doesn't stop, continuing on her way at a good pace. I had never before met a woman with such extraordinary courage in every aspect of her life.

Where she was housed during her time in the Terezín ghetto is now an inoffensive neighborhood block of apartments. Dita looks up at the third floor. She tells me that one of her cousins, who was a carpenter, made her a bookshelf. She tells me much more as we head toward another building where one floor has been preserved as a museum, its rooms full of bunks, just as it was during the ghetto years. It's an oppressive place, too small for so many beds. They've even kept the earthenware basin the occupants used as a communal toilet.

"Can you imagine the smell?" Dita asks me.

No, I can't. We go into another room where there's a security guard. Pictures and posters from the ghetto era hang on the walls. An opera by the famous pianist and composer Viktor Ullmann is playing. He became one of the most active contributors to culture in Terezín. Dita stops in the middle of the room, empty but for the bored attendant. She quietly starts to sing Ullmann's opera. Her voice is the voice of the children of Terezín, which rings out again that morning for a much-reduced but no less surprised audience.

This is another moment when time goes backward and Dita becomes Ditiňka with her woolen socks and eyes of a dreamer, singing the children's opera *Brundibár*.

During our return trip to Prague, Dita energetically asks the coach driver to open the sliding roof so we won't die of asphyxiation from heat in a vehicle with windows that don't open. The driver ignores her, so she starts to pull on the hatch lever herself, and I join her. Between the two of us, we succeed.

It is while we are sitting in the coach that a topic that has been buzzing around in my head for months comes up in the conversation: What happened that afternoon of the 8th of March 1944 when Fredy Hirsch went off to think about the proposal from the Resistance that he lead a camp uprising, given the imminent extermination of the September transport in the gas ovens? Why did a man as composed as Fredy Hirsch commit suicide with an overdose of Luminal?

Dita looks at me, and there's a whole world in her eyes. And I begin to understand. I read in her eyes what I had read in the lines written by Ota in his book, but which I had taken as artistic license or a personal hypothesis. After all, wasn't *The Painted Wall* a novel? Or was it only a novel in order to camouflage certain things which, if Ota had said them in a different context, might have caused him serious problems?

Dita asks me to be discreet, because she thinks that what she's told me might cause her problems.

That's why, rather than explaining what she told me, I'll simply reproduce what Ota Kraus wrote and published in his novel, *The Painted Wall*, set in the family camp. One of the few characters in the book to appear with his real name is Fredy Hirsch, the instructor in charge of Block 31. This is what the novel recounts about that crucial moment when, after the SS have transferred the September transport to the quarantine camp, the Resistance asks Fredy to lead an uprising, and he asks for some time to think about it:

> *After an hour, Hirsch got up from his bed to go and look for one of the medics.*
>
> *"I've decided," he said. "As soon as it gets dark I'll give the order. I need a pill to calm my nerves."*
>
> *. . .*
>
> *A revolt against the Germans was madness, the doctor thought; it was death for everyone: the condemned transport, the prisoners in the family camp, and even the team from the hospital requisitioned by Mengele. The man had gone mad, he was clearly out of his mind, and if he wasn't stopped, the Jewish doctors would die with the rest of the prisoners.*
>
> *"I'll give you something, a sedative," the doctor told him, and turned to the pharmacist.*
>
> *They were always short of medicine, but they had a small stock of tranquilizers. The pharmacist handed him a bottle of sleeping pills. The doctor emptied the contents into his hand and immediately clenched his fist around them. He had some cold tea in his mug into which he tipped the pills, and then he swirled the tea around until they'd dissolved in the murky liquid.*

There are words in penal codes to describe what really happened to Fredy Hirsch that afternoon in 1944. Sometimes, narrative fiction reveals truths that can't be told any other way.

Increasingly, other testimonies contradict the suicide theory that can be found in the official profiles of Hirsch. Michael Honey, a family camp survivor who worked as an errand boy for the medical team, casts doubt on Rosenberg's testimony in his memoir when he speaks of what happened on March 8, 1944: "He was given an overdose of Luminal when he asked for a pill because of a headache."

I hope this book also serves as a vindication of the figure of Fredy Hirsch, somewhat tarnished by the false idea that he voluntarily took his own life. As a result of this notion, his integrity in decisive moments has been questioned. Fredy Hirsch did not commit suicide. He would never have abandoned his children. He was a captain; he would have gone down with his ship. This is how he should be remembered: as a fighter of extraordinary valor.

And, naturally, this book is a homage to Dita, from whom I have learned so much.

The librarian of Block 31 continues to live in Netanya and travels to spend a few weeks each year in her tiny apartment in Prague. And she'll keep doing it as long as her health allows. She is still a woman of unimaginable curiosity, astuteness, kindness, and integrity. Until now, I hadn't believed in heroes, but I now know they exist: Dita is one of them.

WHAT HAPPENED TO . . .

RUDI ROSENBERG

After the war, Rudi Rosenberg changed his name to Rudi Vrba. Following his escape from Auschwitz, he hastened to dictate a preliminary report for Jewish leaders in the city of Zilina about what was really happening to the people deported to Auschwitz. Its contents bore no resemblance to the lies of the Nazis. The report was sent to Budapest, but some of the senior Jewish leaders ignored it, and in May 1944, the Nazis began to transport up to twelve thousand Hungarian Jews a day to Auschwitz. When Rudi reached Britain, he and his fellow escapee Fred Wetzler wrote another, more detailed report that served to inform the world of the terrible truth of what was happening in the concentration camps. This document was one of the pieces of evidence used at the Nuremberg trials. After the war, Rosenberg was decorated. He studied chemistry at Charles University (in Prague) and became a respected professor in the field of neurochemistry. He moved to Canada, where he died in 2006. His bitter criticism of prominent members of the Hungarian-Jewish community, who would subsequently play a key role in the founding of the State of Israel, caused certain sectors of that state to question for decades both his testimony and Rudi himself as a person. To this day he remains a controversial figure there.

ELISABETH VOLKENRATH

Elisabeth Volkenrath was a qualified hairdresser by profession, but her affiliation with the Nazi party led to her enlisting with the SS. She undertook a period of training in the Ravensbrück camp, and in 1943 was posted to Auschwitz as an SS *Aufseherin*, or female guard. In November 1944, she was promoted to SS *Oberaufseherin*, or head female guard, and in this position, she ordered an increased number of executions. Early in 1945 she was transferred to Bergen-Belsen as supervisor. When the Allies liberated the camp, she was arrested by British troops and put on trial as part of the process to determine the responsibilities of the Bergen-Belsen guards. As a result, she was condemned to death by hanging and was executed on December 13, 1945, in the town of Hamelin.

RUDOLF HÖSS

Rudolf Höss, the Kommandant of Auschwitz, received a strict Catholic upbringing. His father even wanted him to become an ordained priest. In the end, Höss opted for the army: order and hierarchy fascinated him. During his term as Kommandant, between one and two million people were killed. When the war ended, Höss escaped from the encirclement of the Allies hunting for major war criminals by using a false identity that suggested he was an ordinary soldier. He worked as a farmer for almost a year, until the Allies forced his wife to reveal his whereabouts and he was arrested. He was tried in Poland and condemned to death. While in jail, before he was executed, he wrote his memoirs, in which he did not deny the hundreds of thousands of crimes he had committed, and justified them by declaring that, given his military rank, he was obliged to obey the orders he received. He was even proud of his organizational skills in managing a death machine as complex as the one at Auschwitz. He was hanged in Auschwitz I, and the gallows still stand where the sentence was carried out.

ADOLF EICHMANN

Adolf Eichmann was one of the primary ideologues of the so-called Final Solution to exterminate the Jewish race. He took charge of the logistics involved in the deportations to the concentration camps. He was also the architect of the *Judenräte*, or Jewish councils, which collaborated in the deportations. Eichmann was captured by American troops at the end of the war, but he passed himself off as Otto Eckmann and they didn't realize he was one of the most wanted Nazis. After hiding in Germany and traveling through Italy, Eichmann boarded a ship to Argentina in 1950. There, he gathered his family together and lived under a false name, working as a machine operator in a car factory. In 1960, thanks to information gathered by the Nazi hunter Simon Wiesenthal, an elite group of the Mossad (the Israeli intelligence service) found him in Buenos Aires. In a daring operation, they arrested Eichmann in the street, bundled him into a car, and headed for the airport. From there, he was secretly taken out of the country in a plane belonging to the Israeli airline El Al, by pretending he was a drunk aircraft mechanic. The incident gave rise to a bitter diplomatic dispute between Argentina and Israel. SS *Obersturmbannführer* Adolf Eichmann was tried in Jerusalem and condemned to death. The sentence was carried out on June 1, 1962.

PETR GINZ

The editor-in-chief of the magazine *Vedem*, put together voluntarily by the youth of Terezín, was born in Prague on February 1, 1928. His parents were passionate advocates of the universal language

Esperanto, and people with a deep interest in culture. In October 1942, the Gestapo ordered Petr and several hundred others to be deported to Terezín, while his parents and sister remained temporarily in Prague. Petr was one of the few unaccompanied children in Terezín, although his parents regularly sent him packages containing food and writing paper. In one letter that has been preserved, Petr asked his family for chewing gum, notebooks, a spoon, bread, illustrations for copying . . . and a sociology book. He shared his packages with his roommates. His generosity, intelligence, and pleasant manner made him one of the boys most loved by both his companions and his teachers. In 1944 he was deported to Auschwitz; he didn't return home when the war ended. But his name didn't appear on any list of the dead, either, and for ten years his family held out the faint hope that they would see him again. At the end of that time, they were contacted by Jehuda Bacon, who had been deported on the same transport. He explained to them that when they were sent to Auschwitz, a selection was carried out on the station platform itself: Those on the right went to the camp, and those on the left went directly to the gas chambers. Jehuda saw Petr being assigned to the left group.

DAVID SCHMULEWSKI

The Polish leader of the Resistance in Auschwitz was already a veteran left-winger before he was detained—he had fought in the International Brigades during the Spanish Civil War, and later against the Nazis. After the war ended, he held several important positions in the Polish Communist Party. A murky business in which he was caught up—something to do with the trafficking of works of art—forced him to step down from the Party, and he ended up in exile in Paris, where he lived until his death. It is not known to what extent his involvement in the trafficking of artwork was a ploy by leaders of the Communist Party to discredit him, since his status as a war hero made him untouchable. His grand-nephew, the polemical and brilliant English intellectual Christopher Hitchens, who died in 2011, talks about some of these matters in his book *Hitch-22*.

SIEGFRIED LEDERER

He was the fellow escapee with SS First Officer Viktor Pestek, whose desertion cost him his life. Lederer escaped from the Gestapo by the skin of his teeth and became an active member of the Resistance. In Zrabaslav he passed himself off as an SS general to help local Resistance groups. He ended up in Slovakia, where he spent the rest of the war helping local partisans.

JOSEF MENGELE

In January 1945, a few days before the Allied forces liberated Auschwitz, Josef Mengele blended into a retreating infantry battalion. In this way, he ended up being one of hundreds of soldiers taken prisoner and managed to pass unnoticed by the Allies. He was assisted not only by the chaos in the first few weeks after the war ended, but by the fact that the Allies were identifying members of the SS by a tattoo they all had on their arms that identified their blood type—something regular soldiers did not have. Mengele, always prudent, had never been tattooed. He managed to escape from Germany with the financial assistance of his influential industrialist family and took refuge in Argentina. He lived an agreeable, upper-class life there as a partner in a pharmaceuticals company. Toward the end of the 1950s, Nazi hunter Simon Wiesenthal picked up Mengele's tracks thanks to divorce papers he signed—an action he agreed to by letter with his wife. But someone managed to warn Mengele that he'd been discovered, and he left for Uruguay. He lived there under a new false identity but in considerably less comfortable circumstances, in a modest shack and with the worry of knowing he was being pursued. He was, however, never caught. He died in 1979 at the age of sixty-eight while bathing in the sea—probably of a heart attack. In the biography of Mengele written by Gerald Posner and John Ware, the authors tell how, after years of intermittent contact by mail, Mengele's son Rolf went to visit him before his death. Rolf was finally able to ask the question that had been eating away at him since he was a child, that is, whether Mengele was really responsible for the atrocious crimes attributed to him. It was difficult for a son to accept that his father—so solicitous and considerate in his letters—could be the vicious monster talked about in the media. When Rolf finally asked him face-to-face if he really had ordered thousands of people to be executed, Josef Mengele assured him that it was just the opposite. Showing absolutely no emotion or doubt, Mengele told his son that thanks to his selections—in which he separated those Jews who were still in a fit state to work from those who were going to be killed—he had saved thousands from death by assigning them to the "suitable" line.

SEPPL LICHTENSTERN

Seppl Lichtenstern was selected for transportation from the family camp to the Schwarzheide camp in Germany in July 1944. There, the Nazis put him to work in a factory that converted brown coal into diesel fuel. At the end of the war, the Nazis organized a macabre march, with no food supplies, of thousands of prisoners from camps that were about to fall into the hands of the Allies. It was a march-flight to nowhere in particular. It was called "the death march" because weapons were fired without warning and those who were dying were summarily executed by the side of the road. Thousands of these prisoners, including Lichtenstern, died during this final act of Nazi madness. His remains lie in the Saupsdorf cemetery in Germany.

MARGIT BARNAI

Margit got married and lived the rest of her life in Prague. Although Dita emigrated to Israel, they never lost touch. They exchanged letters and photographs of their children. Margit had three daughters. The youngest was born when Margit was already forty years old. She was baptized with the name Dita. Dita Kraus continues to keep in touch with Margit's daughters. She's like an aunt to them, and they catch up whenever Dita visits Prague.

PRIMARY SOURCES

Adler, Shimon. "Block 31: The Children's Block in the Family Camp at Birkenau." *Yad Vashem Studies* XXIV (1994): 281–315.

Demetz, Peter. *Prague in Danger*. New York: Farrar, Straus and Giroux, 2008.

Gutman, Yisrael, and Michael Berenbaum, eds. *Anatomy of the Auschwitz Death Camp*. Bloomington: Indiana University Press, 1994.

Kraus, Ota B. *The Painted Wall*. Tel Aviv: Yaron Golan Publishing, 1994.

Křížková, Marie Rút, Kurt Jiří Kotouč, and Zdeněk Ornest. *We Are Children Just the Same:* Vedem, *the Secret Magazine by the Boys of Terezin*. Prague: Aventinum Nakladatelství, 1995.

Levine, Alan J. *Captivity, Flight, and Survival in World War II*. Santa Barbara, CA: Praeger, 2000.

Millu, Liana. *El humo de Birkenau*. Barcelona: Acantilado, 2005.

Posner, Gerald L., and John Ware. *Mengele: La esfera de los Libros*. 2002.

Venezia, Shlomo. *Sonderkommando*. Barcelona: RBA, 2010.

Vrba, Rudolf, and Alan Bestic. *Je me suis évadé d'Auschwitz*. Paris: Éditions J'ai Lu, 1998.

The Librarian
of Auschwitz

A Conversation with

Dita Kraus,

the Librarian of Auschwitz

The Librarian of Auschwitz by Antonio Iturbe is based on your real-life experience as a prisoner of Auschwitz. What do you hope readers take away from this story?

Two, even three new generations have been born since the events described in *The Librarian of Auschwitz*. Most people who survived those times are no longer alive. The guilt of the Nazi perpetrators of the murder of millions of innocent people, families, babies, and old men and women is being forgotten or trivialized, if not outright denied.

The Librarian of Auschwitz is therefore not only a riveting read but also has a mission. It acquaints the public with proof of important historical facts.

How did you meet Antonio Iturbe, the author of *The Librarian of Auschwitz*? What was the interview experience like?

Antonio Iturbe received my name from Beit Terezin in Kibbutz Givat Chaim, Israel. He wanted to get information about the library in the family camp of Auschwitz. To his surprise, he discovered that the librarian was myself. He wrote a very apologetically worded request asking if I would be able to speak about Auschwitz. We began exchanging questions and answers by internet until the day we met in person in Prague. There, after two intensive days of touring Prague and Terezín, he told me: "I am going to write a book about you."

I laughed. He couldn't be serious.

But as you see, he was.

With publication of *The Librarian of Auschwitz* now in English, what are you most excited to share with readers?

The publication of *The Librarian of Auschwitz* in English excites me very much. My children and grandchildren speak Hebrew and English. But the book was written in Spanish and translated into many other languages, including Czech, Japanese, Dutch, and more. Thus, no one in my family could read it. Eureka, now they can.

Reading books is part of my life. I cannot understand how people can spend their days without books. Many books have had a decisive influence on me, even in my childhood.

As a young person I read everything without choosing. But in later years I became more picky. What fascinates me most are novels in which the author creates characters who are so alive that I feel as if I met them personally.

The quality decides the life of a book (like any other product). The best live for ages, the mediocre and trivial are soon forgotten.

DISCUSSION QUESTIONS

1. One of the first things we find out about Auschwitz is that "death has become an industry that is profitable only if it's done wholesale" (p. 1). What does this tell us about the camp? What imagery does it evoke?

2. Alfred Hirsch establishes a school in Auschwitz. He asserts that "Each time someone stops to tell a story and children listen, a school has been established" (p. 1). Do you agree with this? Why or why not?

3. The Nazis have banned school and books in their concentration camps. What does it mean to deprive someone of an education? What's so dangerous about allowing books?

4. When Block 31 receives word that SS guards are on their way for an inspection, Dita makes her way to the center of the hut to hide the books: "Dita Adler is moving among hundreds of people, but she's running by herself. We always run on our own" (p. 4). What do you take this to mean?

5. What is the significance of the story of Prague's astronomical clock and the clockmaker who took his revenge by putting his hand into the mechanism to disable it? Does it have relevance to the larger narrative?

6. Discuss the concept of "living libraries," or "book-people," as they're referred to, such as Mrs. Magda, who performs *The Wonderful Adventures of Nils Holgersson* for the children (p. 25). What's different about this kind of reading? Bringing to mind oral storytelling traditions, what is lost in this way? What is gained?

7. When Dita asks Alfred Hirsch about *The Adventures of the Good Soldier Švejk*, he tries to keep her from read-

ing it because it's "not appropriate for children, especially girls" (p. 27). Dita fires back that, considering her surroundings, there's very little that could shock her. What do you think of this argument, and the attempt to maintain certain rules of propriety (however old-fashioned) in a place where they've been all but eradicated?

8. Of all the books in Dita's library, which one stands out to you the most? Which had the greatest impact on your understanding of the story?

9. In a flashback, Dita recalls telling a classmate the tale of the Golem, a monster made of clay brought to life by a rabbi. At different points in the story, both Dita's books and Alfred Hirsch are referred to as Golems. What does this indicate?

10. What do you think of Professor Morgenstern? Did your feelings about him change over the course of the story? How so?

11. "It's the war, Edita . . . It's the war" becomes a kind of refrain, something Liesl repeats to her daughter with each new injustice they face. What's your reaction to this line?

12. Discuss the complications of being a prisoner given privileges or power over your fellow prisoners (for example, Rudi Rosenberg as registrar and Schmulewski as assistant to the *Kapo* in his barrack).

13. When Dita reads *The Adventures of the Good Soldier Švejk*, the book makes her think of Alfred Hirsch's ever-present smile—an act of defiance in Auschwitz, she realizes. Does the bumbling, secretly shrewd character of Švejk remind you of anyone else?

14. After Alfred Hirsch's death, Dita searches for answers. She thinks to herself that "truth is the first casualty of war" (p. 265). What does this mean to you?

15. Eventually, the Nazis shut down the family camp, and all prisoners are brought before Dr. Mengele for selection. When it's Liesl's turn, she's assigned to the group of the sick and elderly, but instead makes her way to her daughter's group, unnoticed by the guards. Is this unintentional disobedience or quiet rebellion? What leads you to believe this?

16. Most of *The Librarian of Auschwitz* is told through Dita's point of view, but occasional interludes take us inside other characters' heads. What are some advantages of this kind of storytelling? How did you respond to it?

ANTONIO ITURBE lives in Spain, where he is both a novelist and a journalist. In researching this story, he interviewed Dita Kraus, the real-life librarian of Auschwitz.

LILIT ŽEKULIN THWAITES is an award-winning literary translator. After thirty years as an academic at La Trobe University in Australia, she retired from teaching and now focuses primarily on her ongoing translation and research projects.